EXPOSED

The sound of the door closing, combined with the fact that she was wearing nothing but a towel, made Katie burn with embarrassment.

Ethan picked her nightgown up off the bed. "Very pretty," he said, and shot her a look of pure deviltry.

The sight of that wisp of lace in his hands made Katie's heart pound in her chest. She stretched out her arm to take her nightgown, but he pulled it back, just out of reach, and she watched the teasing gleam in his eye. "An interesting situation for a man to find himself in, wouldn't you say?"

Katie lunged for the gown, and he took a step back. "Ethan, give it to me," she demanded.

"Why should I?" he countered softly, slanting her a look from beneath his lashes that made her body flush with heat. "I like you better without it."

Praise for Laura Lee Guhrke's splendid Southern romance

BREATHLESS

"*Breathless* really grabs and holds your interest. Daniel and Lily are friends as well as lovers, and the love scenes will take your breath away. *Breathless* has *keeper* written all over it." —Bookbug on the Web

"Readers who enjoy strongly written books about small t... Laura Lee Guhrk... e this novel above t... *About Romance*

D1053841

Books by Laura Lee Guhrke

Breathless
The Charade

Published by POCKET BOOKS

For orders other than by individual consumers, Pocket Books
grants a discount on the purchase of 10 or more copies of
single titles for special markets or premium use. For further
details, please write to the Vice President of Special Markets,
Pocket Books, 1230 Avenue of the Americas, 9th Floor,
New York, NY 10020-1586.

For information on how individual consumers can place
orders, please write to Mail Order Department, Simon &
Schuster Inc., 100 Front Street, Riverside, NJ 08075.

LAURA LEE GUHRKE

The Charade

SONNET BOOKS
New York London Toronto Sydney Singapore

The sale of this book without its cover is unauthorized. If you purchased this book without a cover, you should be aware that it was reported to the publisher as "unsold and destroyed." Neither the author nor the publisher has received payment for the sale of this "stripped book."

This book is a work of fiction. Names, characters, places and incidents are products of the author's imagination or are used fictitiously. Any resemblance to actual events or locales or persons, living or dead, is entirely coincidental.

An *Original* Publication of POCKET BOOKS

A Sonnet Book published by
POCKET BOOKS, a division of Simon & Schuster Inc.
1230 Avenue of the Americas, New York, NY 10020

Copyright © 2000 by Laura Lee Guhrke

All rights reserved, including the right to reproduce
this book or portions thereof in any form whatsoever.
For information address Pocket Books, 1230 Avenue
of the Americas, New York, NY 10020

ISBN: 0-671-02367-5

First Sonnet Books printing March 2000

10 9 8 7 6 5 4 3 2 1

SONNET BOOKS and colophon are trademarks of
Simon & Schuster Inc.

Front cover illustration by Bradley Clark

Printed in the U.S.A.

For Marie,
who always thought American history was dull.
I hope this book changes your mind.
With much love.

1

Boston, February 1775

At dawn, North Square was seething with activity. Women with baskets stood amid the flimsy stalls of the marketplace, haggling with farmers or their agents over the high prices. Their voices mingled with the crowing of live turkeys for sale, the beckoning calls of merchants, and the rattle of carts that rolled through the square carrying precious firewood, apples, and onions from the country.

Preoccupied with their own business, no one noticed the man who stood in the doorway of an inn on the edge of the square. Perhaps it was because the winter morning was bleak, and his long black hair and black cloak blended into the dark shadows of the doorway. Or perhaps it was because he stood utterly motionless, little more than a shadow himself.

His position commanded an excellent view of the square, and in the dim light of early morning, his gray eyes restlessly scanned the area. He was looking for one man, and that man would tell him that his call for a meeting had been heeded.

Ethan Harding's acquaintances would have been astonished to see him skulking about in doorways in the wee small hours of the morning, since it was common knowledge that he never rose before noon. But then, they would not see him here, for they were fast asleep in their beds themselves, and it was unlikely they would have recognized him in any case. The dark clothing he wore was so unlike his customary wardrobe of colorful silks and lace, and his hair was not concealed by a powdered wig. The wealthy dandy of the Tory drawing rooms was completely unrecognizable in the serious man swathed in black who stood in the doorway of a second-rate inn on North Square. And that suited Ethan perfectly well.

A fishmonger's cart rolled into his line of vision and came to a stop. Ethan let out his breath in a slow sigh of relief at the sight of the driver, a big, bald Scotsman who jumped down from the cart, crying, "Fresh clams today! Fresh clams!"

Colin Macleod's fish were often wrapped in seditious newspapers. Ethan smiled to himself, knowing perfectly well that Samuel Adams didn't mind if his fiery prose smelled of cod or haddock, as long as the public was kept informed of every single transgression committed by the British government.

Ethan started toward Colin, but matrons and housekeepers eager for fresh clams swarmed around the cart, and he stepped back into the shadows, waiting for the women to depart. While he waited, he continued to observe his surroundings, a habit gained from long experience.

The baker, Matthew Hobbs, had a stall beside Colin's cart and seemed to be doing a brisk business. A pity, since the man was a staunch Tory. Ah, well, not everyone wanted liberty from England. What they didn't realize was that it was inevitable.

A young woman of perhaps nineteen or twenty paused beside the baker's stall, less than a dozen feet from Ethan's place in the shadows. Her clothes were rags, too tattered to make her the servant of even the meanest master. Against the chill of the Boston winter, she wore no hat. Her hair, the golden brown color of honey, was cropped short, and Ethan guessed she had probably sold the rest of it to buy food or lodgings. She stood in profile to him, and although the long cloak she wore hid the lines of her body, Ethan could see hunger in the hollow of her cheek and the line of her throat. She was clearly a beggar, a common street waif a man would seldom notice, unless it was with a wary eye and a hand on his purse. But when she turned his way, Ethan drew a deep breath of surprise and revised his opinion. There was nothing common about this girl. She had the face of an angel.

Ethan was not a man to be impressed by a woman's beauty. In truth, he seldom noticed women at all these days, which he considered rather a shame when he took the time to think of it.

There had been a point in his life when women had been one of his major preoccupations, but suspicion was his only mistress now, and he knew all too well that treachery could hide easily behind a woman's charms. Ten years as a spy had taught him that. Nonetheless, he could not help staring.

Her wide eyes were the azure blue of a summer sky, with all the innocence of a child. Yet her thick, dark lashes and soft, generous lips had all the seductiveness of a courtesan. Her features were delicate, her flawless skin the color of cream. But it was her smile that fascinated Ethan. It was a smile that could make a man abandon his ideals, forget his honor, sell his soul. It was a smile that enslaved. It was magic.

He wondered what had brought that smile to her lips, but from this vantage point, he could not tell. She returned her attention to the baker, who, like Colin, was preoccupied with a crowd of customers. Because he was observing her so closely, Ethan did not miss the apparently casual glance she gave her surroundings or the two meat pies that slipped from the baker's table into the folds of her cloak.

Well done, he approved, watching in amusement. Anyone who stole from a Tory deserved high praise indeed. She moved out of Ethan's line of vision, and he leaned forward so that he could continue to watch her, but she disappeared into the crowd.

He leaned back in the comfortable shadows of the doorway to wait for Colin to be free of customers. Even though the two men would speak in seemingly trivial terms, Ethan did not want to run the risk of having anyone overhear their conversation. It was always best to be cautious.

A boy of about twelve stood near Ethan's doorway selling newspapers. Tory newspapers, no doubt, since it was almost impossible for a boy to sell Whig newspapers in the marketplace these days. The soldiers harassed the Whig newspaper sellers so mercilessly that such an occupation was hazardous for a boy. Ethan set his jaw grimly. Soon, boys would be able to sell newspapers with any opinions under the sun without fear of reprisal from the bored and unruly troops of a tyrannical king.

A man paused beside the boy to buy a newspaper, a man who was obviously wealthy. His shoe buckles were cast of silver, his cane was made of gold and ivory, and his wig was of the finest quality. Ethan could not see his face, but the fashionable cut of his clothes, the vivid peacock-blue color of his coat, and the lavish lace at his cuffs proclaimed him an even more dandified Tory than Ethan pretended to be.

"Thief! Thief!"

The sudden cry rose above the noise of the crowd, and Ethan once again leaned forward in the doorway, curious to see what was going on. To his surprise, he saw the angel girl again, but this time, she was in the grip of a prosperous merchant.

"I am no thief!" she said indignantly, trying to

wrench her wrist free of her captor's grasp. "Un-hand me!"

"You took my pocket watch. I know you did." Keeping a firm hold on her wrist, the man looked around for a constable. Ethan watched as she shoved and struggled against her captor, and he caught the glint of silver as she slipped the man's watch into his pocket.

Clever girl. Ethan grinned, knowing no one would be able to prove theft against her now. Unaware that his property had been returned, the merchant continued to shout for a constable, but the only person who came to assist was a young red-coat officer. "What is going on here?" he demanded as he stepped forward out of the gathering crowd.

"This girl stole my watch," the merchant accused, twisting the girl's wrist with enough force to make her cry out.

"I did not! It's a lie!" She looked up at the officer, her gorgeous eyes wide and pleading. She lifted her free hand in a helpless gesture. "A ghastly mistake has been made," she said in a voice that would have melted stone. "This man thinks I have stolen something from him, and I am unable to convince him of my innocence. Oh, Major, you seem such an able and intelligent gentleman. Please help me."

The officer, who was only a lieutenant, puffed up like an arrogant peacock at her flattery. He smiled and patted her arm. "I'm sure everything will be fine," he said soothingly, and turned to the merchant. "When did you lose your watch, sir?"

"I didn't lose it," the other man said angrily, scowling at the officer. "She stole it."

"Have you proof of this?"

"Proof? She'll have it on her, and that's all the proof you'll need."

The girl's expression was one of such martyred innocence that Ethan nearly laughed aloud. "By all means, search me if you must," she said with injured dignity. "I will gladly submit if it will convince you I am innocent. But, if you please, sir, ask this gentleman to search his own pockets as well, for I am sure he is mistaken."

The lieutenant would not have been human if he had not responded to such a plea. He turned to the merchant. "Sir, are you certain your watch is not on your person?"

"Of course I'm certain. Any fool can see she stole it."

Being called a fool did not sit well with the lieutenant. He frowned. "Would you mind verifying that the watch is missing?"

"Of all the ridiculous . . ." The merchant let go of the girl and patted his pockets, muttering impatiently to himself and scowling, but his irritated expression changed to astonishment as he pulled the heavy silver watch out of his coat pocket.

"It appears that you have falsely accused this young lady," the lieutenant said.

"I must have misplaced it," the other man murmured, and Ethan choked back his laughter only with a great deal of effort. Red-faced, the merchant bowed stiffly and walked away without another word.

The girl turned to the officer, her face shining with gratitude. "Oh, Major, I don't know how to thank you."

Now that the excitement had passed, the crowd that had gathered around them dissipated. The dandy with the peacock-blue coat walked on with his newspaper, and matrons returned their attention to Colin's clams.

Ethan, however, continued to watch the girl. After such a close call, he expected her to beat a hasty retreat, but he found he had underestimated her. Instead of counting her blessings and going on her way, she lingered beside the officer, talking with him. One or two more flattering comments, a few moments of rapt, wide-eyed attention, and the lieutenant was completely captivated. He smirked and swaggered, too besotted by his bewitching companion to notice when one of her small, delicate hands slid into his pocket.

Tongue in cheek, Ethan watched her remove the officer's money purse quicker than the blink of an eye and slip it into her cloak. *By the devil,* he thought in admiration, *this girl could get through heaven's gates by stealing the keys.*

Impressed by her audacity, Ethan watched, certain that the officer would come to his senses and realize what had happened. But such was not the case. She touched the redcoat's cheek in a lingering caress of farewell and turned away, leaving the dazed young officer staring after her with an expression on his face similar to that of a bewildered sheep. Giving him one last glance over her shoulder that held all the promise a man could want, she melted into the crowd and disappeared from sight.

Still grinning, Ethan watched her go, feeling a hint of regret. He couldn't recall witnessing anything recently that had given him more pleasure than the past few moments. That girl was one in a thousand.

A movement out of the corner of his eye brought his attention back to the business at hand, and the pretty thief vanished from his mind.

Colin was finally free of customers. Ethan stepped out of the doorway and approached the cart. The gazes of the two men met, but neither expressed recognition. No one watching them would ever be able to discern that they knew each other well.

"No fresh oysters this morning?" Ethan asked.

"No, sir, but we've a good supply of clams."

Ethan waved away clams with disinterest. "I wanted oysters."

The fishmonger made a sound of disbelief. "Fresh oysters? Clams I can dig from shore, but with the harbor closed and the Port Bill in effect, how do you think I'd get hold of oysters, my good man?"

"Is there nowhere hereabouts a man can find fresh oysters?"

Colin heaved a heavy sigh and said grudgingly,

"I'm told the White Swan sometimes serves 'em raw for breakfast, provided you've the money to pay. Although where they get 'em from, I'm sure I don't know. Must bring 'em in overland during the night from Portsmouth."

The White Swan was a good choice for a meeting. At this hour, it was unlikely anyone would be there, despite Colin's words about oysters for breakfast. Ethan nodded, tipped his hat in farewell, and left the marketplace. He made his way through the maze of North Boston's twisting, narrow streets at a brisk pace. His worn and somber clothing of black broadcloth allowed him to blend easily into the crowd around him. He looked like an ordinary merchant, one of many who crowded the streets on early-morning business. He had chosen his clothing this morning for just that purpose. If any of Governor Gage's spies were following him, they would find it difficult to keep him separate from every other man in the crowd. He doubted he was being followed, but one could never be too careful.

Ethan always chose whatever clothing was appropriate to the mission of the moment, but no matter what role he played, there was one thing he always wore: the silver medal concealed beneath his shirt that proclaimed him a Son of Liberty. Wearing the Liberty medal was dangerous, but it was a badge of honor, and Ethan, like all his comrades, never took it off.

The White Swan was known by most people in Boston as a Tory pub, but most people never knew about the politics that were discussed in the attic. When Ethan entered the place, the only people there were the owner, Joshua Macalvey, and his younger sister, Dorothy. Joshua stood behind the bar, and Dorothy, a plump and pretty brunette of twenty-two, was clearing tables of the tankards and trenchers left from the night before.

Neither of them spoke to him, but Dorothy smiled a greeting, and Joshua jerked his head toward the kitchen. Ethan headed in the direction Joshua had indicated, going through the kitchen and up the back stairs to the attic. His knock on the door was answered immediately, and the door swung inward to reveal that the other two men with whom he had arranged this meeting had arrived before him.

Ethan nodded to the man who had opened the door. "Andrew," he murmured in greeting, stepped past his oldest boyhood friend, and entered the room.

Andrew Fraser, with his melancholy face and deep voice, seemed more like an undertaker than a wine merchant. He was worried, but then, Andrew was always worried. Their mischievous pranks at school and notorious escapades with women during their days together at Harvard had long since given way to the hanging offenses of rebellion and sedition, but the seriousness of the situation could never be gauged by Andrew's demeanor. Whether it was putting salt in a tutor's tea, visiting the brothels at Mt. Whoredom, or plotting against the government, Andrew always looked as if doom had come upon them.

"We're taking grave risks by meeting in broad daylight, Ethan," Andrew reminded him.

"Don't waste time telling me things I already know, my friend."

Andrew shook his head in disapproval. "Couldn't this wait for our usual Friday-night rendezvous at the Mermaid?"

"I'm afraid not." Ethan turned to the other man, whom he recognized as Joseph Bramley, one of Samuel Adams's messengers. He knew Bramley only by sight, but Samuel trusted his messenger implicitly, and that was good enough for Ethan.

"I'll make this quick, gentlemen. The less we linger here, the better." Without bothering to remove his hat, he sat down at the table in the center of the room. The others followed suit, and Ethan came directly to the point. "Governor Gage is sending two officers into the country tomorrow morning on a secret mission."

"For what purpose?" Andrew asked.

"To map the countryside from Boston to Worcester. One Captain John Brown and one Ensign Henry De Berniere are to walk on foot to Worcester dressed as countrymen and posing as surveyors. Their mission is to determine the condition of the roads, paying specific attention to possible sites where troops might be ambushed."

The other two men received this news in silence, thinking out its implications. Finally, it was Andrew who spoke. "Gage may be pompous, but as a governor, he is not the tyrant Hutchinson was. Nor is he a fool. It seems clear that he wants to determine the safest, most discreet route by which he can send troops on the march."

"And those troops will be marching straight for our powder stores in Worcester," Ethan added. He leaned forward in his chair and spoke his mind. "Gentlemen, we have to send a courier to Worcester and warn the town."

"So they can move our powder and ammunition to a new hiding place before troops arrive to take it?" Joseph guessed.

"Exactly. My sources tell me Gage knows we have more than fifteen tons of powder and thirteen cannon stored there. We cannot allow that large a cache of weaponry to fall into Gage's hands. A few months from now, we will need all the powder and cannon we can get."

Both men leaned back in their chairs, and a long silence followed. Finally, Joseph cleared his throat and spoke again. "You think it will come to war, then?"

"I do. War became the only possible course when that damned Port Bill was passed." The Boston Port Bill had closed the harbor eight months previously, a move intended to starve Boston into submission. Thanks to the generosity of the other colonies, which sent food and supplies into the city over land by Boston Neck, the marketplaces still managed to conduct business. Boston citizens were still able to eat, despite Crown Law, but it was now nearing the end of a long, hard winter, and food prices were high. As food supplies decreased, hatred increased, and war became more likely with each passing day.

Ethan went on, "How long can colonials live under what amounts to martial law? How long before all our freedom is taken away? It is now impossible for any colonial to get a fair trial in Boston, or speak his mind publicly, or even have a mind of his own. We can't even hold a town meeting anymore without being harassed. Three years ago, we could freely discuss our political opinions. Now, four Whigs can't have a pint of ale together without being suspected of sedition. This situation cannot continue." Ethan took a deep breath and looked at the other two. "Let us be blunt, gentlemen. What we are really coming to is complete independence from England."

Joseph's eyes met his across the table. "Our friends agree with you. I hate to think of it, but I believe it is unavoidable."

Ethan nodded slowly, glad of the reassurance that other Sons of Liberty saw the situation as he did. He had often wished he could communicate directly with men such as Samuel Adams, John Hancock, and Paul Revere, but his public position as a loyal Tory made such a convenience far too risky.

Andrew spoke again. "Let us return to the situation of Worcester. Two officers will not take the powder but will simply report back to Gage on its location and recommend the best route to take for marching there, is that not so?"

"Exactly," Ethan answered. "My sources tell me Gage intends to accelerate his attempts to take our powder, and in the coming months, reconnaissance missions such as this will become commonplace. Despite the failure at Portsmouth two months ago, Gage is convinced he can avoid war simply by relieving us of our gunpowder one storehouse at a time."

"A shrewd maneuver," Joseph commented. "He is absolutely correct. Our lack of weaponry is our greatest weakness if it comes to war." He met Ethan's eyes across the table. "Are you certain this information is accurate? How did you come by it?"

"As Andrew will tell you, my sources are reliable. And confidential."

Joseph appeared satisfied by that. "I'll deliver this news to Paul Revere. He'll want to ride to Worcester tonight and get word to the militia there."

"Tell Paul to have the militia leave the powder where it is until Gage's two officers have passed through. Then move it to a new hiding place."

Joseph nodded. "That way, if the troops do march on the town a few days from now, they'll come up empty-handed."

Andrew also rose to his feet. "I'll pass this information on to the Boston and Charlestown militia so we can be ready for the repercussions. If troops march and find nothing for the trouble, God knows what Governor Gage will do." He glanced at Ethan. "Why on earth did you take the risk of coming out at this hour to bring us this news? Skulking about in patriot taverns at night posing as a dock worker named John Smith is one thing, Ethan, but during the day you could be recognized much more easily."

"I know, but it was necessary," Ethan answered, and rose from the table. "I can usually tell when a Gage spy is following me. I don't believe I was followed."

"If you are wrong, if you are being watched, Gage will eventually learn who you really are. You could be arrested, even hanged, for sedition."

"We all face that risk, if it comes to that," Ethan answered. "But Gage isn't arresting anyone yet. He is a fair man, despite all Samuel's attempts to paint him otherwise in the Whig newspapers."

"I feel compelled to point out that arrest is not the only risk involved here," Joseph interjected. "As Ethan Harding, you have access to many friends of the governor. If Gage discovers that Ethan Harding and John Smith are the same person, we will lose you as our most valuable source of information."

"Gage wouldn't charge me with sedition without better proof than the word of an informant," Ethan answered. "As I said, he is scrupulously fair. And, given my social position and connections, he will be especially careful to obtain irrefutable proof before arresting me."

Andrew came around the table and laid a hand on his arm. "Proof can be fabricated. I'd hate to see you swing on the gallows, my friend. Watch your step."

"Andrew is right," Joseph said. "Be careful."

Ethan smiled grimly. "I am always careful."

2

$\mathcal{H}$ad the pious ladies who ran the Benevolent Home for Unfortunate Girls in London known that Katie Armstrong would turn out to be a natural thief, a talented pickpocket, and an accomplished liar, they would have prayed harder for her soul and applied the willow switch to her backside with even more frequency. Had they known she would never suffer a guilty conscience for her sins, they would have sent her straight to a workhouse, dismissed her soul as a lost cause, and never have bothered with her at all.

At this moment, Katie was nibbling the second meat pie of her stolen breakfast and trying to find the cheapest lodgings she could get with her stolen coins. Guilt was the farthest thing from her mind.

She needed a place to stay. Sleeping outdoors on one Boston winter night had been enough to convince her of that. For lodgings, she needed money. The handful of silver she'd taken from James

Willoughby's strongbox had brought her all the way from Virginia, but that money was gone, and though it was nearly March, Katie had almost frozen to death last night. She cursed herself as all kinds of a fool for heading north instead of south when she'd run away from Willoughby, but there was no help for that now.

The thought of her former master made her shudder. She had seen a great deal of life's dark side, but what Willoughby had done to that unfortunate kitchen maid, Patsy Wells, had been beyond anything she had ever seen, beyond anything she could have imagined. Patsy was dead, and Katie knew she'd have met the same fate if she had not left Virginia. If she were ever caught and sent back, he'd kill her before she could run away again. No matter what she had to do, she would not return to her master.

She forced memories of Willoughby out of her mind. That whoremaster was the last thing she needed to be thinking about just now.

She swallowed the last bite of her meat pie and decided she'd better settle for one of the cheap rooms she'd found earlier around the prostitution district, an area appropriately called Mt. Whoredom. Though she didn't plan to stay in Boston long, she had to remain at least a few days and rest. Two months of hard winter travel from Virginia had been grueling, and she had arrived here yesterday with not so much as pence in her pocket. With what she'd dipped from that lieutenant this morning, she could have lodgings in Mt. Whoredom for at least a month. She knew many of those rooms had fleas, but she couldn't afford to be choosy, and it was harder to dip in a small city like Boston than it had been in London. Too much risk of getting caught and hanged. She had to make her stolen coins last as long as possible.

She wished Meg were with her. Meg had been her partner in crime and the closest thing to a friend she'd ever had. But Meg had died in London courtesy of the hangman's noose, and Katie knew that these days there was no one she could rely on except herself.

Preoccupied with her thoughts, she did not notice the carriage that halted beside her or the two soldiers who stepped down from it, until a pair of hands closed over her arms and seized her.

Struggling against the grip of her assailant, Katie let fly with a string of angry curses as she was turned around and slammed back against the wall of the alley to face the pair of redcoats. Her heart thudded with panic, but neither of these men was the dolt-headed lieutenant she'd fleeced that morning.

The one who held her firmly by the shoulders nodded to his companion. "She fits the description." Looking once again at Katie, he added, "We've been searching for you all morning, my girl."

They must have seen her stealing from their fellow officer. Or worse, they were friends of his, come to find her from his description. She thought of the miserable weeks she'd spent in Newgate four months ago before being transported to the colonies, and she struggled furiously to free herself. Better to die trying to escape than end up in prison living with the rats and facing the gallows again.

A vicious kick to her captor's shin loosened his grip, and she jerked free, but her victory was shortlived. The two men easily overpowered her. Katie struggled in vain as the soldiers dragged her into the waiting carriage.

During the brief ride, there was little chance for escape. Both soldiers kept a firm grip on her, and both were immune to her pleas, questions, and curses. When the carriage came to a halt, she made one last attempt to break free, but it was useless.

Her captors dragged her inside a tavern, past the doorway of a taproom empty at this hour of the morning, and up a set of narrow stairs. Katie was hauled into a large, sparsely furnished room. A man was seated at the head of a long table, and he rose to his feet as she was brought in.

At the sight of him, Katie went still, and her curses died on her lips. This was not the lieutenant. In fact, he was not an officer at all. This man had pale skin stretched tight across his cheekbones, eyes that were dark and expressionless, and a smile that was coldly mocking. His face reminded her of a death's head.

He glanced to the soldiers on either side of her and gave a nod of confirmation. "Excellent work, my good men. You may let her go."

The two soldiers obeyed, and Katie gave each of them a resentful scowl before she turned her attention to the man at the other end of the room. He studied her as he came around the table, and she subjected him to the same thorough scrutiny he was now giving her.

He did not look like a magistrate. Too richly dressed, she decided, studying his powdered wig, peacock-blue coat, and silver buckled shoes. He paused a few feet away from her, and, without taking his eyes from her face, he spoke to the pair of soldiers. "Leave us."

The soldiers departed, closing the door behind them.

"I am Viscount Lowden," he said.

A British viscount? Katie was astonished.

"What is your name?" he asked. When she remained silent, he went on, "I can easily find out. You might as well stop wasting time and tell me."

"Katie," she answered.

"Well, Katie, do you have any idea why you are here?"

Her mind raced frantically, but she could not figure out the purpose of all this. She didn't think she was officially under arrest. She shook her head in answer to his question.

"I summoned you here because I have a task for you to do."

She raised her eyebrows at those words. "Summoned? Dragged is more like it."

"I suggest you curb your insolence, girl." He took a step closer to her and grabbed her hand. Peeling back her tattered glove, he turned her palm upward to expose the *T* branded into her skin. The mark of a thief. "If you do not watch your tongue, I shall find another girl to suit my purpose, then I will find your master and return you to him."

Dread seeped into her bones at the idea of returning to Willoughby, and Katie felt a sickening twist of fear in the pit of her stomach. *Steady,* she told herself, and looked the viscount in the eye. She jerked her hand away and put just the right hint of defiance in her voice when she said, "I don't know what you're talking about."

He smiled. It was a benign smile, but Katie felt the hairs rise on the back of her neck. The survival instincts honed by a life on the street told her that this man was dangerous, and she'd best watch her step.

"Let us stop the pretenses, shall we? I know you are a thief. I know this not only by your brand but also because I myself witnessed your little escapade in North Square this morning."

He grabbed her hand again and turned her around, the movement so sudden she had no time to defend against it. He pulled her back against his body and wrapped his arm around her, but she sensed it was not a sexual gesture. He began fumbling in the pockets of her cloak and pulled out the lieutenant's velvet money bag. The moment he had it, he let her go.

She whirled around and opened her mouth to give him a few choice words, but one look at his eyes silenced her. God, he was a cold one, this man.

He held the purse aloft. "What have we here? The theft of an officer's money is a serious offense."

She licked her dry lips and did not reply.

"You are a thief," he went on, "and I can tell by your brand this is not your first offense. I conclude you are indentured but too young to have worked off your seven-year term. So, you are obviously a runaway. Don't look daggers at me. I am no stupid fresh-faced lieutenant, and I didn't bring you here so I could have you hanged for something as mundane as stealing. Nor am I in the business of finding runaway servant girls for colonists careless enough to lose them."

Katie was fatalistic by nature. She knew when rage was futile and lies became useless. Her only option was to cooperate and see what happened. She shrugged. "Very well, then. What do you want of me?"

He pulled a folded sheet of parchment out of his pocket. "This is an arrest warrant against you for your crime. It is signed by Lieutenant Weston. It was his purse you lifted this morning in the marketplace."

"God's blood, you're a lying bastard," she ground out between clenched teeth. "You just told me that you didn't bring me here to have me hanged for theft, yet you have an arrest warrant!"

He was unperturbed by her rage. "Mind your tongue," he said softly. "Insult me again, and I'll not bother with warrants. Make no mistake, I could kill you right now, and no one would ever know."

She knew he spoke the truth. He was a man with money, title, and power. She possessed none of those things. He could debauch her or kill her or both, and no one would ever know or care. She stiffened and glared at him. "I've faced the gallows before, and I got used to the idea of dying a long time ago, so your threats are wasted. I'm not frightened of you." The last was a lie, but she had her pride. By God, she'd not cower before any man. Katie held out her hand. "Let me see the warrant. I want to read the charges against me."

For the first time, she seemed to surprise him. "You can read?"

His reaction reminded her of Meg, who had also been astonished that she could read and write. Meg had figured out a way to put that particular knowledge to a profitable use, of course. She had concocted a swindle with compromising love letters, forged by Katie, and used against various peers of the realm. It had been a very lucrative scheme. By the shrewd gleam in Lowden's eye, Katie judged he was thinking of how he might also make use of her education, and she decided it would be wise not to mention her talent for forgery.

She gave the viscount a mocking smile. "Don't

expire from the shock, my lord. Yes, I can read. Let me see the warrant."

He handed her the document, and she read it all the way through. It was a detailed account of her escapade that morning. She handed it back. "All true," she said with a blitheness she was far from feeling. "Except about my hair. It's more blond than brown."

"Better and better," he murmured to himself as if she had not spoken. He folded the warrant and put it back in his pocket. "The fact that you can read is an unexpected bonus. Can you write as well?"

"Aye. English and French."

"Excellent." The viscount drummed his fingers on the table beside him, staring at her thoughtfully. "Despite the fact that you can curse like a sailor, you speak with a cultured voice. Despite your insolent tongue, you seem to have some knowledge of good manners, polite society, and civil conversation."

"I am an orphan, my lord," she answered dryly, "not an animal."

He ignored that. "And you can read and write. How does a street thief develop such accomplishments?"

Katie knew from experience that whenever possible, it was best to tell the truth, so one didn't get trapped in one's own lies. "For nearly a decade, my mother was the mistress of a wealthy gentleman. He was married but estranged from his wife, and he lived with my mother quite openly. Most of my childhood was spent in his household. My mother taught me to read and write, both English and French. She came from a good family, but she'd had the misfortune to fall in love with my father, who was a wastrel and a libertine and who refused to marry her. So she became a wealthy man's mistress. She died when I was ten, and her protector packed me off to an orphanage."

"You are fortunate it wasn't the workhouse," he commented.

That was one way of looking at it, she supposed, but she thought of Miss Prudence's thin, cruel lips and sadistic fondness for the willow switch, and she didn't quite see it as fortunate. She shifted her weight restlessly, unable to see the purpose of this man's questions and comments. She didn't know why it should matter to him that she could read and write. Whatever he planned to do to her, she wished he'd get on with it. "Why have you brought me here?"

"You're a very good liar, you know. I think you even manage to convince yourself of your own lies. I suspected as much when I saw you making a fool of that lieutenant."

She did not respond to that. She simply faced him in stony silence, waiting for an answer to her question.

"You are audacious," he continued, "clever, quite pretty, and completely unscrupulous. And that, my girl, is exactly what I want from you."

"I don't understand."

"Danger does not seem to bother you," he went on as if she had not spoken. "Death doesn't seem to frighten you. I have a mission for you that involves the possibility of both."

"Do I have a choice about this?"

"Of course. If you accomplish this mission, I will buy your indenture and set you free. I will also give you a gift of fifty pounds to start a new life. If you refuse my proposal, I will find your master and send you back to him."

Fifty pounds was a fortune, freedom was a gift, and a choice such as this was no choice at all. "Whatever you want me to do, I'll do it, if you set me free."

"It is dangerous work. You might not live long enough to enjoy your freedom."

"I don't care. I'd rather be dead than indentured."

"Very well," he said, nodding as if he had not expected her to say anything else. "But know this. If you betray me, what I do to you will make indenture seem like heaven by comparison."

Katie looked into his dark, empty eyes and suppressed her shiver. He meant what he said. But if he was willing to free her, she didn't care how dangerous he was. "What is it you want me to do?"

"Doubtless you have heard of the Sons of Liberty?"

"The secret society?" she murmured. "Of course I've heard of them."

"Their headquarters are here in Boston, and I

have just arrived from London for the purpose of arresting the ringleaders and demolishing the organization. You are going to help me do just that."

"I?" Katie stared at him in astonishment. "You want me to find the Sons of Liberty for you?"

"I already know who they are. However, confidential information is being passed to them by someone at the highest level. It is being given to the rebel leaders through a man named John Smith."

"Who is he?"

"We don't know very much about him, but we do know that somehow he is receiving information from people close to the governor, and he is passing that information on to the rebel leaders."

"Then why don't you arrest him?"

Though his expression remained cold and aloof, there was no mistaking the anger in his voice when he replied to her question. "Our honorable governor is determined to follow English law to the letter and refuses to arrest any man without proof," he said contemptuously. "Gage will not move to arrest even Paul Revere, and a more seditious traitor than that man never walked the earth. As for John Smith, Gage has flatly refused to investigate unless there is some evidence. Because I have only been in Boston a few days, I have only just begun to gather information about him. We suspect *John Smith* is an alias, but we do not know who he really is. We do know he is supposedly an unemployed longshoreman, which is odd, because he has enough money to spend many of his evenings drinking rum at various rebel taverns in North Boston."

"You have spies in these taverns?"

Lowden's mouth tightened to a thin line, and his dark eyes met hers. Once again, Katie felt that cold prickle of fear. She knew her question displeased him, and she was surprised when he answered it.

"Not yet. Gage has mishandled these rebels from the beginning. His attempts to place spies in the rebel taverns has failed, but I intend to succeed. I already have men watching these taverns from the outside, but since John Smith has only been seen at night and the streets are so dimly lit, it is difficult for my spies to give me a detailed description of the fellow without getting closer to him, and that has proved to be a difficult task. He is as elusive as the wind, and he has the uncanny ability to discover who our informants are long before they can learn anything useful."

"That is why you need me," she guessed. "You want me to spy for you."

"Yes. Discovering who John Smith is, finding out from whom he gets his information, learning exactly how he passes his information to the ringleaders, and finding proof of his sedition that I can submit to the governor will be your tasks. Only I and my immediate subordinate, Captain Worth, will know about you."

Katie frowned, thinking it out. "How am I to succeed where your other spies have failed?"

He shrugged. "As I said before, you are a clever young woman. You'll think of something, I'm sure." He walked over to his chair and sat down, then took up quill and ink. "You might find a way to become the man's lover," he suggested, his quill making scratching sounds against the parchment as he wrote. "Given your beauty, your mother, and your background, that should not be difficult."

Katie wanted to grind her teeth at the viscount's insulting words, but though several stinging replies came to mind, she did not say any of them aloud. She would not risk her chance to be free with fifty pounds in her pocket simply for the momentary satisfaction of returning insult for insult. She remained silent.

"If you don't favor that idea," the viscount continued, sensing her resentment, "you might find a way to work at one of the taverns he frequents— the Green Dragon, the Salutation, or the Mermaid. After that, keep your eyes and ears open." He blew on the paper to dry the ink, then rose and walked back to her side. He handed the paper to her.

Katie ran her gaze down the list of names. "These men are the Sons of Liberty?"

"The ones we know of, yes. Memorize this list, then burn it. Your main concern will be John Smith, but my greatest lack is information, so bring me anything you discover about these men, however unimportant it may seem."

"John Smith is not on this list."

"No. Unlike most of his fellow rebels, he is not willing to advertise the fact that he is a Son of Liberty. Nonetheless, I believe that he has a network of spies that stretches into Governor Gage's office. I want that web of spies destroyed. I want him tried for sedition, and I want him hanged."

She nodded and put the list in her pocket. "How do I report to you?"

"Come to the marketplace in North Square at dawn every Saturday, and Captain Worth will find you. You will need some time to get settled in your new situation, whatever it may be. You will meet Worth a week from this Saturday. That gives you nearly a fortnight."

Katie let out her breath in a sharp sigh. "It's stupid for me to risk meeting with one of your men unless I have something to report, and I doubt very much I'll learn anything of significance in a fortnight."

"Nonetheless, I want to keep an eye on you, my girl, so I will expect you to be there every Saturday. If you have information, Worth will arrange a meeting between us here, at the Stag and Steed Tavern. We shall arrange a signal between Worth and yourself. If you have any news for me, let your bonnet hang down your back."

She gestured to her ragged clothes. "What bonnet?" she countered in a wry voice.

"With what I witnessed this morning, I'm sure you could find the money to buy one."

"Perhaps, my lord, but it is risky. Do you want your spy arrested by the constables?"

"Fair enough." He drew a British half crown from his pocket and tossed it to her. She caught it in her hand.

"If you learn something that cannot wait for a Saturday, you may leave a message for me here with the cook, Mrs. Gibbons. But if you do come here, be careful that you are not followed."

"I understand."

The viscount looked at her, and his eyes narrowed. "I expect you to provide me with John Smith's true identity and tangible proof of his sedition. If I can arrest him based on your evidence, I will have you set free, and you will get your money. If you are found out by the rebels, you'll be tarred, feathered, beaten, and probably killed, and I will not be able to come to your aid. Should you try to play me for a fool and disappear, I will find you. When I do, I'll use the warrant and have you arrested. You'll be tried and hanged for the theft of Lieutenant Weston's purse, which, for the time being, will remain in my possession as evidence of your crime."

Katie swallowed hard, then asked one last question. "What if I do my best for you but fail to find this proof you need?"

"I'll get another spy and return you to your master."

Kate felt herself go cold at that uncompromising answer. Lowden sensed her reaction and the effectiveness of his threat. "I suspect that idea does not appeal to you?" he said, his voice deceptively soft.

"No," she said. "It does not."

"Then don't fail me." He waved her toward the door. "Now, go."

Katie obeyed that order willingly. She paused by the fire in the kitchen of the tavern to appreciate its warmth before returning to the bitter cold outside, and she could not help being stunned by the abrupt turn her life had taken, a turn decidedly for the better. Her indenture paid and fifty pounds more. That was worth more money than she could ever earn by pickpocketing.

Freedom and money. She savored the idea that now she had the chance for both. If she succeeded, there would be no more looking over her shoulder, no more going hungry, no more sleeping in alleys and fields, and no threat of Willoughby in her shadow. Katie thought again of Patsy Wells and vowed that she would be successful in her mission for Lowden. She had to be.

She thought of the list in her pocket, and all her brash confidence came flooding back. Most men could be manipulated easily enough. Her task should not be too difficult.

She spread her hands before the warmth of the fire and realized that if she accomplished this mission, the money the viscount had promised her would be enough to give her coal for many long winter nights to come. She'd eat meat every day, and she'd have a roof over her head. She could start a new life. An honest life. Best of all, she would be free of Willoughby.

Free. Katie hugged herself at the exhilarating thought of freedom, and, ignoring the curious stare of the sour-faced Mrs. Gibbons, she laughed aloud with exultation.

3

The Mermaid was primarily a sailor's tavern, but it was also one of the places where patriots met. The owner, David Munro, was a friend of Ethan's, making the tavern an ideal place for secret meetings.

Ethan knew perfectly well that the pub was often watched by Gage's spies, usually from within a Tory-owned house across the street, and he always had to be careful that he was not recognized. The sailor's cap pulled low over his eyes and the crude oilskins he wore made a suitable disguise, and anyone watching him would conclude he was just another longshoreman thrown out of work by the much-hated Port Bill, out to spend his last few coins on rum. At the Mermaid, as in the other taverns Ethan frequented during the midnight hours, most people knew him only as John Smith. Only a trusted few knew his true identity as Ethan Harding.

Andrew was already there when he entered the

tavern, seated at a table on the far side of the room and drinking a pint of ale with Colin Macleod. Ethan gave the men no sign of recognition. Instead, he passed their table without a glance and took a seat behind them in the darkest corner of the tavern. He ordered rum, a drink all longshoremen favored and he personally detested, then settled back to wait. It would not be long before Joseph arrived; then he and the three men at the next table would move to the private room in the back, where there was no chance of being overheard. There they could freely exchange information. Until then, Ethan preferred to remain in the taproom, where he could see any faces that came in or out of the tavern.

With the news Ethan had conveyed to Joseph, patriots had kept a close watch on Gage's two spies. The moment Brown and De Berniere had returned to Boston, all the Worcester powder stores had been moved. If Gage sent troops to Worcester now, they would come back with nothing to show for it but a tour of the countryside.

Despite their success in keeping the Worcester stores out of Gage's hands, powder supplies were far too low, and Ethan knew tonight they would have to discuss that situation. The plain and simple truth was that they needed more weaponry. If Gage even partly succeeded in his plans, colonists wouldn't have enough powder and shot for any kind of a fight when war broke out. They would have to appeal to France for assistance in any case.

It was all well and good for Samuel Adams to write in the *Boston Gazette* and other Whig newspapers that justice would prevail, Ethan thought in frustration, but Adams was an idealist. Ethan knew that without the weapons, supplies, and powder French loans could provide, King George's troops would pound them to dust in a matter of months. Worse, Gage knew it, too.

The idea of an alliance with France held a rather absurd irony. Ethan could still remember fighting in the colonial militia against the French when he was a very young man. Barely sixteen, he had joined the militia along with hundreds of others to help Britain gain control of all North America.

He had been quite an idealist himself back then, truly believing in king and country. Now, his father was dead at redcoat hands, and Ethan knew loyalty to a king gained a man no reward but iron-fisted tyranny, high taxes, and an untimely death. There had to be a better life than that.

Suddenly, the door to the tavern burst open, interrupting Ethan's thoughts, and a thin, ragged girl ran inside the inn. "The Regulars are after me!" she cried, pushing back the hood of her cloak with one hand as she closed the door behind her with the other. "I have to hide! Oh, please, won't someone help me?"

It was the pretty thief he had seen three days before in the marketplace. Ethan raised his brows in surprise at seeing her again, though after the little comedy he had witnessed in North Square, he was not surprised to find her running from soldiers. He ignored her plea for help, since the last thing he needed was a confrontation with redcoats. There were other patrons in the tavern, however, far more chivalrous than he.

Several men jumped to their feet, but it was Andrew who reached her first. Grabbing her by the elbow, he hauled her across the tavern, yanked open the door that led into the private room, and shoved her inside. He had scarcely managed to get back to his seat before three British Regulars entered the tavern.

One of the soldiers, an officer, stepped forward, and Ethan slouched in his chair, hoping the shadows of his corner hid him from view of the officers. He knew Captain Worth; he'd danced with the man's sister less than a week ago at an officers' ball. Given his attire, his lack of a powdered wig, and the dim light of the tavern, he doubted Worth would even notice him, much less recognize him, but he didn't want to take any chances.

"Where is she?" Worth demanded, his hand on the hilt of his sword.

No one answered. The men gathered around the tables in the taproom simply stared at the hated lobsterbacks and said nothing.

The captain strode to the bar, where Munro presided over his kegs. "You there," he said, leaning across the bar to jab one finger into the tavern owner's shoulder. "Barkeep, we're looking for the girl who stole my pocket watch. We saw her come in here. Where is she?"

David turned his head away, hawked, and spat into a brass spittoon on the bar before he replied. "The only woman here is my wife, Molly." He glanced over at his wife. "Been dipping into soldiers' pockets, Molly, my dear?"

The buxom redhead scowled. "I wouldn't get that close to them!" she called back, setting three tankards of ale at Andrew's table. "I might get a disease."

At the laughter that ensued, Worth whirled around to face the crowd, his cheeks reddening with anger. "I won't let you hide that girl. She's a thief, and, by God, I'll have her swinging on a rope by tomorrow. Where is she?"

After a long moment of silence, Andrew said, "We haven't seen any girl come in here, have we, men?"

All the men in the tavern responded by shaking their heads.

"Lying rebels, all of you," the captain said with contempt. "It is pointless to lie. We can always search the place and find her ourselves."

At those words, every man in the tavern tensed, and some stood up, ready for the fight. Before things could get out of hand, Andrew stepped forward to address the officers. "I am afraid we cannot allow that, Captain," he said with quiet firmness. "Governor Gage has specifically ordered the Regulars not to use force, so I suggest you leave." He smiled politely. "Otherwise, we might have to evict you."

The captain was well aware of the danger he faced. The Boston mobs were a soldier's greatest fear these days. He scowled at Andrew. "You damned rebels won't get away with this impudence much longer!" he shouted. "We'll restore order here, the Sons of Liberty will be hanged for sedition, this little rebellion will be quashed, and British justice will once again prevail in the colonies."

Andrew gestured toward the door. "Save the speech for your troops, Captain," he suggested. "You've no audience for it here."

The officer turned on his heel and left the tavern, his companions right behind him. Once the door closed after them, David turned to his son. "Daniel, follow those redcoats," he ordered. "If they turn around to come back, run ahead and warn us."

He had barely finished these instructions before the nine-year-old was out the door. Andrew then walked over to the back room and let the girl out of her hiding place.

"Thank you," she gasped. "I thought I was done for!"

"Anyone trying to avoid King George's troops finds a welcome here," Andrew said, and led the girl to his table. "Did you really steal his watch?"

"He thinks I did, which would have been enough to have me arrested." She gave him an impudent grin. "He's an officer. He can afford to buy another."

Andrew and the other two men at his table laughed as the girl sat down with them. She was only a few feet away from Ethan, and he took advantage of the fact, studying her.

When he had first seen her in North Square, he had thought of her as having the face of an angel. But looking at her now, he found himself revising his opinion slightly. There was skepticism in that face, and irony. It was the face of one who had lived too long on life's hard edge, a face that knew how to lie without remorse or regret. The candlelight softened but could not hide the hollows in her cheeks that told of years of hunger. Yet there was an elusive quality of sweetness about her that went beyond mere beauty. She might steal a watch to buy food, but he'd wager she would share that food with a starving puppy.

He wondered at the coincidence that had brought her here, into the Mermaid, of all places. But was it coincidence? Ethan frowned, watching her thoughtfully over the rim of his tankard. He went over every event of the last few days in minute detail, every meager scrap of information he knew about the girl, but, try as he might, he could see no connection between a pretty street thief and Governor Gage. He finally concluded that a coincidence was exactly what it was. He would, of course, inquire about her among his sources to make certain.

Andrew shoved a tankard toward her. "Here. I'll have Molly bring you some supper."

She shook her head. "No, sir. I've no money to pay for it."

"Not even an officer's pocket watch?"

Ethan's voice drew the attention of all those at the next table. The girl turned toward him and met his gaze, her eyes wide. "I didn't steal his watch."

Ethan did not know if she was lying or not, but he realized it didn't matter. She had the ability to make others want to believe her, the ability to compel others to give her the benefit of the doubt.

"I almost wish I had stolen it," she went on. "I've been in Boston only a few days. I've nowhere to stay, and 'tis bitter cold tonight." She sighed, her expression suddenly forlorn. Now everyone was expected to feel sorry for her and offer her a place to sleep.

As if on cue, Andrew spoke up. "I'm sure Munro wouldn't mind letting you stay the night here. There's a shed by the alley. He keeps his cow there, but it's clean, and there's straw on the floor. I'll speak with him."

Her smile of gratitude was his reward. "Oh, thank you, sir. You're very kind to go to so much trouble."

"No trouble at all, my dear child." He patted her shoulder, then stood up and started toward the bar to speak with David.

Ethan rose to follow, not missing the apprehension that flashed briefly across the girl's face as she watched him.

"She might have stolen that watch, you know," David was saying as Ethan joined the two men at the bar. He listened to their conversation as he held out his tankard for another measure of rum.

"She probably did steal it," Andrew answered, "but looking at her, I can certainly see why."

"What if she steals from me?" the tavern owner demanded.

Andrew shrugged his shoulders. "What's there to steal in the shed? It's unlikely she'll make off with your cow in the middle of the night."

David hesitated for a moment, then nodded. "Very well. I'll let her stay the night."

"I was hoping we could do better than that," Andrew went on. "You could give her a job."

Ethan listened as his friend championed the girl, and he did not like it. He glanced at David, who made a sound of impatience as he poured a measure of rum into Ethan's tankard. "A job?" The innkeeper echoed Andrew's suggestion in disbelief. "Doing what?"

"She could sweep floors, help in the kitchen, serve the ale with Molly, that sort of thing, couldn't she?"

"And how am I supposed to pay her?"

"Pay her in food. God knows, she could use it."

"True enough." David glanced toward the table where the girl sat, and Ethan turned his head in time to see her smiling shyly back at the innkeeper.

"She's a pretty little thing, isn't she?" David murmured.

Ethan heard the hint of compassion in the other man's voice and knew he'd been right about that girl the moment he had first seen that smile of hers in North Square. She could enslave a man with that smile. He decided it was time to voice his opinion.

"Do you really think giving the girl a job is a good idea?" he asked, glancing at both his friends as he spoke. "We know nothing about her."

"What's there to know?" Andrew countered with a hint of irritation. "She's on the run from Regulars, she's obviously destitute and indigent, and you only need look at her to see she's in desperate straits. Sometimes I think you've no heart left in you."

"I don't." He set his tankard on the bar and turned to the man who had been his friend since childhood. "In these times, a heart is a dangerous thing to have."

"Good Lord," Andrew said, laughing in disbelief. "What, you think the girl's a spy?"

"I don't think anything yet. I just don't see why it's necessary to give a stranger a job."

"Out of simple kindness. Are you so caught up in fighting the king that you've forgotten how to be kind to a stranger?"

That stung, and Ethan frowned at his friend. "Very well. If David wants to give the girl a job, that's his business, but if she overhears something—"

"We meet in the back room to avoid just such a possibility," David interjected. "I agree with Andrew. There's no harm in giving the girl a cot and a few hot meals. And she won't have to sleep in the shed. She can sleep by the fire in the kitchen. It's warmer there. I'll have Molly find her some blankets and get her something to eat."

David went to speak with his wife, and Ethan turned to the man beside him. "I didn't know you felt so strongly about helping street urchins," he commented. "Or perhaps you only take an interest in the pretty ones?"

Andrew actually blushed. "N-nothing of . . . of the sort," he stammered in reply. "As I said, it's just an act of kindness."

"Kindness is fine," Ethan told him as he straightened away from the bar, "but remember that we know nothing about her, an unfortunate circumstance which I'm going to begin remedying right now."

There was something quite exhilarating about being a spy. It reminded Katie of her days as a street thief in London, the dizzying feeling of danger, the edgy taste of fear. There had always been true pleasure in the triumph of planning a coup with Meg, carrying it out successfully, and enjoying the spoils of the victory. She hoped she could succeed as well at spying as she had at pickpocketing.

So far, she thought she was doing quite well. An offer of employment so soon had been far more than she could have expected, but Katie didn't hesitate to take advantage of such a heaven-sent opportunity. She humbly accepted Mr. Munro's offer of a job in exchange for food and lodgings, then followed his wife, Molly, out of the taproom, through a buttery, and into the tavern kitchen.

Molly walked over to the huge brick fireplace that was built into the back wall of the kitchen, and, using two heavy cloth pads, she removed a kettle from the warming oven above the fire. "There's always baked beans kept hot around here," she told Katie. "And plenty of brown bread. Anytime you're hungry, just help yourself."

Katie sat down at the long, narrow kitchen table, and Molly placed a wooden trencher of the beans and bread before her. She stared down at her simple meal and felt the sharp twist of hunger in her belly. Gripping the edges of the table, she leaned forward and closed her eyes, breathing in the enticing fragrance of hot food, a smell that made her dizzy.

"How long?"

Katie opened her eyes and found Molly watching her. "What?"

"How long since you had a hot meal?"

Katie saw the kindness and understanding in the other woman's eyes and turned her head away sharply. "Long enough," she answered, and picked up her spoon. Fighting back the urge to gobble her meal like an animal, she began to eat.

To her relief, Molly didn't ask any more questions. "You can sleep here in the kitchen. We have a cot in the attic, and I'll have David bring it down here for you to sleep on." She pointed to a wooden chest in one corner of the room. "Blankets are in there. Tomorrow morning, we'll start you working. Goodness knows, I could use the help."

Molly returned to her thirsty customers in the taproom, and Katie ate her meal, thinking it had been a long time since anyone had looked at her with kindness.

Suddenly, all the exhilaration left her. She stopped eating and stared into space, realizing that she was going to be spying on people who had been kind to her, a cruel way indeed of paying back their kindness. She felt a sudden twinge of something she had not felt much of since her childhood. Guilt.

She rose to her feet, picked up her trencher, and crossed the kitchen, intending to dish up another helping of baked beans, forcing that unwelcome guilt from her mind. It was too bad, of course, but everyone in this world had to look out for themselves. If Molly foolishly told her things that ended up getting the woman into trouble, well, whose fault was that? Certainly not Katie Armstrong's. Life was a battle, and she was fighting for her own survival. Let Molly and everyone else do the same.

She reached for the ladle that hung on the wall beside the fireplace, reminding herself of the most important lesson she had ever learned about life: *Look after yourself, because no one else will.*

Even Meg, who had been the only person she had trusted since her mother's death, would never have put Katie's needs above her own, nor would she have expected Katie to do so for her. Theirs had been a relationship of mutual necessity, and neither of them had been able to afford the luxury of putting friendship ahead of survival. Survival always came first.

Now, for the first time, Katie had the chance of a life beyond mere survival, and she wanted that chance, wanted it more than she'd ever wanted anything. The hard part was done, and now all she need do was find John Smith. He might be among the men in the taproom at this very moment. Finding him was only the first step, and probably the easiest one. Getting proof of his sedition would be harder, but Katie had no doubt of her eventual success.

When she did accomplish this mission, there would be no more snatching meat pies and pocket watches. No more sleeping in stables. No more fear of prison or the gallows. No more looking over her shoulder for Willoughby.

Katie heard a sound behind her, and she jumped, dropping the ladle back into the kettle with a clang. She whirled around to find a man standing in the doorway, the man in oilskins who had mocked her in the taproom.

She tensed, waiting, wondering what he was thinking. This man wasn't like the others. They had felt sorry for her, just as she had known they would; they had wanted to help her. This man was different.

He watched her with cool, assessing gray eyes, eyes that she suspected could see far too much. His long black hair was caught back in a queue that only served to emphasize the lean planes of his face. He was a full head taller than she, and though his clothes were the rough oilskins of the docks, he wore them with a sort of casual elegance, reminding her of the lords she used to see amusing themselves in the East End brothels of London.

Though it might be a contradiction to describe him as both incredibly weary and vibrantly alive, that was what Katie sensed when she looked at him. There was something about him akin to the restrained energy of a whip just before it lashed out. Katie prided herself on her talent for assessing a person's character, but this was a man she could not fit into any of the usual categories. She was suddenly afraid. "Who are you?"

"There's no need to look so frightened," he said, his voice gentle. Somehow, that surprised her.

"I'm not frightened," she answered. "You startled me, that's all."

He gestured to the pot on the hearth. "If you want a second helping, go ahead and have it. No one's going to brand your hand for it, you know."

Though she wore her gloves and he could not possibly see the *T* burned into her palm, Katie instinctively hid her hand behind her back, then silently berated herself for such a revealing gesture.

"I wasn't stealing anything," she said defensively. "Molly already told me I could have more if I wanted it."

"Then get on with it, and stop looking like a guilty child," he said, his face lighting with an unexpectedly charming smile.

Katie caught her breath, realizing for the first time that here was a very handsome man. But there was something about him that made her wary. Living on the London streets had honed her survival instincts, and she trusted them. She didn't know how or why, but this man was dangerous.

She turned away to ladle another portion of beans into her trencher. She sliced off another helping of brown bread and turned back around to find he was still smiling at her. "Do you enjoy making fun of people?" she asked.

"No, I don't. Forgive me." He lifted his hands, palms facing her in a conciliatory gesture. "We seem to have gotten off to rather a bad start. Shall we begin again?"

She stared at him for a moment, suspicious and skeptical, but that smile of his seemed genuine enough, without a hint of his former mockery, and she found her tension easing slightly. "Very well."

"Then sit back down and eat your meal before it gets cold."

He spoke with the careless authority of one accustomed to being obeyed. He moved into the room with the languid, easy grace of a man who went where he wished and did what he pleased. He placed his tankard on the table, but he did not sit down. Instead, he waited for her to return to her seat, his gaze still fixed on her.

She frowned, uncomfortable with the scrutiny. "Why are you staring at me like that?"

"Was I staring? I apologize," he answered in a voice of silken smoothness, but he did not look away.

Katie returned to her chair and sat down. He pushed her chair in for her, then circled the table to take the chair opposite hers. The simple courtesy startled her. From a man dressed in oilskins, it was an uncharacteristic gesture. His clothes might indicate that he was a fisherman, or perhaps a long-shoreman, but if that were the case, she was a princess. "Who are you?" she asked again.

"My name is John Smith."

Stunned, Katie stared at him, unable to reply. In one of the patriot taverns less than an hour, and she was already having a conversation with the man she had been sent to find. Triumph flooded through her at the ease of her success, but she suppressed it, careful to keep her face expressionless. She said nothing.

"What's your name?" he asked, lifting his tankard to take a drink as he watched her through narrowed eyes.

"Katie."

"So, tell me, Katie, why did you take shelter here in the Mermaid after stealing that soldier's watch?"

Denying his assertion would be pointless, and

Katie did not bother to do so. She shrugged. "I've been in Boston only a few days, but that's long enough to know which taverns are Tory and which are Whig. When being chased by Regulars, it seems to me a good strategy to take refuge in a Whig tavern."

He smiled. "In other words, the enemy of my enemy is my friend? Do you really think the king's soldiers are your enemy?"

"If they had been able to pin theft on me, they would have hanged me. I'd say they were my enemies, yes."

There was a long silence. He took a long draught from his tankard and put it down slowly, then gave her a searching glance across the table. "I mean," he said, his gaze meeting hers, "are you Tory or Whig?"

Katie almost said she was Whig, of course, but in the space of a heartbeat, she decided against it. She would have to walk carefully with this man, and she decided an indifferent skeptic who needed to be persuaded was her best method of approach. "I have no political convictions. The only thing I worry about is having a place to sleep and food to eat. What do I care who rules the colonies?"

"You should care about that if you care about freedom."

She made a sound of contempt. "Freedom is a myth."

He leaned forward, and those gray eyes darkened to silver smoke, almost as if he were angry.

She sensed again the aura of danger that surrounded him. "It doesn't have to be," he answered. "Not if people have the courage to earn it."

"How does disobeying the king prove courage and earn freedom?"

"What choice do people have? Should they allow themselves to submit to slavery? Should they not fight against it?"

"You speak like a rebel," she countered. "Is it not sedition to talk this way?"

His anger disappeared, and his expression was suddenly bland. "What way? We are merely talking of slavery, and slavery is a perfectly legal trade in good King George's colonies."

She stared at him, feeling a hint of admiration. No wonder he was a successful spy. Anyone who wished to lead this man into a trap with words would have a difficult time doing it. "You talk like a rebel one moment and a loyalist the next. Which side of the fence do you stand on, Mr. Smith?"

"The true one, of course," he answered smoothly, and it did not escape Katie's notice that his answer was no answer at all. "Munro and I have been friends for a long time. Provided you don't steal from him, I'll let you stay."

The arrogance of the man almost made her laugh aloud. "You will? And what say do you have in the matter?"

"More than you could imagine." He paused and returned her stare with a long, searching glance of his own. "Andrew persuaded David to give you a job. I'm afraid he is highly susceptible to beauty in distress."

She had the feeling he could see right through her wiles, and she did not like it. "Unlike you, of course."

He grinned. "On the contrary, I am very appreciative of beautiful women."

Katie continued to eye him with skepticism. "But not the sort of man to be concerned with their distress."

"You don't know me well enough to judge what sort of man I am, do you?" he countered softly, and rose to his feet. "You should prove adequate as a kitchen maid, provided you work as well as you talk, of course."

"I'll earn my keep."

"I'm sure you will, my pretty little thief. I'll be around often enough to see that you do."

He turned away and left her. Alone in the kitchen, Katie wanted to laugh aloud at the quickness of her victory. She had found John Smith, and he was already playing right into her hands. How easy this had been.

Too easy. That thought brought her up sharply, and her feeling of triumph vanished as quickly as it had come. Why did he mean to take such a personal interest in her? It sounded as if he had suspicions about her. She knew if she wanted to earn her freedom, she had best watch her step with this man.

Still, she was not intimidated. She was a spy, after all, and she hadn't agreed to be one because it was safe. John Smith was no longshoreman, she knew that well enough from her London street days. She wondered how he obtained his information, and she vowed that she would find out.

If he intended to keep an eye on her, so be it. She was going to do the same, and perhaps what she discovered would be enough to earn her freedom.

4

The following morning, Katie opened her eyes to a shadow hovering over her. Startled, she reacted instinctively, flinging out her arm with enough strength to shove the person standing over her back several feet. The sound of stumbling feet and the crash of a chair to the floor followed.

"Ouch!" a voice objected. "That hurt!"

Katie jumped out of bed, oblivious to the pain she had caused. Being surprised out of sleep by a stranger in the night was a danger she had faced the many times she'd been forced to sleep on the streets. It was not something she had expected in the kitchen of a tavern. It had startled her badly.

She fumbled for the lamp and flint on the kitchen table, and once the lamp was lit, she held it high, turning toward the stranger who had startled her.

She found herself face to face with a boy of about nine or ten, a boy she knew she'd never seen before, but his distinct resemblance to Molly told her he must be that woman's son.

"You're awfully jumpy, aren't you?" he said as he bent down to rub his shin. "I didn't mean to scare you."

She wasn't about to admit she'd been frightened by a boy. "I wasn't scared. It's just that you startled me. I didn't expect to wake up with a stranger standing over me."

The boy righted the overturned kitchen chair and plopped down onto it. He didn't appear to feel any self-consciousness at having been caught studying her in her sleep, and he continued to regard her with unabashed curiosity. "I'm Daniel," he said, and thrust out his hand. "My parents own this tavern. I know your name is Katie. So now we're not strangers anymore."

She grinned and shook his hand. "I'm very pleased to meet you. But how did you know my name? I don't remember seeing you in the tavern last night."

"I saw you. You came running in to hide from the Regulars. After we hid you in the back room, the redcoats left, and my father sent me to follow them so he would know if they came back for you." He leaned forward in his chair. "Are you really a pickpocket?"

She heard the eagerness in his voice, and she had an idea of what was coming, but there was no point in lying about it, since everybody seemed to know. "I used to be."

"But you took that soldier's watch." Before she could open her mouth to protest, he went on, "How do you do it? Will you show me?"

Her suspicion confirmed that he wanted to know about dipping, Katie shook her head. "I'm not sure I should. Your mother wouldn't like it."

"C'mon," he entreated. "Mama won't mind."

Children always said that, she thought wryly, and it was never true.

She shook her head again and reached under her cot for her boots. She put them on, then crossed the kitchen and donned her cloak.

"Aw, c'mon. Show me. Show me."

"No, no, no," she said, laughing as she grabbed the pail that stood on the floor beside the back door. Leaving Daniel and his pleas behind, she walked outside into the frosty morning air. It was not quite dawn, but the sky was lightening with the first gray hint of it. After using the privy, she filled the pail with water from the well and returned to the kitchen. She ignited the banked coals in the hearth with the bellows, heated the water, and washed her face and hands, all the while ignoring Daniel's pleas to be taught the finer points of pickpocketing.

"Stop it," she finally said in a stern voice reminiscent of Miss Prudence. "I'm not going to do it, and that's that."

"Do what?"

Both of them turned around to see John Smith standing in the doorway that led to the taproom. He still wore the tattered brown oilskins of the night before, and there were tired lines around his eyes that showed he had not yet been to bed.

"John!" Daniel jumped up from the table and ran across the kitchen, throwing himself at the man with gleeful abandon.

As if this were a common occurrence, he was ready for the assault. He grabbed the boy, laughing as he lifted him into the air, slinging him over one shoulder like a sack of flour. "Good morning, Daniel."

Katie shook her head, watching him with the boy. "I believe you were here just a few hours ago. Don't you ever sleep?"

He grinned and sauntered into the kitchen, Daniel still slung over his shoulder. "I told you I'd be around to keep an eye on you," he reminded her as he crossed the room to her side. He bent down, dipping his shoulder to slide the boy to the ground. "Where's your father?" he asked. "I need to see him."

"They're both still abed," Daniel replied. "I'll get them."

He left the kitchen. John Smith watched him go, then returned his attention to her. He studied her for several seconds, and she tried not to squirm under the scrutiny. "Aren't you going to answer my question?" he finally asked.

He was standing so close, she felt suffocated. What was it about him that rattled her so? "What question?" she asked, grabbing for a poker to stoke the fire.

"What does Daniel want that you are refusing to do?"

"He wants a lesson in pickpocketing," she said with a sigh.

"I'm not surprised. You refused?"

"I don't think Molly would take kindly to lessons of that sort."

He laughed. "You're probably right." He paused, as if giving the matter further consideration, then he added, "Although that might depend on whose pockets he dipped into."

"Tories, you mean."

"Naturally. Molly might then consider it a patriotic duty." He glanced up and down the length of her, and his smile faded. "Why don't you sell that soldier's watch and buy yourself a decent dress?"

The sudden change of subject surprised her, but when she glanced down at herself, she could appreciate why he had asked the question. Her dress was a revolting shade of brown linsey-woolsey, and because it was the only garment she owned, it served as day dress, Sunday dress, and nightgown. It was tattered and stained and should have been thrown away long ago. But she couldn't very well purchase new clothes by selling a watch that didn't exist. Stealing Captain Worth's watch had been a sham she and the officer had concocted two days ago, with the viscount's blessing, of course. The purpose had been to get her into the Mermaid with a minimum of suspicion, and, except for the man standing before her, the ruse had succeeded well.

"I'm afraid I can't do that," she answered, looking him in the eye. "I told you before that there is no watch."

He started to reply, but at that moment, Molly walked into the kitchen, a pitcher in her hand and Daniel right behind her. "Katie was quite right to say no," she told her son as she crossed the room to Katie's other side.

"But I just wanted her to show me," Daniel said sulkily as he sat down at the table.

"My son is a persistent little beggar," Molly warned as she poured some of the water Katie had heated into her pitcher. "Don't you be giving in to him."

"Don't worry, Molly," Katie assured her. "I'm not going to teach him how to steal."

"She doesn't have to teach me how," Daniel interjected. "I'd just like to see her do it, is all."

Katie shook her head again, but the temptation to show off her greatest skill was becoming too great to resist. She set the poker back in the rack, then turned away, knowing full well that John Smith was directly in her path. The result was that she ran straight into him.

As if it were an instinctive reaction, she brought up her hands between them. In doing so, she managed to slide them inside his jacket to rest against his chest. Beneath his oilskins, she could feel his muscles tense at the intimate contact, and she gave him her most dazzling smile.

"Sorry." She slid her hands down his chest in a

way that was almost a caress and meant to be clearly seductive. His expression did not change, but she heard his sharp indrawn breath, and she realized that though he might hide his emotions well, he was not immune to a bit of feminine charm. She let her hands slide away and stepped around him, but she had taken only two steps before his voice stopped her.

"Give it back."

She turned around and looked at him with her most innocent expression. "Give what back?"

He held out his hand. "The shilling that was in my pocket."

"Spoilsport," she accused, and stepped forward to drop the coin into his palm.

"I didn't even see you take it!" Daniel cried in delight. "How did you do that?"

"By means you're too young to appreciate," John Smith answered for her, his voice wry.

Molly laughed, but her son did not. He frowned, clearly bewildered. "Huh?"

"Never mind." John put the money back into his pocket, then turned to give the boy a stern look. "Shouldn't you be about your chores? You'd best get them done, or you'll be late for lessons this morning."

"No lessons today," Molly answered for her son, turning away from the fireplace. "Parson Gilling is sick. He's been down with the influenza." She glanced at him and went on, "David will be down shortly."

"The sooner the better. I need to get some sleep."

The news that he had not yet been to bed did not seem to surprise Molly, and Katie realized she must be accustomed to this man coming and going from the Mermaid at odd hours.

"I'll see what's keeping him," Molly told him, and turned her attention to Katie. She waved a hand toward the snowy white sheets piled in a large basket in one corner of the room. "It would be a great help to me, Katie, if you start ironing those sheets."

"Of course," Katie answered.

"Irons are in the pantry." Molly left the kitchen with her pitcher of hot water, and Katie fetched the pair of irons and their heating plate to fulfill the other woman's request.

"That was really something to see, Katie," Daniel told her as she laid a sheet across the table to iron it.

He was looking at her with such obvious admiration, she couldn't help telling him, "I can pick locks, too."

"S'truth?"

She nodded, and he laughed. "You are so much fun, even for a girl. Aren't you going to show me how you got that shilling out of his pocket? Please?"

"That will be enough." John Smith's voice cut in with decisive authority, and the boy immediately fell silent. "Stop badgering her, and tell me what you're going to do today, since there are no lessons."

"Mama said I could go to Benjamin's print shop," Daniel told him. "Weeks ago, he said he'd teach me how to set the type for the newspaper if I got better at spelling." He lifted his chin with a proud grin. "And I did."

John laughed. "Yes, I heard about how you won the spelling bee yesterday. I think everybody in Boston knows by now."

Daniel rolled his eyes, and his freckled face scrunched with distaste. "Mama tells everybody. It's embarrassing."

Katie laughed at that, and she found to her amazement that John Smith was laughing, too. She studied him as she worked, listening as he talked with Daniel, and she realized the boy was hanging on his every word. Somehow, that surprised her. She would not have thought him to have a way with children. But then, he and Daniel seemed to know each other well, and the boy obviously worshiped him.

"Tell me a story, John," Daniel ordered, propping his elbows on the table as he looked at the man who sat opposite him.

John groaned, leaning back in his chair and stretching out his long legs beneath the table. "Don't tell me you want to hear about the tea party again."

"No, I want a new story, one you haven't told me before."

Ethan pulled out his watch and shook his head. "We don't have time. If you're going to help Benjamin Edes put out the next edition of the *Boston Gazette,* you'd best get yourself to Edes and Gill. They start before dawn over there. Go on with you."

Katie could not believe what she was hearing. She stopped ironing in astonishment as Daniel shoved back his chair and ran out the back door. The door banged shut as she looked over at John Smith. She found those perceptive gray eyes watching her closely.

"What thoughts are in your head, that you stare at me in such a horrified way?" he asked. "Have I grown a second head?"

She shook her head. "The *Boston Gazette* is one of the city's most radical newspapers. I may have been here only a few days, but even I know that."

"What of it?"

"I cannot believe Molly would allow her son to work for a printer who is distributing seditious literature. He's only a boy. What is she thinking to allow it?"

He shrugged, unperturbed by her ire. "Gage hasn't outlawed the newspapers yet."

She returned her attention to her work. "But he will. And when he does, that boy will be committing treason."

He grinned. "As a lawyer I know named Patrick Henry said once, 'If this be treason, make the most of it.' "

She shot him an unamused look. "You have a glib tongue about your cause, sir."

"Aye, perhaps I do."

"Aren't you afraid of being arrested?"

"For what?" He actually sounded amused. "Talking about rebellion isn't against the law, at least not yet. And if it were, it would be worth it, for this rebellion is a just one."

Katie made a sound of contempt, unimpressed. "All seditionists say that, I'm sure. Besides, whether the words are yours or this Patrick Henry or the scathing articles of Samuel Adams typeset by a boy and printed in Benjamin Edes's newspaper, it makes no difference.'Tis all just words, just talk. In the end, what difference will it make?"

"Words can change the world," he answered, smiling at her sound of disbelief. "And you needn't sound so skeptical." He leaned forward to rest his elbows on the table. "How did someone so young become so cynical?"

"I'm not cynical, just realistic," she answered, and set the now cold iron in her hand back on the hearth. "And I'm not that young," she added, reaching for the second iron that had been heating.

"Of course not," he answered gravely, resting his chin in his hand. "You must be all of nineteen. Clearly in your dotage."

She heard the teasing beneath the seriousness of his voice, and she made a face at him. "I'm twenty," she corrected, "and you needn't laugh." She stopped ironing. Staring down at the white linen, she added softly, "Twenty is old enough to lose one's illusions."

"Oh, I don't know. I still have some, and I'm thirty-three. Stop evading my question. How did you become so cynical?"

Katie sighed and continued her task. Why did he probe so? Still, she wanted to get close enough to him to learn his secrets, and to do that, she needed to reveal a few things about herself and establish some trust between them. "When I was a little girl, my mother was the mistress of a very rich man. Given that my own father was long gone and had never gotten around to marrying her, she didn't have much choice. Life is not kind to unprotected women. I lived among aristocrats, and I saw how they treated my mother. I remember quite well how they treated me." She looked at the man across the table, and she couldn't keep a hint of bitterness out of her voice when she said, "My mother died when I was ten, and her protector had no use for me. I was sent to an orphanage. Six months there was long enough for me. I ran away."

"And you've been on your own ever since?"

She heard the hint of compassion in his voice, and she turned on him savagely, hating it. "Don't you dare feel sorry for me!" she ordered, slamming the iron down on the heating plate in front of the fire. "I've done all right on my own. And I'll tell you what life has taught me—that no matter what people say, no matter how much they talk about freedom, if you don't have money or the proper line of ancestors, you can't ever be truly free."

He acknowledged her words with a nod.

"Under a monarchy, you are absolutely right. But what if the people governed themselves?"

"Without a king? Impossible."

"Why?" He leaned forward, his eyes burning into hers. "Why is that impossible? What if we elected our rulers, what if we could choose who governs us? Don't you see, Katie? That would make all the difference. That would mean a better life for people of all classes."

Katie stared at him, and for a moment, she imagined it. For a moment, she believed him. A spark of his idealistic hope flickered inside her, then died.

"It will never happen." She grabbed the finished sheet and folded it. "Class, money, breeding, and the quality of one's connections are what matter, and kings rule because they have the most money, the best breeding, and the highest status. Fine speeches don't mean a thing. Talk all you want about changing the world, but it won't change. If you weren't born into the privileged class, you have to make your own way and do the best you can, and life isn't fair. That's just the way it is."

She set down the sheet and turned away. She left the kitchen without a backward glance, despising him for making her hope, even for one tiny instant, that he might be right. Her only hope of a better life was in the hands of the viscount, a man who had more money and power than she would ever have, and she'd do well to remember that.

* * *

After a little more than a week at the Mermaid, a week of carrying firewood and scrubbing pots, a week of stoking fires and stirring stews, and only a fleeting glimpse or two of John Smith, Katie knew changes would have to be made. She'd never accomplish anything if she remained stuck in the kitchen all the time. She was supposed to meet Worth in the marketplace the following morning, and she had to find a way to get to North Square for that meeting. Not that she had anything to tell once she got there.

Katie picked up another dirty trencher and scraped the scraps of food it contained into the bucket beside her. Not too long ago, scraps like these had been her usual meal. James Willoughby had always been stingy with food and lavish with punishments. She was well away from him, but if she didn't learn something valuable, she just might find herself on her way back to his farm in Virginia. She knew it was probably unrealistic to think she could learn anything of significance so soon, but that didn't stop her from hoping she would.

She had to find out more. She guessed the room where they had hidden her that night a week ago was used for John Smith and his fellow spies to meet in private, because the night of her arrival at the Mermaid, she had seen him go into that room, along with Andrew Fraser and two other men. They had remained there for several hours with the door shut, pretending to be engaged in a long drinking bout. Molly had helped carry out the pretense, going in and out of there carrying trays of ale, but Katie had seen the frozen puddle of ale outside the window the next morning and had not been fooled. She suspected that John and those other men were exchanging information and plotting sedition against the king. If she could find a way into that back room, she might overhear something important. It still wasn't the proof Lowden demanded, but any information she could glean would help her find that proof.

Persuading Munro to let her help Molly serve those men probably wouldn't be too difficult. He'd looked at her with the wary eye of a good innkeeper the first few days and kept a close watch on his liquor supplies, but after over a week of her charm, he was putty in her hands. No, she wasn't concerned about Munro. John Smith worried her far more.

Katie stopped scrubbing trenchers and stared out the back window of the kitchen. John Smith. He dressed like a longshoreman, but he had the manners and attitude of a gentleman. Where did he get the information he passed on to his cohorts at the Mermaid, and from whom? She had to find out, but she did not know how she could ask questions about him without arousing suspicion.

"Daydreaming isn't part of your job, Katie."

Molly's amused voice broke into her thoughts, and Katie gave a start. "I'm sorry. I don't usually daydream. It won't happen again."

Molly set a load of pewter tankards beside Katie

to be washed. "That's all right. I know what it's like to wash all these dishes. Daydreaming is certainly more fun. So, what were you thinking about?"

Katie dunked a tankard into the basin of hot, soapy water. "Oh, nothing important," she answered with a shrug. "I was—" She broke off, struck by a sudden idea, an idea that was perfect for finding out more about the enigmatic man who dominated her thoughts.

She cleared her throat. "I was thinking . . . that is, I was wondering . . . umm . . . about John Smith."

Molly chuckled as she picked up a towel and began to dry the tankards Katie had washed. "Were you, now? Well, that's understandable."

Turning to the other woman, Katie hoped she looked slightly lovestruck and very embarrassed. "He seems like a . . . a very nice man."

Molly's chuckle turned into laughter. "John Smith might be many things, but nice isn't one of them."

"Well, I thought he was nice."

Molly leaned on the table and gave her a questioning stare. "Did you?"

"Yes, I did. But he looks rather sad, I think. And lonely. Does he have any family?"

"Not that I know of."

"That's a shame," Katie murmured. "He and Munro are very thick."

"They are friends," Molly agreed. "Of course, he's known David a long time."

"Your son worships him."

"Aye." Molly breathed the agreement with a resigned sigh. "And I'm not sure I'm glad of it."

"Why not?"

"Smith is a very private man. He doesn't get too close to anyone, and children don't much understand the bounds of privacy. He doesn't like to talk about himself."

"That makes him rather mysterious, doesn't it?"

"I suppose that's one way of looking at it," Molly answered, and fell silent. Katie waited, but the other woman said nothing more, obviously unwilling to discuss the subject any further.

Katie, however, was not deterred by Molly's hesitation. She persisted. "Is John coming to the Mermaid tonight?"

"Aye, a bit earlier than usual. I promised to make him some of my codfish cakes. Eth—" She broke off whatever she'd been about to say and said instead, "He loves my codfish cakes."

"Well, I'm glad. At least he'll get a decent meal for once. With all this coming and going at such odd hours, he can't be eating well. I'm certain he doesn't get enough sleep, either."

Molly's expression became concerned. "Now, don't you go getting any ideas about him, Katie. He's a handsome fellow, sure enough, but he's not one to set your cap for, if that's what you're thinking."

"I'm not!" she denied with just enough heat to make the words seem like a lie. "I'm just a little worried about him, is all. And I can't help being curious."

"Aye, and curiosity killed the cat. Katie, heed my words. John Smith is not the steady sort that makes a good husband. He's had many a girl thinking what you're thinking, and it never came to anything. Don't go setting yourself up for heartbreak. Find a nice, reliable fellow who doesn't come and go like the wind. That's my advice."

Molly straightened away from the table. "I'd better return to the taproom. By the way, I'll be going to North Square tomorrow morning to do the marketing, so you and I will need to make a list tonight." She sighed. "I do hate going to the marketplace. I've never been much of a bargainer, and now, with the shortages and high prices, it's even worse."

A heaven-sent opportunity if ever there was one. Katie took a deep breath. "If you hate it so much, why do it?"

"If I didn't, who would?"

"I could do it for you."

Molly raised her eyebrows and laughed. "And why would I let a slip of a girl who has a fondness for other people's watches do my marketing for me?"

"Because I could get you better prices," Katie answered confidently. "I'm very good at negotiating."

"Aye, and sure of yourself as well."

Before Katie could answer that, another person entered the conversation. "She has good reason to be sure of herself," said a wry voice behind them. Both women turned around to see John Smith in the doorway, leaning indolently against the door-jamb, arms folded across his chest. "This maid could charm King George himself. And she's right, Moll. You'll get better prices if you let her do the shopping. Just don't let her go alone with your money purse, or you might never see her again."

He always appeared out of nowhere. Katie saw the cool amusement in his eyes, and she felt her insides twist with sudden dread. He always looked at her as if he knew all about her, as if he understood every trick in her repertoire, as if he knew the truth behind every lie she told. Damn, he looked at her as if he knew she was spying on him, and the knowledge amused him.

He doesn't really know anything about me, she told herself. *He can't possibly know.* But she had the feeling that he was determined to find out, and that could jeopardize everything, including her life.

5

Molly glanced from Katie to John Smith and back again. She seemed to sense the sudden tension in the air and cleared her throat nervously. "Well," she said, and started for the door leading into the taproom, "if you think you can get me better prices, Katie, I'll let you do the shopping tomorrow, and we'll see." She looked up at the tall man, who moved out of the doorway to let her pass. "I'll tell David you're here," she added, and left the kitchen.

Katie returned to her work, hoping he would leave, but he did not. She could feel his speculative gaze burning into her back. Finally, she could stand it no longer. She turned and faced him, drying her hands on her apron. "Why do you always stare at me?"

"I'm trying to make up my mind about you."

Katie's dread deepened. "Why? What do you want of me?"

A smile lifted one corner of his mouth. "I don't know yet. I'll think of something."

"Oh, really?" Katie scowled at him, knowing he was playing games with her. She did not like the feeling of being a mouse in a cat's paws. "When you do, pray let me know."

"I will." He straightened away from the door-jamb, but he did not leave. "Tell me why you were asking Molly questions about me."

"I wasn't—" Katie drew a deep breath, exasperated. It was useless to deny that she'd been asking questions. He had obviously overheard at least part of the conversation. What was it about him that rattled her so? "I was just curious."

"Indeed?" He began walking toward her slowly. "Why?"

Katie took an involuntary step back and immediately hit the table behind her. She watched as he came closer, and she found herself unable to resume her pretense of being interested in him for romantic reasons when he watched her so closely. Her mind raced, searching for a lie plausible enough to satisfy him, but she could think of none.

He came to a halt in front of her, so close that she could feel the heat of his body even though he was not touching her. Suddenly, she wanted to know the truth about him, not because she was a spy. No, she wanted the truth for another reason, a reason she could not define even to herself.

"Who are you, John Smith?" she whispered. "Who are you really?"

He bent his head, and the rough stubble of his unshaven face brushed her cheek. His breath was warm in her ear as he said, "If you're curious about me, I'd be happy to answer any of your questions. I would, of course, expect something from you in return."

The implication was clear, and Katie shivered with fear and more as his lips brushed her ear. All her senses told her she was in danger, and she had to think. But she could not think.

This man was unlike any other she had ever met. This was a man she could not manipulate with a melting glance and a few sweet words. This was a man she could not fool with a few glib lies or beguile with a few compliments. In fact, when it came to guile, she'd wager John Smith could teach her a thing or two.

He lifted his hands, slid his fingers into her short hair, and tilted her head back. She realized he was going to kiss her, and a quivering excitement began deep inside her, an excitement she had never felt at the touch of any man before. Lost in the sensation, she closed her eyes, and she forgot that this man was her enemy. She forgot that he was a traitor and she was a spy. She forgot to breathe.

His lips grazed hers lightly, brushing her mouth in a slow, maddening caress that robbed her of the ability to think. Katie leaned into him, silently pleading for more than this feather-light kiss.

"If you keep responding so sweetly," he murmured against her mouth, "I might be able to make you forget your questions altogether, and you'll come to know me in the truest sense of the word."

He was laughing at her. Somewhere past her drugged senses, she could hear the amusement in his voice, and she realized that amusement was at her expense. Anger doused the excitement inside her, and Katie opened her eyes, feeling like an utter fool. She tried to pull away from him, but his arms wrapped around her, and her attempts to free herself were useless.

"What, you don't want to take me up on my suggestion?" he asked, smiling in the face of her futile struggles. "Katie, you wound me."

"I am very sorry to hear it," she answered, glaring up at him. "Let go of me."

The laughter faded from his expression, and his face hardened into uncompromising lines, but, to her surprise, he complied with her demand and let her go. "I hope we understand each other," he said softly as he took a step back. "From now on, keep your curiosity and your questions to yourself. Stay out of my affairs."

He turned away and left the kitchen. Katie watched him go, berating herself for losing her head in such a silly fashion. She was going to prove a poor spy indeed, if a rogue's kiss could divert her so easily.

And he was a rogue. He was also a traitor. He was in the thick of this rebellion, yet no one seemed to know anything about him. That was very odd in itself. Most people had family, friends, a history of sorts, and were not so unwilling to talk about them. John Smith was a man who kept his own counsel very well.

Katie's humiliation gave way to her innate stubbornness. He might be clever, but so was she. She'd lived all her life by her wits, and she intended to use them to discover the truth about John Smith. If he thought a kiss and a few orders were going to divert her from that purpose, he was sadly mistaken.

"Doesn't that fancy chef you've got ever feed you?" Molly muttered under her breath, watching in good-humored exasperation as the man beside her helped himself to another heaping plateful of codfish cakes and succotash from the pots on her hearth.

"Of course," Ethan answered, "but the poor fellow's fallen on hard times. With the Port Bill in effect, there's not an oyster or lobster to be got anywhere, and with butter so scarce, he can't make his elaborate sauces. Besides, not even the fanciest chef could make better codfish cakes than you."

"I didn't make them. Katie did."

His expression of surprise made her laugh. "While you were meeting with David, I gave her a cooking lesson. She knew you would be having supper here tonight, and she asked me to teach her how to make your favorite dish, so I did." Molly gave her fish stew another stir, then straightened to give the man beside her a searching glance. "You realize the girl's infatuated with you."

Ethan laughed. "You think Dorothy, the barmaid over at the White Swan, is in love with me, too."

"So she is," Molly answered promptly. "Liberty isn't her cause. You are."

"Tell me something, Moll," he said, looking at her in exasperation. "Is there any woman in Boston that you *don't* believe is in love with me?"

She scowled. "Well, I'm certainly not," she answered tartly. "And I wish you would take this seriously. The hearts of young women are easy to bruise."

"Perhaps," he answered skeptically. "In Katie's case, I have my doubts."

"She might have had a difficult life, and she might appear a bit hard on the outside, but really, I don't think she is. You know she's asking me questions about you."

"Yes, and questions make me suspicious."

"That's nothing new," Molly answered. "You're always suspicious."

"True." Ethan pinched off the crispy edge of a codfish cake from the trencher in his hand and popped the morsel into his mouth. He added, "I confess that I see conspiracies everywhere."

"In this case, I think your suspicions are groundless. She didn't ask about anyone else. Just you."

Those words caught his attention. Ethan leaned close to the woman beside him. "Pray tell me," he murmured, "exactly what questions did she ask?"

"None of the questions a spy would ask, if that's what you're thinking," Molly answered, her voice as low as his. "She didn't ask what you discuss with the others in the back room. She didn't ask about anyone's political opinions. She wanted to know if you get enough sleep because you look so tired all the time. She asked about your family and your friends, saying they don't seem to take very good care of you. That's hardly the talk of a spy."

"True." He thought of how Katie had melted against him when he held her in his arms, of how sweetly she had responded to his kiss, and his instincts told him that the pleasure she had taken from that kiss had been genuine. If Molly was right, if she was infatuated with him, her questions were natural enough. Still, he could not quite believe it. That girl looked out for herself.

Molly tapped her spoon on the edge of the pot, then set it aside. "You don't really think she's in Gage's pay, do you?" she asked, looking up at him. "That slip of a girl who looks like a nor'easter would blow her away?"

"No, I don't, Molly, not really. Gage is too compassionate to use a starving girl. He'd at least feed her enough to keep body and soul together if she were in his pay. So, stop fussing like a hen with one chick. Besides, I've made inquiries about that girl, and she has absolutely no connection with Gage that I can discover."

"You investigated her background?"

"Of course I did. She is an indentured servant

from Virginia, and her master has reported her as a runaway. I cannot be certain, but I believe she entered the city only a few days before she came bursting through the doors of the Mermaid with Regulars on her tail. I don't see how she could possibly know Gage or anyone working for him, and she's not had time to develop the contacts she would need in order to be a spy for hire."

Molly shook her head sadly. "You have a beautiful girl infatuated with you, and the only thing you can think about is whether or not she's a spy. Any other man would just kiss her and get on with it."

"I did kiss her," Ethan answered, grinning at the surprised look Molly gave him.

"You did? When?"

"Only a few hours ago."

"Indeed?" Molly gazed at him curiously. "And how did she react?"

His grin widened. "She kissed me back but glared at me afterward as if she wanted to slap my face."

"That proves my point," Molly countered with triumph. "That just shows that she's half in love with you already. I warned her off you, of course, because I knew that would be what you'd want me to do. I told her you weren't the steady kind, but I'm afraid that only made her more curious about you. And, to be honest, I can't say I'm all that unhappy about her feelings for you."

Ethan gave her an exasperated look in return. "You are hopelessly romantic, Moll," he accused.

"There is no place in my life for pretty girls who have the silly idea of being in love with me, especially if they are too clever for their own good and have a penchant for other people's watches."

"Can you blame her for that? She needed a warm place to sleep, and you only have to look at her to know how life has treated her. Believe me, I know what it's like to be indentured. It's no better than slavery. Besides——"

David Munro entered the kitchen, interrupting his wife's defense of Katie. "Andrew and Colin are finally here."

Ethan stepped away from the hearth to follow David out of the kitchen, and the subject of Katie was forgotten. "Then, since Joseph is also here, we can begin," he answered. "I have important news for them."

Andrew Fraser, Colin Macleod, and Joseph Bramley were all staring at him, dismayed by the news he had brought.

Ethan leaned back in his chair and remained silent, letting the information sink into their minds.

Joseph was the first to speak. "Gage is to be supplanted by this Lowden fellow?"

"No," Ethan answered. "Gage is still in charge, and Lowden will make a show of reporting to him. I suspect, however, that Lowden's primary responsibility will be quite different—to report directly to London."

"Still," Joseph said, "Gage has always been

highly regarded by the king and his ministers. Why the sudden loss of faith in him?"

"This news is not really surprising," Ethan countered. "After all, Gage has not been particularly effective in dealing with us. I'm sure London will welcome any recommendations Lowden might have."

Colin spoke up. "Just who is this Lowden?"

Ethan opened his mouth to answer, but a soft knock on the door kept him silent. At Andrew's order to come in, Molly entered with fresh rum and ale. It was not until she had taken away the empty tankards on the table, left the room, and closed the door behind her that Ethan spoke again.

"Viscount Lowden," he said in answer to Colin's question. "Eldest son of the earl of Ravenstock. Ambitious, ruthless, and just arrived from London, eager to make a name for himself and return to England in glorious triumph. He is also said to be a more fashionable dandy than Ethan Harding."

"But what is his true purpose here?"

Ethan shook his head. "I don't know. The official word from Province House is that he is here as a liaison between Lord North and Gage, but that is ridiculous. Why shouldn't Gage just communicate directly with the king's minister? I intend to find out what he's really doing here in Boston."

"What makes him a danger to us?"

"I am told he is quietly approaching men of influence, lawyers, merchants, and the like, who are known to be sitting on the political fence and are undecided about which side to support."

"That makes sense," Andrew said. "A fence-sitter is more likely to be persuaded to the Tory side. Especially if they are offered lucrative rewards direct from a representative of Lord North, who everyone knows has the king's ear."

Colin gave a snort of contempt. "A fence-sitter is the worst sort of coward. Let's find 'em, and I'll heat the tar myself."

Ethan turned to Joseph. "You'll need to warn Samuel Adams, Paul Revere, and Dr. Warren about this as soon as possible. I will do all I can to identify Lowden's true purpose here, and if it poses a danger to us, we will need to take steps to deal with it."

Joseph tilted his head to one side, eyeing Ethan across the table. "You sound confident of success."

Ethan shrugged. "I don't mean to imply that it will be easy. But we are usually able to find out what the Tories are up to fairly quickly." He gave them a wry smile. "Unfortunately, they are able to do the same."

"Not to you," Colin said. "At least, not yet. God willing, it will stay that way."

Ethan glanced at each man in turn. "Gentlemen, if you hear anything about the viscount through your own sources, let me know. I must know what his intentions are. In that, Ethan Harding, loyal Tory, will be of great use, I think."

Joseph shook his head in amazement. "Sir, you

have my admiration. I don't know how you manage to maintain these two identities of yours without getting caught."

" 'Tis very simple, my friend," Ethan answered, meeting the other man's gaze across the table. "I don't get caught because I never trust anyone until I am absolutely sure of their loyalty."

Following someone was not as easy as it used to be, Katie acknowledged to herself as she pulled her cloak more tightly around her body to shield herself from the cold February wind. Far ahead of her, John Smith paused beneath the light of a streetlamp, and Katie ducked swiftly into the closest alley, afraid he would turn his head and see her behind him.

She waited, remembering the old days in London, when Meg had taught her the fine art of shadowing someone. It was a useful skill, for they would sometimes have to follow their intended target for blocks before finding an opportunity to deprive him of his purse, and Katie had become very good at it. Meg had taught her well, but it felt like a much more difficult and risky task now than it had then.

The thought of Meg was painful, but as she followed her quarry through the dark streets of Boston, she could not help remembering the other girl. They had both been eleven years old when they met, but Meg had always seemed far older. It was Meg who had taught her how to survive on the streets. It was Meg who had shown her how to dip into men's pockets and women's reticules. It was Meg who had taught her theft, forgery, and swindling so that she could survive without resorting to prostitution, which was the usual fate of girls in her situation.

She pushed memories of Meg out of her mind and returned her full attention to the man far ahead of her. His meeting with the others tonight at the Mermaid had lasted more than three hours, and she would give a great deal to know what they had discussed, but she had not been able to get anywhere near that back room.

Instead, when the clock struck midnight, Molly had dismissed her and sent her to bed. There on her cot in the kitchen, she had waited beneath her blanket, awake and listening for the meeting to end and the men to depart for home. John Smith had been the last to leave, and she had slipped out to follow him, determined to find out something she could tell the viscount tomorrow.

After a few seconds, she dared a look out into the street and found that John Smith was nowhere to be seen. Cursing herself for losing him, she leaned back against the alley wall and decided it was probably best to return to the Mermaid.

But when she took another look out into the alley, she caught a brief glimpse of his black-clad figure far ahead of her. He was almost indiscernible at this distance, and Katie slipped out of the alley and continued to trail silently after him.

They passed the Old Granary Burying Ground and turned onto Beacon Street, where luxurious mansions backed up against Boston Common. When he turned onto a narrow side street, she followed as closely as she could. When he turned another corner, she was afraid she might lose him altogether, but she did not dare quicken her pace to run after him. The night was cold and silent, and her footsteps would surely be heard if she broke into a run.

When she reached the place where he had turned, Katie came to a halt and cautiously took a peek around the corner. She saw a lane of sorts, with a high wall running along one side and stables along the other. Beyond the stables lay the huge expanse of Boston Common. Fifty yards or so down the lane, she saw John Smith slip through an opening in the wall and disappear from view. The iron bars of a gate made a slight clanging sound as they closed behind him.

Katie cautiously approached the gate he had slipped through and looked between the wrought-iron bars. In the moonlight, she could see graveled paths and boxwood hedges, a gazebo and a fountain, all the accoutrements of a wealthy man's garden.

Between the bare branches of the shrubs and trees, she could see the back wall of a redbrick mansion that rose three stories high. In one of the rooms on the ground floor, lamps were burning, and through the expensive leaded window glass, she could clearly see the luxuries within the house. Gilt mirrors, woven tapestries, lavish furnishings, a pianoforte, oil paintings. He must live here.

Katie smiled with satisfaction. She'd been right about him all along. Longshoreman indeed! Now that she knew where he lived, finding out his identity would not be difficult at all. The viscount would be well pleased with this information.

"Is your curiosity finally satisfied?"

She whirled around to find John Smith scarcely a yard behind her, one shoulder against the wall of the alley, arms folded across his chest. Katie went cold with fear.

She was quick, but he was quicker. When she tried to dart past him, his hands closed over her shoulders in a merciless grip, and she was shoved back against the wall beside the gate. His face in the moonlight gave no clue what he was thinking.

"What good will running do?" he murmured. "Where could you possibly go?"

"Anywhere as long as I'm away from you!"

"Katie, you astonish me. A short time ago, you were willing to follow me anywhere. Now you wish nothing but to be away from me." He sighed in mock exasperation. "Women are so fickle. Can't ever make up their minds."

The usual ironic amusement was in his voice, but beneath it was something else, a weariness, as if he gained no pleasure from baiting her.

"You knew I was following you?"

"Not until I was inside. I could see you from my

bedroom window, standing by the gate. You're very good at shadowing someone, but may I give you some advice? If you're going to skulk outside a man's house and don't want to be seen, then don't stand in the moonlight, in plain view of the house."

Katie silently berated herself for making such a foolish mistake. She had been so pleased with her own cleverness in managing to discover where he lived that she had forgotten caution. Now, if she could not find a way out of this mess, she would pay the price for her carelessness.

The viscount's ominous warning came back to her. *If you are found out by the rebels, you will be tarred, feathered, beaten, and probably killed.*

She licked her dry lips, trying to think of a plausible reason she could give for following him, but it was for naught. She had survived most of her life by using her wits, but now at the most crucial moment, her wits chose to desert her.

John Smith had her imprisoned in his hands like an animal in a trap, and the strength of his grip brought the sickening certainty that nothing she said would make a difference now. She looked into his eyes, eyes as cold and hard as granite in the moonlight, and she had no doubt about his intentions. He was going to kill her.

6

What the hell was he going to do with her now? Ethan stared down into Katie's pale face, and he knew what he ought to do, he knew what his safest option would be, and he was angry enough that he almost found that option appealing. Now that she knew where he lived, she could easily find out his true identity. What she did with that knowledge could jeopardize not only himself but the cause he had spent ten years fighting for.

But he had to shoulder his share of the blame. He had been so preoccupied with the matter of Viscount Lowden that he had not noticed her following him until it was too late. He didn't often make such a careless mistake. Damn his preoccupation, and damn her curiosity.

But was it only curiosity that had led her to follow him?

He studied her in the moonlight, but he could find no answer to that question in her expression.

The only thing he sensed from her was a hint of fear. He could feel her slender body trembling in his arms.

What had impelled her to follow him? She was a thief and a liar, and despite Molly's romantic ideas, he doubted very much that she was infatuated with him. She could be a Tory spy, but he had found no connection between her and the governor. She had been in Boston less than a fortnight; his sources had already verified for him that she was a runaway.

Was she a spy? Or was she just an infatuated girl?

Ethan didn't know, but he bloody well intended to find out. Keeping one arm wrapped securely around her, he reached into his pocket for his gate key. "Come with me," he said, and unlocked the gate. She seemed to sense struggle would be futile, for she did not even try to escape as he hauled her across the back gardens and into his house.

Once inside, Ethan lit a lamp and took her into his study, where he pushed her into a chair. He removed his cloak and tossed it over the settee, then made a fire in the grate. He chose not to sit down. Instead, he stood with his back to the fire, thrust his hands into the pockets of his oilskin trousers, and studied her for a long time without speaking.

She pushed back the hood of her cloak and sat rigidly in the chair, lifting her head to meet his gaze straight on. "Well, now what?" she demanded.

He did not reply. There was defiance in her

voice and in the blue eyes that looked back at him, but despite her attempt at bravado, it was clear that she was still badly frightened, and he knew the idea that he might put a permanent end to her curiosity had occurred to her. *Good,* he thought with some satisfaction. That would probably make it easier for him to find out what he wanted to know.

"Yes," he finally said, "now what?" He stepped away from the fireplace. "Brandy, I think, would be a very good idea."

He crossed the room to the cherry-wood liquor cabinet and poured a measure of his best brandy into a crystal tumbler. Thinking perhaps it might require more than one drink to loosen her tongue, Ethan brought both bottle and glass to her. He set the bottle on the table beside her chair and held the tumbler out to her, but she did not accept it.

"Take it," he urged. "You are definitely in need of a drink. God knows, you look like a frightened rabbit."

She bristled at his words, clearly not liking the comparison. "I'm not frightened of you."

He reached for her hand. "Liar," he said, and curled her gloved fingers around the tumbler. "You are scared to death, and well you should be. Now, drink."

He stood beside her chair and watched as she downed the brandy in one swallow. She immediately choked, a clear indication that she was not used to spirits. But then, he already knew that. David had already assured him that she had made no attempt to dip into the tavern's supply of ale and rum.

"Excellent," he said as she set the glass down on the table beside her. "Some color is coming back into your face now. For a moment, I thought you were going to faint on me, and that would have been very inconvenient."

"I've never fainted in my life."

"There's a first time for everything." He shifted his position so that he was standing directly in front of her. He placed one hand on each arm of her chair and bent his head until his face was only inches from her. It was a dominating position and told her he had all the advantage. "Tell me," he murmured, looking straight into her eyes, "why this passionate desire to know all about me? Why does a runaway bondswoman have such an interest in my life?"

She tensed, and he knew she had not reckoned with the possibility that he would discover the truth about her. She leaned back as best she could within the confines of the chair and glared at him. "I am no runaway!"

He shook his head slowly. "Katie, I will have the truth from you this night if I have to beat it out of you."

"I'm telling you the truth."

"I doubt you've ever told the truth in your life."

"Then why ask me any questions?" she countered, and he caught a hint of despair behind the defiance in her voice. "Why not just kill me and be done with it?"

"My dear girl," he replied with mock astonishment, "I wouldn't dream of killing someone with your talents. It would be such a waste."

Her hands clenched into fists—to stop their shaking, he suspected. But he could not afford to take pity on her. There was too much at stake. He leaned even closer. "Answer my question. Why are you asking questions about me and following me?"

Ethan waited several seconds, watching her, but she stared right back at him and said nothing. Bullying her wasn't going to work. He decided to try a different approach. He straightened away from the chair and tilted his head to one side, eyeing her speculatively. "Tell me, Katie, what do you think Mr. James Willoughby will do to you when I send you back to him?"

He expected a very convincing denial that she knew any such person. He expected anger, or possibly an attempt to charm her way out of the situation. She did not do what he expected.

She grabbed the bottle beside her, then smashed it against the edge of the table, spraying brandy and shards of glass in all directions. She slashed at him with the broken bottle, forcing him to jump back. The moment he did, she was out of the chair.

She faced him with her makeshift weapon and moved slowly toward the door, her gaze never leaving his face. "I'll not go back to Virginia," she said through clenched teeth. "I'd rather die."

The vehemence of her reaction was startling. At this moment, she was poised for flight, her eyes wide with a terror far greater than any he had provoked in her thus far. He wondered what this Willoughby had done to her. He could well envision the possibilities, and he was sickened by them.

Just now, she reminded him of a wild, cornered animal, and he treated her as one, speaking in a gentle voice as he walked slowly toward her. "It's all right, Katie. Provided you start telling me the truth, and provided we can come to some sort of agreement, I'll not send you back to him. You have my word on it."

His word did not seem to be enough for her. She lifted her weapon higher, pointing the sharp, jagged edge of the broken bottle at his face, and continued to move backward until she hit the door behind her. Her hand was shaking badly, and he had no doubt she would attempt to use her weapon if she felt she had to do so. That did not worry him, since he could easily overpower her by force, but Ethan simply held out his hand. "Give me the bottle, Katie."

She did not comply. She did not move.

"Even if you manage to get away from me, all I need to do is send the constables after you," he pointed out. "You have no horse, no friends, and no money. You would be found before you could even get out of the city, and you would be packed off to Virginia. Wouldn't it be better for you to take your chances with me?"

With those words, all the fight seemed to drain out of her. She sagged back against the door, and he took advantage of the moment. He seized her wrist and wrenched it with just enough force to make her drop the broken bottle. Still holding her wrist firmly, he bent and picked up her makeshift weapon, then led her back to her chair. He put the jagged bottle far out of her reach in the opposite corner of the room and resumed his place in front of her.

"Now, let's return to the matter at hand, shall we?" Ethan suggested, his voice once again becoming hard and implacable. "As flattered as I am at the idea that a beautiful girl such as yourself would be infatuated with me, I don't believe it for a moment. So, tell me the real reason you are asking people questions about me. Tell me why you followed me tonight."

When she still did not answer, he shrugged and said, "Very well. I'll have the constable fetch you. You'll spend the night in stocks, and tomorrow I'll see that you are returned to Virginia. I'm sure your master will be overjoyed to see you again."

Her lip trembled, and she suddenly capitulated. "All right, all right!" she cried. "I confess, I am not in love with you at all. I had other reasons for my interest."

"Which are?"

"From the way you talked, it became obvious that you are a Whig rebel and one of those Boston revolutionaries," she told him. "I also realized that the Mermaid is one of the places where you meet with other rebels."

"So?"

She took a deep breath. "So, I thought if I could find out something important about you and the others, something damaging, then it might..." Her voice faltered, and she fell silent.

"I am losing my patience. It might what?"

She licked her dry lips. "I figured it might be worth something to the government here. If I found out some things about you and your rebel friends, I thought somebody might pay me for the information."

Now, that was an answer with a ring of truth in it. The girl was an opportunist, and she was definitely in need of money. "And to whom did you think you would sell this information?"

She shrugged. "I thought the governor, perhaps. Or his aide-de-camp."

"What do you know of the governor?"

"I know he wants to find out everything he possibly can about the Whigs."

"And how do you know that?"

"For heaven's sake," she said impatiently, "I can read a newspaper."

Katie was full of surprises. Most girls in her situation couldn't even write their own names. "I see. So you assumed Governor Gage would find information about me and my friends valuable?"

"There is talk on the streets that Gage has paid private citizens for information in the past. When I realized you were a seditionist and the Mermaid a rebel meeting place, I figured I might just as well take advantage of that and see what I could get."

"Let me assure you that at this point, you don't have any information Gage's spies don't already know."

A shrewd look came into her eye. "Except where John Smith, longshoreman, really lives."

Ethan well appreciated the danger of that knowledge. He fell silent, thinking over what she had told him, and she seemed to take his silence for condemnation. "I'm just trying to survive," she said defensively. "I can't remain in Boston long, or Willoughby might find me, and as I told you before, I would rather die than go back to him. But to move on, I need money. I thought this would be a quick way to get it."

That was probably true enough. He folded his arms, studying her. He could see no sign of deception, but he also knew that didn't mean a thing. Still, her story made sense, and given what he knew of her character, it was likely she would take advantage of the opportunity she had been given. After all, starving and on the run, why shouldn't she?

"How did you find out about Willoughby?" she asked.

"They keep lists of runaways. It was a simple matter to check them. One James Willoughby of Norfolk, Virginia, reported the loss of an indentured servant matching your description and giving the name of Katie Armstrong. Armstrong is your surname, is it not?"

"Yes," she said with a sigh.

"At the very least," he continued, "you should have changed your Christian name to something more common—Jane or Anne, perhaps."

She turned her head to look up at him, meeting his gaze steadily. "You should know. I think you change identities as easily as other people change clothes." She leaned back in her chair. "So, you aren't going to send me back?"

"That depends."

"On what?"

He did not answer immediately. She was in a dangerous and difficult situation, and he held a great deal of power over her. Given that, he wondered if he might be able to make use of her. She was unknown to both sides, she was beautiful and clever, and she was a very good liar. He thought again of Lowden, and he wondered if he could make use of this girl to find out what Lowden's purpose was in Boston. Though she had stumbled into the idea of being an informant by accident, he appreciated that she could be a very good spy.

She knew where he lived. She would be able to sell what she knew to Gage. Though Gage would never arrest him on the mere word of a street waif, he would probably lose his ability to get information on the governor's activities, and he certainly wouldn't be able to find out more about Lowden.

Letting her go was not an option. If he returned her to her master, she could still sell what she knew, and Gage might pay enough for the information to buy her indenture and free her.

So, the question remained, what was he going to do with her now? If freedom from Willoughby and the money to enjoy that freedom were what Katie wanted, he had the ability to give them to her. Perhaps all he needed to do was offer them. She had been thinking to sell information to Gage. Why not sell information to him instead? Information about Lowden. A specific plan began to form in his mind.

"Depends on what?" she asked again, breaking into his thoughts.

"On whether or not you and I can reach some sort of agreement."

She folded her arms, and a wary look came into her eyes. "Such as?"

He gestured to the luxurious furnishings around them. "You have discovered where I live. Based on that information, it would be a simple matter for you to find out who I really am."

"Do you mean you're not John Smith, longshoreman?" Her eyes widened. "I'm shocked."

"Mmm. I can see that."

"So, save me the trouble of finding out. What is your name?"

"Ethan Harding." He gave her his most gallant bow. "Your servant, ma'am."

His name clearly meant nothing to her. She continued to stare at him, and a skeptical frown knit her brow. "Is that your real name?" she asked.

"Of course. It's useless to continue pretending with you. As I said before, now that you know where I live, you could find out my true identity without difficulty."

"And how many of your Whig friends know who you really are?"

"Very few, I'm afraid," he admitted. "I do not tend to display that fact openly."

"David and Molly know," she guessed. "Daniel does not, for he calls you John. Probably Andrew knows, and a few others as well."

"Only about half a dozen people know that Ethan Harding and John Smith are the same man."

"How have you managed to keep this a secret?"

"Until you came along, it was relatively easy. The two men do not have the same acquaintances. They move in very different circles."

As he answered her questions, he continued to think out the idea in his mind. *Would it work?* he wondered. It was risky, but he had never minded taking risks. Not if they were necessary.

She took a look around the room. "Your oilskins do seem ludicrously out of place in this house. Revolutions against the king must be quite profitable, or else Ethan Harding has another means of earning a living."

"Shipping," he answered. "It's a family business. It is also in danger of becoming insolvent if the king's taxes and punitive policies continue to bleed it dry."

She smiled. "So all your noble talk the other

night about freedom was meaningless," she said. "Your true motive for this revolution of yours is money."

He had no intention of telling her his true reasons for becoming a rebel. "Sheath your claws, Katie." He took a step back from her chair and sat down on the settee opposite. "A person always acts in his own self-interest. The fact that my own livelihood is at stake doesn't mean I don't believe in the Whig cause. If I didn't believe it, I would not be involved, and the money be damned."

"I see. What are you going to do with me?"

"I think it's obvious that I can't simply let you go as if this night never happened, although I do have some idea what to do with you." He paused, forming his next words carefully. Years of skulking about in the night, living two lives, the danger of discovery always hanging over him like the blade of a guillotine, had trained Ethan well. Discretion was ingrained in him, and he intended to tell Katie only what she needed to know in order to do what he was about to demand of her. Taking a deep breath, he said bluntly, "I want you to become my mistress."

Of all the things she might have expected him to say, Ethan could tell that was not one of them. She stared at him in blank surprise, but after a moment, Ethan saw a change come over her. A knowing look came into her eye, and one corner of her mouth curved upward in cynical derision, as if such propositions had come her way from other men in the past. Somehow, that look irritated him. It was clear that in her mind, he was now just another man with dishonorable intentions, and she had met that type of man before.

"I would provide you with a house," he went on, "so you needn't wash dishes in Molly's kitchen in exchange for a place to sleep. I would also provide you with a household account, a new wardrobe, and a generous income, so depriving soldiers of their pocket watches would, I hope, not be necessary."

"You are very generous," she murmured, and there was a hint of sarcasm beneath the words. "And what do you receive in exchange for your largesse?"

"Do you really need to ask?" he countered softly.

To his surprise, she blushed. "I may be a thief," she said, drawing herself up stiffly in her chair, "but I am no strumpet, sir, despite what you obviously think. I refuse your offer."

"Don't be so hasty. You could gain a great deal out of this."

"I became a pickpocket so that I would not become a whore," she said through clenched teeth.

"What I am proposing would not make you a whore."

"Really? A mistress is a woman who gives a man her sexual favors for a house, clothes, and jewels. A whore gives a man sexual favors for money. What is the difference?"

"None, except that our arrangement would be a pretense."

"What do you mean? I will only pretend to be your mistress?"

"Exactly."

"Do you really think we'll deceive anyone?"

"I have a great deal of faith in your acting ability. And you have some knowledge of the role already."

She scowled at the reminder of her mother. "But what is the purpose of such a charade? I don't understand."

"I don't expect you to," he replied. "Despite your assumptions, I do not take advantage of unwilling women, and I assure you, I do not need to do so."

The skepticism did not leave her face. "Why would you want me only to pretend to be your mistress?"

"Because it suits me."

She scowled. "You are the most aggravating man. You have a way of answering questions that provides no answers at all."

Despite the seriousness of the situation, he could not help a smile at her accurate observation. "So I've been told before."

She shook her head, still confused. "There is more to this than meets the eye. What else do you want of me?"

He leaned back against the settee, hands in his pockets. Instead of answering, he said, "Scarcely a week ago, I was standing in the doorway of an inn at the edge of North Square, and there I witnessed a scene of such mischief and devilish skill that I will never forget it." He paused to look at her. "Would you like to know what I saw?"

Dismayed, she stared back at him. She swallowed, tried to speak, and swallowed again.

Without waiting for her to gather her thoughts enough to answer, Ethan went on, "I saw a ragged street waif with the face of an angel steal a watch, then completely bewitch the British lieutenant who intended to arrest her for that crime, just before she deprived him of his purse. It was a comedy worthy of the theater. She disappeared into the crowd, but fate put her in my path a second time, and I decided it was wise to find out more about her. I discovered that she was also a runaway indentured servant. Tonight, I discovered she has a very strong reluctance to return to that indenture, and I cannot help but think it was rather unpleasant for her."

She went pale. "You've made your point," she whispered. "So, I ask again, what more do you want of me?"

"It is quite simple. I can use you, Katie. I can use your clever mind. I can use your brash confidence and your audacity. I can use your glib ability to lie. What's more, by following me, you have left me few options. You were willing to spy for Governor Gage. I propose that you spy for me instead. I assure you, I will pay you more than he would."

For a long moment, she simply stared at him in disbelief. Then, suddenly, she jumped to her feet. Thinking she meant to run again, he stood up to prevent her. But once she was on her feet, she did not move. "You can't be serious!" she cried, her voice cracking with obvious agitation.

"I never joke about revolutions."

She laughed, but there was a hysterical edge to it. "I don't believe this," she cried. "It's too much! It is just too much." Still laughing, she sank back down into her chair, bent her head, and covered her face with her hands.

Ethan was not surprised by her reaction. He knew she'd had plenty to frighten her this evening, and it was understandable that the strain had become too great for her. He also sat down and remained silent, watching her struggle to regain control of herself.

Finally, she lifted her head. She took a deep breath. "So, my being your mistress must be some sort of act to cover my real purpose as a spy?"

"Ethan Harding is known throughout Boston to be a Tory, a loyal subject of the crown. You are one of the few people who know the truth about me. I warned you to put aside your curiosity and stay out of my affairs, but you did not. Now you have forced my hand. I know about Willoughby, and I choose now to hold that piece of information over your head in order to maintain your silence. But I also can appreciate your talents and your need for money."

"You mean, you intend to blackmail me into committing sedition along with you."

"*Blackmail* is a very ugly word," he admonished. "Besides, I am willing to provide other incentives."

She stared at him in disbelief. "What incentives?"

"Playing the charade of being my mistress will give you the house, clothes, and jewels you mentioned before, without having any of the obligations, shall we say, of the job. In addition, if you prove satisfactory, I will buy your indenture from Mr. Willoughby."

"I would be trading one master for another. What is the good of that to me?"

"When I no longer need you, I will set you free."

"How do I know you will do what you promise? All I have is your word."

"That will have to be enough, I'm afraid. Are we agreed?"

"What sort of spying would I have to do?"

"I have a few ideas of how I might make use of your talents, but I haven't really thought it all out yet. Having you follow me home was not something I planned on. It was a careless mistake."

"And you don't make many of them, I'll wager." Katie thought it over for a moment, then shrugged. "Hanging as a rebel would be better than returning to Virginia." She rubbed her temples with her fingertips, as if their verbal dueling had given her a headache. "I agree to your arrangement."

"Good." He rose and walked toward the door of the study, beckoning her to follow. "It's nearly dawn. I'll escort you back."

Neither of them spoke as they retraced their steps to the Mermaid. She had a great deal to think about, and so did he.

Was he doing the right thing? Or was he making a terrible mistake? It was rare for Ethan to have doubts about his decisions, but he'd never been spied upon by an unscrupulous girl who could probably lie to God and get away with it.

Whether he had made the right decision or not really mattered very little at this point, anyway. If he had not taken steps to ensure her silence, if he had not given her the incentive to work for him instead of the Tories, he would have run the greater risk of losing all that he and his comrades had been working for.

That was something Ethan could not have allowed. If she had refused his proposal, he probably would have been forced to ensure her silence in a far more permanent way. He was very glad she had not refused.

7

$\mathcal{I}$nside the Mermaid, all was dark and silent. Ethan lit a lamp and started for the door through the buttery. "I probably won't be back here until next Friday, so I'm going to wake David and Molly to tell them about your little adventure this evening and of our new arrangement."

"You mean before I have the chance to give them my version of events."

"Exactly. God knows what lies you'd spin for them. I suggest you stay here. You've gotten into enough trouble tonight, as I think you'll agree, so I wouldn't recommend you try tiptoeing upstairs and listening."

"I wouldn't dream of such a thing," she answered with dignity. "I don't eavesdrop on people's conversations."

"I'm very glad to hear it."

"Besides, I'd never get away with it," she added as he left the kitchen. "The stairs squeak abominably, and you'd hear me coming by a long way."

Her words made him grin. She was right about the stairs. He went up to David and Molly's bedroom, listening to the creaking and groaning of the steps as he mounted them. The noise was loud enough that it woke the innkeeper and his wife, and when he reached their bedroom door, he found it open. Both of them were standing just inside the room, and Molly had a lit lamp in her hand.

"What is it?" David demanded. "What's happened?"

"We have a problem, but I believe I have resolved it." Ethan entered the room and shut the door behind him. He told the couple succinctly of the events of that evening and his agreement with Katie.

When he had finished, both David and Molly stared at him as if he'd lost his mind. Neither of them spoke for a long moment. Finally, Molly let out a heavy sigh and shook her head in disapproval. "And Katie agreed to this insane arrangement?"

"Of course. She has little choice but to agree."

David pushed back his nightcap, setting it askew. "This is a fine kettle of fish," he muttered. "Using innocent girls as spies."

"That girl is no innocent," Ethan countered harshly. "She intended to spy on us and sell that knowledge to Gage. She knows her way about well enough."

"Aye, perhaps she does, but you can see why by

just looking at her. What is the purpose of making her your mistress?"

"If everyone thinks she's my mistress, she can move in my Tory circle and help me find out Lowden's purpose in Boston. I can let a house for her nearby and use it as an alibi for myself."

"An alibi?" David repeated. "What do you mean?"

"If Ethan Harding is ever suspected or followed, it will be assumed that my carriage has stopped in front of her house because I am staying the night with her. I can then change clothes there and sneak out the back for my nighttime activities. Katie can also carry messages for me."

"This could be dangerous work for a slip of a girl."

"Can you think of anyone more suited to the task?" Ethan countered. "She is intelligent, resourceful, and she's an even better liar than I am. In fact, she has all the qualities needed in a spy." The scene in North Square flashed through his mind again, and he added, "She has another extraordinary talent. She has the ability to captivate any man she chooses."

"Except you, it seems," Molly put in.

"Except me," Ethan agreed, ignoring the sarcasm.

David spoke again. "All this may very well be true. But the real question is, can she be trusted? Given her intention, I doubt it."

Ethan shrugged. "Katie has no political convictions, but she is not a fool. She knows her refusal would be a worse option. Besides, I had little choice, and I have a very powerful incentive for her to keep silent. She is a runaway bondswoman who made it very clear to me this evening she does not want to be returned to her master."

"And you threatened to do exactly that!" Molly shot him a furious look. "I can't believe what I'm hearing! You would really have sent her back to indenture if she had refused? That young girl who's had nothing in her life but misery? Really, Ethan, sometimes you can be incredibly cruel."

He was not perturbed by Molly's outrage. He had expected it, given that she had become inconveniently fond of the girl. He returned her hostility with a cool glance of his own. "I warned her to stay out of my business, and she responded by following me home, hoping to betray me to Gage for money. I cannot afford to let her sell what she knows about me. Can you think of any other way to ensure her silence?"

"So you will use threats and intimidation to force her into committing sedition? What if something happens to her? It's not as if you can protect her from getting arrested."

"I already told her I will buy her indenture and free her. She'll be getting her freedom out of this, and that is what she truly wants. So we all benefit by this arrangement."

"How convenient," Molly responded tartly.

"Would it be better to let her go and have her

running to Gage at the first opportunity?" Before she could answer, he went on, "Or perhaps you think letting the girl steal on the streets and run the risk of getting hanged for theft is a better choice? Or perhaps you think it's better for her to remain on the run from a lecherous master who will eventually find her and drag her back to what was no doubt a sordid life?"

He rose to his feet. He'd had no sleep for two days, he was tired, and he was in no mood for Molly's moral recriminations. To his relief, she made no further arguments, and Ethan started for the door. "I'd best go before it gets light. I'll make the arrangements to let a house for Katie. I should be able to find something suitable nearby within a day or two. Until I get her settled in her new situation, let her continue working here. Molly, I want you to keep a close eye on her. God only knows what she'll take it into her head to do next. She bears watching."

"Aye," the woman said heavily, "I'll do it. I don't like it, but I'll do it."

"Good." Ethan paused in the doorway and glanced back at the couple. "I told her only what she absolutely needed to know and no more. I did not mention Lowden to her, and I'm not going to do so until I must. I'm certain she'll be asking more questions, but hold your tongues. The less she knows, the better for us all, including her."

Both of them nodded their agreement, and Ethan left their bedroom. He returned downstairs, where he found Katie still sitting in the same chair by the kitchen table where he had left her. As he entered the room, she stood up and followed him to the door without speaking.

Before he departed, Ethan felt it necessary to remind her once again of her position. "I've told Molly to keep an eye on you when I'm not around. I'll find a house for you in the next few days. Until then, you'll continue to work for Molly, and I've instructed her to keep close watch over you. Remember, Katie, if you betray my trust, I'll not hesitate to send you back to Mr. Willoughby."

"Of that I have no doubt," she answered, and shut the kitchen door in his face.

Ethan stared at the closed door for a long moment, oddly reluctant to leave. He remembered the terror in her face at his threat to send her back to her master, and he could not help wondering what this James Willoughby had done to her. Even more important, he could not help wondering why he cared.

Stunned, Katie stared at the closed door of the kitchen. This whole situation was so incredible, so damned funny, she was finding it hard to believe.

With David, Molly, and their son in the house, Katie dared not laugh out loud, but she was hard-pressed to smother her jubilation. She'd been a spy for the Tories less than two weeks, and already she had the information she had been sent to find. Now she knew all about John Smith. She knew he was his own informant—Ethan Harding found out what the governor was up to, and, posing as John Smith, he passed that information to the rebel leaders. Lowden would surely give her the freedom she desired in exchange for news as valuable as this.

But would he? She froze, and her jubilation evaporated as she remembered the cruelty in Lowden's eyes. She could not afford to trust him, either. First, she would need proof of what she knew. But if she told Lowden what she knew, handed over the proof he required, there was no guarantee he wouldn't send her back to Willoughby anyway. She would have to protect herself. Before she handed over the proof that the viscount required, she would require papers signed by the governor that she was indeed a free woman, and she would demand the money Lowden had promised her. With working papers and money, she would run as far away from Willoughby, Ethan Harding, and Viscount Lowden as she could get. Then she would be safe. She would be free. No man would control her. Not even Ethan.

She remembered how he had kissed her in this very room, how that kiss had scattered her wits and robbed her of the ability to breathe. She'd been kissed before, but always she had been in charge of the situation, her goal to get something from a man, usually his purse. She had always thought kissing a necessary but rather repugnant activity. She hadn't known it could make a girl feel as if she were melting like butter.

Katie scowled, still frustrated by her body's traitorous response to that kiss and the man who had caused it. He could kiss her like a lover, sure enough, but he could also send her to her death the next day without losing any sleep over it.

Well, the tables were turned now. She was the one in charge of the situation. She held his life in the palm of her hand. All she had to do was find the proof Lowden required, and she would be free. She thought of Ethan leaning over her, his eyes as bleak and gray as a winter morning. He might mask his ruthlessness with good looks and charm, but she had no doubt that he was as merciless as Lowden, perhaps more so. She could not trust Ethan, either.

Look out for yourself. No one else will.

The sound of footsteps interrupted her thoughts, and she grabbed for the broom that stood in one corner of the kitchen. When Molly entered the room, she found Katie busily sweeping the floor.

Uncertain how much Ethan had told the other woman about her midnight activities, it was hard to know what manner she should adopt. After all, she had been caught where she had no business to be. Katie decided saying nothing was her safest course. She could feel Molly watching her, but she kept her head lowered and her gaze fixed on the floor.

Molly watched her for a long moment without speaking, then heaved a sigh. "Come along, Katie. It's dawn. We'd best get ourselves to North Square and do our marketing. If we dally too long, all the fresh vegetables will be gone."

Leaning back in the doorway, Molly shouted, "Daniel, you'd best milk that cow and fetch water from the well. David, don't you let him shirk his chores. Katie and I will be back in a few hours." She crossed the kitchen to pull her cloak from one of the pegs on the wall beside the door. Then she glanced at Katie. "Come along."

Katie set aside her broom and donned her cloak. She'd pocketed that extra half a crown from the viscount instead of purchasing a bonnet, but she figured the hood of her cloak would work just as well as a signal. She pulled the hood up around her face as an indication that Captain Worth should stay away. She did not want to meet with the viscount until she had the proof that would ensure he kept his part of their bargain. Besides, she could not very well arrange a meeting with the viscount as long as Molly was with her.

The sun was just coming up as she followed Molly out of the tavern and into the street. The two women headed toward the marketplace in silence, and it was not until they had walked several blocks that Molly finally addressed the situation on both their minds.

"Well, Katie," she said, her breath coming in white puffs from the cold, "you're in a fine mess now."

Katie suppressed a smile. If Molly only knew the truth! But her voice was meek and—she hoped—contrite when she answered, "Yes, ma'am."

Molly turned to give her a disapproving frown. "What on earth were you thinking of, following him through the streets in the middle of the night and thinking you could sell the information? I warned you. Didn't I tell you to stay away from him?"

"Yes, ma'am."

"But no, you wouldn't listen," Molly went on as if she had not spoken. "That's the worst of girls— they never do listen. Always think they know best." She shot Katie a warning glance from beneath the brim of her bonnet. "Ethan has his cause, and that's all that matters to him. You interfere in that, and he'll cut you to ribbons without a qualm."

Katie had no doubts about that. Yet she could not help but wonder if there was any heart at all beneath his ruthless ambitions. She remembered him sitting in the kitchen with Daniel, the coldness gone from his eyes and the weariness gone from his face as he talked with the boy. She remembered the affection he had shown the child, but she also remembered his callous treatment of her last night, and she wondered how a man could be so tender one moment and so ruthless the next. It was such a contradiction.

She could still hear the passion in his voice when he had spoken of a new world, a world where people controlled their own destinies. An absurd notion, of course, and one that King George would never allow. Ethan and his friends were fighting a losing battle, and Katie knew that being on Lowden's side was the only choice for her.

Molly spoke again, breaking into her thoughts. "I thought you an intelligent girl, but now I'm beginning to think you've no more sense than a hen. By casting your lot with Ethan, do you realize the danger you are putting yourself in?"

"You and David have obviously cast your lot with him as well," she pointed out. "So who has no sense?"

"Aye, you've the right of it there," the other woman agreed. "But I never claimed to have any sense, and I know for certain that husband of mine has none, either. We're idealistic fools, I suppose. Still, we would follow Ethan into hell and back if he demanded it." Before Katie could ask the reason why, Molly added, "Instead, he has demanded it of you."

"Indeed?" Katie murmured. "Perhaps you are right, but he gave me little choice."

"Aye. He would have returned you to your master."

"And that would be worse than hanging." She took a deep breath. In a hard voice, she added, "I will never go back to Virginia. I will never be indentured again. In truth, I'd prefer to be hanged for sedition."

Molly turned her head to look at her, and her brown eyes were not without sympathy. "Beat you, did he, that master of yours? Or something even more cruel, perhaps?"

Katie shuddered. "You don't know what it was like," she whispered. "You can't possibly know."

"Can't I?" Molly pulled off her knitted glove and turned her palm up to reveal the *T* that marked her skin, a brand identical to Katie's. "I was indentured myself once. I know exactly how you feel. All you can think about is surviving one day to the next."

Katie knew that wasn't enough. She didn't want merely to survive. She had done that nearly all her life. She wanted to be free and secure enough that she never need worry about going hungry or being a man's property or sleeping in the cold.

She had no doubt that Ethan intended to use her to gain his own ends, but she had intentions of her own. She had to bide her time, keep him dangling until she could find the proof Lowden required. Then, and only then, Ethan's threat to send her back to Willoughby would mean nothing. She would have freedom, money, security. Everything she had ever wanted. As for Ethan, he would be hanged for sedition.

Katie abruptly stopped walking.

He'll hang. The thought whispered through her like a cold wind, and she shivered at the vision in her mind of Ethan swinging lifeless on the gallows. If he died, it would be at her hands.

Suddenly, all her triumph left her, and all her brash self-confidence disappeared. Suddenly, the situation was not amusing or exciting, and the idea of the reward she would receive no longer brought any sense of satisfaction or relief.

Katie shook her head, fighting back the guilt

that was suddenly twisting her insides. Now was a damned inconvenient time to develop a conscience.

She pushed guilt aside. After all, it would not be her fault if he died. Ethan had chosen his course, with all its dangers, knowing that sedition was a hanging offense. And it was not as if she had the luxury of other choices. She would not go back to Willoughby and sacrifice her own life to save a man she barely knew from his own folly.

Katie knew she had not chosen this course—it had been forced on her—and she could not change that now. She told herself not to think about the price Ethan would pay for her freedom. She told herself not to think about the fact that he would die because of her. But no matter what she told herself, the harsh truth remained. A new life for her meant death for him.

Lord North would be expecting a report. Viscount Lowden frowned down at the letter he was composing to the king's chief minister, not at all pleased with it. North would be impatient for results, and there were no results yet. He was going to New York to determine the extent of rebellion there. Perhaps he should wait until he returned to send North a dispatch.

"In any case, I have nothing to tell," the viscount muttered, addressing the empty room around him. "I've been in this godforsaken place for less than a month. I can't very well set up an entire network of spies in a month."

A knock on the door of his office interrupted his thoughts, and the viscount hastily pushed the letter beneath the blotter on his desk, concealing it from any prying eyes.

At his command, Captain Worth opened the door and entered the office, presenting himself to the viscount with a formal bow.

"Well, Captain?" Lowden demanded. "Did our pretty little spy go marketing this morning?"

"Aye, but I had no opportunity to speak with her. She had another woman with her." Worth paused to remove his hat and take a pose of respectful attention before he continued his narrative. "She had the hood of her cloak pulled up to show me to stay away, but she was there, all right. She stayed about an hour. Then she returned to the Mermaid, and I came here."

"You watched her the entire time?"

"Aye, but I kept a fair distance behind them so the other woman would not see me."

Lowden leaned back in his chair. "And?"

A slight smile lifted one corner of the captain's mouth. "And she managed to buy two turkeys, a sack of flour, a jug of molasses, and four bushels of dried cod for a price any merchant would consider criminal."

The look the viscount leveled at the captain was a frosty one. "Is that relevant?"

Worth's smile disappeared instantly. "No, my lord."

"Who was with her?"

"A woman named Molly Munro, wife of the Mermaid's owner. They were together the entire time."

Despite the fact that he could hardly expect any news from the girl so soon, Lowden was frustrated that he could give Lord North no information in his answering letter. "She gave you no indications of her progress?"

"No, but she is working in the tavern. That much has been confirmed by one of my men."

Lowden nodded. At least there was some satisfaction in knowing the girl was well positioned to hear any news about the mysterious John Smith. "I am relieved to know that the scene you played out with her in the Mermaid was a success."

"Indeed, sir. A clever idea she had, to pretend she stole my watch."

"Yes, the girl is rather clever, isn't she? Let us hope she can produce some results." He stared into space for a moment, wondering what he was going to tell Lord North. He began composing possible replies in his mind. Perhaps he could tell North about Katie. No, he decided reluctantly. Only he and Worth would know about her. That would ensure security. Dispatches to London could be read by many prying eyes and never delivered.

Lost in thought, he had forgotten all about Worth's presence, but when the officer gave a discreet cough, Lowden came out of his silent reverie. "You have not forgotten that I am leaving for New York today?" he asked Worth.

"I had not forgotten, sir."

"I will return in a fortnight, in time to attend the Governor's Ball at Province House. While I am away, continue going to the marketplace on Saturdays. If Katie has any information for me, send a courier to New York. I will be staying with my wife's cousins there."

The captain nodded to show his understanding. "Very good, sir. Is there anything else you wish me to do while you are away?"

"No. That will be all." He gave Worth a nod of dismissal. "You may go."

"Yes, my lord." The officer gave him another formal bow, donned his hat, and clicked his heels sharply together before he turned in precise military fashion and departed from the room, closing the door behind him.

Viscount Lowden turned to gaze out the window. His suite of offices at Fort Hill gave a splendid view of Boston Harbor, but Lowden scarcely noticed. He could find no beauty about anything in this city. He hated everything about it. He hated the primitive conditions and the lack of refinement. He hated the uncivil and hostile populace, with their seditious literature, their defiant disregard of the king, and their bullying mob tactics against the king's loyal subjects and soldiers.

Lowden sighed wearily. The sooner he was on a ship back to England, the better.

Perhaps it was best not to think of home. He

knew he was going to be marooned in this barbaric place for many months yet, and he needed to resign himself to that.

To that end, Lowden turned his thoughts to his newest spy. She had only been in her position for a little more than a week, so he could not expect any news from her yet. But he could live with that. He had patience. A man could gain anything in life if he was patient.

Lowden pulled out a sheet of parchment, picked up his quill, and began to compose his report to Lord North. It was the letter of a true politician, full of platitudes and subtle flattery, and he hoped the king's chief minister would not notice the fact that it contained no news whatsoever.

8

$\mathcal{W}$hen Lord Percy invited his intimate friends for an evening of playing cards, the port was plentiful, the play steep, and the news always interesting. Though forced to act the part of a man more interested in fashion than politics, Ethan usually came away from such evenings with valuable information, making it worth suffering through hours in lace cravat and powdered wig. Both itched intolerably, and he longed for his comfortable oilskins.

This evening, however, proved to be well worth the suffering. Lord Percy was Governor Gage's lieutenant. In addition, Sir William Holbrook, one of Gage's closest aides, was also there, and both men were full of the latest news of their superior, news that confirmed all Ethan's suspicions of Governor Gage's plans. Arnold Travertine, another Tory who worked in Province House in a minor capacity, made up the fourth for whist.

Only two bottles of port had been emptied by the

four men at the card table before Percy's tongue was loose enough to convey the governor's newest strategy for dealing with the rebels.

"Gage plans to confiscate every stockpile of Yankee weaponry in New England, one by one." Percy emptied his glass in one swallow and refilled it from the bottle on the table. "He thinks that will prevent the rebels from waging a stand against British interests. With no weapons, there can be no rebellion."

Ethan took the deck of cards from Arnold Travertine, who sat on his left, and began to shuffle them as he listened. Since Gage had already sent out spies into the countryside, Ethan was not surprised by this news, but he needed to know the details of any future missions. "Just how do they plan to do this?" he asked, deliberately adopting a supercilious tone of voice. "Ask the Massachusetts farmers where they've hidden their guns?"

Travertine chuckled, but Percy and Holbrook did not join in their humor. "Close enough," Holbrook said. "Gage's spies are mapping out the condition of the roads, and trying to find as many of the rebels' powder and weapons stores as possible. As each location is discovered, he'll send troops to confiscate the weaponry."

"It's about time Gage took some form of action," Travertine put in. "He's been sitting on his hands for far too long."

"I think we are all in agreement there," Percy replied. "I don't know why he doesn't just arrest the ringleaders and be done with it. His leniency only makes these rebels more defiant."

"Hear, hear," Holbrook put in, lifting his glass in approval. "I've advised him many times to arrest the rabble. After all, the crown has suppressed insurrections in Ireland, and never has there been a more fractious race than they. Our own countrymen here would surely be easier to subdue than the Irish."

"So why doesn't he do so?" Travertine asked.

"Gage insists on proof of the sedition, my friend," Holbrook told him. "Letter of the law and all that. Very tiresome, but there it is."

"If these rebels continue, he may not be so finicky about British justice," Percy pointed out in reply. "Besides, if he needs proof, he will eventually get it."

"I hope so," Ethan said. "But tell me of this new plan. I confess, I am intrigued."

"If he continues to send spies into the countryside, I hope Gage is choosing men with cool heads who can pass for locals," Travertine said thoughtfully.

"He is," Percy assured. "Every officer in the garrison with any knowledge of the countryside has been interviewed, and Loyalist agents are being recruited from the local population."

Every nerve in Ethan's body tensed. It was crucial that he find out details, but he dared not risk suspicion by asking any direct questions. He knew from experience that while a direct question might fail to elicit information, a skeptical attitude often brought forth an instant response. "Ridiculous, all this talk of spies and informants," he drawled, sorting his cards. "We're not at war, you know. You've been listening to too much gossip at Province House, my friends."

"It's not gossip," Percy insisted.

Ethan did not reply. He merely eyed the other man with good-humored indulgence, as an adult might look at a child who insisted that fairy tales were true.

As he had hoped, Percy bristled at that disbelieving look. Provoked, he leaned forward in a confidential matter and added, "This is not gossip, Harding. I am among those chosen for future missions. In addition, I have heard that several other men of our acquaintance are also participants in this plan."

Ethan wanted to laugh. Percy couldn't pass for a Boston artisan or country farmer if his life depended on it. But there were other men in his Tory circle who could. Perhaps Katie could help him find out who those men would be.

Ethan betrayed nothing of his thoughts in his expression. "Gad, Percy, you'll be running about the countryside in late winter? How dreary."

"Powder isn't the problem, anyway," Travertine said with a sigh. "What Gage really needs to do is find a way to contain these outrageous Boston mobs. They become bolder every day and have gone from being a petty inconvenience to a real source of danger. A man loyal to our king can't walk the street without taking his life in his hands. Something must be done."

"Absolutely," Holbrook said, and lifted his glass. After taking a drink, he turned to Ethan. "Are you coming to my party week after next? It's only supper and cards, but it should be quite entertaining."

Ethan hoped so, but not quite for the reasons to which Holbrook referred. Thomas Flucker, a friend of his who was also an aide to Gage and the father-in-law to Whig bookseller Henry Knox, had already informed him that Holbrook kept most of his secret dispatches and documents in a locked desk at his home. Ethan intended to have a look at them to see if he could discover any information about Viscount Lowden. In that task, he suspected Katie would be of great assistance to him.

"That depends," he answered. "May I bring a friend?"

"Certainly. To what friend do you refer? A gentleman or a lady?"

"Neither." Ethan flashed him a grin of one man of the world to another. "A man's mistress should never be a lady."

The other men at the table laughed with him. Holbrook slapped him on the shoulder. Conversation then shifted to talk of the Governor's Ball scheduled to take place in two weeks' time, and Ethan knew he would probably learn no more information tonight. He had a great deal more to do before the evening was over, including a meeting with Katie, and he needed to make his exit.

At the end of the next round of play, he rose from the table. "Gentlemen, I must be on my way."

The other three looked at him in dismay as he began to gather his winnings.

"But it's early still," Percy said, pulling out his watch. "Only quarter to eleven."

"Quite." Ethan stood up and removed his black and gold dinner jacket from the back of his chair and slipped it on. He put the profits of the evening in his pocket and adjusted his lace cravat. "But I have another engagement."

"Another engagement?" Holbrook repeated. "Something to do with this new mistress, I'll warrant?"

Ethan let a secretive smile play at the corners of his mouth, but he said nothing.

Travertine put in, "It's going to be rather inconvenient for the rest of us if this mistress will always be taking you away in the midst of an enjoyable evening's card play. Who is she? An actress, perhaps?"

He thought of Katie's dramatic abilities and found Travertine's comment quite appropriate under the circumstances. Besides, making her an actress would provide a perfect background for her, and he silently thanked Travertine for the suggestion.

He had his carriage brought around to the front of Percy's lodgings and instructed his driver to take him to the White Swan, where he was to meet Katie.

He wondered what she would think of the house he had leased for her. It had taken his secretary, Adam Lawrence, only the better part of the morning to find a property that met his requirements. Adam had warned him that the house needed repairs, but its location made it so ideal, Ethan had been willing to overlook a few minor deficiencies. It was directly across the alley from the Mermaid and a block away from the Salutation, another of his midnight haunts. Though Ethan had not had time to take a look at it himself, he had leased it furnished for six months. If it needed repairs, he would order them, to make the house suitable for Ethan Harding's mistress.

He had sent Katie a note this afternoon with instructions to take a look at the house, then meet him at the White Swan that night to give him a report of what repairs would be necessary.

The tavern was crowded when he arrived, but Dorothy knew to expect him that night and had kept the small table in the corner free for him. He did not see Katie as he crossed the room and took his seat, so he settled back to wait.

He did not have to wait long. Within moments of his arrival, he saw her enter the tavern. She glanced around as if looking for him, but when she caught sight of him, she made no move toward his table. Instead, she hesitated in the doorway, and Ethan beckoned to her with a wave of his hand.

She waited a moment longer, then circled the room to his side. She sat down opposite him, and he immediately discovered the reason for her hesitation.

"Are you out of your mind?" she muttered, pushing her tattered cloak off her shoulders. "This tavern is filled with soldiers. What were you thinking?"

"Don't worry. The lieutenant whose purse you lifted is not here. Nor is Captain Worth, whose watch you supposedly didn't steal. Besides, if either one of them presses charges against you, I have enough money to buy your way out of the stocks."

"I can't tell you how much that relieves my mind. As for your money, if you have so much, couldn't you have found me a better house?"

He laughed, and she shot him a look of exasperation. "What is so amusing?"

"You sound more like a wife than a mistress."

"I am not your mistress, and I don't have to talk like one when no one else is listening to our conversation. Couldn't we have met somewhere other than a tavern full of soldiers?"

"Not tonight. I have things to do here, and until you are settled in the house, I cannot be seen there. Ethan Harding would have no reason to park his carriage in front of an empty house."

"If it's empty, I can understand why. The two front windows have broken panes, the larder is empty, and everything is covered with dust. Worst of all, the house has mice."

She shuddered, and Ethan lifted his brows in some surprise. "You're not scared of a few mice, are you?"

"I hate them," she told him, her expression clearly conveying her distaste.

"We'll get you a cat."

Katie made a sound of disdain, showing just what she thought of that suggestion. "Unless you're suggesting that we import a tiger from India, a cat is out of the question. An ordinary house cat wouldn't have a chance. Those mice would eat *him.*"

She shuddered again, and he realized she was genuinely afraid. "This is something I never would have expected," he said. "You, a girl who has lived on the streets of London, afraid of a few mice. Katie, you astonish me."

"Mice are too much like rats to suit me, and God knows, I've seen enough of those disgusting creatures to last a lifetime. You have no idea what it's like to fight with them for your bread. Especially when they win. I want the mice out of the house. Until then, I don't sleep one night in that place."

"I don't expect you to do so. I wanted to know from you what repairs might be necessary, since I have had no time to look at the house myself. Now that I know what needs to be done, I will tell my secretary, and he can arrange to make the house comfortable for you. Until everything is in readiness, you don't have to sleep there."

"I was hoping I could, though. To live in a real

house again, sleep on a real bed, will be heavenly. You have no idea how I am looking forward to it."

To hear her talk so wistfully about two things he took for granted was rather disconcerting. It reminded him of how hard a life she lived. "By tomorrow night, you'll be able to do both," he promised her.

"Can I have a bathtub, too? A real one, big enough that I can sit down in it?"

She suddenly sounded like a child asking for a special treat. "Of course you may have a bathtub if you want one."

She propped one elbow on the table and rested her chin in her hand with a dreamy sigh. "Oh, that will be lovely. I've always wanted a bathtub." She cast a slow glance over him and straightened in her chair as if she had suddenly noticed something odd. "What are you all dressed up for? Are those fancy clothes supposed to be some sort of disguise?"

He smoothed his gold brocade waistcoat. "In a way. I was with some very influential Tories, and this is how I usually dress when I have social obligations of that sort."

"Perhaps those clothes help disguise you from other people but not me. Even with that stupid powdered wig you have on, I could recognize you a mile away."

"Most people cannot say the same, thank God."

"It is fortunate for you that most people are not as observant as I."

"Nor as modest."

She grinned at that. "You never fooled me for an instant. I've yet to see a man who works on the docks put on Sunday manners for a kitchen maid. He wouldn't pull out a chair for her and wait for her to sit down before he takes his own seat. That's how I first came to realize you were not the long-shoreman you pretended to be."

"Since you are so adept at dispensing advice, I want you to apply a bit of it to yourself. Tomorrow, you will begin pretending to be something you're not—my mistress. Remember, you aren't a street waif any longer."

She looked down at the clothes she wore. "Really? I never would have guessed."

"Hmm. You have a point. Perhaps that's why I made you an appointment for tomorrow at Elizabeth Waring's to be fitted for a new wardrobe. We will meet there at ten o'clock in the morning. Elizabeth is Boston's finest dressmaker."

She looked at him across the table and bit her lip. An expression of uncertainty crossed her face. "You're buying me an entire wardrobe?"

"Certainly. For my mistress, only the best."

An unexpected smile lit her face, a smile of such childlike beauty, he was startled. God, her smile could light up even the darkest shadows of a room. He realized the reason for that sudden smile. "You've never had new clothes before, have you?"

Still smiling, she tossed her head with a show of bravado. "Of course I have," she answered. "I used to wear beautiful clothes all the time, even ball gowns of silk and lace, diamonds. I attended all the assemblies at St. James's Court, of course."

A vision came into his mind of her plundering the pockets of unsuspecting peers in an opulent ballroom, and he couldn't help grinning. "I see."

"My company was in demand among all the fashionables of London."

"Katie, if you're going to lie to a man, at least tell him a lie he can believe."

"It's true," she assured him. "I had half a dozen men madly in love with me."

His grin faded. "Now that," he said slowly, "I can believe."

Ethan heard her sharp intake of breath. Her smile vanished, and he sensed the sudden tension in her. He thought of her sweet response to his kiss in the kitchen of the Mermaid, and just the memory of it aroused him. He wanted to kiss her again.

It had been such a damned long time since he had made love to a woman. Too long. But he could afford to trust no one, and he knew there was nothing on earth more likely to loosen a man's tongue and steal his common sense than a woman. He drew a deep breath and leaned back. "As for the house, I will have workmen in to make repairs first thing tomorrow. I promise you, they'll get rid of every last mouse. I also had Adam hire servants for you."

Her eyes widened. "I'm going to have servants?"

"Of course."

"A house, a real bed and a bathtub, as well as

clothes and servants," she murmured. "All for a pretend mistress." She suddenly looked troubled. "You are being very generous."

He heard the wariness enter her voice, and it made her seem oddly vulnerable. On impulse, he reached out and lifted her chin with one finger to look into her eyes. "Don't worry. You will be able to carry out this charade with a clear conscience, because despite what people will think, your virtue will not be compromised." His gaze roamed over her face, appreciating the stunning beauty of it, and he added, "From my point of view, that is most unfortunate."

Abruptly, he let his hand fall away. "Besides, before it's all over, you'll have earned your rewards."

"I don't doubt it." She leaned forward in her chair. "Perhaps, then, it's time you told me exactly how."

Ethan met her expectant gaze with a steady one of his own. "All in good time."

"Really, Ethan, you are a human oyster," she told him, aggravated by his unwillingness to give her any information. "How am I to spy for you if I don't know what I'm looking for?"

Before Ethan could reply, they were interrupted. Katie looked up to find the barmaid standing there with two brimming tankards of ale. She set them on the table, and Katie took a few seconds to study her. She was a voluptuous girl with long, loose dark hair, who gave Katie a hard, unfriendly stare in return for her scrutiny before she turned to the man seated opposite. Her gaze softened immediately. "Ethan," she greeted him. "I'm sorry it took me so long to get ale for you, but it's quite crowded tonight. It's good to see you."

The flush in the girl's cheeks could be from the heat of the blazing fire in the hearth nearby, but there was no mistaking the warmth in her voice. *Besotted,* Katie decided. *Poor girl.*

He replied to her greeting but did not introduce her to Katie. "I believe you have news for me?" When she nodded, he went on, "We'll talk later, then."

It was a clear dismissal. The barmaid hesitated a moment, then bit her lip and turned away, but not before casting another suspicious glance at Katie.

"Who was that girl?" she asked after the barmaid had departed. "She glares at me as if I'm after stealing her money bag."

"Dorothy is a very perceptive woman. She has you pegged quite well." He smiled as he spoke, but he was not looking at her. His restless gaze scanned the room beyond her shoulder. In the dim light of the candle that burned between them, Katie studied him from beneath her lashes as she sipped her ale. It was a harmless pursuit to observe him at this moment, since he was not looking at her. He was always tense and alert, always cognizant of possible danger. Yet he did not realize that his greatest danger was right in front of him. His greatest danger was her.

Suddenly, it hurt to look at him. Katie turned her face away and took several gulps of ale.

"Careful." His amused voice had her returning her gaze to him. He was looking at her now, his elbow on the table, his chin in the palm of his hand. "The ale is strong, and the last thing I need is a drunken spy."

A teasing gleam came into his eyes, and Katie caught her breath, feeling suddenly giddy. She knew it was not the ale that rushed to her head. It was him. He made her feel as if she were walking the edge of a cliff, exhilarated and dizzy, yet never forgetting that one missed step could mean her life. "I'm not going to get drunk."

"I'm glad to hear it."

Katie took another sip of ale. "So, answer my question. What are we doing here, anyway?"

"I had you meet me here for several reasons. There are two people I wanted to introduce to you. Dorothy is one."

"And the other?"

He gestured toward the bar and the burly, barrel-chested man who stood behind it tapping ale. "That is Joshua Macalvey," Ethan told her. "He owns this tavern. He and I are good friends."

"You are friends with a man who owns a Tory tavern?"

"He can't help it if his establishment is conveniently close to Fort Hill and the Regulars have taken a liking to it. Actually, it is very convenient for us. It's amazing the news and gossip officers impart when they've tipped a few pints."

"I take it Joshua's politics differ from those of his patrons?"

Ethan smiled at her. "You might say that."

With that smile, Katie noticed for the first time the laugh lines at the corners of his eyes, and she realized that he must be a man who smiled often. With her, he was usually so serious, sometimes even menacing.

"Joshua and I have known each other for many years," he went on, bringing her attention back to their conversation.

"Boyhood schoolmates?" she guessed.

"No," Ethan answered. "War. We fought together against France. We were in the colonial militia."

"You fought for England?"

"Believe it or not, yes. Many men, including myself, felt differently then. England was our country. Long live our king, and all that."

He lowered his gaze to the tankard of ale in his hands and fell silent. He sat rolling the tankard idly back and forth between his palms, frowning at it. It was almost as if he had forgotten she was there, but after a long pause, he spoke again. "That was over seventeen years ago. Joshua and I were sixteen then. Too young to think for ourselves. We were told that England needed us, and we simply did what we were expected to do."

"And now?"

He lifted his head to meet her gaze, and she did not miss the momentary flash of anger that crossed his face. "Now we are not boys but men. We pay attention not only to what we are told but to what we see with our own eyes and hear with our own ears."

Before she could ask what had brought about his change of mind and heart, a voice interrupted them. "I see that you have ale, my good man, but is there anything else you require?"

Katie turned her head to find Joshua Macalvey beside their table. Her gaze swept downward as she cast a quick glance over him, and she saw that the lower half of his right leg was gone, replaced by a wooden peg. She had not noticed it when she first came in, for he had been standing behind the bar.

The tavern owner leaned down to say something to Ethan, and the two men talked for several minutes. She tried to hear what they were saying, but they kept their voices low, and with all the noise surrounding them in the crowded tavern, there was no way Katie could discern even one word of their conversation.

Finally, Joshua straightened away from the table, and Ethan rose to his feet. "I'll be back shortly," he told her, and turned away. Joshua took the vacated chair opposite her, while Ethan crossed the room to the bar.

She watched him greet a pair of redcoat soldiers as if he knew them well. He lounged with casual elegance against the bar, and all the tenseness she had seen before was hidden behind his easy, careless pose. She wished she could hear what they were saying, and she wondered how she was ever going to ferret out the proof she needed for Lowden if she could never listen in on Ethan's conversations with others.

"Ethan tells me you are going to be one of our friends," Joshua commented, and she returned her attention to him. "I can scarce believe it."

Her heart skipped a beat, and Katie drew a deep, steadying breath. "What makes you say that?"

"You look more like a waif whose main concern would be her next meal." Joshua tilted his head to one side, studying her. "I wonder what sword Ethan is holding over your pretty head."

"I don't know what you mean."

"Perhaps you don't. I'll wager he could bind you to him with nothing more than a few sweet words and a kiss. Ethan has a way with women when he chooses."

"Does he? I hadn't noticed." She turned her head once again toward the subject of their conversation. Ethan and the pair of soldiers had moved to take seats at a nearby table. Dorothy stood beside his chair, and he was deep in conversation with her. Her generous breasts spilled over the edge of the tightly laced corset she wore over her chemise, and when she leaned down to whisper something in his ear, Katie was certain those breasts were going to fall out of her corset and right into his face.

"If you hadn't noticed," Joshua's teasing voice interrupted her thoughts, "why are you glaring at him?"

"I'm not," she lied, and forced the scowl from her face. She turned her attention away from Ethan and his barmaid and back to the man opposite her. "I was just worried, that's all."

"Worried?"

"If she gets any closer to him, he'll suffocate," she said sweetly.

Joshua chuckled. "There are worse ways for a man to die."

She cast another glance at the subjects of their conversation and found the girl with her hand on Ethan's shoulder. She was whispering something in his ear. Katie forced herself to look away. "They seem to be more than friends."

"That sounds like the tone of a jealous woman."

"Nonsense." Never in her life had Katie felt jealousy toward another woman over some man, and she resented the notion that she felt it now, especially about a man who cared naught for her, a man she knew was capable of slitting her throat should he find out the truth about her. "You are mistaken, sir. The loose women he trifles with in taverns are no concern of mine."

"Loose women?" Joshua threw back his head and laughed. Katie stared at him, unable to understand what she had said that was so amusing. After a moment, he stifled his laughter and took a long draught of ale. "Dorothy," he said, striving for a serious expression, "is my sister."

Katie stared at him in dismay, her face heating with embarrassment. "I'm so sorry. I didn't realize that."

Joshua dismissed her embarrassment and her apologies with a wave of his hand. "My sister dresses as she does and acts as she does for very good reasons, not because she is a loose woman."

"Because that sort of demeanor elicits more information from the soldiers who drink here than she would get otherwise," Katie concluded, guessing what Joshua had not explained.

"You are a shrewd young woman and seem to know your way about. I can see why Ethan has chosen you to assist him. But I wonder what your reasons might be for agreeing to do so, since you insist he holds nothing over your head."

Katie was silent a moment, thinking how best to proceed. Here was a chance to find out more information about Ethan that might prove useful, and she did not want such an opportunity to pass. But if she wanted to get information, she would have to establish some credibility with Ethan's friends. "Death does not frighten me," she said, choosing her words carefully, "and my alternatives to being Ethan's friend are worse than death."

"You intrigue me. I cannot help but wonder what those alternatives might be."

"They are rather unpleasant, to say the least. I would rather not talk about them." She turned her face away and took that opportunity to divert the conversation. "Ethan has told me that the two of you fought together against France."

"We did. And I thank God every day for that. If Ethan had not been with me, I would not be alive."

"He saved your life?"

"He did. We were in the same regiment, and we had become friends. We were fighting near Albany and getting badly beaten. Our sergeant gave the call to retreat, but just then a spray of grapeshot hit us. I was wounded, and so was a friend of mine. The French were pounding us with cannon and grapeshot, and we knew we would be killed if we did not get back behind the lines, but neither of us could retreat with our regiment."

"What happened?"

"Ethan had already fallen back, but he saw us in the distance. I'll never forget the sight of him, crossing that field toward us, dodging the cannon fire. He carried me out of there."

Joshua paused in his story, shaking his head as if in disbelief. "Once he got me to safety, he went back for David. He took a musket ball in the shoulder, but he saved both of us."

Katie remembered the comment Molly had made the morning before as they had walked to the marketplace. Perhaps here was the story behind it. "Was your friend's name Munro?"

He looked at her in surprise. "Yes, David Munro. You've heard the story already?"

"No, but I have met David and his wife. Molly

told me both of them would follow Ethan into hell and back. Now I know why."

"Aye. We would willingly give our lives for him."

She thought of the part she might be forced to play in making that happen, and she felt again that inconvenient prick of her conscience. "That could happen."

He smiled at her. "I had received a letter from my wife the day before I was wounded. She'd been expecting a baby, and she told me she'd just had twins. If not for Ethan, I never would have seen my daughters, the two loveliest girls in the world. I will never be able to repay Ethan the debt I owe him."

"What happened after the war?" she asked. "What changed the two of you from supporters of the king to his enemies?"

"Many things can change a man," he answered in a noncommittal voice. "My reasons and Ethan's may be different, but our goal is the same."

Before she could ask another question, a shadow crossed their table, and both of them looked up to find the subject of their conversation standing there. Joshua rose to his feet. "I look forward to seeing more of you, Katie." He turned to Ethan, his face grave. "Take good care, my friend."

Katie watched the tavern owner for a moment as he walked away amid the many bright redcoats that filled the room. "How can you frequent a tavern filled with soldiers?" she asked as Ethan set down his tankard of ale and resumed his seat. "Isn't it dangerous? Aren't you afraid you'll be recognized?"

"The only way anyone here would recognize me would be as Ethan Harding, who is known to be a Tory. No one here is likely to have seen me in the Mermaid or any other Whig tavern. British Regulars know they are not welcome in those places."

"What about informants and spies?"

He did not seem particularly worried. "You'll find that we usually discover Tory informants very quickly. Of course, they have the same ability to discover ours. Very little stays a secret in Boston."

Katie hoped that maxim would not apply to her.

"Besides," he continued, "a spy's word would not be enough to have any of us arrested. I hate to give Gage credit for anything, but he is a scrupulously fair man. He insists on having just cause to arrest someone, and having a pint of ale in a particular tavern and complaining about English policies is not against the law. Proof of sedition is hard to obtain."

Katie was already beginning to appreciate that point. "Still, it is fortunate you can count on Joshua's loyalty."

"Aye, but his true loyalty is to freedom."

"From what he told me, his true loyalty is to you."

A slight frown creased his brow, and she could tell that he was displeased that she knew. "Joshua talks too much."

"Why? Our conversation was harmless enough. He told me of how you saved his life, and how he would give his in return."

Ethan made a sound of impatience. "He should not have told you. People know I was in the colonial militia during the war, of course. It would be impossible to keep that a secret. But if people knew what happened with David and Joshua, they would find my actions rather at odds with my image as a fatuous fool."

"So no one knows about it?"

"You do. Somehow that worries me."

"You do me little credit. I can keep your secret."

Ethan tilted his head to one side, studying her, his gray eyes thoughtful. As always, his discerning stare made her uncomfortable, and she started to look away, but he reached out to cup her chin in his hand and hold her still, smiling at her as he caressed the curve of her jaw with his thumb.

When he smiled like that, it was as if the sun had come out, yet she could not say why. He was handsome, true, but that was not the reason. Perhaps it was the sudden warmth that smile brought with it, as if they had shared a moment of intimacy, a rare thing from a man with so many secrets.

"I can't really blame Joshua for his lack of discretion," he murmured. "Those angel-blue eyes of yours could pull secrets out of a statue. 'Tis no wonder Joshua paid no heed to what he said. Almost any man alive could make that mistake."

She caught her breath. "Even you?"

"No," he answered, and let his hand fall away. "I said *almost* any man. I make myself the exception."

"Do you indeed?"

"I am never indiscreet." Ethan lifted his tankard, and his smile changed to a careless, impersonal one. The intimacy they had shared was gone, and she was once again sitting with a stranger. "But then," he continued, "I have also had the advantage of watching you use your charms on that poor lieutenant whom you deprived of a purse, and I have profited by his example."

She scowled at the laughter in his voice. Even above the noise in the tavern, she could hear it. "That poor lieutenant was a fool. He let a smile and a pretty face manipulate him so easily."

"Don't be so hard on him. He was young, and too inexperienced to have learned that beauty does not necessarily go hand in hand with goodness and virtue."

That stung. "Isn't your defense of him misplaced? As a soldier of the Regulars, is he not your enemy?"

"Not really. The Regulars are simply a tool."

"So the king is the true enemy?"

"I did not say that."

"You don't have to say it. It is obviously what you believe." Here was a chance to get back at him for his stinging comments and to prove him wrong about his ability to resist what he called her considerable charms. The opportunity was too good to miss, and Katie took it. She widened her eyes with deliberate innocence. "And how you can believe such things is incomprehensible to me. The king is the head of state, and he is the head of the church, akin to God. Not only is it sedition to think otherwise, it is blasphemous."

"Rot! The king is mad; that is common knowledge. And his ministers care only for what comes off the tax rolls. Though bishops might feel differently, I doubt God would consider greed a church sanction." His voice was low, but anger vibrated within every word, and Katie felt a sudden rush of triumph. At last, she had provoked him beyond prudence. Here, in a Tory inn, he had forgotten about caution, and, surrounded by King George's soldiers, he was speaking to her of treason and rebellion. Say what he would about discretion, even Ethan Harding could abandon it, given the right inducement.

"The king and his ministers care naught for this land and naught for its people," he went on. "England is using us, as a man might use a prostitute, with no thought to woo her before he takes what he wants. Why should we suffer such treatment? For an insane king?"

"There are some in this very room who would call what you are saying treason," she said blandly, and watched the anger vanish from his face as if it had never been there. A flicker of wry acknowledgment came into his eyes.

"Aye, so they would," he murmured in agreement. " 'Tis fortunate that the noise in here prevents anyone from overhearing my seditious talk. It might ruin my image as a loyal Tory. It was not wise of me to speak so." One corner of his mouth turned up in a rueful half smile. "It would seem even I can forget discretion when you choose to turn your wiles on me."

She laughed, thoroughly enjoying her momentary victory. "Wiles? I used no wiles on you, Ethan. We were simply talking."

"No. I was talking, you were listening, and that is the danger. The knife is silent, too, until it's in a man's back."

"I have no knife." She leaned closer to him across the table. "I am your colleague, Ethan. Don't you trust me?"

He mirrored her, leaning forward, so close that his lips almost touched hers. "My darling girl," he murmured, his voice so low and seductive that Katie's heart began pounding wildly, "I don't trust you at all."

She jerked back, all her brash confidence gone. He was so much better at this game than she, and no matter what she did, he always managed to stay one step ahead of her. Katie opened her mouth to give him a scathing reply, but before she could do so, he spoke again, all mockery gone from his voice. "Finally," he murmured, almost as if he were talking to himself. "I thought she'd never finish with him."

He caught Katie's inquiring glance, but he did not explain. Instead, he stood up and circled the table to stand beside her chair. He grabbed her hand and pulled her to her feet. Before she could realize his intent, he wrapped his arms around her and kissed her, in full view of all the men in the tavern.

Katie heard several ribald chuckles from the surrounding tables, and she pushed against his chest, but he did not release her. Caught within the tight circle of his arms, she could not move as his mouth opened over hers. His tongue slid past her parted lips, and he tasted deeply of her. An aching warmth spread through her entire body. She could feel the hard muscles of his chest beneath her palms. Everything else in the world faded away until there was nothing but him.

As abruptly as he had kissed her, he stopped. He did not let her go, but he pulled back to look into her eyes. Shaken, Katie stared up at him, but she could read nothing in that hard, enigmatic face. He might have been made out of stone.

No, not quite stone, she suddenly realized. His face might give nothing away, but she could feel his heart thudding beneath her fingertips as if he'd been running. "Ethan," she whispered, and felt herself melting in his arms.

More male laughter from the tables around them brought her to her senses and reminded her that they were standing in a room full of soldiers. She jerked back hard, but his arms remained around her, and she could not break free.

"Why did you do that?" she asked, her cheeks burning, acutely aware of all the staring soldiers.

"Now it's clear that you belong to me," he murmured. "I can leave you alone in a room full of soldiers while I meet with Dorothy, and none of them will bother you."

He didn't seem to care that it made her look like a doxy. She did not glance around, but she could well imagine the speculative gazes and knowing smirks of the soldiers. She knew what they must be thinking, and she did not like it.

Ethan seemed oblivious to her discomfiture. He turned away, and her resentful gaze followed him as he moved through the crowded taproom. He may have given all these men the impression that she belonged to him, but she did not belong to him. She was no man's property. At least, not for long.

It wasn't even as if he thought of her as a colleague. His light, mocking words came back to her, and Katie set her jaw stubbornly. *You may not trust me yet, Ethan,* she thought, watching him disappear through the door out of the taproom. She pressed her fingers to her lips, which still tingled from his kiss. *But you will. Before this is over, you'll trust me completely.*

9

$\mathscr{B}$ecause they had met this way so many times before, Ethan knew which of the tavern's bed-rooms Dorothy would be in. The light of only one candle illuminated the room at the end of the up-stairs hall, but he could see Dorothy was already there, seated on the edge of the bed. As he stepped inside and closed the door behind him, she rose to her feet.

"Who is that girl with you?" she asked in an anxious voice.

"She is working with me. I brought her along so that you and Joshua could meet her."

"Working with you? What do you mean?"

"I have heard certain things, and I want to investigate them. Katie is going to help me."

"Katie?" Dorothy frowned, clearly skeptical. "But who is she? Where did she come from?"

"She's a pickpocket. I found her hiding from British Regulars at the Mermaid. She got a job working there for a time, but now she is working for me."

"I don't like it, Ethan. Is she trustworthy?"

That idea amused him. "Trustworthy? No, I'm afraid not."

Dorothy started to speak again, but he forestalled her. "Don't worry, Dot. Katie has very powerful incentives to remain loyal to me. If she wants to stay alive, that is."

He could see that did not satisfy her, but he didn't care overmuch about that. "Forget about her. We are wasting precious time. What news have you for me?"

She stepped closer to him. In a low voice, she said, "The officer I was talking with just arrived from London to be under Gage's command, and he says the news there is that Parliament is tired of what they call our childish tantrums. Word is that Lord North will soon be sending specific orders to Governor Gage to arrest Samuel Adams, John Hancock, and all other principal leaders in the Massachusetts Provincial Congress. In addition, anyone caught in possession of a Liberty medal will be arrested for sedition." Her round face creased with worry. "Ethan, please throw that thing away. If you are caught wearing it—"

"Your brother wears one, too," he reminded, and watched her shoulders slump in weary acknowledgment.

"Aye," she murmured. "I have not forgotten."

"And has he tossed his in the gutter?"

Wordlessly, she shook her head.

"And he will not do so. Nor will I. It is something we wear with pride, regardless of what danger may ensue. Throwing it away would be as unthinkable as turning aside from our families." He knew he was starting to give a damn speech, and he had no time for it now. "Did this officer say anything else?"

"They want all the weaponry of the colonial militia confiscated."

"That is nothing new. Gage just doesn't know yet how to mount an effective campaign to steal it."

"Well, this Captain Montrose told me North is becoming increasingly infuriated with Gage for not taking more aggressive action against us. In any case, Gage has not yet formally received these orders to arrest Whig leaders, and until he does, he cannot very well act on them."

"Even when he does receive them, he will take his time in carrying them out," Ethan replied, "because he will be reluctant to move against people he considers to be fellow Englishmen. He also knows that for every Whig arrested, there will be ten more to take his place."

"True," she agreed, and glanced past him at the closed door. "We should not linger here, and I have more to tell you." She took a deep breath. "Will you be attending the Governor's Ball?"

"Aye." He gave her a brief smile. "Ethan Harding is invited to all the social events of the season, my dear."

"Good. There is talk that a certain Jean-Paul Chevain will be there. He is a French aristocrat, though I don't know his title. More important, he is an official emissary of King Louis, though his stated purpose in Boston is supposed to be a friendly one."

"The French and the English are never friends," Ethan said with some humor. "But what is said to be his true purpose here?"

"Evidently, he has been in secret correspondence with Benjamin Franklin about gaining French support for our cause. Loans, in particular."

"Excellent. I have been wondering how we might approach France. Trust Franklin to have done so already."

"There are those who think you might perhaps talk to him about the possibilities. Perhaps even negotiate the terms of a loan for us if war breaks out."

Ethan thought about that for a few seconds. "The French love to irritate the English, especially at a profit, but I don't see how I can negotiate anything at the ball. Unless I can get him alone, there is too much chance of being overheard."

"Some feel that it would be a perfect opportunity."

He nodded in agreement. "It would, but Gage will be watching him during his entire visit. Let me think about how it might be managed. Have you any other news? What about Lowden?"

"I have not been able to discover anything about him we don't already know. If he is here for some deeper purpose than he claims, I don't believe any of the officers are aware of it. Even Captain Worth, who is his aide-de-camp, claims to know nothing."

"Someone always knows something." A noise on the other side of the closed door caused him to glance uneasily in that direction. "We'd best go back down."

He started to turn away, but her voice stopped him. "Ethan?"

He looked at her over his shoulder. "Yes?"

"About that girl—" She broke off and took a deep breath, then said, "Remember your own rule. Trust no one."

He smiled at the woman he had known for more than fifteen years, a woman who was the sister of one of his best friends, a woman who had proved her loyalty many times. "Even you?"

Her plump and pretty face took on a hardened expression. "Even me," she whispered.

Although Ethan had ensured that soldiers would not approach her while she waited for him to return, that did not stop them from staring at her. When an officer at the next table lifted his tankard to her in an admiring salute and licked his lips, Katie gave him a fierce scowl. "Shame on you," she rebuked him in a censuring voice reminiscent of Miss Prudence. "Shame, shame. You are an officer of the British Army. Behave yourself."

The officer's mouth fell open in astonishment at her words as his fellow redcoats laughed. Katie remembered how Ethan had been talking to some redcoats earlier, and though these were not the men he had been talking to, she wondered if she might engage them in conversation and see if they knew anything about Ethan that might be of use.

But before Katie could put this plan into operation, the door of the tavern opened, and another British officer entered the White Swan. It was Lieutenant Weston.

Katie cursed Ethan for bringing her here and decided it would be wise to make a hasty retreat out the back before the lieutenant saw her. Ethan's assurance that he would buy her way out of jail was not very comforting, and Lowden had already told her if anything should go wrong, he would not come to her aid. Avoiding a confrontation with Weston was clearly a good idea.

Katie sidled out of the taproom, hoping the lieutenant would not see her. Once out of the room, she raced through the tavern kitchen and out the back door, but she had barely taken half a dozen quick steps down the alley before a pair of strong hands grabbed her from behind and turned her around. She looked up into the angry, flushed face of Lieutenant Weston and knew she was going to have to do some pretty fast talking.

"I knew it was you!" he shouted. "You're the witch who lifted my purse."

"Mother of God," Katie muttered under her breath, not knowing herself if it was a curse or a prayer. She did not want to deal with this man.

He was drunk and angry, and the malevolence in his eyes was unmistakable. She was in serious trouble.

She gave him a dazzling smile as her mind rapidly invented possible strategies. She could pretend she didn't know anything about the disappearance of his purse. Or she could give him a hard-luck story about a dying little sister. Maybe a starving mother. Or . . .

Weston shoved her back against the wall of the alley before she could put any of her ideas to work. "You owe me three guineas," he told her, "and you can pay it back right now."

Katie could feel his hands groping beneath her cloak to pull up her skirt. Panic flooded through her, but she wouldn't show it to this lout. She'd be damned first.

"Let me go, you bastard!" She clawed and kicked at him, trying to get away, but her efforts were in vain. Lieutenant Weston had all the strength of a seasoned soldier. When she heard the ripping sound of her skirt, she realized with sickening certainty that she was going to be raped right here, in an alley, against the wall of a tavern.

She caught a movement out of the corner of her eye, but before she could assimilate what it was, Lieutenant Weston was pulled away from her. She sagged back against the wall, trying to catch her breath as she watched Ethan drag the other man into the center of the alley. He gave the soldier a shove that sent him stumbling back a step or two, then he pulled off his cloak and evening jacket and tossed them aside.

Even in the dim light of the moon, Katie could tell that Ethan was furious. She could feel the anger emanating from him like heat from an oven. The soldier sensed it, too, for he glanced about as if for help.

Ethan's mouth curved upward in derision. "What is it, sir? If you have friends inside, I'm sure they are too drunk to come to your aid. You planned on having only a woman to fight with, but you were wrong."

"She's a thief. I was only getting what was owed to me. Cease this interference, or I'll slit your throat and take my payment from her anyway."

Katie saw Ethan suddenly jump sideways. She realized Weston had pulled his knife from his belt and that Ethan was trying to avoid the slash of the blade. The redcoat was surprisingly quick for a drunken man and lashed out again with the knife, this time slicing open Ethan's shirt. Katie saw a flash of silver against Ethan's chest, and though she did not know what it was, Weston obviously did.

"Well, what have we here?" the officer asked, pointing at Ethan's chest with the knife. "A Liberty medal. Who'd think a fancy toff like you would be one of those rebel curs who commit treason against the crown? Now I really have reason to kill you."

He lunged forward, and Katie cried out in alarm, thinking Ethan had been stabbed, but he gave no sign that the knife had found its mark. Instead, when Weston pulled back, he grabbed the soldier by the wrist and wrenched it sideways with a hard yank, forcing the knife to fall from his hand. Then he brought his other hand up in a fist and slammed the soldier hard in the solar plexus. Weston doubled over, and Ethan grabbed his arm, twisting it behind him. "I suggest you drop this matter," he told the lieutenant softly. "Or I will give you more than the loss of three guineas for your trouble."

He did not give Weston the chance to respond. Instead, he slammed his fist hard twice against the back of the other man's neck, and the lieutenant fell facedown to the ground.

Ethan stood over him, waiting, but the man did not move. He stepped over the unconscious soldier and came to her. "Are you hurt?"

She shook her head. She could see Ethan's bare chest where the knife had cut open his shirt and waistcoat. The Liberty medal he wore glinted silver in the moonlight. But the moonlight also revealed the dark stain of blood. It stained the slashed remnants of his shirt and the skin just beneath his ribs. "But you are!" she cried, and looked up into his face. "Oh, Ethan, you've been wounded."

He glanced down. "So I have," he said calmly.

Katie could not be so sanguine about it. "We need to get a physician."

"It's only a scratch."

"Any knife wound, even a scratch, can turn septic." She grabbed his hand, pulling at him to follow her, but he did not move. "Ethan, come on. Why do you just stand there, bleeding all over your shirt?"

"Does the sight of my blood bother you so much?" He leaned back against the wall and smiled at her. "If I died, you would be free of our bargain."

"God's balls, Ethan," she cursed in frustration, "this is no time to make jokes. You are hurt. At least let me see it." She let go of his hand and tried to pull aside the edges of his clothing to have a look at his wound, but he seized her wrist.

"Can it be?" he murmured, his thumb caressing her palm. "Katie, can it be that you are concerned about me? I am touched."

She stiffened at the light, mocking tone of his voice and jerked her hand free. "I assure you, my concern is not because I have a tendresse for you. If you were to die—"

To her astonishment, her voice broke. She realized suddenly that she was actually worried about him, afraid that he was badly hurt, and she could not understand herself. After all, her whole purpose was to trap him so that he could be hanged. Why on earth should she be upset that he was wounded in a knife fight?

Katie told herself not to be ridiculous. "If you were to die," she said in a hard voice, "I would remain a runaway indentured servant and no better off than I was before. That is the only reason for my concern."

His free hand slid into her hair, and he tilted her

head up, forcing her to look at him and not his wound. "You are such a liar," he muttered, staring into her face as his hand slid down to the nape of her neck. "A beautiful, clever, bewitching little liar. But tell me the truth now. Why should it matter to you if I am wounded? What if I died? Would you care?"

She didn't care. It would be stupid to care about a man who thought only of his revolution, a man who was ruthless and mocking, a man who spent most of his time in a shadowy world of intrigue and danger, a man she had been sent to destroy. It would be very stupid.

Even as these thoughts ran through her mind, she could feel his fingers lightly caressing the back of her neck, and without even understanding her own actions, she reached up to touch his cheek. "Perhaps because when that redcoat tore my dress, you came out of the dark like an avenging angel, and I saw the look on your face," she whispered. "Were you afraid he would extract his payment from me by force?"

He let her go abruptly. "No," he answered. "I was afraid I would lose my best spy before she ever had the chance to do anything."

There was a lightness to his voice that stung. "Then we are both fortunate, for we are both safe," she shot back, then turned on her heel and started toward the end of the alley, not looking back to see if he followed her.

He isn't worth worrying about, she told herself.

Let him bleed all over the alley. It made no difference to her because she didn't care. Caring about Ethan Harding would probably destroy her only chance for freedom and put her life in serious jeopardy. By the time they reached the Mermaid, Katie had reminded herself at least a dozen times that she was not that stupid.

Dawn was breaking when Katie left the Mermaid and started toward the marketplace to meet with Captain Worth. Even though her bargain with Ethan meant she no longer had to do Molly's marketing, the other woman had willingly handed over her basket and a shopping list, even entrusting her with a handful of silver to pay for the purchases. Molly had seen the tear in her skirt and the clumsy mending Katie had given it on her return from the White Swan last night, but though she asked what had happened to her gown, Katie had not explained. Weston's attempt to assault her was not something she wanted to talk about.

She now had exactly what she needed to obtain her freedom, but there was no lightness in her step as she walked to North Square. She would be able to tell the viscount that John Smith's true name was Ethan Harding, that though he posed as a Tory, he was in reality a traitor to the king. Her proof would be the Liberty medal he wore. Surely, Lowden would agree that she had fulfilled her part of their bargain, and he would fulfill his part in return.

She would be able to collect her reward and

leave Boston. She could settle anywhere she chose. She would have enough money to live comfortably, and she would have the freedom that ensured she would never again be at any man's mercy. She would gain all the things that were most important to her.

So why was she not happy?

Katie tried to remind herself of her own rules—nothing mattered but her own survival, caring about other people was pointless and painful, to look out for herself because no one else would—but somehow she found no solace in the bitter truths life had taught her.

Ethan was going to be hanged because of what she told Lowden. She thought of the way he had come to her rescue the night before, and now she was about to repay his good deed by sending him to the gallows.

And who knew what friends of his might follow him to the hangman as a result of her information? Lowden would investigate every part of Ethan's life, and that could eventually lead them to discover evidence against David and Molly.

Once again, she heard that pesky little whisper of her conscience, and she made a sound of vexation. What was wrong with her?

If she did not tell what she knew, Lowden would eventually grow tired of learning nothing from her, and he would send her back to Virginia. And why shouldn't she tell? Wasn't Harding a traitor who deserved to hang for rebelling against the king? Weren't David and Molly traitors as well? What of Daniel? Would he be hanged, too? Surely not. He was only a boy.

These people mean nothing to me, she told herself fiercely. *They have made their choices, and I must make mine.*

With every step she took closer to the market-place, the more Katie hardened her heart. Through Worth, she would inform Lowden that she had accomplished her mission and assure him that what she had discovered would be well worth the price of her indenture. She would also be sure that Lowden understood her demands. She wanted her indenture paid, papers guaranteeing her to be a free woman, and the fifty pounds the viscount had promised her. Only then would she tell him what he needed to arrest John Smith.

Resolute, all the foolish whispers of her conscience pushed aside, Katie entered North Square and immediately saw Captain Worth standing beside the baker's stall waiting for her. The image of Ethan swinging on the end of a rope flashed before her eyes, but Katie squared her shoulders and ignored the image.

Over the top edge of his newspaper, Worth was watching the crowd that streamed past him, and he saw Katie approaching from some distance away. He met her gaze for a brief moment, then tipped his tricorn hat to her as she went by. She knew he would follow her, and she was right. After a moment, he fell in step beside her.

"You have news?" he murmured as he walked beside her.

"Perhaps," she answered.

"What is it, girl? Tell me quickly."

She cast him a contemptuous sideways glance. "You think I would entrust it to you?"

"Take care, little thief," he warned in a whisper. "I have Lowden's trust. You do not."

They paused before an onion seller. Katie closed her eyes, swallowed hard, and told herself not to be a fool. *Tell him you have news for Lowden and you want a meeting. Tell him.* But the words stuck in her throat.

Worth leaned closer to her. "Do you want to go back to Virginia?"

This game had barely begun, and already she was sick of it—sick of the tension she felt at having to be always on guard, sick of trying to remember which side she was on, and sick of the two men who held her life in their hands. Suddenly, she wished both Ethan and the viscount to perdition, and their causes with them.

She looked at Worth, her chin high. "I want a meeting with Lowden, alone. Only then will I tell what I know."

"The viscount has left Boston. He has gone to New York on business for a fortnight. But he has ordered me to write him with whatever news you have."

The knowledge that Lowden was away gave Katie such an overpowering feeling of relief that her knees nearly gave way. "I have things to tell the viscount, but I am not going to entrust them to you. If he is away, I will wait." Striving to keep her voice brash and sure, she went on, "By then, I will have even more to tell him."

Worth laughed low in his throat. "You are a confident hussy," he said, then turned and walked away.

No, what I am is a fool, she thought angrily, as she began picking the best onions off a farmer's cart for Molly and plopping them into her basket. She could not understand why the idea of a two-week reprieve should have brought her such an overwhelming sense of relief. She wanted her freedom, didn't she? She wanted her silver, didn't she? Then what the bloody hell was wrong with her?

When Lowden returned, she was going to march right into the Stag and Steed and hand Ethan Harding over to the king's justice, get her money, and leave Boston for good. And damn the consequences. She would have her freedom, and that, she told herself firmly, was all that mattered.

Despite the adventures of the night before, Ethan was up early. He had breakfasted and was in his library to meet with Adam by seven o'clock. Before he took Katie to the dressmaker this morning, he needed to tell his secretary what he had learned last night so that Adam could get word to his contacts.

Last night. Ethan closed his eyes. Thoughts of

the night before reminded him of how Weston had touched Katie, what had almost happened to her, and how powerful his own rage had been.

He could not remember the last time anger had ruled his actions, and the depth of his anger last night astonished him. He could easily have killed that redcoat. If he had, there would have been questions, and interrogations, and inconvenient probing into his life. When a man spent half his time committing sedition, attention of any sort from authorities was unwelcome. And risky.

What was it about that waif that made him lose his senses? For a waif she was, her loyalty to him gained only by blackmail and bribery. He must not forget that.

A sound caused him to open his eyes, and he found his secretary standing in the doorway, a ledger tucked under his arm and an inkwell stand and blotter in his hands. "Adam, come in."

The blond young man in black broadcloth entered the study and sat down in the chair opposite Ethan's desk. He opened the ledger on his lap and set his inkstand on the desk. He paused with a quill poised over the inkwell, but he did not look at all ready to begin work. Instead, he gave Ethan a searching glance and frowned, his concern obvious.

"Is there something you want to tell me, Adam, that you stare at me so worriedly?"

"Your valet tells me the shirt you wore last night was cut to shreds and had blood on it."

That irritated him. "Honestly, can't a man keep anything a secret in his own household?"

"Not from his valet. And not from his secretary, when said secretary is a cousin of that valet."

"Indeed, and do the two of you discuss my shaving habits and the state of my wardrobe as well?"

"What happened last night, Ethan?"

"Nothing."

That, of course, did not satisfy Adam, who continued to look at him with grave concern.

Ethan shrugged. "It was a small matter that does not have anything to do with our cause. A drunken soldier wanted a fight, and I was forced to oblige him. I received a scratch or two from his knife, but I was not badly hurt. Neither was he."

"Did this fight have anything to do with the Armstrong girl?"

"As a matter of fact, yes. What of it?"

"How sure can you be of her?"

"I can't be sure of her at all," he admitted. "But I am keeping my fingers crossed."

"Your shirt was cut to ribbons. Did she see your Liberty medal?"

"Possibly. If I am arrested this afternoon, I will know my attempt to bribe her to our side has failed, and I probably should have offered her more money."

"Damn it, Ethan." Adam tossed the quill in his hand onto the desk with a sound of frustration. "Must you make light of this?"

"What would you have me do, Adam? Slit her throat to silence her?"

"Of course not."

"Then, if murder does not suit you, and you don't like my solution of bribery, I would welcome your suggestions. Should we lock her in a farmhouse in the country to ensure she holds her tongue?"

His secretary heaved a sigh. "I have no suggestions. But you are so cool-headed about things. Sometimes it is very exasperating. Aren't you worried?"

"I let you and Andrew do my worrying for me," Ethan answered, and changed the subject. "I am taking Katie to Elizabeth Waring's this morning to get her some decent clothes. While we are out, I want you to arrange for workmen to make repairs to her house." He enumerated the flaws Katie had told him the night before.

"I knew it needed work," Adam answered when Ethan had finished dictating the required repairs. "But once those are done, it will be a perfect house for a man to keep his mistress. Not too down at heel but not too lavish, either."

"Good. Get started immediately. Also, I want to have a small supper party at my house to introduce her to my acquaintances. Thursday evening should do. Get the invitations out immediately. The usual crowd. See if you can arrange for Viscount Lowden to attend. Perhaps I should call on him."

"You can't. He left yesterday for New York. He will be gone for a fortnight."

"He arrived in Boston scarcely a month ago. Why is he going to New York already?"

"I don't know."

"Find out. If the gossip is true that he has come to Boston for some official reason, his trip to New York could be part of that reason, and very important."

"Is Katie Armstrong going to help you find out about Lowden's purpose here?"

"I hope so."

Adam looked at him curiously. "Is making her your mistress really only a ruse, or do you intend to make it a reality?"

A vision of Katie lying naked across his bed, giving him that extraordinary smile of hers as she opened her arms to him, flashed through his mind and sent waves of pure lust through his body.

Ethan pushed that delectable vision out of his mind. When he spoke, his voice was cool and betrayed nothing of his thoughts. "Even if I do choose to make her my mistress in fact, it is not your concern," he answered. "Now, don't you think it's time you stopped fretting about my new mistress and started carrying out my orders?"

His secretary held up both hands, palms out in a gesture of surrender. "Of course. Is there anything else you need me to do?"

"Yes, as a matter of fact. Last night, I learned from Dorothy that orders will be coming from London to arrest all rebel leaders as soon as North can gain enough support in the House of Lords for such a move."

Adam gave a low whistle. "The way things are progressing, that will not take long."

"Exactly. I estimate that by the end of March, there will be arrest warrants issued, and Gage's insistence on proof will go to the dogs. Have Adams and Hancock left the city yet?"

"Not yet. They want to wait until after the public meeting today at Old South Meeting House."

"Damn Samuel," Ethan muttered. "I don't like the idea of having a public meeting in open defiance of Gage."

"They want to mark the five-year anniversary of the Boston Massacre to keep people's memories and anger fresh."

"I know what they want to do, but I still have grave misgivings. It will only lead to more riots."

Adam shrugged. "I daresay you're right, but you try telling him that."

"I know, I know. He is a stubborn man. I just hope after this meeting, he and Hancock leave Boston for the countryside. It's safer for them there, especially given what Dorothy told me last night."

"Did she have any other news?"

He told Adam of the French emissary, Chevain. "Find out all you can about the fellow. And if you can figure out a way for me to get him alone at the ball, let me know."

Adam nodded. "Is that all?"

Ethan did not answer at once. He drummed his fingers on the desk for a few seconds, lost in thought, then said, "I want all the Whig newspapers to report the impending Whig arrests as if they are imminent and wholly unwarranted." He met the other man's eyes. "You understand my meaning?"

"Of course. Hint that Gage is prepared to arrest Whigs without cause, play up the unfairness of it all, with emphasis on the arrogance of the king and the foolishness of his ministers. Yes, I understand perfectly. Samuel will revel in it."

"He knows this is a fight that will be won with propaganda." Ethan pulled out his watch, glanced at it, then said, "You'd best get started if we want this news in the evening editions."

"Does this take precedence over the project of renovating Katie Armstrong's house?" Adam asked in a teasing voice. "Or is making your mistress comfortable a more important task?"

"Don't be impudent. The newspapers come first, of course." The mention of Katie reminded him of something else, and as his secretary rose to leave the study, Ethan spoke again. "Adam, I want those repairs made today. Hire as many workmen as needed, and get them over there now. Also, the house has mice. Be sure the workmen get them out. Every last one of them."

Adam grinned. "You just told me the newspapers were more important."

Ethan frowned. "I also told you not to be impudent."

10

Ethan was a man of his word. When Katie returned from the marketplace, it was half past nine o'clock, and she found a slew of workmen had already descended on her new home. From the kitchen of the Mermaid, she watched them across the alley as they swarmed over the roof and walls of her house like a mass of bees. They were repairing roof shingles, replacing windows, patching crumbling brick, and giving the shutters a new coat of paint. She watched them for some time and concluded that given the number of men and the speed at which they were working, they would probably finish all the repairs in one day.

Molly echoed this conclusion when she came into the kitchen a few moments later. "You'll be sleeping in a bed tonight, that's my opinion."

Katie smiled, savoring the prospect. "I was thinking the same thing."

The other woman caught sight of that smile and

frowned at her in return. "Katie, don't be getting too fond of it. It isn't your home, remember."

Her smile faded. "I haven't forgotten that," she said. "But if I have to play a part, I might as well enjoy myself."

"Aye," Molly said with a resigned sigh. "Just be careful of your tongue in Ethan's circle. Those Tories have spies everywhere."

And she was one of them. Katie wondered what Ethan would really do to her if he discovered her secret. She shivered, remembering the night of their bargain and the cool, impersonal way he had contemplated her fate.

Once she turned him over to Lowden, she wouldn't have to worry, she reminded herself. Ethan would be dead.

"Katie, what's wrong?"

"What?" She looked at Molly blankly, and it took several seconds for the other woman's question to sink in. "Wrong? Nothing."

"Suddenly, all the color just drained out of your face. Are you ill?"

"Of course not. I—"

She was saved from making up some excuse by the arrival of a boy at the back door. Grateful for the interruption, Katie opened the door. "Yes?"

"Katie Armstrong?" When she nodded, the boy thrust a folded sheet of parchment toward her. "Note for you. I'm to wait for a reply."

Katie took the letter from him. It was closed with a seal of red wax, and the initials *E.C.H.* set into the wax told her the identity of the sender. She broke it open and scanned the lines of handwriting that reminded her to meet Ethan at the dressmaking establishment of Elizabeth Waring at ten o'clock. She nodded to the boy. "Tell him I have not forgotten, and I will be there," she instructed, and thrust the note into her pocket as the boy departed.

She turned to Molly. "Where is Elizabeth Waring's shop?"

"West Street. Near the Mall by Boston Common."

"That's a bit of a walk from here." She glanced at the battered enamel watch pinned to Molly's dress. "I'd best be on my way if I'm to be there by ten."

"Why are you going there?"

"Ethan seems to think his mistress should have a new wardrobe."

Molly frowned, clearly conveying her dislike of the plans Ethan had made. But then she shrugged, as if telling herself there was nothing she could do about it. "I suppose that one good thing to come out of this is some decent clothes for you."

"Or indecent ones," she answered with a grin. "After all, I'm supposed to be a mistress."

Molly seemed slightly shocked. "Elizabeth Waring's is a respectable establishment, and Ethan would never buy you anything that was not perfectly respectable. He is not that sort of man."

Katie wanted to laugh at that. "He is willing to blackmail me into spying, coerce me into playing the part of his mistress, and let me suffer the consequences if I'm caught, but he is not the sort of man to buy me wicked underclothes?"

Molly pressed her lips tightly together and did not answer for several seconds. Finally, she said, "He does what he has to do. You should not have tried to spy on him. Or on the rest of us, for that matter." Katie started to speak, but Molly stopped her. "Katie, girl, I've been in your shoes. I know you were only trying to keep body and soul together. But that doesn't mean I can condone what you've done. And don't expect any tender regard from Ethan because you've had a hard life."

"I don't," Katie answered. She knew better than to expect anything from anyone.

Elizabeth Waring's dressmaking establishment was indeed a respectable one. Clearly, it was also the best of its kind in Boston. Katie came to these conclusions before she even reached the front door of the shop. Luxuriant carriages clogged the tiny street outside the entrance, and a group of liveried footmen stood by the front doors, ready to handle any packages brought out by the ladies inside.

When she stepped into the shop, she could see that the showroom itself was filled with ladies of Boston's highest social echelons. One quick glance around enabled Katie to pigeonhole the women into various categories. There were several debutantes wrapped in swaths of pastel silk, discussing their coming-out balls with a great deal of giggling.

Their mamas, obviously the grand dames of Boston society, were also in evidence, examining bolts of aubergine velvet and burgundy wool as they spoke in autocratic tones to fawning shop assistants. Another quick glance around told Katie that Ethan had not yet arrived in this feminine domain.

Uncertain how to proceed without him, Katie halted just inside the entrance. She caught the attention of a shop assistant, whose expression immediately changed from a welcoming smile to a look of dismay. She crossed the room, taking in Katie's tattered cloak and dress with one horrified glance. It was incredible, Katie reflected, just how effectively a shop girl could look down her nose. Given that her social class was probably not much of a cut above Katie's own, she didn't have cause to be such a snob.

"I am here to purchase an entire wardrobe," Katie told her, pretending blithe indifference to the girl's obvious scorn.

"If you are here to pick up a wardrobe order for your mistress, you must use the servants' entrance in the back."

As the woman spoke, Katie could hear the room quieting down and feel the stares of other women in the showroom, as her appearance began to be noticed by the ladies present. She lifted her chin a notch. No mere shop assistant was going to get the better of her.

It would take gall, but gall was one thing Katie possessed in abundance. It also helped that she knew Ethan would be arriving at any moment. "I am not a servant," she informed the girl coldly. "As I said, I am here to purchase a complete wardrobe, and that wardrobe is for myself."

The girl smiled with obvious contempt. "If you have the money to purchase even a handkerchief, you must have stolen it. This is a ladies' establishment. Women of your sort are not welcome here."

Those words stung like a slap, as they had been meant to do, but Katie refused to show that they had any effect on her. She opened her mouth to dress the girl down as she so richly deserved, but another voice entered the conversation.

"My dear, I'm so sorry I'm late."

Katie let out her breath in a sigh of relief at the sound of Ethan's voice. She turned to him gratefully. "Darling, thank God you're here. I am having the most dreadful time." She stuck out her lower lip in a fretful pout and made a gesture of tearful feminine distress. "This woman is being incredibly rude to me."

She didn't miss the slight tilt of his mouth that told her he was doing his best not to laugh. But when he turned to the girl, he raised one eyebrow, and with that tiny gesture, he managed to show all the disdain of his class for a mere shop assistant. "Rude to you?" he repeated, as if incredulous at such a turn of events. "I am appalled."

The girl swallowed hard, and her eyes widened as she realized she had made a serious mistake. Katie simply could not resist giving her a triumphant smile. The girl practically wilted on the spot.

"Where is Mrs. Waring?" he asked. Before the shop assistant could gather her wits enough to answer, he went on, "Find her, and tell her that Ethan Harding is here and requires her attention."

The girl bobbed a quick curtsy and departed, disappearing from view through a set of curtains at the back of the shop.

"How do you do that?" Katie asked in a whisper. "Do you practice that haughty, contemptuous look in front of a mirror?"

"Every day."

At that moment, another woman emerged from the back of the shop and came toward them, holding her hands out to Ethan in greeting. "Ethan, how lovely to see you," she cried, clasping his hands in hers and kissing him on both cheeks. "And I was delighted to know you had made an appointment, but my curiosity was piqued by your note. You have, I believe you said, a project for me." She glanced at Katie and back to him. "I believe I can guess what that project might be."

"You have always been a shrewd woman, Betsy." He gestured to Katie. "This is a friend of mine, and I am putting her into your capable hands. From head to toe, I want her turned out in every particular. Hats, shoes, stockings, gowns, underclothes, everything. I presume she will also be able to take away a few ready-made things with her today. As you can see, she is in need of them."

"If you are paying the bill, Ethan, my dear, I would be delighted to give her every gown I have." She turned to Katie and gave her a long, sweeping glance. Katie was somewhat relieved that there was no disdain in that look.

Elizabeth studied Katie for several minutes with the professional thoroughness of a dressmaker. Then she gave a decisive nod and took Katie by the elbow. "Come with me, my dear," she said, and waved farewell to Ethan with an airy gesture of her hand. "Darling, you may leave her with me," she told him over one shoulder. "By this evening, you won't recognize her."

Ethan departed, and Katie was left in the hands of the dressmaker and her assistants. Some of the customers looked at her askance, making her feel defensive and wary, but Elizabeth ignored them. "Now, my dear," she said, leading Katie into the back of the shop, "let's have some fun. Have you ever had a milk bath?" Without waiting for a reply, she turned and led Katie up a set of stairs to what were obviously her own apartments.

During the next two hours, Katie was given several luxuriant beauty treatments, including a milk bath to enhance her complexion, followed by a rinse in icy water and a rubdown with fragrant oil. Warm oil was also poured onto her hair, and afterward her hair was washed with the finest soap and trimmed at the ends. She suspected that dressmakers did not usually offer baths and other such attentions to their clients, but she didn't know if it was her own disreputable appearance and stained clothes or Ethan's influence that had given her these uncustomary treats.

Her old clothes and boots were consigned to a dustbin, and she was dressed in a ready-made day dress of willow-green wool. Elizabeth then led her back to the showroom, where she spent the remainder of the day lounging on the fat cushions of a chaise and selecting her new wardrobe.

Katie savored every pleasure that came her way that day. She studied the beautiful clothes being paraded before her with a feeling akin to awe, but she acted as if she bought beautiful clothes all the time. She sent the shop girls scurrying to and fro for bonnets and shoes to match, and she took what she had to admit was a wicked delight in turning thumbs down on some of the most beautiful gowns she had ever seen. She nibbled sweet biscuits and sipped mulled Madeira. She discussed laces and trims, tried on numerous bonnets, and paid careful attention to Elizabeth's recommendations for colors that suited her complexion and clothing styles that suited her figure. She soaked up the attention of the women who waited on her as the parched desert soaked up rain. By the end of the day, she felt exhausted. She also felt more beautiful and alluring than she ever had in her life before.

Money, she decided, was a wonderful thing indeed.

Ethan approached the Old South Meeting House with the casual demeanor of a man simply out for a stroll. As he passed by, he noticed that quite a crowd had already gathered in front, though the meeting was not scheduled to begin until later. He saw many familiar faces. Aside from Whig leaders such as Samuel Adams, John Hancock, and Dr. Joseph Warren, he also saw many of his own friends and acquaintances, including David, Colin, Adam, and Joshua.

Another group was also gathering nearby, a group that caused Ethan grave concern. A group of British officers lounged on the corner, wisely remaining separate from the Boston citizens who were eyeing them with clear hostility. To Ethan, the troops looked bored, idle, and in search of trouble, and the sight of them only increased the misgivings he had expressed to Adam earlier that morning.

Recognizing one of the officers, he approached the group of redcoats and paused to make conversation. "Lieutenant Chase, what have we here?"

The young officer scowled. "They're having some kind of meeting. Defying the king, that's what they're doing."

Ethan nodded as if in agreement. "With these Whigs getting all fired up, there could be trouble."

"Don't you be worried, Mr. Harding. If they get out of line, we'll soon put them in their place."

His hand closed over his musket, and Ethan felt his lip curling with contempt. He quickly concealed his expression, but inside he felt his anger growing. God, was there no end to the arrogance of the king's troops? Couldn't a group of citizens even gather for a town meeting without being afraid of reprisal?

Ethan tipped his hat and gave Lieutenant Chase a suave smile. "I'm certain you will, Lieutenant," he murmured. "Good day to you."

He walked away from the officers, but he bought himself a mug of hot cider from the stand nearby and took up a position on the opposite corner from the meeting house. Sipping his cider, he watched and waited with a tense feeling in his guts. Before the end of the day, there was going to be serious trouble. He glanced at the stand where others were gathered to buy mugs of cider as he had done, and he concluded ruefully that the cider seller was probably going to be the only one who profited by today's events.

Despite Ethan's concerns, nothing happened during the several hours he waited outside the Old South Meeting House. He watched the crowd of Bostonians go inside when the doors opened, and he saw several of the officers follow them in. When he left to return to Elizabeth Waring's shop, the meeting was in full force, and nothing untoward had happened. For that Ethan was grateful. Perhaps, he thought in some surprise, it would all end peacefully. He hoped so.

When he arrived at the dressmaker's, he found a second surprise awaiting him. It took him several moments to find Katie in the crowded showroom, and when he did, he almost did not recognize her.

For several seconds, he simply stared at her, unable to think of a thing to say.

Even in rags, she had been a beautiful woman, but there was something about her now that came from more than physical beauty. She was dressed in fine clothes, and her short hair gleamed with all the warmth of polished amber, but her beauty, her clothes, and her hair were not what made him unable to take his eyes off her.

It was something else. Elizabeth, being a woman of sense, had left Katie's face free of cosmetics, but her complexion glowed with a radiance that came from inside. There was something about her, a nuance of pride in the lift of her chin, a soft smile of quiet confidence in the curve of her lips, a knowing look in her eyes as she studied him from beneath the velvet brim of an absurdly small bonnet.

Elizabeth, standing behind her, smiled at him. "She looks a picture, doesn't she?"

Katie laughed with mischievous delight. "Elizabeth, he seems to be stunned."

"I am," he assured her. "You've stunned me."

She ducked her head and smoothed her skirt. Then she looked up at him again and smiled almost shyly. "I do look rather good, don't I?"

"Good?" He laughed. "*Good* is hardly the word. My God, you were beautiful enough before, but now—" He broke off and shook his head. "There isn't a woman in Boston to touch you."

"I hope he still feels that way when he gets the bill," Elizabeth told Katie. She held out an armful of wrapped packages to Ethan, but it was to Katie she spoke. "Here is another ready-made dress for you, as well as a change of linen and nightdresses. The rest of your clothes should be arriving to you during the next week or so."

"Thank you."

Elizabeth glanced at Ethan. "The bill will be high," she said. "Be prepared."

Ethan waved away the cost with such disinterest that the dressmaker raised her eyebrows at him.

"Whatever it is, Elizabeth, I'll pay it willingly," he assured her, and turned to offer Katie his arm. "Come with me, and I'll wager ten guineas that half the men walking down the street will turn their heads to look at you."

If it had been a true wager, he would have won hands down. As they strolled back toward North Boston, nearly every man who passed them gave Katie an admiring glance, an appreciative smile, and a friendly tip of the hat.

"You were right," she told him as they turned onto her street. "I am beginning to feel a bit self-conscious."

"I don't believe that for a moment. You're a beautiful woman. Surely you know that."

"Yes," she admitted matter-of-factly. "I have always known that. But this is different. The men we are passing look at me differently from the way men have looked at me before, admiring but restrained, as if they think I'm a lady. I've never really thought about how much difference clothes can make to what people think of you." She gave him a shrewd sideways glance. "But you know that, don't you?"

"Clothes can be a very valuable tool in creating a certain impression, yes."

"Mmm," she murmured in assent, and studied him thoughtfully as they walked. "You use clothes very effectively yourself, although I have to say that I like you better when you aren't wearing that wig."

"You and I are in complete agreement about that," he told her. "Unfortunately, wigs are in high fashion, and I am a fashionable man."

She laughed at his unenthusiastic tone. "Ethan Harding, perhaps," she agreed in a low voice. "But what about John Smith?"

"I believe that man prefers oilskins."

Katie shook her head and murmured under her breath, "It's so astonishing that no one ever recognizes that you are both men."

"Not so astonishing. The two fellows have an entirely different group of friends, and it is highly unlikely they would have any mutual acquaintance."

"Perhaps, but what is even more astonishing is how you can talk about them both as if they are totally separate from yourself."

"They are."

She frowned, looking at him in some uncertainty. "What do you mean?"

"John Smith is an invention of my mind. I created him, as if I were writing a novel. I gave him a family, conveniently dead, of course, with graves on the frontier. Native savages, you know."

She nodded with pretended sympathy. "How tragic."

"Indeed. So tragic that he came to Boston and began working on the docks."

"I can understand thinking of John Smith as someone wholly separate from yourself, but how can you say that about Ethan Harding?"

"I am not the same Ethan Harding I was ten years ago."

"What do you mean by that? What changed you? The war?"

"Many things changed me," he said vaguely. He had no intention of telling her anything about himself that he did not need to. Instead, he paused on the street and said, "This is indeed a day for transformations. Look at your house. You won't recognize it."

Katie turned her head and stared at the house in obvious astonishment. It was no wonder. Ethan, too, was amazed at the changes that had been wrought in one day.

The soot accumulated over the winter from Boston's many coal fires had been washed away from the exterior, and the brick looked almost new. The shutters had been given a new coat of dark green paint, and a shiny new brass knocker and kick plate had been added to the front door, which had been painted the same dark green as the shutters. The walk had been swept, the two front windows had been given new panes of glass, and all the dead weeds had been cleared from the yard. The house now looked like any other upper-class home in the neighborhood.

"My goodness!" Katie gasped, laughing. "You're right. I hardly recognize it."

They walked up the front steps, and before Katie could even open the door, it was opened for them by an elderly man with the typical expressionless face of a well-trained butler. So stoically did he look at them, he might have been carved out of wood.

"You must be Stephens, the butler," Ethan greeted him. "I am Ethan Harding. This is Mrs. Armstrong."

Katie gave the servant an imperious nod perfectly suited to her role as mistress of the house. Stephens also found it so, for he held out one gloved hand for her cloak without any change in his impassive expression. If he disapproved of the fact that his wages were paid by a man not her husband, he was clearly too well bred to show it. One of Adam's greatest talents, Ethan knew, was hiring servants. They were always impeccable.

Stephens accepted her cloak, then held out his hand for Ethan's. He removed it and handed it over to the butler, then removed his hat. The impassive Stephens did not blink an eye when he pulled off the damned wig as well, dropped the wig into the hat, and thrust the hat into the butler's outstretched hand.

"There is a fire in the parlor, ma'am," he said, and pointed to a room to her right. "Would you like tea, ma'am?"

"Yes, thank you."

After hanging their cloaks and Ethan's hat and wig on the coat tree, Stephens left them, presumably in search of the tea tray, and Ethan followed Katie into the parlor.

"I thought tea had been banned in Boston," she said.

"Not banned," he corrected her. "Boycotted. And only by Whigs. You, my dear, are a loyal Tory, like myself."

Their gazes met in tacit understanding. "Of course," she said with a straight face. "Good thing, too. I am very fond of tea."

His hair felt matted from the wig, and he raked his fingers through it. He glanced around. "What do you think? Does it please you better now than it did last night?"

Katie glanced around, clearly just as surprised at the changes that had taken place inside the house as she had been by those outside. The white sheets that had covered the furniture had been removed, and though the furnishings were plainer than the luxurious ones of Ethan's house, they were quite comfortable. There was a colorful chintz sofa with two matching wing chairs facing the fireplace, as well as a few side tables and several additional chairs. Behind a beautiful brass fire screen, a coal fire heated the room. For entertainment, there was a small pianoforte, a chess set, and a card table. It was a cozy room, meant to make one feel at home.

Katie found it so as well. "I haven't lived anywhere this comfortable since I was a child," she told him, clearly well pleased. "It's lovely."

"Better than it was yesterday."

"Much better."

"I'm glad you like it. Shall we have a look at the rest?"

She agreed to that suggestion with a wide smile, and they left the parlor to tour the remainder of the house.

She expressed her relief that there wasn't a mouse to be seen anywhere. He was amused that she spent at least twenty minutes at the linen cupboard, fingering the sheets and towels almost with reverence.

He followed her through every room, and her delight was such a pleasure to watch that Ethan knew no matter how much it had cost, it was worth every cent.

Though she seemed pleased with all the rooms in the house, it was her bedroom that seemed to give her the most pleasure of all. To Ethan's mind, it was a nice, perfectly ordinary bedroom, except for the huge copper bathtub that reposed in one corner. There was a large mahogany four-poster, with two matching bedside tables, a washstand with a porcelain pitcher and bowl, and a huge armoire that, if he knew anything about women, still wouldn't be big enough to hold all her new clothes.

There were lace curtains at the windows and several nice paintings on the walls, but Ethan couldn't see anything particularly extraordinary about it.

But Katie entered the room with a cry of pure delight. At first, he thought it was the bathtub that she found so wonderful, but he was mistaken. "Ethan, look, a real bed. It's a real bed with a feather mattress!"

Before he could remind her that all the other bedrooms she had walked through had real beds as well, she ran to the four-poster, turned around, spread her arms wide, and fell back onto the mattress with the uninhibited joy of a child. "Oh, this is heavenly. You don't know how long it's been since I've slept in a bed like this."

He laughed, and she lifted her head to look at him. "Laugh all you want," she told him. "I don't care. This is the greatest luxury there is."

He watched her as she settled into the softness of the pillows with a smile of pure pleasure on her face. With a suddenness that startled him, Ethan was suddenly hot and hard, and he had to grip the edge of the door frame to keep himself from moving toward her, from burying himself in her, burying them both in the softness of the mattress she was enjoying with such innocent abandon. He set his jaw and did not move. One second went by, two, three. He did not know how long he stood there, watching her.

With a sigh, she rolled onto her stomach, and he gripped the door frame harder, until his hand ached. His body ached as well, ached with the effort of holding back. "Are you going to fall asleep?" he asked, his voice strange to his own ears, barely audible to him past the rush of his blood pumping in his veins.

"I might," she answered, her voice muffled by pillows. "I just might."

But she rolled again onto her back and sat up, her skirts billowing around her and that absurd little hat resting crookedly over her eye.

It was the hat that was his undoing, his excuse, his reason for slamming the door shut and moving toward her, for sitting on the edge of the bed with the vague idea of straightening her hat. But somehow the hat ended up tossed on the floor instead, and his hands were on her shoulders, pushing her down into the mattress.

He thought he heard her make a sound of surprise, but he covered her mouth with his, kissing her as he caught that little feminine sound and smothered it. Though he had kissed her twice before for reasons that had nothing to do with desire, this time, desire was the only reason. His tongue entered her mouth, tasted deeply of her, as his hands slid beneath her. He rolled them both so that she was now on top of him, so that his hands could undo the buttons at the back of her dress.

She arched her back with a moan of pleasure, exposing her throat. He pressed his lips to the pulse at the base of her neck and felt her body move against him in an erotic, rolling motion of her hips against his that sent him spiraling past reason, his only coherent thought a curse for Elizabeth, who had sold his mistress a dress with too damned many buttons.

But he had barely unfastened the third one down her back when she went limp against him, her body suddenly weighted and unmoving. "You promised me," she whispered, her face buried in the curve of his shoulder. "You gave me your word."

Christ, Katie, not now. Don't do this, don't stop me now.

But it was useless; those whispered words were a woman's best defense, and he could not go on. He shoved her off and sat up, breathing as if he'd been running. Katie, too, was breathing hard, and he didn't know whether it pleased him or not to know she had been just as aroused as he.

Neither of them spoke, and after a few minutes, Ethan got up from the bed with an abrupt movement. "I'm sorry about that," he said roughly, knowing he didn't sound sorry at all. "It won't happen again."

He opened the door, but before he could walk through it, her voice stopped him. "Ethan?"

"What?"

"Will I see you tomorrow?"

"Probably not. I'll be having a dinner party Thursday night to introduce you to a few acquaintances. I'll have my carriage fetch you at seven o'clock."

He took a step through the door.

"Ethan?"

He smothered a curse and waited.

"Thank you for the clothes. And for having the house repaired and for getting rid of the mice because you knew I hate them . . . and I just wanted to say thank you because . . . well, because I wouldn't want you to think I wasn't grateful for what you've done. I mean . . ." She paused amid the tangle of sentences and took a deep breath, then burst out, "Thank you for keeping your word."

"For God's sake," he ground out between clenched teeth. "Don't thank me for that."

He walked out of the room and closed the door behind him. He didn't want her thanks for keeping that promise. He had the feeling that before it was all over, it was a promise he was going to break.

11

The following morning, Katie was awakened by a light tap on her bedroom door. She opened her eyes as a girl about her own age wearing a mobcap and apron entered the room bearing a laden tray. "Breakfast, ma'am," the girl said with a timid smile as she paused beside the bed.

It took Katie a moment to realize she was actually being served breakfast in bed. She sat up, and the maid placed the tray across her lap. A boiled egg, kippers, a pot of tea, and a piping-hot stack of buttered toast with marmalade filled the tray, and she sniffed appreciatively. Though it was beyond her experience to be waited on, Katie decided she could easily get used to it. "It looks wonderful. Thank you."

The girl smiled. "I'll tell Mrs. Clapham you said so, ma'am. She asked me to say if eight o'clock be too early for you, to tell her when you'd like it served, and she'd rearrange things to suit you."

Katie smiled at that. What a luxury, to have a hot breakfast when she chose and to eat it in bed. "Eight o'clock is fine."

"I'll tell her."

The girl bobbed at the knees and started to turn away, but Katie stopped her. "What's your name?"

"Janie, ma'am. Janie Duncan." She gestured to the window. "Shall I open the curtains, ma'am?"

"Yes, please," she answered gravely, but she wanted to laugh. She was going to have to become accustomed to being called *ma'am*. It was not a title she was used to. "I'm glad to meet you, Janie," she said as the girl pulled back the curtains from the window and sunlight flooded the room. "I'm sorry we didn't meet last night."

A slight frown creased the maid's brow. "I hope I didn't do wrong about that."

"Wrong?" Katie was bewildered. "Wrong about what?"

"I'm to be your maid, ma'am. That's what Mr. Lawrence said when he hired me." Before she could ask who Mr. Lawrence was, Janie rushed on, "But I wasn't able to start work until late in the evening, and your door was closed, and I took that to mean you was asleep already and wouldn't be needing me until morning. But I don't see how you got undressed by yourself." The maid picked up Katie's green dress from the chair where she had left it the night before and eyed it doubtfully. "There's an awful lot of buttons down the back."

Katie felt the heat rush into her cheeks, and she

quickly ducked her head. She wondered what the girl would say if she explained that the top three buttons had already been unfastened by the man who paid the wages in this household. She took a gulp of tea and figured that there were some things servants just didn't need to know. She'd probably learn of the arrangements soon enough, anyway.

Suddenly, the door burst open, and Katie found another visitor entering her bedroom. This visitor, however, was no servant. Daniel Munro came into the room with all the force of a hurricane and all the enthusiasm of a half-grown puppy. " 'Morning, Katie," he cried, and slammed the door behind him. He plopped down on the edge of her bed with enough force to rattle the dishes on her tray. "Have you heard the news?"

"Daniel Munro!" Janie grabbed the boy by the ear and dragged him off the bed. "Don't you know better than to just burst into a lady's bedroom?"

Daniel rubbed his sore ear. "What are you on about, Janie Duncan?" he demanded resentfully. "There's no lady here. It's just Katie."

Katie looked from one to the other. "You two know each other?"

"Yes, ma'am," the maid answered. "Second cousins." She turned to the boy and pointed to the door. "Out."

"It's all right, Janie," Katie told her. "He can stay. What news, Daniel?"

"The riot yesterday." Daniel resumed his seat on the edge of her bed, and as Katie ate her breakfast, he launched into a rambling account of how there had been some big meeting at a place called the Old South Meeting House, and how Samuel Adams had been there, and Dr. Warren, too. And how Dr. Warren had made a speech, and how there were lobsterbacks there who booed and hissed.

"And one of 'em yelled, 'Fire! Fire!' and that was it," Daniel concluded in a rush. "Only John thinks the redcoat didn't really say 'Fire.'"

Katie shook her head, thoroughly confused. "What did Eth—" She broke off and corrected herself. "What did John Smith think he said?"

"He thinks the redcoat was booing Dr. Warren and really said, 'Fie, fie,' but Samuel says no, and told Benjamin to put it in the *Gazette* that he actually said 'Fire' to cause a riot. And it did."

"You mean people thought he said there was a fire, and they panicked?"

"That's it. People started running for the doors and screaming, and some people were trampled. And just then, the redcoats of the Forty-third came marching by with their fifes and drums going, and people really got scared, thinking the Regulars were coming out. Lots of people got hurt. John was really angry, and he told my father how it was stupid of Sam Adams to even have a town meeting right now. He said if anybody had gotten shot like what happened at the massacre five years ago, the war would've started then and there. I don't understand why he was so angry. I mean, John wants war as much as any of us. He's said so often enough."

Janie sniffed. "Don't be wishing for war, Daniel. No good can come of it. I don't care what this John Smith says, whoever he is."

Katie looked at her curiously. "You don't know John Smith?"

"No, ma'am, but then, I don't know many people in Boston. I'm from Cambridge myself. Daniel's father sent for me, saying he knew a Mr. Lawrence was hiring a maid for a lady, and how he knew my family needed the money. I came straightaway."

"Janie, how can you say you don't want the war?" Daniel demanded. "You're a Whig like any of us."

"It doesn't mean I want a war," the girl answered with a sigh. "I wish they'd just let us go."

"They won't," Daniel told her. "My father says we'll go to war with the Regulars before it's all over, you just wait and see." He pointed to the tray. "Those look like smashing kippers, Katie. May I have one?"

David Munro might have been right about an impending war, but the quiet atmosphere of Boston during the three days that followed the incident at Old South Meeting House seemed to belie that prediction. The streets were quiet, there were no riots or mob scenes, and nothing happened to fuel the fires of rebellion. It appeared that each side was making a supreme effort to be civil to the other, as if mere civility could prevent war.

During those three days, Katie saw nothing of

Ethan, and she spent her time enjoying her life of luxury. Every day, she dined on wonderful food, took carriage rides on the Common, and tried on every gown as it was delivered from Elizabeth Waring's shop. Every night, she took a long soak in the bathtub Ethan had provided for her and slept dreamlessly in the plush softness of her feather bed. She knew that all of this high living would end when Lowden returned, but she fully intended to enjoy it while it lasted. Ever since she was a child, Katie had lived for the moment, and if she had vague moments of uneasiness or guilt, she pushed them aside.

Thanks to the comforts Ethan's money afforded, her life was perfect. In fact, it was almost too perfect. After three days of it, Katie was actually in danger of becoming bored. She was accustomed to living on the hard edge of life, and after three days of luxurious living, she began to realize that, while enjoyable, luxury could easily become monotonous. She found herself looking forward to Ethan's dinner party.

As he had told her, his carriage came for her promptly at seven o'clock, and by quarter past the hour, she was standing in the wide foyer of his elegant house, handing her sable-trimmed wrap to a butler even more staid and impassive than her own.

The night she had followed Ethan home from the Mermaid, he had taken her inside through the back door, and the house had been dark and silent. She had known by the plush comfort of his library that he lived well, but now, standing in the marble-tiled front entrance of his home, with an immense crystal chandelier high over her head and a thick Aubusson rug beneath her feet, she could truly appreciate that fact.

"Mr. Harding is in the music room, ma'am," the butler told her. "This way."

Katie followed him past the sweeping staircase and through a set of double doors. After announcing her, the butler departed, closing the doors behind him. Ethan rose to greet her, and she couldn't help laughing at the sight of his elegant, almost dandified clothes.

"What are you laughing about?" he asked.

"I'm sorry," she said, pressing her fingers to her lips in a futile attempt to suppress her amusement, "but I can't seem to get used to seeing you in lace cravats and breeches. And a purple waistcoat, for heaven's sake. You look so different in your oilskins."

"That's the idea," he said dryly. "But I thought you said you would always be able to recognize me, despite my attire."

"So I would." She didn't tell him it was because she always pictured him the way she had first seen him—dressed in the rough clothes of the docks, with his black hair caught back in a queue, leaning back in a tavern chair, looking as dangerous as a cobra ready to strike. Elegant clothes and powdered hair could not change that.

"Would you like a sherry?" he asked.

"Yes, please." She settled back on the gold brocade settee as he poured her wine. "What is the purpose of this party, anyway?" she asked. "Is there something specific you wish me to do?"

"Not tonight." He handed her the glass of sherry and sat down beside her. "I have a specific assignment in mind for you, but tonight, I am merely establishing your acquaintanceship with me to my Tory friends."

"Don't you think it's time you told me exactly what this bargain of ours will entail for me?" She took a sip of wine. "I have the right to know."

"Yes," he said with a sigh. "I know you do." He set his glass aside and turned to her. "Katie, I have one task for you, and one task only. If you can fulfill it, your freedom from indenture to Willoughby is yours."

"What is it?"

"I want you to find out everything you can about one man. Viscount Lowden."

She froze with her glass raised halfway to her lips, but somehow she managed to recover her poise after only an instant and took another sip of wine. "Who is he?"

"He has come from London, supposedly to be a liaison between Governor Gage and Lord North, who is the king's chief minister in London."

"Supposedly? What do you mean?" Katie's mind raced as she asked these questions. Lowden wanted her to spy on John Smith, who was really Ethan Harding, and Ethan wanted her to spy on

Lowden. This was getting complicated, and Katie began to feel as if she were a circus juggler with too many balls in the air.

"I believe Lowden's declared purpose is not his true one, and I want to know what he is really doing in Boston. My normal channels of information have been unable or unwilling to tell me that information, so I am hoping you can help me find out."

"I see." Katie already knew Lowden's true purpose—to find proof against Whig seditionists—and for a moment, the thought crossed her mind that she could pretend to find that out somehow, tell Ethan, and have him buy her indenture. But then she remembered the arrest warrant Lowden held against her and dismissed the idea. No, Lowden was her only choice. She had to remain on his side. "But you don't wish me to begin this assignment tonight?"

"There is no point. Lowden is away. He is in New York for another week or so. But in the interim, our time will not be wasted. This week gives me the opportunity to establish you in my circle of friends. I will also have other tasks for you to do. Tomorrow, for instance, we will spend the afternoon together, and the following day, you will run a very important errand for me. By the way, beginning tonight, you're an actress."

"What?"

"You are a London actress, a protégée and understudy of Mary Black, and you have just arrived in Boston."

She took a sip of sherry. "And why did I leave my promising career to come here?"

"You had a very severe illness and, as a result, lost your voice for a long time. Because of that, you also lost your mentor. Though you have recovered and are no longer ill, you wanted a change of scene and society. So you decided to come to the colonies for an indefinite stay. Your name is Mrs. Armstrong."

"And what happened to Mr. Armstrong?"

"He died. You're a widow."

"And because I'm an actress, I'm also of a loose moral character and very likely to be some man's mistress," she concluded. "In this case, yours."

"Quite so."

Katie had no doubts about her acting ability and was able to play her part easily enough that evening as she was introduced to Ethan's acquaintances, and the story he had concocted regarding her background was put to good use. She also fancied that she came across convincingly as both an actress and a mistress.

Her memories of life with her mother were somewhat vague, but during the course of the evening, Katie discovered how much of her childhood she actually remembered as she took on the role her mother had played in life. She found herself adopting her mother's demeanor, meeting the speculative looks of Ethan's guests with a naturalness that somewhat surprised her.

Because Ethan was an unmarried man, and she

professed to be a widow with her own household, total discretion regarding their relationship was not required, and Katie was glad of it. Her mother had been in a different position, the unmarried mistress of a married man with whom she had lived openly, and the veiled contempt with which she had been treated was something Katie did not particularly wish to experience.

Instead, when Ethan introduced her as his friend, Mrs. Armstrong, most of the guests accepted the relationship without raising an eyebrow. They must surely have concluded she was Ethan's mistress, but most were too well bred to show it. There was one exception, a man named Holbrook, and his reaction was far more boorish than that of any other guest. "An actress, eh?" he said, giving her a wink. "I didn't know Ethan even liked the theater. He must be able to see some plays that we don't."

He laughed heartily at his own words. Ethan gave the other man a polite smile, but Katie could see it was a smile that did not reach his eyes. He took her elbow and steered her away from Holbrook, insisting there were other guests she had to meet.

"Thank you," she whispered as he guided her away.

"I'm sorry about that," he said as they took up a place at the opposite end of the room. "Holbrook's a pig."

She glanced up at him in surprise. "You're angry."

He didn't answer, but the tight set of his mouth

confirmed her conclusion, and she felt a tiny throb of pleasure. "Be careful," she murmured, unable to resist teasing him. "You might start falling madly in love with me."

"God, I hope not. You'd lead any man in love with you a sorry chase."

That was so true, she couldn't help laughing. "Thank you very much. You know, Ethan, if you don't flatter your mistress occasionally, you just might find she's left you for another man."

"I see. And of the other men in this room, which would you choose?"

She pretended to give the matter serious consideration and finally settled on the tall, blond man standing nearby. "That one."

"Not possible. Travertine wouldn't be at all attracted to you."

"You are overwhelming me with flattery this evening. And why would he not find me attractive?"

Ethan flashed her a grin as she took a sip of sherry. "You're a woman."

She choked. "He likes boys?"

"I believe I've shocked you."

"Not at all. 'Tis a pity, though. He's so handsome." She gave an aggrieved sigh. "Why is it the handsome ones always prefer boys?"

"That hurts, Katie. Do you feel better now that you've evened the score?"

"Yes," she said, aware that she was smiling like a cat who'd found the cream pitcher. "I believe I do."

"My opinion remains unchanged. God help any man who falls in love with you."

Katie caught Holbrook studying her across the room, and when he began moving toward them, she groaned. "Holbrook is coming this way."

"Don't worry. I'll protect you."

"If Holbrook is such a pig, why do you invite him to your parties?"

"He is one of Gage's aides, and he gives me a great deal of valuable information. Especially when he's drunk, which is quite often. Besides, his wife, Rosalie, is a nice and lovely woman."

"He has a wife? A nice, lovely one?"

"Hard to believe, but yes. Even more surprising, his wife is actually said to love him dearly."

"Perhaps," Katie said with all the cynicism of her lifetime. "But I just hope he stays away from me. If he doesn't, I'll do something rude."

"You have my permission to kick him under the dinner table."

To her relief, and probably Ethan's as well, that action did not prove to be necessary. They were seated at opposite ends of the table, and Ethan was quite skillful at keeping Holbrook away from her. As the evening went on, Katie found herself rather enjoying her part. There was a certain excitement in it, especially when she glanced up to find Ethan watching her, with that half smile on his face, and she would find herself smiling back. Whenever their eyes met, it was curiously intimate, as if they shared a secret.

Which was true, she supposed. They did share a secret, a secret she would be forced to reveal to his enemy in only a few days' time. But whenever she looked at Ethan and found him smiling at her, she wished she did not have to choose between his destruction and her own.

The following day, Ethan called for her as he had told her he would, and if he had some treasonous deviltry in mind for their afternoon and evening together, he gave no sign of it. He simply suggested they take a stroll toward the marketplace.

Though the day was cold, the sun was shining, and the skies were crystalline blue, making it a perfect day for walking, but from what Ethan had told her the night before, he had a deeper purpose for their afternoon than simply being seen strolling together.

When she asked him what that purpose might be, he smiled and said, "You are very fond of bookstores."

"I am?"

"Indeed. You have been told that the London Bookstore is the place to find an excellent bound copy of Shakespeare's complete works."

Katie gave an unladylike whistle. The London Bookstore was owned by Mr. Henry Knox, and the patriot sentiments of Mr. Knox himself were common knowledge. He was a Whig down to his fingertips. "Is it wise for you to be seen in a patriot bookstore?"

"No, and that is why you are going there instead of me. Being a stranger in Boston, posing as someone who has no political sentiments, you can enter a Whig bookstore without suspicion. No one will think it odd."

"And while I am shopping for Shakespeare's complete works, what will you be doing?"

"Having a cup of tea at the coffeehouse down the street. When we get close to Knox's establishment, we will part company. When you've finished there, you can meet me at the coffeehouse."

"But what is my real reason for going there?"

"As I said, you are buying a book." Before she could ask more questions, he spoke again. "Are you settled into your house? Is everything comfortable for you?"

"Yes, thank you."

"Have any mice returned?"

"Not a mouse in sight," she assured him. "Though mice do have a habit of coming back."

"Perhaps that's why I brought you this." Ethan came to a halt beside a newspaper seller and reached inside his cloak. "I have a gift for you."

First the cloak, then the house, the servants, and the clothes. Now he wanted to give her another present? Katie was dismayed. She thought of her mother, dependent on gifts from a man, but she was not in that position. Even more important, she was there to find evidence to betray this man. She didn't want gifts from him. "You don't need to be so nice to me," she told him. "Just because we're playing out this charade that I'm your mistress, giving me presents is carrying it a bit far, don't you think?"

He started to speak, but she forestalled him. "It isn't necessary. Men do buy their mistresses expensive gifts. I know that my own mother received diamonds, gold, and all sorts of other baubles, but I don't want them."

"I understand," he began, "but this isn't much of a gift, believe me. It's a trifling thing—"

"Perhaps it is," she interrupted as she held up one hand to stop him from speaking, "but I cannot accept it. Ethan, the clothes and the house are necessary for me to play my part, I understand that. But beyond that, I won't be beholden to you in any way."

During her little speech, he watched her with an intent expression on his face, as if every word she uttered was vitally important, but Katie did not miss the slight tilt at one corner of his mouth. He was really the most unaccountable man. She frowned, suddenly suspicious. "Are you laughing at me?"

"I wouldn't dream of it," he said gravely. "But I must confess that the idea of giving you gold and diamonds never occurred to me." He pulled something out of the inner pocket of his cloak and held it out to her. "Although if you were to insist upon it, I could have the jeweler make him a diamond-studded collar, I suppose."

Katie stared at the small bundle of orange fur he

held out to her, and she could not think of a thing to say. She opened her mouth, and closed it again.

In his hand was a kitten, still quite young, and small enough that Ethan held it easily in the palm of his hand. It looked at her and gave a faint, mewling cry.

To Katie, that helpless sound was like a rock hitting a window. It shattered something inside her—the hard and brittle armor of cynicism and detachment she had worn for most of her life, armor so comfortable to her that she hadn't even known it was there until now, when she felt it falling around her in pieces on the ground.

She stared at the kitten, looking into the round green eyes that peered at her from between Ethan's fingers, and she felt herself coming apart.

Ethan did not appear to notice. He turned the kitten's face toward his own and studied it for a few seconds. "I got her from my kitchen maid," he said nonchalantly. "If she turns out anything like her mother, who is the destroyer of rats in my household, she'll weigh a full stone or more, and she'll be as big and fat as a Christmas ham."

No man had ever done anything thoughtful for her, at least not without the expectation of something in return, and she could not quite take it in. She stood there, staring stupidly at the animal cradled in his hand, and she was unable to utter a word.

"I think she'll be able to dispatch any mice that dare to invade your larder," he told her, and turned the animal back around so she could see its face. "Wouldn't you agree? I mean to say, who needs a tiger from India when you have a fierce mouser such as this?"

Katie started to laugh, but her laughter changed to a sob, and she found to her mortification that she was doing something she had not done since she was a little girl. She was crying. She was standing in the midst of a public street, with hordes of people all around her, with tears falling down her cheeks.

She reached for the kitten and took it from his hand. She buried her face against the soft fur to brush away her tears, and though she struggled to regain control, she could not seem to manage it. The worst part of it was that she could not even understand why she was crying. She never cried. Never.

Ethan said nothing. He simply reached into another pocket and pulled out a handkerchief. He held it out to her without a word, and when she took it, he turned away, giving her time to compose herself. He pretended to study the newspapers stacked nearby, while Katie tucked the kitten into the warm shelter of her cloak pocket and put his handkerchief to good use.

Once she had her emotions in check, she and Ethan continued their walk down the street as if nothing had happened. Neither of them spoke. Ethan made no attempt to talk, and for that she was grateful. She could not have managed conversation just now.

She had spent most of her life hardening herself against the world by caring for no one, protecting herself from painful disappointments with a jaded mind and a jaundiced eye, always believing the worst and keeping fear at bay with a shell of brash self-confidence.

A lifetime of self-protection had been shattered in an instant. One man and his gift of a common household kitten had stripped away all her protective barriers and left her feeling raw, vulnerable, and very much afraid. She was trying to harden her heart against him, and he was making it impossible. Damn him, anyway.

12

 $\mathcal{T}$ he London Bookstore was packed when Katie entered. Amid the array of books, telescopes, wallpaper, and baskets available for sale, customers chatted with one another as they sipped steaming cups of chicory coffee.

Mr. Henry Knox proved to be a plump, cherubic-faced young man, and he must have been expecting her, for scarcely a minute after she entered the shop, he came bustling across the crowded room to greet her.

"Mrs. Armstrong," he exclaimed as if they had already met. "I am delighted to see you again. You have come for your book?"

"I have," she answered, taking her cue from him.

"Excellent. I will wrap it up for you. In the meantime, feel free to browse as much as you like."

Their gazes met in understanding, before the bookseller departed in search of what Katie knew was more than a copy of Shakespeare's complete works. Perhaps there were letters or secret papers inside, but if so, she would have no opportunity to have a look at them, for when Knox returned, the package he handed her was wrapped securely in brown paper and closed with sealing wax.

"Would you like it charged to your account?" Knox asked her.

"Of course." Katie accepted the package from him and left the shop. She tucked the package under her arm and her hands in the pockets of her cloak against the cold wind of early spring. One of her hands closed around the warm, furry bundle in her pocket, and this time she didn't cry. Instead, she smiled. So much for gold and diamonds.

She found the coffeehouse Ethan had described, and when she went inside, she found him waiting for her at a table in the corner, surrounded by several other ladies and gentlemen, most of whom she had met the night before. William Holbrook was among them, and he greeted Katie with a rather lecherous wink that she found quite irritating.

"My dear Mrs. Armstrong," he greeted, casting a long and lustful look at her body as Ethan pulled out a chair for her. "By Jove, what is that thing?"

She looked down to discover the kitten had poked its head out of her pocket and was blinking sleepily at Sir William. "It's a kitten, my dear sir. A present from Ethan."

Holbrook glanced at the man beside her with a dubious shake of his head. "It won't do, my dear fellow. You really must find more lavish gifts for your—er—friend than that."

The implication was clear, but Katie ignored it. She pulled the baby cat out of her pocket and held it up for everyone to see as she sat down at the table. "I prefer this," she said softly. "I've never had a pet." She looked at the man seated beside her. " 'Tis a better gift than diamonds."

"Mrs. Armstrong, you are a very unusual woman," Arnold Travertine told her with a shake of his head, watching as she tucked her present back into her pocket, "to prefer a common house cat to jewels."

"And less of a strain on the accounts, eh, Harding?" Holbrook said, laughing at his own joke. Titters from two of the ladies present echoed him, but most people at the table just looked uncomfortable. "I'm so glad you could join us, my dear lady."

"I'm afraid I can't say the same, Sir William," she answered with a yawn. "It's barely noon, too early in the day for shopping."

"You surprise me. I thought all women love to shop." He shot a meaningful glance at her companion. "Especially when it is a man's money she's spending."

Katie was getting quite tired of the man's innuendoes. "Where is your wife, Sir William?" she asked sweetly. "I have yet to meet her."

Sir William was not a discerning man, but even he knew he had gone too far. He made no more references to her position as Ethan's mistress, and talk shifted to music and art, two topics Holbrook clearly knew nothing about. After perhaps half an hour of conversation, Ethan rose to his feet. "Mrs. Armstrong and I should be going. She still has at least four other shops to visit."

He bade the group of his society friends farewell, and they departed. When they were out the door, Katie drew a deep breath, glad to be gone from there.

"I see you have the package from Knox. Keep close watch on it."

"Why?" she asked. "Are there secret papers hidden inside?"

"No secret papers," he answered. "I assure you, there is a copy of Shakespeare's plays inside that package."

"And something more, I'll wager. My curiosity almost led me to take a peek."

"It wouldn't matter if you did," he answered. "Anything that might be inside would mean nothing to you."

"I don't understand."

"You don't have to."

She scowled. "Must you always be so circumspect?"

Ethan shrugged. "Since you will have charge of the book in a few days, and knowing your insatiable curiosity, I fully expect you to look it over."

"What do you mean, I'll have charge of the book after a few days?"

"There is a man in Cambridge who is very fond of Shakespeare. You will need to take the book to him at the Blue Boar Inn there. A man named Joseph Bramley."

"Who is he?"

"No one important, I assure you. He is a mechanic, I believe."

"So is Paul Revere," she pointed out. "Would you call him unimportant?"

"Unimportant enough that he hasn't been arrested yet."

Katie remembered what both Lowden and Ethan had told her about Governor Gage requiring proof of sedition before he would arrest anyone. "Because they cannot prove anything?"

"Exactly."

"And what about you?" she whispered, and turned her head to look at him. "How long can you keep up this charade before you are suspected?"

"As long as I have to."

That answer and the uncompromising tone of his voice reminded her of how determined, how ruthless, he could be. Yet he could also give her a kitten because she was afraid of mice.

That consideration, that thoughtfulness, was something she would not have thought him to have, and suddenly, she wished she could see more of that side of his character. She knew she would never get to know him that well, and she wondered why that bothered her so much.

*　　*　　*

Every time Ethan thought he had Katie figured out, she surprised him. He knew she was cynical, tough, and realistic, a survivor. He would have been hard-pressed to believe anything could make her cry, and yet the gift of an ordinary kitten had caused her to dissolve into tears on a public street. He could not understand it. Katie was not a woman who easily displayed her true feelings, probably because it made her appear too vulnerable, a protective defense he understood very well, for he was the same way, although for different reasons.

Ethan could believe Katie capable of using tears to manipulate a man, but he knew that had not been the case today. Her response to the kitten had been genuine, he was certain of that. He wondered what had caused it, what thoughts and emotions had gone through her mind at that moment, but had he asked her directly, she would not have told him the truth. In fact, she probably would have told him to sod off.

They spent the remainder of the afternoon strolling through Boston, looking in shop windows and sipping hot coffee as they watched children skate on the ice of the Mill Pond. She made no reference to the kitten in her pocket, and it was not until they had returned to her house that evening that Ethan found the opportunity to bring up the subject again.

Stephens greeted them at the door, and the butler's expression did not change at the sight of the kitten she pulled from her pocket. He took her cloak and Ethan's, then told them that there was a fire going in the parlor if they wished to warm themselves after their walk.

Katie laughed as she and Ethan entered the parlor to follow the butler's suggestion. "That man never changes expression. I believe I could have pulled the head of John the Baptist out of my cloak, and Stephens wouldn't have raised an eyebrow."

"You are probably right," Ethan answered, watching as she knelt on the rug before the fire, cradling the kitten in her hands. "Stephens is an impeccable butler."

He saw her press a kiss to the top of the kitten's head before she set the tiny animal on the rug, and he found that almost as surprising as her tears had been. "I can see you like your gift," he commented. "Have you thought of a name for her yet?"

She nodded. "I think I'll call her Meg."

"Why Meg?"

"Meg was a friend of mine. At least . . ." She fell silent, and he thought she wasn't going to finish what she had been about to say, but after a long pause, she spoke again. "At least," she whispered, "Meg was the closest thing to a friend I've ever had."

She looked up at him, and a shadow of something—sorrow, perhaps—crossed her face. "I envy you. You have several close, loyal friends. That is extraordinary. You are very fortunate. Don't ever take them for granted."

He started to assure her that he did not do so,

and yet the thought suddenly occurred to him that he probably did. He knew David, Molly, Joshua, Andrew, and Adam would follow him without question down any road he chose to take, and he had never before thought of that as extraordinary or considered himself fortunate. "Thank you for reminding me," he said gravely. "Sometimes we do tend to take our friends for granted, and we shouldn't."

He wanted to ask her about Meg, but before he could do so, she spoke again. "Thank you for your gift. It was very thoughtful of you." She smiled suddenly, and the shadow was gone. "Although I don't think it's the usual gift a man gives his mistress."

Ethan knelt down beside her. "Why is it so unusual, Katie?" he asked. "Because you're not accustomed to receiving gifts from men? Or because you know from your mother's experience that men don't give gifts without exacting a price?" He leaned closer to her. "Or perhaps," he added softly, "it is the thoughtfulness of it that you find surprising?"

"All of those," she confessed. "But the last most of all." She leaned back and lifted her chin, returning his gaze with an almost defiant one of her own. "No man ever gave me anything before, at least not anything I accepted, and certainly nothing that had special meaning to me. I am not accustomed to that sort of consideration from men. From anyone, really."

As if suddenly thinking she had revealed too much, Katie looked away, glancing at the animal that had begun this conversation. At present, the kitten was curled up in a ball beside her, sound asleep. "She looks so small. If I get any rats, I hope they won't hurt her."

"It's supposed to be the other way around," he reminded her. "And don't worry. She'll grow into the job. I told you before, her mother is the terror of rodents. My kitchen maid assures me that no mouse or rat would dare invade our kitchen as long as Libby is anywhere in the vicinity."

"Libby? Short for Elizabeth, I imagine."

"My Tory friends would think so. But actually, you are wrong. Libby is short for Liberty."

She laughed. "Even your cat has a political significance. Why doesn't that surprise me?"

"And what about your choice of name? Meg is probably short for Margaret."

Katie's smile faded. "I imagine so, but actually, I don't know for certain."

"You don't know? Who was this Meg, then?"

"We met when we were both eleven years old. I had run away from the orphanage, and it was my second night alone on the streets. I was in an alley in East London. I was cold and hungry and so scared that I just started crying. Then I heard this voice in the dark telling me to quit bawling like a baby since people were trying to sleep."

"That was Meg?"

"Yes. The next morning, she woke me up with a

kick in the shin and handed me half a loaf of bread still warm from the baker's oven."

Ethan grinned at that. "Stolen, of course."

"Of course." Katie shook her head as if in disbelief. "To this day, I don't know what made her decide to help me, but she did. She taught me how to steal food off a cart in the marketplace. She also taught me how to pick a man's pocket or a woman's reticule without getting caught, where to sell the stolen goods, and how to know I was getting a good price for them. She even taught me some confidence swindles. We worked as a team for nearly eight years, which is safer than doing it alone."

Katie looked at him. "Meg saved my life. If I had not met her, I might have died of hunger or cold. Or I might have been forced into prostitution, which would have been worse than death."

"Yet you say she was only the closest thing to a friend you've had. I would call her a special friend indeed."

Katie shook her head. "Oh, no. It isn't the same thing as your friendship with, say, Joshua. You see, on the streets, what matters is to survive. If it had come down to saving me or saving herself, Meg would have let me hang without blinking an eye. Because of that, you don't get too close to people. You can't."

"A hard way to live," he commented, and watched her jaw set.

"That's the way it has to be. You get used to it."

"What happened to bring you to the colonies?"

"Meg and I got caught lifting the purse of a West End toff, who turned out to be an earl, a very wealthy and powerful man. Stealing is always a very serious offense, but in this case it was especially so, as you might guess. I went to prison and was committed to transportation to the colonies. Meg was not so fortunate."

"What happened to her?"

Katie's lips tightened, and she looked away. "They hanged her in the public square. The only reason I didn't hang with her was that the judge thought I was pretty and took pity on me. But I was forced to watch them hang Meg—to teach me a lesson, I imagine, and to help me realize the error of my ways." She shook her head and stood up. "For goodness sake, let's talk about something else. Or better yet, let's play chess. There is a set on that table."

He was surprised. "You know the game?"

"My mother taught me. She felt it was an accomplishment every mistress should have."

Her words struck Ethan like a punch in the stomach. "What do you mean?" he asked, following her across the room. "Your mother expected you to follow in her footsteps?"

She shrugged as if it was a matter of no consequence. "I am sure she knew it was a possibility for me when I grew up. After all, she taught me to read and write both English and French, she taught me cards and chess, and she drilled etiquette, manners, and the peerage into me as if it were military training."

"In other words, she gave you all the accomplishments required of a mistress?"

"Well, it wasn't because she hoped I would marry above my station."

"But you were only a child." Ethan was not a man to be easily shocked, but the idea that a woman would prepare her young daughter for such a life did rather shock him. "My God."

Katie shrugged as if it didn't matter. "Look at it from her point of view. We had no money, no influence, and no connections. And I was illegitimate. What other ambitions could she possibly have had for my future?"

He remembered her words that morning in Molly's kitchen about connections and money being so important, and he knew the answer to her question was none. "Let's play," he said abruptly, and sat down.

She took the chair opposite him at the small table. "Keep in mind that I'm not very good at it," she warned him. "Partly because I've had little practice, and partly because my mother did not teach me to play well."

"Of course not," he muttered. "It wouldn't do for a mistress to be skilled at the game, because she should always lose to her lover anyway, isn't that right?"

"But I won't let you win," she told him firmly, "despite what you told Holbrook today. And I don't have to, since I'm not really your mistress."

"If you really were my mistress, I can assure you,

I would not want you to lose a chess game on purpose to bolster my pride."

If you were really my mistress, we would be too busy making love to play chess, anyway.

Ethan studied her in the lamplight as they played, and he took a great deal of pleasure in imagining all the delights having Katie for a true mistress would offer. God, he wanted her.

He would not have thought it possible, but she was even more beautiful now than she had been the day he first saw her in the marketplace. The three weeks that had passed since then had brought about some subtle but unmistakable changes in her face and form. Good food had caused her to gain some much-needed weight, though she was still far too thin. The sharp lines of hunger and deprivation he had first seen etched into her face had softened, showing her beauty more plainly than ever. And yet it was not her beauty alone that intrigued him and ignited his desire for her. It was something else.

She looked like an angel, but she could lie like a demon. She could steal a man's watch quick as lightning, but she would refuse any jewels he might give her. She was so jaded, but the gift of a kitten could make her cry. It was the astonishing contrasts within her that he found fascinating.

She moved her bishop and glanced across the table at him, realizing for the first time that he was staring at her, not at the board. Something of what he was thinking must have shown in his face, for a slight blush tinged her cheeks, and she spoke hastily as if to divert his attention. "I've told you a few things about my past. Why don't you tell me something about yours?"

"What do you want to know?"

"I want to know how a man who once fought for the king could change into a radical rebel and fight against him."

"Radical?" He lifted an eyebrow. "Is that what I am?"

"Very much so, as if you didn't already know it. Ethan, what happened to change your outlook?"

He did not answer at once. He lowered his gaze to the chessboard and looked at it for a long time. She waited, and finally, he gave a slight laugh and returned his gaze to her face. "If I told you it was because my father was one of the most loyal Tories in the king's possessions, would that make sense?"

"Because you hated your father?"

"Because I loved him."

"I don't understand."

He picked up one of the chess pieces he had taken from her and rolled it between his fingers, studying it. "My father was a very straightforward and plain man. He believed your king was your sovereign, and you had no right to question anything he did. I believed it because he believed it, and he was my father."

"And then?"

"Then, the Stamp Act was passed in 1765, and the riots broke out all over Boston. My father tried to intervene when a group of redcoats beat up one of the rioters." Ethan set down the chess piece. "One of the redcoats shot him." He looked down at the board. "It's your move."

"Is it?" She took no time to consider but simply shoved her rook sideways. She wasn't interested in the chess game now.

Ethan immediately moved his knight, took her rook, and sat back. "Checkmate."

She made an exclamation of vexation and stared down at the board, clearly trying to discern what she had missed and where she had gone wrong. Finally, she sat back, laughing. "I cannot believe I didn't see that!" she cried. "Your strategy seems so obvious to me now."

She glanced at the clock on the mantel, then sighed and returned her attention to the board. "Playing against me is too easy for you. You won that game in less than two hours."

"Don't be so hard on yourself. You played well, but I've been playing chess since I was a boy, and it's a game of experience as well as ability. You said yourself, you don't play often. You simply need more practice. Dorothy plays the game. You might practice with her when she has free time."

Her expression did not brighten. "I take it that idea does not appeal to you?" he asked.

She shook her head. "Dorothy does not like me."

"She doesn't trust you. There's a difference."

"Perhaps, but that still doesn't make me want to play chess with her."

He laughed. "She is only trying to protect me

from possible Tory spies. I didn't tell her that you were considering becoming one until I made you a better offer."

She propped her elbows on the table and cupped her chin in her hands, looking directly at him across the chessboard. "You realize, of course, that she is madly in love with you."

"Molly says the same."

"It's true. My guess would be she doesn't give a damn about colonial liberty. It is you she cares about."

Ethan shook his head with a sigh. "Why do women always attribute everything to love? Don't you think Dorothy is like her brother, a believer in freedom and self-government?"

"Rot." Katie made a face. "Women don't do anything for an ideal. They do it for a man. Dorothy is involved in this for you."

"Perhaps." Ethan leaned forward in his chair. "But you are different. You do this neither for an ideal nor for a man. You do it for yourself."

She sat up abruptly, and her eyes narrowed. "Of course I am doing this for myself," she said in a cool, passionless voice. "I told you, for me, survival is what matters. That and my freedom."

"Why?" he asked. "Why is freedom so important to you?"

"I found being indentured intolerable."

He leaned forward. "Intolerable in what way?"

"It was . . ." She jerked her chin, looked away, hedging now. "I didn't like it."

He would not be denied. "Why?"

She let out her breath in a sharp, impatient hiss. "For heaven's sake," she muttered. "Why all the questions? Why does it matter?"

He was honest in his reply. "I don't know why it should matter," he answered. "But it does. It matters to me. Katie, what happened?"

She stiffened in her chair, a brief, fleeting stiffness that melted away as suddenly as it had come. She leaned forward, mirroring him, smiling that angel smile. "Why do you want to know?" she murmured in a teasing voice. "Do I matter to you so much, Ethan?"

He was not fooled. "You're not answering my question. What happened?"

Her ploy having failed, she leaned back with a sigh, of irritation or resignation, he could not tell. She picked up a chess piece from the table and focused her attention on it as she spoke. "I knew the moment I saw him what he was like," she said, and he knew she was speaking of Willoughby. "I was standing on the docks in a line with the other prisoners, and I saw him walking along the line, picking the ones he wanted. I could tell that he was a man of some consequence by his clothes, the way he walked, the way he spoke. He stopped in front of me, and when I looked in his eyes, I knew."

"Knew what?"

"I knew he was going to buy my indenture, and I knew why. At that moment, on the docks, both of us were fully aware of what would happen, even though neither of us said a word."

Ethan was aware of it, too. He knew there were men who abused their indentured servant girls and slaves, and he could well imagine Willoughby's intentions, especially toward a woman as lovely as Katie.

"He just turned to the captain, who told him how much," she went on, her voice flat and matter-of-fact, as if she were speaking of the price of eggs, not the price of herself. "Female indentures aren't usually worth much, but the captain got five pounds British sterling for me. You see, he knew what Willoughby was looking for, and he knew how much Willoughby was willing to pay for it."

Even though he had suspected this, Ethan felt sick. "Because you were still innocent," he said harshly. "Is that what you mean?"

"Yes."

Her eyes were dry, and something in their depths made him feel as if he were looking into a dark and bottomless chasm. Somehow her lack of any visible emotion hurt him more than sobs or tears ever could. It cut him deep down inside.

"I assumed he would do it right away, that very day. I was wrong. Oh, God, I was so wrong."

She choked on the last word, the first inkling of her inner feelings, but she closed her eyes for a moment, swallowed hard, then continued in that same dead voice, "I underestimated his cruelty. He kept me on tenterhooks for six weeks, just looking at me in a way that made me want to bathe in hot water and lye soap. Then he showed me what his intentions were. He took another girl and made me watch them. I had no idea what he was going to do to her until he did it."

She looked at him, her blue eyes huge and expressionless, like dead lakes, and Ethan could imagine what she had seen, because he saw it reflected in her eyes. He wanted to grab her, hold her, tell her to stop. He did not want to hear the rest of the story, but it was too late to stop her. She was speaking again, telling him the rest.

"I did not know such sick things existed," she said. "I have slept in alleys. I've lived in brothels. I've seen a great many things in my life, but I had never seen anything as sick as what Willoughby did to that poor girl. She died."

Katie looked at him, her eyes glazed with pain for that other girl, a girl who was dead because of one man's sick perversions. Though she was looking straight at him, Ethan knew she did not see him. In her mind, she was reliving what she had been forced to watch. She began to shake. She covered her face with her hands.

The things she had seen were beyond his experience, but he could feel the pain inside her. "Katie—"

She lowered her hands and sat back, struggling to regain control. "That night, I picked the lock on Willoughby's strongbox, stole the silver that was inside, and ran for my life."

"Then he didn't . . ." Ethan could not finish the

sentence, but Katie understood what he wanted to know.

"No," she said flatly. "I never gave him the chance. I got out of Virginia as fast as I could, and I ran as far as I could before my money ran out. I stopped here."

Ethan sucked in a deep breath of relief. But, though he was relieved, Ethan saw the pain in her eyes, and relief did not diminish the rage he felt. He knew there was nothing he could say to ease her pain, but he knew what he wanted to do. He wanted to find that bastard Willoughby and kill him. He wanted to take back the threat he had made to send her back to her former master. Most of all, he wanted to hold her, protect her, keep her safe. Damn it all, she needed that.

"Why didn't you tell me this before?" he demanded hoarsely. "If I had known . . ."

His voice trailed away as he looked at her, and his words seemed ridiculous. He *had* known, in a way. He had been given an inkling of the truth that night when she'd waved the broken bottle in his face. He had seen her loathing of her former master. He had seen her fear. But he had not been able to risk letting her go. So, he had used her instead, not wanting to know where her loathing and fear of her master came from, not wanting to think about the brutal reality to which he had threatened to return her.

"If you had known," she repeated thoughtfully. "If you had known, what would you have done?

Would you have done anything differently? Knowing that I would never have agreed to help you without the threat of Willoughby over my head, would you have let me go?"

He stood up so abruptly that his chair tipped over backward, and the clatter of it hitting the floorboards echoed through the room like a musket shot. "It's late," he muttered, raking a hand through his hair as he turned away and started for the door. "I'd better be on my way."

He took the package from the hall table and paused by the door. "I'll bring this back to you in a day or two. Then you can take it to Cambridge."

He did not wait for a reply. Turning away, he opened the door. He strode down the steps and got into his waiting carriage.

He should just let her go, end their charade, and release her from their bargain, but he could not. It was too great a risk. He had no illusions that she would stay for him or his cause. As she had told him, she was not in this for an ideal or for a man. She was in this for herself. Nonetheless, Ethan remembered that dead look in her eyes as she had told him about Willoughby and why she would rather die than go back to that life. He had the feeling that look would haunt him for many days and nights to come.

He was threatening to send her back to that life if she did not cooperate with him. Doubts about his decision to involve her assailed him, and he shifted guiltily on the carriage seat. Perhaps he should find someone else to go to Cambridge. He could afford to buy her indenture and free her. Perhaps he should just let her go.

No, she knew too much. She wouldn't stick at handing him to the governor for money if he no longer had anything to hold over her head. He could not let her go. Once again, guilt and doubt overtook him. Was he doing the right thing by making her stay? So many people depended on him to make the right decisions, to find the right information, to keep danger at bay, and he had never been uncomfortable with the role. Until now.

He smiled to himself, but there was no humor in it, only irony. He was getting too softhearted, it seemed, and for a spy who was committing sedition, plotting revolution, and preparing for war, a soft heart was a very inconvenient thing.

13

For the next two days, Katie heard nothing from Ethan, and she occupied her time doing things she had never had the means or opportunity to do before. She visited as many dressmakers and haberdashers in Boston as she could find. She found it amusing that shop assistants fawned all over her, now that she had fine clothes and a fancy carriage. Only a few weeks ago, any shopkeeper would have taken one look at her and chased her out with a broom and threats of the constable. Now, they tripped over themselves to assist her, and she took a somewhat wicked enjoyment in sending them running for the richest foodstuffs and fabrics for two or three hours and then walking out after buying only a ha'penny box of sweets or half a yard of lace.

She also savored her comfortable house and the servants who fetched and carried for her. She knew she had only a few more days before Lowden returned and she would be forced to end this charade, but she wanted to take all the pleasure from it that she could, for she doubted she would ever have the chance to live like this again.

One of the most enjoyable pleasures of her new life was a nightly soak in the huge copper bathtub Ethan had bought for her, a luxurious ritual complete with lavender-scented soap and warm towels. This evening bath enabled her to forget, at least temporarily, about the price she would pay for the enjoyments of her new life, to forget about the dangerous line she was walking, to forget about the control two men had over her life. Until one of them intruded on her nightly bath and reminded her.

"Now, that is how a mistress ought to look."

Katie knew it was Ethan before she even opened her eyes. With a startled gasp, she turned her head and saw him standing in the doorway to her room, dressed all in black, tricorn pulled low over his eyes, the copy of Shakespeare in his hands. He leaned with one shoulder against the doorjamb in that languid yet alert stance she was coming to know so well. Instinctively, she crouched down in the tub in an effort to shield herself from him, but she knew he had probably already seen everything there was to see.

She grabbed for one of the towels that lay on the floor beside her and took the offensive. "What do you mean barging into my room?" she demanded as she stood up, hoping to brazen things out while shielding her nakedness from his intense perusal with a towel that suddenly seemed far too small.

He grinned at her awkward efforts, unperturbed by her bravado. "Since it is my money that pays for this room, I think I have the right to enter it if I choose to do so."

Katie made a sound of outrage, but it was hard to express it effectively when she was dripping wet and a towel was all the protection she had. Before she could figure out how to respond, Ethan entered the bedroom and shut the door behind him.

She watched with growing dismay as he sauntered over to the bed where Janie had laid out a nightgown for her earlier. He set down the book and picked up the filmy garment of lawn and lace. To her acute embarrassment, he held it up for a good, long look. "Very pretty," he said, and shot her a look of pure deviltry. "I'm so glad I bought this one."

The sight of that delicate wisp of fabric in his hands made Katie's heart begin to pound hard in her chest. Her throat went dry. "What are you doing here?" she asked, trying to sound blasé, and ashamed that her question came out in nothing more than a hoarse whisper.

She wrapped the towel securely around herself and stretched out her arm, but Ethan did not give the nightgown to her. Instead, he stayed well out of her reach, that teasing gleam in his eyes. "An interesting situation for a man to find himself in, wouldn't you say?"

She lunged for it, but she was hampered by the fact that she was still standing in the bathtub. With a sound of aggravation, she stepped out of the tub, but Ethan took a step back, still keeping the gown out of her reach. "Ethan, give it to me," she demanded.

Tongue-in-cheek, he considered that for a moment. "Why should I?" he countered softly, slanting her a look from beneath his lashes that made her body feel flushed with heat. "I think I like you better without it."

He took a step toward her and reached out his hand to her face. When his fingers traced a delicate line across her jaw, down the line of her throat, and across her collarbone, she forgot all about her nightgown.

Paralyzed by the intensity of his gaze and the light touch of his fingers as they moved further down, Katie could not seem to move, or breathe, or even think. She felt him trace a line over her skin at the edge of the towel, just above her breasts, and knew she should do something to stop this intimate exploration, but she could not seem to find the will to move. Slowly, ever so slowly, he leaned toward her.

She thought of the other times he had kissed her, and she felt again that trembling excitement, knowing that he was going to kiss her again. Her lips parted in anticipation, and she swayed closer to him, silently pleading for him to continue.

But Ethan did not do so. He stepped back with

an abruptness that startled her, and he thrust her nightgown toward her as if it were suddenly a barrier between them. Katie's pleasurable anticipation evaporated, and she felt all her previous embarrassment return.

When she took the nightgown from him, he turned his back to her. She hastily cast aside the towel and slipped the gown over her head.

Clothed, more or less, she felt much more in command of herself and the situation. "What have you been doing for the last two days?" she asked.

He turned around and smiled at her. "Katie, that is none of your affair."

"You disappear for two days, then arrive in my bedroom out of nowhere and interrupt my bath . . ." She knew that comment was heading her into dangerous territory, and she took a deep, steadying breath. Pointing to the book on the bed, she said, "If giving me that was the purpose of this visit, you've done what you came for."

"Actually, I really came to see you naked."

Those words sent a rush of tingling pleasure through her entire body. It was a sensation she had never felt for any man before, and she did not like it, for it also made her feel far too vulnerable.

Somehow, in the three weeks since their first meeting, Ethan had become more than just a traitor to be captured. Now, she knew him, she knew his kiss, his touch, and somehow that made him more dangerous than before—dangerous to her peace of mind. When he was the cool, impersonal stranger, it was easier to keep her own distance. But the man standing before her now, the man who was looking at her with desire—that man was dangerous indeed.

She knew he wanted her. She could see it in his eyes, hear it in his voice, feel it in his touch. There was no doubt about it. He wanted her.

Katie closed her eyes for a moment, feeling again that dizzying sensation of walking the edge of a cliff. The realization that Ethan desired her was exhilarating, but it was also frightening.

It was exhilarating because this was the first time in her life she could honestly say she welcomed a man's desire without wanting to use it against him in some way. It was the first time she could remember ever holding her breath in anticipation of a man's kiss and feeling such bitter disappointment when that kiss never came.

It was frightening because she could feel herself falling under his spell the way men had always fallen under hers. She had told him things the other night that she had never told anyone. She was standing in front of him in a gown practically sheer enough to see through, and all she wanted was for him to kiss her again. She felt as if her entire world were turned upside down, and the only right thing in it was him.

"That's the second time I've seen you blush," he said, breaking into her thoughts. "I never would have thought you the blushing type," he added, sounding surprised.

Katie told herself not to be a fool. She could not start getting all calf-eyed about Ethan Harding. No man was worth risking her life. She held out one hand impatiently. "Stop blathering, and give me the damn book."

He held it out to her, and she took it, irritated by the fact that he was so cool when she felt so flustered. "When do you want me to take this to Cambridge?" she asked.

"You'll need to leave at first light. If you know how to ride, then go by horseback. That way, you won't have to worry that your carriage driver will talk afterward."

"You hired my carriage driver. Don't you trust him?"

"I don't trust anyone. Make certain you're not followed. And for God's sake, be careful."

"I will," she promised.

"Send me a note when you return from Cambridge that all went well, but mention no names, and give me no details. Holbrook is having a card party the following night, and I will call for you in my carriage at seven."

He opened her bedroom door to depart but paused in the doorway to look at her over his shoulder. His grin was wicked, and she saw that teasing, dangerous look return to his eyes. "By the way, Katie, there's no need to be embarrassed," he told her. "I didn't see a thing."

She did not believe him for an instant, but she could not help laughing as he departed. He was such an outrageous liar, she thought as she crawled into bed.

He was a liar, a rogue, and a spy who came and went like the wind. But he had convictions, and he had courage. And though he had blackmailed her into working for him, he was capable of surprising gallantry. Though he had threatened to send her to Willoughby, he had saved her from Weston.

And now you are going to repay him by betraying him to his enemies.

Katie slammed her hands over her ears, but she could not shut out the guilt that whispered to her. She closed her eyes and tried to go to sleep, but the awful image of Ethan swinging on the gallows came into her mind, making sleep impossible.

She squeezed her eyes more tightly shut, working by sheer force of will to banish that horrible image from her imagination, but this time she could not succeed. It haunted her mind like a shadowy ghost, and try as she might, she could not dismiss it.

Suddenly, she found it hard to breathe. She sat up, flinging back the sheets and trying to banish her rising panic, but it was a futile attempt.

I can't do it, she thought wildly. *I can't turn him over to Lowden. I could never live with myself.*

She curled up into a ball, wrapping her arms around her bent knees. She gulped in deep breaths of air, trying to calm her jangled nerves. "You can do it," she murmured over and over. "You can do it because you must. You have no choice. You have to do it. It's your life or his. You have to do it."

When she thought of him, when she remembered the thrill of being in his arms and the delicious warmth of his kiss and the way he had come to her rescue, when she contemplated actually betraying him, it was so hard to accept.

Katie leaned back against the fat pillows of her luxurious bed, and for the first time, she took no pleasure in the softness. She did not sleep well that night. Truth be told, she did not sleep at all.

The Blue Boar Inn was located only half a mile north of Cambridge on the Lexington Road, and Katie found it easily. It was a simple two-story clapboard house set well back from the road, but the sign that hung at the roadside, a large painted affair of bright yellow with a blue boar insignia, was difficult to miss.

When she walked inside the tavern, it was empty save for the barkeep, who stood behind the bar drying freshly washed tankards from the night before. He looked up as she entered, and he frowned as she paused just inside the door.

"Yes?" he asked, looking at her with such a fierce scowl that Katie felt her face grow hot. Was this fellow naturally of a sour disposition, or was it perhaps that she seemed untrustworthy?

She slid her saddlebag off her shoulder and told herself not to be silly. No one could tell she was really a Tory spy just by looking at her. And if this barkeep had suspicions, what of it? She had valuable information, and that gave her the upper hand. "I am here to see a man named Joseph Bramley," she said firmly. "I was told I could find him here."

The barkeep's frown deepened. "He's still abed. What do you want him for?"

"I'm afraid that is a personal matter," she answered, forcing herself to give the man her most charming smile and thereby take any possible sting out of her words. "I have been instructed to speak only with Mr. Bramley and no one else. It is very important, and I believe he is expecting me."

The man tossed down his towel. "Wait here."

Katie moved over to the fire to warm herself as the barkeep went upstairs. It was several moments before the man came back down. He jerked a thumb over his shoulder to the stairs. "Go on up."

Katie mounted the stairs. When she reached the top, she peered down a long, dark hallway. At the end, she could see a short, stocky man in breeches and shirt standing by a doorway. His face was vaguely familiar, and she thought he might be one of the many shadowy figures she had seen slipping in and out of the Mermaid during her first week there as a spy, but she knew she had never been introduced to him. He beckoned her with an impatient wave of his hand. "Come, lass. Don't just stand there."

Katie walked down the narrow corridor and followed the man into one of the bedrooms.

"I recognize you from the Mermaid Tavern," he

said in a low voice as he closed the door behind him. "What is your name?"

"Katie," she answered, also keeping her voice down.

"Who sent you?"

"A friend to us both. The man some call John Smith."

The corners of his eyes crinkled with sudden amusement, and he chuckled. "Lucky man, Smith. I should have such pretty friends as you." He paused, then asked, "Has he given you a message for me?"

"Not a message, sir." She opened the saddlebag, cast a quick glance at the door and windows, then pulled out the book and handed it to Bramley.

He opened it and scanned a few pages, nodding his head several times as he did so. His understanding of what was inside was clearly much greater than hers.

Before leaving Boston early this morning, she had spent more than two hours poring over that book. She could see that some printed pages had been pasted over the existing ones, but the words were rhymes that might be read in a nursery, rhymes of nonsense that Shakespeare never wrote. It was obvious they were coded messages, and as hard as she had tried, she could not understand their meaning.

She was glad that she could not have kept the book to give Lowden. The viscount would not be back for several more days, and if she had not brought the book to Cambridge, Ethan would surely have discovered her treachery long before the viscount could return and protect her.

"Excellent!" he exclaimed. "It never ceases to amaze me how he obtains his information."

"It astounds me as well, sir," Katie admitted. "Do you wish to send a reply?"

He shook his head. "No, except to say that I will pass this on to the proper people."

She nodded and turned to go, but she had taken only a few steps before Bramley's voice stopped her.

"Katie?"

She paused and glanced at him over her shoulder. "Yes, sir?"

"You are a stranger to Boston, I'm told. Why do you involve yourself in our cause? Do you dream of liberty?"

"No," she answered. That was a lie. She was in this for liberty—her own—but somehow she was reluctant to explain this to Bramley. Instead, she asked, "What about you, sir?"

"Eh? What do you mean?"

"Why do you risk all you have in a cause that seems impossible to win?"

His reply came without hesitation. "Because I believe that the will of common men should prevail over the whim of kings."

A smile lifted the corners of her mouth. "You sound like the one who sent me."

"Aye. He believes the same." Joseph tilted his head to one side. "And you, miss? What do you believe?"

Katie opened her mouth to reply, but she could think of nothing to say that would answer that question. She used to believe only in herself and surviving one more day. Now, she didn't know what she believed anymore.

"Molly tells me you are rather fond of our friend Smith," Bramley murmured. "So perhaps what you believe in is a man with stormy gray eyes and enormous courage, and perhaps that is enough."

Katie thought of how Ethan had looked at her last night, and she turned away without answering. If that was what she believed in, if she took her life in her hands because of the way a man looked at her when she wore nothing but a towel, then she was a simpleton indeed.

14

After her trip to Cambridge, Katie had no opportunity to see Ethan until the following night, when he escorted her to William Holbrook's supper party. During the carriage ride there, she told him all had gone well with Joseph Bramley, and his response was, as usual, an enigmatic one. "Yes, I know."

"How could you possibly know?" she countered. "It happened only yesterday."

He gave her a smile far too secretive for her peace of mind. "I have my sources."

Katie prayed those sources wouldn't find out which side she was truly on. "Before we arrive at this party, are you going to tell me what I'm supposed to do?"

"I actually have two purposes in mind for you this evening. The first will be simple." He turned toward her on the carriage seat. "Lowden is away, but one of Holbrook's guests tonight will be his wife, Lady Lowden. When you are partnered with her at cards, see what you can discover about her husband. Any information would be useful, but as I've already told you, I want to know what he is really doing in Boston."

"And you think his wife might tell me?"

"Possibly. It is certainly worth the effort to try. Engage her in conversation, use flattery or charm or whatever you think might work. Do you think you can do it?"

"I expect so," she said serenely. "That kind of thing is usually simple enough."

"I'm glad you are so confident."

Katie shrugged, knowing it didn't really matter if she succeeded in that assignment or not. She just had to pretend to make an effort at it until Lowden returned. "I am confident. After all, didn't you make this bargain with me because I am clever, audacious, and a very good liar?"

Ethan laughed at how she threw his own assessment of her back in his face. "Did I also tell you that you are far too conceited for your own good?"

"There is no sense in downplaying my talents, since you already know what they are," she countered. "What is the other task you have for me?"

"That will not be as simple. Holbrook is one of Gage's closest aides. He keeps his private papers in the desk of his study, and I am hoping there is some information about Lowden among them. During the party, I want to take a look through his desk to see if we can find anything that might be valuable."

"Why do you need me for this?"

"Holbrook keeps his desk locked. I don't know how to pick a lock. But if I remember one of our conversations at the Mermaid correctly, you do."

Katie wanted to groan. This was not something she could simply pretend to do. If Ethan was with her and wanted the papers in Holbrook's desk, she would have to play along. "You really expect me to break into the desk of one of Gage's aides?"

"Yes."

"How?"

"I was hoping you would have some ideas on that score. You are so much better at this sort of thing than I am."

"And if we are caught by Holbrook or one of his servants or one of his guests, what explanation could we possibly give for rifling through his desk?"

"I'm hoping you'll be able to think of a plausible story for us to offer should that happen. I have faith in your cleverness, your audacity, your talent for lying—"

"Enough already," she interrupted. "All this flattery from you, and I will end up conceited. But there must be a simple way to do this so that we don't get caught." She frowned and fell silent, chewing on her lower lip as she stared out the carriage window. Life, she decided, was so much simpler when she was merely a thief, not a spy.

She couldn't very well refuse. And if Ethan were right that there was information about Lowden in those papers locked inside Holbrook's desk, it would probably be worthwhile for her to know it. After all, she couldn't trust the viscount any more than she could trust Ethan, and it would be wise to have all the information she could get her hands on.

Suddenly, she straightened on the seat. "Aren't we on the west end of Beacon Street?" She pointed out the window. "Isn't Mount Whoredom right up there?"

"Yes."

"Stop the carriage."

"Why?"

"I have a plan, but to carry it out there are some things I need. Stop the carriage."

Ethan rapped heavily on the roof of the carriage, and the driver slowed to a stop. Katie opened the door and jumped out. "I'll be back in a few minutes."

"Where are you going?"

"Just wait here." She started to turn away but paused and held out her hand to him. "Do you have any money?"

Ethan dug into his pockets and fished out several Massachusetts Old Tenor coins. She shook her head. "I'd prefer British sterling. At least a guinea."

He gave her the needed money. "A full guinea is enough to buy your way onto a boat out of Boston," he said. "I hope that's not your intention."

"I couldn't live for long on a guinea, so don't worry," she told him. "I expect far more generosity out of you than that. Willoughby won't sell my indenture for a mere guinea." With those words, she took the money, closed the carriage door, and vanished into the darkness. It was a full twenty minutes before she returned.

"I was about to go in search of you," he said as she climbed in. "What were you doing for so long?"

The carriage lurched forward to continue on toward Holbrook's house as Katie pulled the two items she had acquired with Ethan's money out of her cloak pocket. "Buying these," she told him as she held up a small vial of blue glass and a flat leather pouch about three inches square.

"What are those?"

"The weapons of choice among thieves."

"Weapons? What do you mean?"

She saw the frown on his face, and she responded with a tiny smile. He looked worried now, because he didn't feel in control of her or their situation. She was rather pleased about that. Ethan was always so cool, so calm about everything. It would do him good to sweat a bit. "You'll see."

"Katie, what are you scheming?"

She thought of the other night, when he had interrupted her bath, and she decided it would be fun to make him sweat a bit more. He deserved it. She rested her feet on the carriage seat opposite and pulled back the hem of her skirt to reveal her legs, which were encased in the finest, wispiest silk stockings Elizabeth Waring had to offer. "You want to get into Holbrook's desk, don't you?" she asked as she tucked the small glass bottle into the garter at her knee.

"Of course," Ethan answered, but it didn't escape her notice that he was looking at her legs, and the look on his face told her quite clearly that Holbrook's desk was the last thing he was thinking about just now.

She slid the leather pouch into her other garter. "And you don't want to get caught, do you?"

"No."

"Well, then," she said, pulling her skirts back down and turning to him with a wicked grin, "you'll just have to trust me."

In Katie's opinion, Lady Lowden proved to be the two worst things any woman could be: dull and stupid. Two hours of card play with her were more than enough for Katie to decide she and the viscount deserved each other. Holbrook's wife was also at her table, and Katie found her to be just as Ethan described—lovely and nice. Holbrook was not worthy of her. But Rosalie Holbrook made no secret of the fact that she actually loved her husband. She must know the man was rude, overbearing, blatantly sexual, and probably unfaithful, but if she did know these things, they did not alter her good opinion of him. Katie found her oddly touching and very sweet. Lady Lowden was another matter entirely.

When she managed to finagle a moment with Ethan at the punch table for a whispered exchange of information, she gave him her opinion of the viscountess.

"Yes, but are you learning anything?" he murmured, handing her a crystal goblet of rum punch.

"Oh, heaps of things."

"Good." Ethan put a hand beneath her elbow and steered her to an upholstered bench in an unoccupied corner of Holbrook's card room. He sat down beside her. "What have you learned?"

"Lady Lowden misses London, is hopeless at cards, and her pug dog doesn't like sea voyages." Changing her voice to a well-bred nasal tone, she drawled in a low voice, "My darling little Pudding was so ill, and the captain just refused to do anything about it."

Ethan threw back his head and laughed at her excellent imitation of the viscountess, causing several people in the room to look in their direction.

"Shh," she admonished, but she laughed with him. "People are staring."

"They'll think you are simply doing what mistresses do best."

"And what would that be?" She shot him a flirtatious glance and took another hefty swallow of punch. "You have all your clothes on."

He looked down at the almost indecently low neckline of her gown. "Unfortunately."

Katie caught her breath. It was unnerving when he looked at her like that, when he let her know he wanted her. It did something to her, something warm and melting, something dangerous and irresistible.

She leaned closer to him, close enough to feel the heat of his body.

"Careful," he said softly. "As you said, people are staring."

She sat back, hating herself for being susceptible to a man's desire, even for a moment. It was foolish and futile and would only make things more complicated than they already were.

She drew a deep breath. "Anyway, I didn't like the woman at all. She's simply awful."

" 'Tis fortunate I'm the only one listening to you speak of her in such a way. She is the daughter of an earl."

"That doesn't mean she isn't a horrid woman. I think she loves her dog more than she loves her husband." She shivered suddenly. "I don't blame her."

Ethan tensed beside her. "What do you mean?"

Katie felt her insides twist at her careless slip, and she decided she would be wise to drink no more rum punch this evening. It appeared to be having a dangerous effect on her—loosening her tongue and lowering her guard. She could not afford to make mistakes of that nature. They could cost her life.

She hastily improvised a reply for Ethan to cover her mistake. "You're the one who told me Lowden is ruthless and ambitious. Besides, he's a peer, and I've seen enough of those to know they are all alike. Cruel, greedy men with stupid wives, and Lady Lowden did not alter my opinion of that class tonight."

"Indeed?"

"She cares for naught but her dog and her position in society, her favorite pastimes are piquet and scandal-mongering, and her greatest ambition is to possess more clothes than she could ever wear. Did you see those jewels draped all over her?" Katie gave a wistful sigh. "I could live like a duchess for two years on that necklace of hers."

"Don't even think about taking it," he murmured in her ear. "Should you get caught stealing the jewels of a peeress, even I don't possess enough money or influence to save you."

"I wouldn't get caught. I could slip it off her neck, have it in my pocket, and be out of Boston before she even realizes it's missing."

"Forget it, Katie. Did you learn anything about Lowden from her?"

She would have lied if necessary, but in this case she didn't have to. "I learned nothing of importance. She believes her husband is here as the liaison he claims to be and says she knows nothing more about it. Perhaps there is nothing more to know."

Ethan shook his head. "A man as ambitious as Lowden would not come all the way to the colonies to take up a position clearly below his station. There is more to this than we know. Perhaps Holbrook's desk will reveal more. When do we implement this plan of yours to get into his desk?"

"We have to be the last guests to leave the party."

"Shocking bad form, my dear, but if we must, then we must."

"When we are the only ones left, you must insist that we adjourn to his study for a glass of port to finish out the evening. Say you find that room to be the most comfortable or something, and we'll go in there for a drink."

"And once we are having this cozy drink with our host? What then?"

"Wait until you see Holbrook set his glass down for some reason, then distract his attention. I'll do the rest."

It was nearly dawn before the other guests had departed and they could put Katie's plan into effect. Ethan was successful at finagling their way into Holbrook's study about half past one in the morning with the express wish of seeing his collection of erotic art before they left. Katie had seen enough dirty pictures in her life to know Holbrook's sketches were anything but art, and she heartily wished Ethan had found some other pretext. Fortunately, she had been forced to endure only one lewd comment from their host and one quick glance through his collection before Ethan called the other man's attention to a particularly disgusting pen and ink drawing, and Katie was able to make use of what she had purchased in Mt. Whoredom.

Holbrook had turned his back to her, but Ethan was watching Katie out of the corner of his eye as she pulled the tiny blue bottle out of her stocking. She opened it, dumped the contents into Holbrook's port, and had the bottle tucked back into her garter in scarcely more than the blink of an eye.

Five minutes later, Holbrook was unconscious.

Ethan raised one eyebrow as he watched the fellow slide off the end of the settee and onto the floor. Holbrook's head hit the floorboards with a thump, and Ethan turned to her, that half smile curving one corner of his mouth. "I become more grateful every day that you are on my side."

"I'm glad to hear it." She pulled the pouch out of her garter, then sat down at Holbrook's desk. "Lock the door in case one of the servants decides to come in."

Ethan complied, then crossed the room to stand beside her as she pulled her leather pouch out of her garter and bent her head to the drawers of the desk so that she could examine the locks. "What did you put in his drink?" he asked.

"Holy water." Katie laid the small pouch on the desk, opened it, and selected one slender metal pick from the half dozen in the pockets of the pouch.

"Holy water?" he repeated in disbelief. "You're joking."

"That's what thieves call it. A few drops of holy water in a man's drink, and within minutes he falls asleep. Then it's a simple matter to fleece him of his money purse, watch, jewelry, and anything else of value he might be carrying. Meg and I often used that trick. Very handy stuff, holy water."

Ethan shook his head, watching as she put the end of the metal pick into the keyhole of the desk's top drawer and began to work the lock open. "I must confess, you are the most intriguing woman I have ever known. The depth of your knowledge regarding matters of swindling, chicanery, and theft never ceases to amaze me."

"Thank you, I think." The lock clicked, and Katie removed the pick. She then tackled the second drawer. When that one was unlocked, she began work on the third.

"So," he said as he watched her, "the servants will think he has passed out from drink, and no one will ever know we had a look through his papers."

"Exactly." The last lock of the desk was opened, and she stood up. "We can rifle through his desk to our hearts' content, and I assure you, he won't wake up. When we leave, we tell the butler that the master has passed out, and he needs to be put to bed. He'll wake up with one hell of a headache, but he'll never know what really happened."

Ethan laughed low in his throat as he sat down at the desk. Katie leaned down beside him. Pressing her lips to his ear, she whispered, "Now, tell me again how clever I am."

"You're very clever," he said, pulling open the first drawer. "As I said before, I'm glad you are on my side."

She gave a sigh of satisfaction and tried to remember she was not on his side as he pulled a sheaf of documents from the first drawer of the desk. He perused them quickly, then set them aside and turned his attention to the next drawer. It took several minutes, but finally Ethan seemed to find something significant. He let out a low whistle.

"A complete dossier of Lowden from Gage to Holbrook. We are fortunate William has already read this, or I would have had to break the seal."

"That would not have been a problem," she assured him. " 'Tis a simple matter to undo a wax seal without breaking it."

"Really? You'll have to show me that trick some other time." He began reading.

Katie leaned over his shoulder, but he turned the sheaf of notes away so that she could not read any of the information, and he frowned at her. "Do you mind sitting over there?" he asked, gesturing to the settee. "I'll be done in a few minutes."

"Ethan, if you think I'm going to let you be the only one to read this, you're barmy," she said in a fierce whisper. "I didn't do all this work only to have my curiosity remain unsatisfied. You have to let me read it, too."

He remained unmoved, and Katie scowled at him. "If you don't let me read it, I won't lock the desk back up again, and Holbrook will know what you've done."

"What we've done," he corrected her, but he relented and allowed her to lean over his shoulder to scan each page along with him. It took some time, but they finally found one entry in the dossier that made the entire adventure that evening worth the risks they had taken, an entry that outlined Lowden's true mission.

When they had finished reading it, Ethan tucked the dossier back into the desk and returned the seat to her so she could begin locking the drawers.

"So that's why Lowden's here," she whispered in pretended surprise, as if she didn't already know the man's true motives. "To recruit spies and find proof of sedition against the Sons of Liberty."

"It makes sense. After all, Lord North has been trying to force Gage to take action for months, but Gage has refused to act without proof."

"Why do they need proof? Can't North just order Gage to arrest the Whig leaders?" she asked as she locked drawers one by one. "Isn't he the king's chief minister?"

"Yes, but he needs support in Parliament to force Gage to act, and he has been unable to get it. So he sent Lowden here to obtain the evidence that will force Gage's hand. If—"

The sound of the door handle rattling interrupted his words, and both of them froze, looking at each other in dismay. On the other side of the door, a concerned male voice spoke. "Sir William? It's Roberts. Why is the door locked? Are Mr. Harding and Mrs. Armstrong still in there with you?"

Katie was out of the chair and out from behind the desk before the butler finished speaking, her leather pouch tucked safely back in her garter. She waved Ethan to open the door and bent down beside Holbrook. When the butler entered the room, he found Mrs. Armstrong gently slapping his master's cheeks and looking quite distressed.

"Oh, dear," she said with a sigh as she leaned back on her heels. "Ethan, darling, I'm afraid that last glass of port proved to be too much for dear William. Roberts, you couldn't have arrived at a better moment. We were just about to fetch you."

Katie rose to her feet as the butler crossed the room to stand beside her. He stared down at his master's supine body and shook his head. "He usually holds his port better than that, madam. I don't understand it." The butler looked at Ethan. "Why was the door locked, sir?"

Ethan frowned and tugged on his ear, looking like a man utterly perplexed. "It wasn't locked, Roberts. I opened it without unlatching it. Does it tend to stick?"

"Aye. It does." He looked down at Holbrook's stout form again and sighed. "Well, I'd best put him to bed. I'll see you both out first."

"Oh, no," Katie said hastily. "Please don't bother with us, Roberts. Tend to your master. We'll see ourselves out."

They left the room together, and the butler's voice drifted toward them as they walked to the foyer. "If you say so, madam. Good evening."

They managed to get into Ethan's carriage and be halfway down the street before they looked at each other and burst out laughing. Katie felt that familiar rush of exultation and energy that always came after a successful coup. Her entire body tingled with the excitement of the moment. When she looked at Ethan, she knew he felt it, too.

"Does it tend to stick?" She mimicked his words to the butler between gasps of laughter. "Ethan, I believe you would have made an excellent swindler."

"I believe you're right, especially with you as my tutor. Did you manage to lock all the drawers before Roberts arrived?"

"Of course I did."

"Very good."

"Very good?" she repeated. Still laughing, she grasped the edges of his cloak and leaned closer to him. "Very good? I drug the drink of our host, pick open the locks on his desk, and help you find exactly the information you're looking for, and all you can say is 'Very good'? I was a damn sight better than good, Ethan Harding. I was bold, brave, and daring. I was brilliant."

She gave his cloak a hard tug, pulling him close, close enough to feel his warm breath against her mouth. "Say it. I was brilliant."

"You were brilliant."

His mouth came down on hers before she could reply, and a heady thrill of triumph swept over her, but that feeling was almost immediately replaced by a feeling so potent, so raw and powerful, that any idea of triumph was forgotten.

Her mouth opened freely beneath his, and he tasted deeply of her with his tongue as his hand slid into her hair and he pressed her down into the seat of the coach, overwhelming her with the weight of his body. "Ethan," she gasped against his mouth.

He tore his lips from hers and pulled back to look into her face, as if he were giving her a chance to call a halt. But she did not want to call a halt. She wanted more of his kisses. She reached up and removed his hat and wig, tossing them onto the floor of the carriage. Then she pulled away the queue that held back his long, black hair, wrapped the thick strands in her fists, and pulled his face down to hers. "Don't stop now," she ordered. "Not yet."

He gave her a quick, hard kiss but then pulled back again to tug at the ties that held her cloak together. His hands pulled her cloak apart, and he lowered his head to press kisses along the bare column of her throat. His hands slid up her ribs, to close over her breasts, and even through the layers of her clothing, she could feel the heat of his hands.

His fingertips caressed the bare skin at the top of her breasts above the low neckline of her gown, and Katie moaned at the sweet sensation. He kissed her and touched her everywhere his lips and his hands could find bare skin in the close confines of the carriage—her throat, her face, her mouth, her collarbone, the tops of her breasts—until she was sobbing each breath, arching up to him, wanting more and more.

The carriage halted so abruptly that it startled both of them. Ethan lifted his head, uttering a curse worthy of the longshoreman he pretended to be. He sat up, pulling her with him, then yanked open the door of the carriage and got out. He held out his hand to assist her, and as soon as her feet touched the cobblestone walk in front of her house, he was pulling her toward the front door.

"Wait here," he told his driver over one shoulder. "I'll be out later."

As Ethan led her toward the house, Katie felt a flash of sanity. She could see the inevitable conclusion of this night, and a little voice of caution whispered to her, reminded her of her mother. Even if Ethan never discovered her secret, even if the war he talked about did not come, it did not matter. Men like Ethan Harding did not marry girls like her. They kept them as mistresses, but they did not marry them. They certainly did not fall in love with them. Hadn't her mother's experience taught her anything?

The moment they were inside the house, he shut the door and wrapped his arms around her waist and bent his head to kiss her again. Katie knew she had to end this now, before she did something she would surely regret, before she became his mistress in truth, before the charade became reality.

She turned her face away to elude his mouth. "Ethan, what are we doing?" she gasped, pressing her hands against his chest to keep him at bay. "I think—"

"Don't." He pulled her hard against him and cupped her chin in his hand, lifting her face for another kiss. "Don't think," he said fiercely against her mouth. "Not now."

He kissed her again and again, long, drugging kisses that robbed her of coherent thought and banished any foolish, fleeting idea of ending what they had begun. There was no way to see the future. Now was all that mattered—this moment with him. Bloody hell, she could die tomorrow. Tonight she was going to live and love with everything she had within her.

Still kissing her, he reached behind her and began to unbutton her gown. When he reached the last button at the base of her spine, Katie felt as if she were sliding off the edge of the world, drowning in him, in the heat of his mouth and the hard contact of his body. Her knees buckled beneath her, and she curled her hands around the lapels of his evening jacket to keep herself from falling.

After a long moment, she pulled back, breaking the kiss, but this time it was not to stop, it was not to think. It was to push his jacket off his shoulders. The jacket slid to the floor, and she began unbuttoning his waistcoat. Ethan stood motionless, his breathing hard and fast, his heart pounding beneath her hands as she slipped the silver buttons free with frantic fingers. She started to remove his waistcoat, but he grasped her wrists and gently pulled her hands away.

"Katie . . ." Her name was a groan on his lips. "On second thought, we need to stop this for—"

She shook her head, not wanting to stop. She had chosen this course, and there was no going back. If she stopped, she would think. If she thought, she would change her mind. She didn't want to change her mind. "Bloody hell, Ethan," she muttered. "You say women can't make up their minds?"

"You misunderstand me, love," he said, half laughing as he unexpectedly released her wrists. Bending slightly, he slid one arm beneath her knees and the other behind her shoulders, then lifted her into his arms.

"We need to continue this where we can be assured of privacy. One of the servants might wake up, hear us, and think thieves had invaded the house."

"They'd be right," she whispered. "Remember Holbrook."

"We didn't steal anything." He nodded to the table beside them. "Grab the candle."

Katie did so, and Ethan carried her up the stairs to her bedroom. Anticipation curled inside her like tongues of fire, making the journey up the stairs seem to take forever.

Inside her room, he kicked the door shut and set her on her feet. He took the candle from her and grabbed her hand, then led her across the room to the bed. He set the candle on the bedside table and turned to her.

Katie looked at him in the candlelight. She could see all his desire for her in his eyes, and it gave her a feeling of feminine power that rushed to her head like strong wine. For tonight at least, he would belong to her and she to him.

Their gazes locked. Simultaneously, they began taking off layers of clothing.

Her dress slid down her legs in a swish of silk.

His boots hit the floor with a thud.

Her stays and petticoat landed in a far corner of the room. His waistcoat and breeches followed them.

Neither of them spoke as, piece by piece, they removed the last barriers that separated them. But when he was naked and she was down to only her chemise, he broke the silence.

"I remember the last time I was in this room," he said, and reached out to touch the soft cotton of her chemise. "When I saw you wrapped in nothing but a towel, your skin still damp from your bath. You have no idea how hard it was for me to leave you that night."

Katie drew a deep breath, then let it out slowly. "Why did you leave?"

Ethan lifted one hand to brush aside the golden wisps of short hair that curled against the base of her neck. He kissed her there, savoring the velvety softness of her skin. Arousal was coursing through his body with all the furor of a hurricane, and he knew that nothing could make him stop this time. Tonight, King George's whole army couldn't stop him from having her.

"Damned if I know," he answered her question, and lifted the hem of her chemise. She raised her arms toward the ceiling, and he pulled the chemise over her head, then sent it flying across the room.

He reached for her, but, unexpectedly, she stopped him. She drew back a little, tilted her head to one side, and gave his entire body a speculative, sidelong glance from beneath her lashes. Somehow, that look made him want to smile. Trust Katie to see if she'd gotten a bargain.

She must have thought so, for she looked up at him and smiled as if very well pleased. Her smile, his greatest weakness. At that moment, if she had asked him for his soul, he would have handed it to her.

He slid one arm around her waist and ran the palm of his other hand up her ribs to cup her breast. When she melted back against him with a moan, he laughed with satisfaction. What a beautiful, vibrant woman she was. He loved it.

He spread his hand against her side, his thumb caressing her ribs as he bent his head to press a kiss to her shoulder, his breath blowing warmth against her skin and making her shiver.

Against the palm of his other hand, the nipple of her breast was hard and pebbled, and he closed his thumb and forefinger around the tiny nub as he trailed kisses along her shoulder and up the side of her neck to her ear.

As he nibbled her earlobe, he rolled her nipple gently back and forth between his thumb and forefinger, savoring the soft moans of feminine desire that his hands and mouth tore from her throat.

The sounds of her pleasure were so incredibly erotic that his own body shuddered in response. With his hands on her shoulders, he moved several steps sideways toward the head of the bed, taking her with him as if they were caught up in a slow, erotic dance. He stepped around her and pulled the sheet and counterpane down to the foot of the bed. Then he lay down and reached for her.

Katie felt her body falling forward beside his into the soft feather mattress and her heart falling into his hands. She rolled onto her back, and he moved closer until his hard arousal was pressing against her hip. Slowly, he lifted his hand to touch her face.

She closed her eyes and felt his fingertips lightly brush her jaw, her throat, and her collarbone, on a slow and inevitable journey to her breast. The tip of his finger touched her nipple, but his hand stopped there, and he made no move to continue his exploration of her body.

Why did he stop? she wondered wildly. *What on earth is he doing?*

She opened her eyes and found to her amazement that he was staring not at her body but at her face, as if he had been waiting for her to open her eyes. Then he spoke.

"Since I saw you in that damned towel the other night, I have imagined this moment at least a hundred times," he said in a low, hoarse whisper, "but even in my imagination, you were not as beautiful as this."

"I'm glad you think so." She reached up and touched his cheek, then slid her hand into his hair. She wanted this man, wanted him as she had never wanted a man before. She pulled his face down to hers for a long, hard kiss.

She felt his hand glide down her ribs and across her hipbone, then move lower still, parting her thighs. She cried out against his mouth as he touched her, shocked not only by the scorching intimacy of it but also by how that touch made her feel, as if she were melting into liquid fire.

Jolted by the pure pleasure of his stroking fingers, Katie could not help the moans that broke from her lips as he caressed her. She felt an odd, breathless tension rising inside her. "Ethan," she cried. "Ethan, please."

She felt as if she must be burning alive. She could hear her own voice calling his name over and over, but she could not seem to stop. That queer, piercing tension inside her rose higher with every caress of his hand, building until she was sure she could no longer stand it. Then, suddenly, everything inside her seemed to ignite and explode, sending rippling waves of exquisite pleasure through her entire body.

She was still tingling with the delicious sensations when he withdrew his hand. She felt him move, felt his weight and strength as he rolled on top of her, pushing her into the mattress with a sudden, masculine urgency, overwhelming her with the power of his body.

She cried out as he entered her, a startled cry of pain at his hard invasion, and he must have known it hurt, for he stilled above her. She felt his arms slide beneath her to hold her close, and he bent his head to nuzzle her neck.

He held her tight for a long moment, and, slowly, the stinging pain began to ebb away as he kissed her throat and murmured soft, unintelligible words against her skin. Though she did not know what he said, there was a coaxing reassurance in his voice that both soothed and aroused her. She could feel him, hard and heavy inside her, and an aching warmth spread through her limbs. She moved her hips against his experimentally.

"Katie," he groaned against her neck. "God, don't do that. Not yet. You're not ready."

Katie felt more than ready for what she knew lay ahead. She sucked in a deep breath and began to move beneath him.

"Katie, no," he said again, but she did not heed his command, and with a hoarse cry he responded, his breathing harsh and ragged as he moved forcefully within her. She buried her face against his shoulder and wrapped her arms around his broad back, caressing him as her body rocked in rhythm with his, tightening and releasing in time with each thrust he made.

The tension inside her began building again, growing stronger until, suddenly, without warning, she felt again that exquisite explosion of carnal sensation. Her body tightened convulsively around him as the pleasure washed over her. She cried out, thrusting her hips upward against his, an urgent demand for him to take his pleasure, as she had taken hers.

As if he had been waiting for that, he answered her demand with a visceral sound of purely masculine exultation, and she felt him shudder with the force of his climax. His body thrust hard against hers one last time, then stilled.

Her hands caressed his back as she felt the tension slowly leave his body and lethargy take its place. When he rolled to his side, he took her with him, cradling her against his body. Within minutes, she heard his breathing deepen into sleep. She slid out of his embrace long enough to blow out the candle and pull the sheet that had tangled at the foot of the bed over them both. Then she snuggled back against his body. Though he did not waken, his arm wrapped itself protectively around her.

Katie welcomed the shelter of his arms. She had just been ravished, and yet she had never felt more safe than she did right now.

Deep down in her heart, she knew safety was an illusion. She knew none of this would last, that she could not keep her secret forever. One day, when he discovered the truth about her, when he realized the extent of her deceit, he would surely despise her. She prayed she would be gone by then, and she refused to spoil the beauty of this one night with painful speculations about the future.

She rested her cheek against his chest and felt the hard, round shape of the Liberty medal he wore against her skin. She closed her eyes tight, willing herself to forget about his cause, about Lowden, about everything but him.

I have him tonight, she told herself, listening to his strong heartbeat beneath her ear. *Tonight is all that counts.*

15

Katie woke to a flood of sunlight that told her dawn had given way to day. She blinked against the brightness and came fully awake to the knowledge that Ethan was asleep beside her. She could feel his arm across her waist and his thigh against her hip. The warmth and scent of him filled her senses, and she turned her head to look at him. He lay facing her, half covered by the counterpane, one arm curled around the pillow beneath his head, the other draped over her. He was asleep, and she eased her way out from beneath his arm. She sat up, studying him as he slept.

He needed a shave, she thought, noting the shadow of beard stubble on his face. His long hair lay in a rippling black stream across the white cotton sheeting of the pillow. The muscles of his chest, shoulder, and arm looked as if they had been carved from stone—hard, strong, and impervious to danger. But in the bright morning light, his face showed something else—a vulnerability she had never seen before.

She smiled with the quiet pleasure of simply watching him sleep. At this moment, he looked so different from the cynical stranger who had first mocked her in the taproom of the Mermaid.

The lean line of his profile seemed less harsh now than it had then. His mouth had lost that sardonic curve. His eyes were closed now, but last night she had seen no coldness in their gray depths, only tenderness. Here beside her, there was no ruthless, enigmatic spy or elegant, unreachable rich man. No earnest patriot, no mocking stranger. Instead, here was the man who had kissed her and caressed her, the man who had showed her the meaning of passion. The man who had become her lover.

Filled with an overwhelming tenderness, Katie reached out to touch his face, but she hesitated and drew her hand back. He was sleeping so soundly, she didn't want to wake him. He needed the rest. It would probably do him good to sleep all day.

She glanced at the window. Much longer, and he probably would. It was broad daylight.

Daylight.

That realization doused her contentment as effectively as a bucket of ice water, and Katie felt a sudden, suffocating fear. It was long past dawn, and it was Saturday. She should have been at the marketplace to meet Worth long before now.

She pushed back the sheets and slid out of bed,

wincing at the soreness in her body, a disconcerting reminder of what had happened the night before. She crossed the room to the armoire and began to dress hurriedly, hoping Ethan did not awaken before she could leave.

As she dressed, all the ramifications and consequences of the last night played across her mind, and, try as she might, she could not banish them with her usual brash confidence and optimism. Last night, she had not allowed herself to think. Now, she could not seem to do anything else.

Lowden would be returning any day, and he would want a full report from her on John Smith. What was she going to tell him? If she did not hand Ethan over to him, how long could she play for time before he grew tired of her incompetence as a spy and send her back to Willoughby?

There could be a child as a result of last night. Then what would she do? If she were pregnant, would Ethan marry her? She wanted to laugh at that notion the moment it entered her head. She knew full well how these things turned out. And if their difference in station weren't enough, there was also that inconvenient little fact that she was the spy for his enemy.

She might be able to persuade Ethan to buy her indenture. That would save her from Willoughby, but it would not save her from the gallows if Lowden decided to use that arrest warrant against her.

There was also another hard fact to be faced. The charade was reality now. She had become

Ethan's mistress in truth. She had broken the one and only vow she had ever made to herself, a vow made when she was eleven years old and on the London streets. She had become her mother. Just like her mother.

Life, Katie decided, was hell on earth.

"Where are you going?"

Katie froze at the sound of Ethan's voice. Her hands stilled in the act of buttoning her dress. She turned her back to the bed, knowing she could not bear to look at him now, and finished buttoning her dress. "I am going out."

"Out? Where?"

Katie began searching through the armoire for her cloak, wishing only to be gone as quickly as possible, but then she remembered her cloak was still in Ethan's carriage. With a muffled oath, she jerked a knitted shawl off one of the shelves. The last thing she wanted to do at this moment was answer questions and make up lies. She felt suffocated, with the weight of deceit smothering her, and all she wanted was to get out of this room. Flinging the shawl across her shoulders, she grabbed a bonnet out of the armoire and whirled around to face him. "Am I a prisoner here?"

"Of course not."

"Then I will go anywhere I please, and where I go is not your concern. You don't own me." She slapped the bonnet down her head, and she didn't give a damn that it didn't match her dress.

"Running away, are you, Katie?"

"Yes!" she flung back over her shoulder as she headed for the door.

"Why?"

She didn't answer. Instead, she reached for the door handle, but he was out of the bed and behind her before she could get the door fully open. He flattened his hand against it and slammed it shut.

She could feel the heat of his naked body as he leaned into her, his arms trapping her against the door. His breath was warm in her ear. "What are you running from?" he asked again. "Me or yourself?"

"Don't!" she cried, and turned in his arms, feeling trapped, defensive, and very frightened by the tangled web of lies she had woven around them both. She took refuge in the only truth she could tell him, the only part of her fear she could explain to him. "I watched my mother's life, I saw her self-respect erode away because she was a man's mistress, because she was not his wife. I saw how she was treated, how she loathed herself."

"Katie—"

"I vowed I would never allow that to happen to me." Her voice began to shake, and she knew she was panicking, but she could not help it. She flattened her palms against his chest and pushed him back. "I vowed no man would own me, no man would buy me. But it has happened, hasn't it?"

"Katie, don't turn what happened last night into something sordid. It wasn't like that."

She paid no attention to his words. "I have become exactly what my mother was. I have become a rich man's mistress. How could I have been so stupid?"

"Making love is never stupid," he shot back. "But the morning after is hell."

"Indeed it is."

"Katie, you are not your mother."

"What is the difference, Ethan?" she asked, her voice hard, brittle. "Are you going to marry me now?"

He didn't answer, and with his silence, her mouth twisted in a cynical curve. "Don't worry," she told him. "I never expected you to." She turned her face away, staring at the wall. "Now, please let me leave."

"Are you leaving for good?"

"If I say yes, will you send the constables after me? Will you have them send me back to Willoughby?"

"If you say no, I will believe you."

"So I am your prisoner?"

He lifted his hands to her face, forced her chin up so she was looking not at the wall but into his eyes. "Katie, the governor is having a ball tonight, and there will be an emissary there from the French government. I need to meet with him in secret at that ball, and I have a plan for how to accomplish that, but I can't do it without your help. Everything we have been working for hinges on that meeting."

Katie was dismayed. "But you said if I helped

you find out Lowden's purpose, you would let me go."

"I will arrange to buy your indenture and free you, Katie, as I promised. But these things take time to arrange."

"And in the meantime, I am to continue committing sedition with you?"

"Katie, I need you tonight. If you help me at the ball, that will be the last thing I will demand of you. I swear it. Help me one last time."

She felt his thumbs caress her cheeks, and she closed her eyes, trying to shut him out, keep the hard armor around her heart that had always protected her so well. *Don't touch me. Don't. I can't bear it.* "Will Lowden be at this ball?" she whispered.

"He was invited, but I don't know if he has returned from New York yet or not. Will you help me?"

She opened her eyes and pushed his hands away. "I'll help you," she told him, and turned her back to him. "I'll help you. I don't really have a choice, do I?"

Without another word, she opened the door and walked out of the bedroom. He did not stop her. She arrived at the marketplace and went directly to the onion seller's stall, where she usually saw Worth waiting for her, but he was not there. It was long past dawn, and she knew he had probably given up on her and left the marketplace. She turned and began retracing her steps to the house.

As she walked, she tried to think of a way out of

the mess she was in, but she knew there really was no way out. Ethan had told her he would buy her indenture, but that would not save her from arrest if she did not do what Lowden wanted.

If the viscount had returned from New York, he had probably already discovered that his pickpocket spy had moved up in station to become a mistress, and he would wonder why. He might realize the truth at once, that Ethan and John Smith were one and the same. At the very least, if he came to the ball, he would demand to know what she was doing gallivanting around Boston with Ethan Harding when she ought to be working at the Mermaid to discover the truth about John Smith.

None of that would matter, she supposed, when she turned Ethan over to the viscount. Suddenly cold, Katie wrapped the shawl more tightly around her ribs against the chilly spring wind, but she could not keep the chill out of her heart when she thought of what she had to do.

"What happened at Holbrook's last night? Did you find out anything about Lowden?"

The question only vaguely penetrated his thoughts, and it was not until Adam shouted his name that Ethan paid attention.

Startled out of his reverie, he looked up, frowning at his secretary across the desk. "Sorry, what did you say?"

Adam repeated the question.

"Yes. It seems the viscount has been sent here for

the sole purpose of finding proof of sedition against the Sons of Liberty and forcing Gage to make arrests."

His secretary let out a low whistle. "And how is he planning to do this?"

"He is recruiting spies and informants. Katie and I discovered letters written to Holbrook from Gage that confirm this fact."

"Katie assisted you in this? She is proving to be a rather good spy, isn't she?"

The mention of her name was enough to send Ethan's thoughts back to that morning once again. Adam continued to speak, but Ethan didn't really hear what his secretary was saying. All he could hear was Katie's voice, filled with bitterness and fear.

I am a rich man's mistress. I have become my mother.

To Ethan, her fear seemed out of proportion. She wasn't at all like her mother had been. Couldn't she see the difference? But then, women could be the most unpredictable, unaccountable creatures God ever made. He would never use her as her mother had been used. It wasn't the same thing at all.

"Ethan, have you come up with a plan for the ball tonight?"

He heard the tenor of a question from across the desk, and he nodded absently in reply, but his thoughts remained with Katie.

If I say yes, will you send the constables after me? Will you have them send me back to Willoughby?

He tried to see the situation from her point of view. He could understand that she was scared. He knew she was afraid of going back to Virginia, and he knew he had always used that threat to ensure her silence and her loyalty, but after last night, how could she still believe he would do that to her?

Because you didn't deny it, that's why.

He hadn't denied it because he could not afford to let her go. Not now, not yet. He had told her the truth this morning that he needed her help at the ball. He had a plan to meet with Chevain, but it would only work with her help. If he freed her from their bargain, he could not use her. Guilt washed over him, for the first time overpowering the fact that she had brought their bargain on herself.

"Ethan, what the hell is wrong with you?"

Adam's explosive question forced thoughts of Katie from his mind. He couldn't think about her right now. He had crucial things to do and not much time. "Let's discuss the Governor's Ball tonight."

"That's what I'm trying to do," his secretary said with some exasperation. "If you're ready to stop wool-gathering and listen." He pulled out a sheet of foolscap from the leather portmanteau at his feet and handed it to Ethan. "This is a list of everyone in Chevain's entourage. The whole party arrived from Quebec yesterday."

Ethan scanned the list quickly. "Marie LeBlanc will be there. Excellent."

"Marie LeBlanc is Chevain's mistress."

"Yes, I know. I have been making inquiries."

"If you make your own inquiries, I don't know why you ask me to do so," Adam complained good-naturedly. "What do you have in mind for tonight?"

"This visit is a diplomatic one, made in the guise of friendly relations, is it not?"

"Yes."

"But you know as well as I that France will take any opportunity to irritate England that it can get. So, Chevain will probably be willing at least to listen to me if I can get him alone."

"Agreed. But getting him alone will not be easy. You have spent many years making yourself known among your Tory acquaintances to be notoriously uninformed about politics, though you are the man to consult if one wants a well-made waistcoat or a fashionable new way to tie a cravat. Are you planning to use that as a basis for conversation?"

"No. Chevain is known to be completely uninterested in fashion, and I'm sure Gage's spies will be watching him very closely. If we are seen talking together, it will arouse suspicion."

"Do you have to meet with him at the ball? Is there any other way to have a meeting?"

Ethan shook his head. "I don't see how. His schedule for today is completely filled with diplomatic talks, and his ship departs for France tomorrow afternoon. No, I must talk with him tonight. It's my only opportunity. And not meet-

ing with him is unthinkable. I must know that
we have French support. If we cannot count on
help from King Louis, we have no hope of freedom from England."

"But how are you going to get him alone? And
what does his mistress have to do with it?"

"If I remember the way rooms are laid out at the
governor's mansion, some of the bedrooms on the
ground floor have doors leading into the gardens."

"I believe so, yes."

"People have romantic liaisons at balls all the
time," Ethan went on. "Both Chevain and I will
have our mistresses at this affair. If we were to lead
them into bedrooms that were side by side, each
with a door giving onto the garden—"

"You would simply switch places with Marie
LeBlanc," Adam finished for him. "If people think
you are with your mistress and Chevain is with his,
no one would disturb you."

"We would also have good reason to lock the
doors," Ethan pointed out.

"How are you going to inform Chevain that this
is what you wish to do?"

"I already know from my informants in France
that Chevain is willing to meet with me. I'll dance
with Madame LeBlanc and tell her. The only concern is not being seen slipping in and out of the bedrooms by anyone in the garden. We can only hope
that the early spring chill in the night air discour-
ages people from strolling outside in the gardens."

"Is it wise to involve Katie in this?"

"I don't have a choice." Remembering his promise to her that morning, Ethan went on, "By the way, I want you to make arrangements with Willoughby to purchase her indenture. Go to Virginia to conduct the transaction yourself."

His secretary frowned, looking troubled. "If she is afraid to return to indenture and you free her, what will you have to hold over her head in future?"

"I promised her I would buy her indenture and free her if she helped me to discover Lowden's purpose here, and she has kept her part of the bargain. I intend to keep mine."

"But there is nothing to prevent her from selling what she knows and making more money."

Ethan rubbed a hand across his forehead. God, he was tired of this—of leading two lives, of never letting down his guard, of questioning the motives of everyone he met. "If she wanted to betray me for money, she could have done it two weeks ago. She knew my identity, and she saw my Liberty medal. Yet I am still getting accurate information from Gage's officers. If Gage knew I was passing secrets to Whig leaders, my sources would certainly not be so forthcoming." He shook his head. "No, she has not told anyone about me. Nor has she tried to blackmail me with what she knows."

"But—"

"For God's sake, Adam," he interrupted impatiently. "Just do it, would you? And stop worrying about it."

"All right, all right. But as you once told me, you

pay me to do your worrying for you. I'm just doing my job. There's no need to be cross."

"I know." He held up one hand in a gesture of apology. "It's just that after my adventures at Holbrook's house last night, I haven't had much sleep. To return to the subject at hand, what do you think of my plan to meet with Chevain?"

"I think it's perfect."

"Perfect, perhaps," Ethan conceded. "Let us pray it works."

16

$\mathcal{M}$onsieur Jean-Paul Chevain, the French ambassador, might indeed be one of the most influential statesmen of Europe, he might have the respect of kings and the power to alter the fate of nations, and his support might be vital to Ethan's plans for revolution. But all that didn't change the fact that the man could not dance.

Ethan watched as the Frenchman danced with Katie, and though the seriousness of the evening's events made him feel tense and on edge, he could not help some amusement as he watched Chevain's hapless attempts to master the minuet. The poor fellow missed steps, bumped into other people by turning the wrong way, and caused such havoc that Ethan was sure all the participants were dreaming of ways to kill him before the dance was half done. The entire process was made worse by the fact that Chevain was enormously fat.

Katie, however, handled her partner with skillful finesse. Though her hair was concealed beneath an elaborate powdered wig just like those of all the other women dancing, and her blue silk gown was the exact shade of at least four others on the ball-room floor, Ethan had no trouble keeping her in view. Even without the clumsy maneuvering of her partner, her slender, graceful figure would have been easy to find.

He had already made his suggestion for a meet-ing to Marie LeBlanc, and during a previous dance she had informed the ambassador of Ethan's plans.

Now he was watching Katie and Chevain, wait-ing for some indication on the ambassador's part that the other man would agree to meet with him.

Only moments before the dance ended, Chevain turned in his direction, met his gaze, and nodded slowly. Ethan nodded in reply. The die had been cast, and Ethan was about to have the most impor-tant meeting of his life. In one hour, he would try to persuade King Louis's emissary that France needed to provide the colonies with powder, weapons, and money, and the fate of a new nation could very well depend on how persuasive he could be.

A few moments later, Katie rejoined him, and Chevain returned to the members of his own party on the other side of the room.

"Well?" he asked Katie in a low voice, keeping his gaze fixed on the ambassador, who was now talking with Governor Gage, Sir William Hol-brook, and Holbrook's wife.

"You will need to dance with Marie LeBlanc just

before eleven," Katie told him. "By then, Chevain will have inquired of his host which rooms are free for romantic liaisons."

Ethan cast a sideways glance at her, and he knew she was thinking of the night before. Memories of it flooded his own mind, and it must have shown on his face, for she hastily turned away and grabbed a glass of Madeira off the tray of a passing maidservant. She swallowed the wine in one quick draught.

"Have you spied Lowden in the crowd?" she asked, tossing her wineglass into a potted fern and earning a stern look from the man by her side.

"No," he answered. "But Holbrook might know. He is headed this way."

"Oh, how lovely." Katie made a face.

Ethan threw back his head and laughed. "Be polite," he ordered. "Our good governor is with him."

"Well, Harding," Holbrook said as the two men approached them, "every time I see you with this woman, you are laughing."

"And that surprises you, Sir William?" Ethan asked.

"Not at all. I know Mrs. Armstrong to be quite entertaining company."

His implication was clear, and Ethan's mouth tightened. Katie spoke quickly to fill the awkward silence. "He only says that because I can dance an Irish jig on my fingertips."

"A skill I would dearly love to see firsthand," Holbrook said, and gestured toward the ballroom floor. "I'm sure there is room for you to demonstrate."

"And show my knickers to a Frenchman?" she countered in mock horror. "Laud, Sir William, I couldn't possibly."

The men laughed at that, including Governor Gage. When she was introduced to him, Katie engaged the governor in conversation, and Ethan did the same with Holbrook, much to her relief. She found that Thomas Gage was not what she would have expected. He was an intelligent and soft-spoken man, with deep lines of worry carved in his forehead that spoke of heavy responsibilities. Katie sensed that he was also very kind.

When she expressed this opinion to Ethan after the two men had strolled on toward the refreshment tables, he agreed with her, much to her surprise.

"Isn't he your enemy?" she murmured, glancing around to make certain no one could hear them.

"That doesn't mean I cannot appreciate the man's good qualities, Katie," he answered, his voice as low as hers. "In truth, I have a high opinion of Thomas Gage. He is just, which is more than I can say for his predecessor, Hutchinson."

She shook her head. "You astound me, Ethan, to speak so fairly of the man who could end up hanging you for sedition."

"If it were up to Gage, that would never happen. He believes very strongly in the letter of the law. Unfortunately, the decision to arrest the Sons of

Liberty will be made by Lord North, and that man is anything but just."

"Then let us hope Lord North decides to retire to his country home and grow a new species of rose or something."

Ethan smiled, but there was a grave expression in his eyes. "If he does, it will have to be soon. By the way, Holbrook did not know if Lowden would be here this evening or not. The viscountess has already arrived, so perhaps he has been detained in New York."

Katie heartily hoped so. In her opinion, Lowden could stay in New York until hell froze over.

During the hour that followed, there was still no sign of the viscount, and Katie began to hope he was not coming. Ethan did as Chevain had instructed and danced with the ambassador's mistress, who told him which bedrooms they would use. A few minutes before eleven, he and Katie each took a glass of wine and slipped out of the ballroom, leaving the impression on anyone watching them that they were departing for a romantic tryst. They went into the bedroom Marie LeBlanc had instructed them to use. Once inside, Ethan slid back the bolt that locked the doors leading into the back gardens, then sat down beside Katie on the edge of the bed in the dark and waited.

Neither of them spoke, and with every passing moment the tenseness in the air grew. After they had waited a few moments, her hand reached for his, as if seeking reassurance. He entwined their fingers and held her hand in his. "Everything will be fine," he whispered.

"What if this meeting does not go as you hope?" she whispered back. "Would all be lost?"

He simply lifted her hand in his and kissed her fingertips, but he did not answer her question, and both of them fell silent, waiting.

It seemed like an eternity to Ethan before he heard the sound of a door handle turning. One of the double doors leading out to the garden opened with a lingering squeak and swung wide. In the moonlight, he could see the shapely silhouette of a woman framed in the doorway.

He let go of Katie's hand, set aside his glass of wine, and stood up. As he approached the doorway, the moonlight spilling into the room confirmed that the woman was indeed Chevain's mistress.

Without wasting any more time, he nodded to Marie LeBlanc and slipped past her through the doorway into the cold night air outside.

"Good luck," Katie whispered.

"Wait here, and keep quiet," he ordered both women in a soft whisper, and closed the doors behind him.

No light illuminated the room next door, but when Ethan turned the door handle, he found it unlocked. He drew a deep breath and stepped inside the room. Though no lamps were lit, moonlight through the windows and the glass doors he had entered enabled him to locate Chevain. The stout, balding diplomat was seated in an overstuffed chair in one corner of the room, a glass of wine on the small table beside him.

Though Chevain might not cut an impressive figure, Ethan knew better than to be fooled by appearances. Chevain could doom the rebel cause to fail or enable it to succeed. It was Ethan's task to persuade Chevain to present the latter course to King Louis, but he did not have much time to do so, since neither of them could afford to linger too long.

Fortunately, Chevain was of a like mind and wasted no time on preliminaries.

"So, monsieur," he said in a low voice, "if I have correctly grasped the situation here, if my sources are correctly informed, you plan a war with England." He leaned back in his chair and folded his hands over his generous belly. "But you need the help of France to accomplish this, and that is why you come to me?"

Ethan sat down on the edge of the bed so that he might face the other man. "Yes."

"And why should France agree to help a group of paltry colonials fight a war they cannot win?"

Ethan felt his jaw tighten, and he forced himself to relax. He leaned back on the bed, resting his weight on his arms and smiling at Chevain with a confidence he was far from feeling. "With French weaponry in our hands and French loans to back our efforts, we cannot fail to defeat England," he said. "We can succeed, sir, and we will."

"Not without our help. And I do not recall agreeing to anything as yet. Again, why should

France finance a losing cause? What is in this for us?"

"A very generous usury rate," Ethan answered, his smile widening as he dangled the bait. "Loans to us would generate a high profit for France in the form of interest."

"Only if you are able to pay those loans back," Chevain answered dryly. "Even with our assistance, there is no guarantee that you will defeat England. Financing a war is expensive, and you colonials have nothing—few weapons, little powder, and no means of manufacturing what you need. We know of your discontent with your king, and we are sympathetic, since George is known across the Continent to be insane, but we are not certain it is in our best interests to become involved in your squabble. France would have to make enormous loans to you to finance your efforts, and the profits you promise are by no means assured. I am not at all sure Louis would be willing to plunder our treasury for a venture of such high risk."

Ethan's fingers pressed into the mattress so tightly they began to ache. He studied the ambassador's face, but diplomacy was ingrained in Chevain, and Ethan could read nothing in his expression. A sudden fear gripped him that all his efforts would be for naught. France would refuse her assistance, and without it, Ethan knew he and his comrades could not hope to defeat the most powerful nation in the world.

"What you say is highly sensible, sir, but there is one thing you have not taken into account."

"What is that?"

"The West Indies." Ethan leaned forward on the edge of the bed with sudden urgency. "If England has her way, French trade will be winnowed out in those islands. You know that as well as I do. Your only hope of continuing to profit from the spice trade there is to assist us."

He could tell Chevain appreciated the truth of that, and he pressed his advantage. "There is no reward without risk, sir, and the higher the risk, the more lucrative the reward. If we can defeat England, France would be able to increase its control in the West Indies and make a great deal of money."

He waited, holding his breath, knowing he had done all he could.

After a moment of silence, Chevain spoke. "It is very sound, what you say. We know England is forcing us out of the West Indies, and we have been concerned about the spice trade there for quite some time." He paused, then slowly nodded his head. "Very well. If rebellion does break out here in America, if armed conflict happens, I will present your case to our king and urge him to grant the assistance you request. To what extent he will agree, I cannot say."

Ethan let out his breath in a slow sigh of relief. "That is all I hoped for, sir. My thanks."

"You seem a sensible young man," Chevain said, "despite this impossible cause you fight for. Do you really think you can defeat the English?"

"We don't have to defeat them," Ethan answered, and rose to his feet. "We only have to make them so sick of us that they let us go."

When Ethan returned to the other bedroom, Katie asked no questions until Chevain's mistress had left them. With the doors closed and safely locked, she lit a lamp, then looked at him anxiously. "Well?" she whispered. "What happened?"

Ethan lifted his glass of Madeira from where he had left it on a bedside table. He lifted it high and grinned, feeling jubilant. "To France," he said, and downed his wine in one swallow, then set the glass aside.

Katie laughed. "You succeeded, then, in what you meant to do?" When he nodded in the affirmative, she followed his example and emptied her glass. The gesture left a tiny drop of wine clinging to her upper lip, and Ethan caught his breath as he watched her sweep it away with her tongue. At that moment, every coherent thought but one went out of his head. Suddenly, the only thing he could think about was how much he wanted her. Even the sweetness of the evening's victory was forgotten.

She looked up at him, and her smile vanished. She stared at him, wide-eyed and silent, for a long time.

He reminded himself of the resolutions he had made only this morning, and though it took all the strength he had, he made no move to touch her.

"Wait here a few moments," he instructed her, "then return to the ball."

"Wait? Why?"

"You will need time to straighten your hair and clothes."

"Whatever for?"

"We've just had a romantic liaison, remember?"

She frowned as if perplexed. "We did? Hmm, I must have missed it. If you ask me, Ethan, romantic trysts at balls are highly overrated."

He laughed as he headed for the door, but his laughter faded as he walked down the long hallway toward the ballroom. After tonight, he would have to let her go. He knew she would leave Boston the moment her indenture papers were rescinded, and he did not want to think about what his life would be like when Katie was not there to make him laugh.

Katie did as Ethan instructed, waiting what she judged to be a suitable interval before leaving the bedroom. She opened the door, and, after a quick glance up and down the long hallway, she started back toward the ballroom. Out of the corner of her eye, she saw that one of the other bedroom doors giving onto the hallway was open, but she scarcely noticed it. Preoccupied with her own thoughts, she continued down the hall, but she had only taken a few steps further before a voice stopped her.

"So, here you are."

The voice was frighteningly familiar, and Katie froze, paralyzed with fear. She did not need to turn around to know that Viscount Lowden was standing behind her.

She couldn't just stand there with her back to him, and she couldn't run away. Katie turned around to find Lowden standing in the doorway of the bedroom she had just passed. He must have been lurking in that room, waiting for her to pass by.

He was smiling at her. Somehow, that only increased her fear.

"Well, my girl, I knew I was right to have chosen you." He took several steps forward, then seized her arm and dragged her through the doorway of the room where he had been waiting for her.

He shut the door behind them and faced her, shaking his head as if in disbelief, chuckling as if greatly amused. "You truly have a gift for chicanery. So, Ethan Harding is the betrayer I have been looking for. I never would have believed it."

Katie felt that knot of fear twist into agony. *No!* she wanted to shout. *You are mistaken!*

"What do you mean?" she whispered.

"I returned from New York only a few hours ago and have had no time to find out what has occurred in my absence. Imagine my astonishment when I arrive at this ball only to discover that my spy has become the mistress of Ethan Harding."

Katie could not quite assimilate what was happening. He couldn't possibly know Ethan was the traitor, she told herself desperately. He could not be certain. He did not have proof.

Lowden laid a hand against her cheek with something almost akin to affection, and she had to fight to avoid turning her face away. "I told you to find the spy and become his mistress, and it seems you have followed my suggestion admirably."

She wanted to deny it, but she could not seem to speak. She said nothing, and Lowden's smile slowly faded at her silence, finally turning to a frown.

"Somehow, you discovered that Harding is the one we've been seeking, and you are finding the proof of it, is that not so? What other reason could you have for becoming his mistress?"

Seconds ticked by as he waited for her answer.

It was so simple. It was so easy. Now was the moment she had been waiting for, the moment when she could tell what she knew and claim her reward. All she had to do was confirm his suspicion and tell him about Ethan's Liberty medal. For that, she would be free of Willoughby. She would save her own life and have enough money to start a new one. Katie bit down hard on her lower lip and remained utterly still.

Freedom and money, the two things she had wanted more than anything else in the world, were now hers for the taking, but she could not take them. The price of her life was Ethan's, and that price was too high. She could not pay it. She would not. All this time, she had been deceiving herself. She would not betray Ethan. She had fallen in love with him.

She had no illusions that he might love her, and there was no hope of a future with him. Nonetheless, Katie knew that whether he loved her or not did not really matter. For the first time since she was a child, she knew what it was like to love someone with all her heart, because she would rather sacrifice her own life than his, and she would do it willingly, without hope of his love in return.

She lifted her chin, looked into the merciless face of Viscount Lowden, and put on the most scornful expression she could manage, knowing the only way out of this situation without betraying Ethan was to bluff her way out. "My lord," she said with thorough disdain, "I never took you for a fool. At least, not until now."

Lowden's brows rose at the accusation, and he said in a low, dangerous voice, "Perhaps you had better leave off insulting me and explain yourself, girl."

Her heart was thumping so loudly in her chest that Katie was sure he could hear it, but she forced herself to play out the hand she had chosen. She just had to do it convincingly. "Ethan Harding the rebel spy? Are you mad?"

A flicker of uncertainty crossed Lowden's stony countenance, and she hastened on, pressing her advantage. "Harding cares naught for politics, and even if he did care, he's hopelessly slow-witted, poor fellow. He couldn't possibly comprehend the intricacies of politics." She laughed, shaking her head gently to show the viscount how ridiculous that theory was. "Harding a spy? That is rich indeed, considering that the greatest passion of his life is finding the perfect knot for his cravat."

Lowden's frown deepened. "Do you mean to tell me that you are not his mistress? That the gossip is false? That I did not see the two of you slip out of the ballroom just as I arrived?"

She made an exclamation of impatience. "My lord, of course all that is true. I am Harding's mistress. But Harding is not your traitor. I know this for a fact. Besides, as I said before, he's too dim for the task."

"Then I hope for your sake that there is a deeper purpose behind your new profession than having a wealthy man take care of you."

"Of course I have a deeper purpose." Her mind raced as she began to invent a tale that would satisfy Lowden and get her safely out of there, but before she could say another word, footsteps were heard coming down the hall, and a fretful female voice began calling for the viscount.

"James, darling, where are you?"

Katie recognized the well-bred accents of Lady Lowden, and though she had never believed in God, she was grateful enough for the reprieve to offer a silent prayer of thanks. Then her mouth curved into a mocking smile. "You'd best go, James, darling," she told him in that excellent imitation of the viscountess which had so amused Ethan the night before. "Otherwise, people will start to think I've become *your* mistress."

Unamused, Lowden muttered a curse and

started for the door. "I still expect a full report of your activities during my absence. Worth told me you have news for my ears alone."

"So I do," she assured him. *But I have to think of it first.*

"Be at the Stag and Steed on Monday night, and be prepared to tell me everything you know." He paused with his hand on the door handle. "Midnight."

"I'll be there," she told him.

He left her, closing the door behind him.

"James, here you are!" Lady Lowden exclaimed, her reproachful voice drifting to Katie from beneath the closed door. "People have been telling me they saw you arrive here tonight, but I had no idea you had even returned from New York. Imagine my feelings when I had to be told by other people that you were here."

Whatever Lowden's reply, Katie did not hear it, for his answer was too low for her to make out his words. The pair of voices faded as Lowden and his wife walked back toward the ball. Katie waited a few minutes, then followed them to the ballroom.

Fate had smiled on her tonight, giving her until midnight Monday to spin a tale for the viscount, but she knew it had to be a plausible one. Lowden was no fool.

What would she tell him?

It had to be something convincing enough to divert his suspicions from Ethan. She also hoped whatever tale she concocted could keep her from going to the gallows for theft or being returned to Willoughby before Ethan could complete the transaction to buy her indenture.

She sighed, almost wishing she could go back and do the whole thing over. Everything had been so simple at first, and she had genuinely believed she would have no problem turning Ethan over to the viscount. Now she was in love with him, and nothing was simple anymore.

You're in a fine mess now.

She recalled Molly's words to her the morning after her bargain with Ethan had been made and almost wanted to smile. Molly had been wrong. Katie knew now that she hadn't been in a fine mess then, only a minor predicament. Now she was in a fine mess, and she had no idea what she was going to do about it.

When Ethan saw Lady Lowden return to the ballroom, she was accompanied by a man so dandified Ethan knew he had to be the viscountess's husband. When they paused just inside the ballroom doors to speak with Governor Gage, Lord Percy, Sir William Holbrook, and their respective wives, Ethan nudged Travertine, who stood beside him, and gestured to the couples across the room. "Is that Viscount Lowden?"

Travertine lifted his quizzing glass and took a closer look. "Yes, indeed."

Though it only confirmed what he already knew, Ethan felt his pulses quicken at the name.

So this was the man who had been sent to destroy the Sons of Liberty. Ethan's lip curled slightly, and he vowed that would happen only over his dead body.

"What's wrong, Harding?" Travertine asked, observing his disdainful expression. "You are glaring daggers at the man."

Ethan masked his distaste with a smile. "The fellow is rumored to be one of London's most fashionable fellows, and I can scarce believe it. His waistcoat is the most hideous shade of puce I have ever seen."

"I detect some envy in that statement," Travertine joked. "Perhaps you should learn the identity of his tailor."

Ethan made a sound of scorn. "My own tailor is far superior."

At that moment, he saw Katie enter the ballroom. She was immediately accosted by the group near the door and pulled into conversation with them. As she talked with the viscount, she caught sight of him watching her across the room, and she slowly shifted her position so that she faced away from him. Even among the dancers that crowded the ballroom floor, he saw her hand reach behind her and make a frantic beckoning gesture in his direction.

Excusing himself from Travertine, he crossed the ballroom to her side. "My darling girl," he said in his most fatuous voice, "where have you been?" Without waiting for an answer, he turned to the man beside him expectantly, and Holbrook performed the necessary introductions.

"Your servant, my lord." Ethan bowed to the viscount in his most dandified fashion, and Lowden mirrored him. That politeness taken care of, Ethan held out his hand to Katie.

As she took his hand, her fingers squeezed his, and he did not miss the look of gratitude she gave him. Her gaze met his, and he saw her mouth the words "Let's leave now" as she cast a pointed glance toward the door.

He lifted her hand and kissed her fingers. "You look tired, my dear," he said. "I'll escort you home now."

The viscount protested. "But it is quite early still. You must stay a bit longer."

Ethan smiled and shook his head. "I'm afraid that won't do, my lord. We couldn't possibly stay a moment more. I have an appointment early tomorrow morning, and I wouldn't want to be late."

Lowden protested again, but Ethan was adamant, and a few minutes later, they were in Ethan's carriage and on their way back to Katie's house. Safely inside the carriage with no chance of being overheard, Ethan said, "Did you find out anything interesting from Lowden?"

She looked at him blankly for a moment, then shook her head. "Oh, no, but . . . I didn't . . . I mean, I hadn't expected to learn anything. I was merely . . . umm . . . trying to determine his character."

"And?"

"I don't know." Katie leaned back against the seat and pressed her fingertips to her forehead as if she had a headache.

"I saw him pull you into their circle and make conversation with you. I wonder if he suspects something about you?"

"What could he possibly suspect?" she mumbled. "He's been back in Boston less than a day."

"I don't know, but I hope he arrived too late to notice our little jaunt to the bedrooms and the fact that Chevain and his mistress did the same."

Katie made no reply, and Ethan glanced over at her. By the light of the carriage lamp, he could see that her eyes were closed and her lips were slightly parted. She had actually fallen asleep.

He studied her in exasperated amusement, wondering how she could possibly sleep now, after the exciting events of the night. He had finally met Lowden face to face. He was also exhilarated by the success of his meeting with Chevain. He was not tired in the least.

But then, Katie was not in this cause because she was a patriot who wanted freedom for the colonies. She was in it because she wanted freedom for herself. Once she had it, she would leave, and Ethan knew he had nothing that would make her stay.

17

$\mathcal{K}$atie had two days to fabricate a story for Lowden, and by the time she arrived at the Stag and Steed on Monday night, she had what she felt was a convincing one. Nonetheless, her palms were sweating in their gloves, and she knew she would be glad when the meeting was over.

The tavern was very similar to the White Swan, with its taproom filled with redcoats gulping down ale and meat pies. One glance at the taproom, and Katie decided it would be wise to use the rear entrance through the kitchen. She circled around to the alley and entered the Stag and Steed by the back door. Mrs. Gibbons, her gnarled face flushed from the heat of the ovens, jerked a thumb toward the stairs. "He's waiting for you. Same room as before."

She nodded and walked through the buttery, then mounted the stairs to the upper floor. Lowden was indeed waiting for her, for when she tapped on the door of the room where they had first met, her knock was promptly answered with a command to come in.

She entered the room, closing the door behind her, and the viscount rose from the long table that stood between them, looking just as ruthless as he had the first time she had seen him. She swallowed hard, but she pasted an expression of supreme self-confidence on her face. "Good evening, my lord."

He didn't bother to give her any answering pleasantries. "Be seated."

She took off her cloak and draped it over the back of the chair he indicated, then sat down. "I assume you would like me to tell you the full story." Without waiting for confirmation of that assumption, she swept on. "The plan that Worth and I concocted about the watch succeeded admirably. In fact, I was able to begin working at the Mermaid right away. But Molly Munro, the wife of the owner, put me in the kitchen, cooking and washing dishes, not letting me serve ale in the taproom as I had hoped."

She knew she was talking too fast, and she prayed that to the viscount's ears she sounded confident rather than nervous. "This, of course, presented a problem. You cannot see into the taproom of the Mermaid from the kitchen, and you certainly can't overhear anything from there. So, I—"

"Who is John Smith?"

"I'm getting to that. So, I knew I'd have to take further action if I were going to learn anything of significance. I did learn that John Smith always comes late in the evening, and he doesn't drink in the taproom with the others. There is a private room where he meets with other Whigs, and—"

"What other Whigs?" He leaned forward in his chair, and his black eyes seemed to grow colder. "Give me names."

Katie had been expecting this demand, and she was prepared to fulfill it. Crossing her fingers beneath the table to wish that Ethan had been right when he'd told her Gage would not arrest anyone just for talking about sedition, she said, "David Munro is always there, as well as a man named Joseph Bramley, who I am given to understand is a messenger for both Paul Revere and Samuel Adams."

He nodded. "I am aware of Bramley already."

"They meet in that back room so that Smith can give him information to pass on to Adams and Revere. I figured that out right away, so—"

"But what information is Smith giving them, and how is he getting it?" Lowden interrupted, clearly impatient to get to the heart of the matter.

Katie had no intention of letting the viscount's impatience control this meeting. If she allowed that to happen, her well-rehearsed story would become much harder to tell. "I'll give you all the information I have, my lord, but everything I'm telling you is important, so let me tell it my own way, if you please."

Lowden's black eyes snapped with irritation at her autocratic tone, and Katie knew she had best tread carefully, or she would push him too far. "It will be worth the wait, I assure you. To continue, I knew that if I were going to find out anything, I had to find a way into that back room, but I just couldn't see how to manage it. Then I figured out how to do it. I invented a reason to be away one evening when I knew Smith would be there, but instead of leaving the tavern, I slipped into that private room and concealed myself in the cupboard that stands in the corner."

"That was clever of you."

She heard the grudging hint of admiration in his voice, and that took away some of her nervousness. So far, her plan was working. In response to his compliment, Katie lifted her chin with a conceited smile. "Yes, it was rather clever of me, wasn't it? You'll think me even more clever when I tell you what I heard."

She took a deep breath and leaned forward, implying that she was eager to tell what she knew. "I heard Smith tell the other two that he had learned Gage's plans to confiscate all the rebel powder stores. He gave them details, saying how Gage was sending officers into the countryside dressed as colonials to spy out the powder stores, then send troops to confiscate it. He—"

"But how does he know this? Cease prattling on, and tell me who the traitor is, girl."

She frowned at him to convey some vexation. "If you would stop interrupting me, my lord, I might be able to tell you."

The viscount swept one arm wide with exaggerated politeness. "Please forgive me. Continue."

Katie had known she would have to give Lowden an alternative suspect to Ethan, and she had no qualms about doing so. "David Munro became so excited by the news of Gage's plans that he called Smith by his real name."

"What name?" The viscount straightened in his chair. His gaze bored into hers with such intensity Katie felt her throat go dry, and her palms started sweating again. "What name?" he repeated.

Katie threw the dice. "Holbrook."

"Holbrook?" he repeated in clear disbelief. "You're joking."

Katie felt reasonably safe throwing Sir William to the wolves, and the man was such a lout she could not drum up much remorse about doing it. Besides, she knew that without proof, he could not be arrested, either. Since he was innocent, proof would not be forthcoming. She nodded emphatically. "I am not joking. That is the name Munro called him. He said, 'By God, Holbrook, it is amazing how you learn these things.' And Bramley cried out, 'Holbrook? So that is who you really are!'"

"So Holbrook is the traitor," Lowden murmured, drumming his fingers on the table. "I always knew that man's hearty Tory loyalty was an act."

"I did not know who Holbrook was, of course, but I could tell from his voice that he was a gentleman, so I knew it would be best to search for him among the elite of Boston society. That's why I became Harding's mistress."

The viscount gave her a hard stare, and she knew he was not swallowing her story without question. "If Holbrook is the traitor, would you not have learned more by becoming his mistress?"

She shuddered in revulsion that was not altogether pretended. "What, that lecher? Absolutely not. There are some things I won't do, my lord, not even for freedom and money. Harding, at least, is a reasonably good lover."

"I'm so glad you are enjoying yourself," the viscount drawled with unmistakable sarcasm.

Katie ignored the caustic tone of his voice and grinned, pretending to find his comment amusing. "A girl has to be convincing in her role, my lord. And I must say, I have enjoyed myself. Harding has taken me to parties and balls, he has given me clothes, jewels, even a house. The poor fool. I've milked him for quite a haul."

"No doubt," Lowden said dryly. "And have you been able to take time out of your social calender to find proof of Holbrook's sedition?"

Now she was coming to the tricky part. "Not yet," she answered. "I am working to discover it."

The viscount leaned forward. His voice was ominously low, and Katie swallowed hard, fighting back the cold fear that seeped into her bones. "I hope, for your sake, that you find that proof."

"I will. The house I persuaded Harding to lease for me is directly across the alley from the Mermaid, and I have been watching the tavern and visiting with Molly Munro as much as possible. The problem is, I have not seen Holbrook going in and out of the tavern, at least not by the back door. I have higher hopes for finding the proof from another angle. Harding takes me to all the fashionable functions, and I make every attempt to converse with Holbrook and others in his circle, including the governor himself. I am certain that my efforts will lead me to the proof you require that Holbrook is John Smith, but I need more time."

She could tell that Lowden was not pleased by the delay, but if she had been convincing in her story, he would agree to grant her request. After what seemed an eternity, he nodded. "Very well. I received a dispatch from London, stating that Gage will be receiving orders to arrest all Sons of Liberty by mid-April. That gives you more than three weeks to find proof against Holbrook so that he can be arrested with the others."

Katie rose to her feet, displaying none of the relief she felt. Instead, she acted as if she had expected nothing else. She stood up, pulled her cloak from the back of her chair, and flung it over her shoulders. "You'll have your proof," she told him. "By the way, Harding has insisted on buying my indenture and has already begun making arrangements with my master. So by the time I have your proof, you won't have to bother setting me free."

"How convenient for you that Harding finds

you so charming. But I still hold an arrest warrant against you for theft."

"I have not forgotten that. All I ask from you is that you keep your part of the bargain. When I have the proof of Holbrook's sedition, you will give me the money you promised me, and you will tear up that arrest warrant and give me an assurance signed by the governor that I cannot be prosecuted for the theft of Weston's purse. Then, and only then, I will give you your proof."

A flash of anger came into his eyes. "Careful, Katie," he warned, rising to his feet. "Do not dictate demands to me. Remember, you are not free yet."

She turned and walked away without a backward glance. Just before she stepped out of the room, she replied over her shoulder, "That, my lord, is something I never forget."

During the fortnight that followed, Ethan was kept very busy. He began receiving reports from all quarters that activity of British Regulars was increasing. Troops were reported making marches through the countryside west of Boston and were often seen in their off-duty hours repairing their tents and breaking out their field equipment. In addition, on April 5, longboats were launched from British naval ships anchored in the harbor and moored under their sterns ready for use, a clear indication to the citizens of Boston that something serious was in the wind.

One afternoon two weeks after the ball, Ethan

learned that a party of British officers had been sent to examine the roads to Concord. That night, Ethan called an emergency meeting at the Mermaid.

"The word from Fort Hill is that Gage will definitely be sending troops to march on Concord." Ethan glanced at the other three men seated with him in the Mermaid's private back room. David, Andrew, and Colin all remained silent, and Ethan knew they were thinking the same thing as himself. War with England was very near at hand.

Finally, it was David who spoke. "When do they march? Do you know?"

"Probably within a week. There has been a great deal of activity among the regiments, as you know, and my guess is they will move very soon. But I cannot say for certain. My sources at Province House are being very silent about this mission."

"Do you think this is part of Gage's plans to steal our powder stores?" asked Andrew.

"I do," Ethan answered. "Concord has a very large arsenal of weapons, cannon, and gunpowder. I know Gage would love to get his hands on it."

Colin spoke for the first time. "If they march, what are we to do?"

Ethan shook his head. "I don't know. I wish I could talk with Adams and Hancock about this. Have they left Boston?"

It was Andrew who answered. "When all the activity began in the harbor, they finally became convinced it would be wise. Those orders from London to arrest all Whig leaders should be arriving any day. Joseph Bramley is with them, but he is prepared to return to Boston, if you need his assistance."

"I don't believe that will be necessary. He's better off to stay out of the city if he can. It is going to become more and more dangerous to be a Whig in Boston with each day that passes. Already, the tension is thick enough you can almost see it in the air. Where are Adams and Hancock staying, Andrew?"

"Right now, they are in Lexington, at the parsonage."

"Then I must go to Lexington. I'll go on to Concord from there."

Immediately, there were protests from the other three. "Ethan, you could be followed," David told him. Colin said that if Gage's orders came through and he were caught with Adams and Hancock, he would be arrested as well. Andrew pointed out that if the city gates at Boston Neck were closed in his absence, he could be prevented from returning.

"I know there are risks," he said, cutting through their protests in a voice like steel. "There are always risks. I'm going anyway. I must sit down with Samuel and John so that we can discuss what happens if Gage's troops march. Concord will need to be warned. Powder and ammunition will need to be moved. I don't want to trust this information to a courier. I'm going myself."

"What do you want us to do while you are away?" Colin asked him.

"Colin, I want you to keep a close eye on activity in the harbor. Being a fisherman, you won't cause suspicion if you do. Andrew, you meet with Paul Revere often in the Green Dragon. I want you to talk with him and determine ways to warn the countryside if the troops march on Concord. My opinion is that a system of couriers would be best. These couriers could ride through Massachusetts by various routes and raise the militia."

"Paul is of the same opinion."

"Good. Figure out a way to make it work. If they do march, send Paul to bring the word to Concord. David, I want you to see what you can find out in the taverns. Send Daniel if you have to, and see what Dorothy and Joshua have heard at the White Swan."

The three other men at the table nodded their heads in agreement, and all of them stood up to leave. "I'll ride to Lexington tomorrow night. If you hear anything before then, let me know as soon as possible."

David laid a hand on his shoulder. "Ethan, this could be dangerous. I would hate to see you arrested if those orders come through. Keep your wits about you."

"I always do, my friend. I always do."

During the two weeks that had followed her meeting with Lowden, Katie had been given plenty of time to think about the choice she had made. Lowden had given her a reprieve, and Ethan seemed inclined to do the same, for she neither saw nor heard from him during the fortnight following the ball.

She tried to tell herself that it was all for the best. After all, she already knew she had no future with Ethan, and once his purchase of her indenture was arranged and she was free, she would have to run as far from Lowden as she could. There was no way she could find proof of Holbrook's sedition, since he was wholly innocent, and without that proof, Lowden would surely have her arrested, unless she was able to escape before he could exercise the warrant he had against her. She knew that once she left Boston, she would be on the run from Lowden for the rest of her life, but she did not regret her choice. She had not betrayed Ethan, and that was all that mattered.

Katie spent her days in the Boston shops and her evenings wrapped in the comfort of a warm house, delicious food, scented baths, and a soft bed, but somehow these luxurious comforts she had enjoyed so much in the beginning no longer gave her the pleasure they once had. The only pleasure she truly had was Meg, who was growing from a little ball of fluff into a bigger ball of fluff, and because the animal had been a gift from Ethan, Meg was a bittersweet reminder to her of the wonderful moments she'd had with him. Only a fortnight without seeing him, and she missed him terribly.

Every morning for the past two weeks, she had waited anxiously for the post, hoping there would be a note from Ethan requesting her assistance on some adventure, but the days had come and gone with no word from him at all, and with each day that passed, she missed him more and more.

After fifteen days, she had been unable to stand it any longer, and she had finally sent him an invitation to supper and chess with her for that night. To her surprise, he came, but, to her chagrin, he said very little. He was polite, cool, and very distant. It was as if their adventures together had never happened, as if they had returned to being mistrustful strangers, as if the night they made love had never been. She saw no desire in his eyes, no welcome in his smile, no enjoyment in being with her.

Katie studied him across the chess table from beneath her lashes. He wore no wig, and his black hair was caught back in a simple queue at his neck. It gleamed in the candlelight like a raven's wing, and she remembered how the strands had felt like silk in her fists.

She watched him as he contemplated his next move, and she contemplated hers as well. Somehow, after their night together, the events at Province House, and a separation of more than two weeks, a wall had come between them. She should be glad of it, she supposed. She should be grateful he did not expect her to help him spy on the Tories any longer, for she did not relish being caught between Ethan and the viscount at some party or assembly. She should thank the heavens above he did not want her anymore, for she had meant her words to him that she would not lead the life her mother had. If this wall remained between them, he would never learn of her duplicity. He did not love her, but if he never discovered her secret, at least he would not hate her, either.

Katie told herself all of these things over and over as they played out their chess game in silence, but none of it proved to be any comfort. Finally, she could stand it no longer.

"Why haven't you come to see me?" she asked him, breaking the silence between them that had lasted at least half an hour.

He did not look up from the board, but she saw his hand tighten around his glass of brandy. "I have been quite occupied with business matters, my dear," he said, and pushed his rook two spaces forward.

"Don't you need my help any more?"

He leaned back and slowly raised his gaze to hers as he lifted his brandy snifter to his lips. "I told you, you have fulfilled your part of our bargain. Helping me now is not required." He took a sip of brandy and gestured to the board. "It is your move."

Katie glanced down, moved a pawn, and refused to be diverted from the subject. "I know it isn't required, Ethan," she said softly, "but you need my help just as much now as you did before. I thought—" She broke off abruptly at the coolness in his gray eyes, eyes that had looked at her with burning desire two weeks before. She took a deep breath. "I thought you might want my help."

"Are you offering it?" He leaned forward, reminding her of her first impression of him, that he was tense as a coiled whip ready to strike. "Are you now embracing the cause of liberty?"

She didn't care about his cause, and she tried not to care about the mockery in his voice that told her he knew that fact perfectly well. She loved him, she wanted to be with him as much as she could before she was forced to leave him, and she knew time was running out. "No," she answered. "It's just that I . . . I've missed our time together."

He shoved back his chair so violently it screeched against the floorboards. He set down his glass and stood up. "I think I should go. It's quite late."

He started past her chair toward the door, but Katie rose and put her hand on his arm to stop him from leaving. Before she could even speak, he pulled his arm free with a savagery that startled her. "Must you torture me?" he said through clenched teeth. "Have you forgotten your words to me about not wanting to become your mother? About not wanting to be a man's mistress?"

Katie was startled by the fierce anger in his voice. "No," she answered calmly. "I have not forgotten. But I—"

"Being my mistress is all that I can offer you. Marriage is out of the question."

His statement seemed so abrupt, Katie shook her head in confusion. She hadn't ever expected him to marry her, and she had told him so. Why did he feel he needed to hammer that fact home? "I know marriage is not possible."

"War is coming," he went on as if she had not spoken, "the future is uncertain, and I have many dangerous responsibilities. Even now, I am getting ready to leave Boston."

"Leave?" Katie was dismayed. "What do you mean, leave?"

"I have business outside the city and will be gone for a week, perhaps two."

"But where are you going?"

"That is not your concern."

"Is it dangerous?" she asked, but before he could answer, she knew from his expression that it was very dangerous indeed.

"It could be. Gage is accelerating his efforts to confiscate our powder. And until England withdraws her troops from Massachusetts or the war begins, I will probably go on many missions just as risky as this one."

"Whatever it is, why do you have to be the one to go?" she cried. "Why you?"

"Because there is no one else able to leave the city who can be trusted."

"But if it is dangerous—"

"I've done many dangerous things before in support of liberty. This is no different."

Katie closed her eyes. *It is different!* she wanted to shout. *It's different because I love you.*

She could not tell him that, not when there was no future in it. "Why?" she asked, despreate to understand. "Why do you do these dangerous things when it seems to be such a hopeless business? Why?"

"Because I believe we all have the right to live within a government that is just and fair."

"And I believe you live in a dream," she shot back. "There is no government that is just and fair."

"That's why we are going to invent a whole new one."

"How on earth are you going to do that? Would you listen to yourself? You talk as if inventing a new government is like inventing a new recipe for lamb stew."

He did not reply, but one corner of his mouth lifted in that half smile that she loved. Just now, however, that smile only fueled her fear. "I do not understand you. Why do you risk your life for something unknown that might happen someday?"

"Of all the people of my acquaintance, I should think you would be best able to understand the appeal of liberty."

"This is not liberty. It is madness."

Ethan put his hands on her shoulders. "Katie, listen to me," he murmured. "I do this because I believe that there is a better way to live than at the whim of another, be he a king or a master, and I am willing to risk my life to find it. I believe that we can create something extraordinary, something that has never been done before—a country where people govern themselves. One where we decide who our leaders will be, one where we can say what we feel and think what we please without fear of reprisal. One where we are not at the mercy of those who know nothing about us."

She could not even conceive of such a thing. Survival was what mattered, not putting yourself in danger for something as nebulous as an ideal. "It all sounds very high-minded, very intellectual and noble," she said, "but you are not doing this for ideals. You are doing all this fighting against the crown because of your father. You want revenge."

Ethan's mouth tightened, but, as always, he was cool, calm, and distant. "That was true at first. But over the years, I have come to realize none of this is about me, or my petty grievances."

"It is still insane. The odds are overwhelmingly against you. You cannot win."

"Sometimes it is more important to pay attention to what is right than to the chance of winning. Besides, as I told Chevain during my meeting with him, we don't have to win. We just have to make them so sick of us they let us go, and that, Katie, is perfectly possible."

She could not win, either, it seemed. "Go, then," she whispered, sick with fear. "I can't stop you, and I won't waste my breath trying."

He met her gaze straight on. "So you see, I am in no position to offer you marriage, Katie, and I know anything less would make you feel degraded."

"Friendship would be perfectly acceptable to

me." That was a lie, but friendship was better than nothing for as long as it might last.

"Friendship? God!" He raked a hand through his hair, pulling it loose from its queue and paying no heed when the wide black ribbon drifted to the floor. "Don't you understand, Katie? I'm trying to be a gentleman, but I'm not made of stone. Don't you realize that all evening I've been fighting to keep myself from touching you?"

He drew a deep breath and stepped back from her before she could recover her surprise enough to reply. "I have given you exactly what you wanted. I sent Adam to Virginia to make the arrangements to purchase your indenture. Once that is done, our bargain will be complete, and you will be free to leave. Before another month has passed, I suspect Boston will be in chaos, so it would be very wise of you to leave as soon as Adam returns from Virginia."

With those words, he turned on his heel and left her. Katie watched him go, and she knew she was crying because she could feel the hot tears on her face. She rubbed her hands across her cheeks to wipe them away, and she hated herself for being so weak, for loving a man who did not love her, could not marry her, and would probably die before the week was out.

By the devil, she could count on one hand the number of times she had cried in her life, but falling in love with Ethan had shattered all her protective barriers. Her armor was gone, and she hated how vulnerable that made her. If he hurt, she hurt. If he died, a part of her would die with him.

The slamming of the front door told her that he was gone, and deep down inside, Katie felt as if she were dying already.

18

𝒥t was nearly midnight the following night when Ethan arrived at the Hancock-Clarke Parsonage in Lexington. It was dawn when he traveled on to Concord, and his six hours at the parsonage were not spent sleeping.

Samuel Adams and John Hancock felt as worried as he by the activity of Regulars in Boston. They were pleased that Ethan's meeting with the French had succeeded so well and were in agreement with him that the cache of munitions stored in Concord must be moved. Thanks to the book of Shakespeare Katie had delivered to Bramley, hiding places for the weaponry had already been prepared. By the time the sun rose, Ethan was speeding his horse down the Lexington Road to Concord.

In that town, locals proved to be angry rather than frightened by the impending conflict and more than willing to help John Smith move their weaponry out of Gage's hands. Nor were they surprised by the news. Gage had already sent several of his men to the town on secret missions of reconnaissance to map out the roads and locate powder stores, and since that sort of news always leaked out, Gage's spies had been spotted for the redcoats they were almost immediately.

Ethan spent the next two days helping the citizens of Concord move their munitions. It was a slow process, for the supplies had to be scattered throughout the surrounding communities in small loads. That way, Gage's troops couldn't possibly get their hands on all of it. Activity in Concord and the anger of the locals increased to a frenzy when Paul Revere came with the news that Gage's troops would march on the town the following day.

"Trust the redcoats to make war on the Sabbath," one gnarled old farmer growled to Ethan over a pint of ale at Brook's Tavern in Lincoln, where they had just deposited a pair of cannon in the local granary. "Godless, I call it."

"They did it at Salem," the barmaid reminded them, setting another tray of ale on the table. "Marched into that town on the Sabbath day."

Ethan listened as outraged locals discussed every sinful, evil act ever committed by the king's troops, and the strength of their resentment only confirmed Ethan's belief that there was no going back. War was inevitable now.

Stories of the king's atrocities, many of them highly exaggerated, flowed through the taproom as quickly as the ale, but when the door opened and two strangers entered the tavern, the resentful voices faded to quiet murmurs. The two seemed harmless enough, dressed as they were in the rough garb of country farmers, but with Gage's spies combing the countryside and troops ready to march, suspicion quieted the tongue of every person in the room.

When Ethan saw the faces of the two men by the door, he knew their mistrust of these two strangers was justified. One of the men was Lieutenant Charles Weston.

Ethan turned his face away and leaned closer to old Farmer Hampton. "Those are redcoats," he said softly as the two men called for the barmaid to bring ale and food. "Spies for Gage. One of them knows me, and I fear I must leave. Is there a way out the back?"

"Aye." The farmer rolled his eyes toward the back of the taproom. "That door goes through the kitchen and out to the stables. Get your horse and ride. I'll meet you in Concord tomorrow."

Ethan nodded and rose from his chair. Hoping Weston was too preoccupied with the charms of the pretty, pink-cheeked barmaid to notice him, he made for the door Farmer Hampton had indicated. He slipped out the back and crossed the barnyard, making his way through the muck by moonlight, but he had barely made it halfway to the stables before a warning shout and the crack of a pistol broke the stillness of the night. He thought he heard the outraged voice of Farmer Hampton just as a searing pain sliced across the side of his head. He was unconscious before he hit the ground.

Katie had no idea how long Ethan would be gone, but her worry for his safety escalated with every moment he was absent. Two months ago, she wouldn't have spared any man a second thought, but she was not the same woman who had arrived in Boston two months ago. She was a woman in love.

After seven days with no word from him and seven nights of waiting for him in vain, she could not stand the suspense. She had to see if anyone knew his whereabouts.

She tried the Mermaid first, but David was not at home that evening, and Molly had heard no word from Ethan at all. She studied Katie's face for several seconds, then said, "My girl, there's no sense in worrying. Worry never did a soul any good at all. Besides, Ethan's done this sort of thing many times before, and nothing has ever happened to him."

"Is that supposed to make me feel better?" Katie asked, sinking into one of the chairs in the kitchen.

"No, but I have something that might." Molly poured a dollop of rum into a mug and handed it to her. "Get that down, and it'll calm your nerves. You look all in."

Katie swallowed the rum and choked as the burning liquid seared her throat. After a few moments, she gave a shaky laugh. "It didn't help, Molly. I'm still worried to death."

Leaning forward, she rested her elbows on the table and cradled her head in her hands. "This is the first time in my life I've ever done this," she confessed without lifting her head.

"Done what?"

"Worried about someone else more than myself." It was a painful admission to make. She straightened and looked the other woman in the eye. "I'm not handling it very well, I'm afraid."

Molly did not look at all surprised. "With the life you've had, that's understandable. I know, because I led that life myself. I was an orphan. I stole on the streets in Glasgow and got shipped here for my trouble. That was before I met David, and once I met him, everything changed for me."

She reached out and laid her hand over Katie's. "I know what it's like to always look after yourself first because that's the only thing you can do, I know how you're always afraid to think about anyone else. But then one thing happens, and everything you thought about life goes by the wayside. Everything is different when you fall in love with a man."

Katie sucked in a sharp breath and drew her hand away. "What makes you think that?"

"Katie, girl, it's written on your face. Ethan once told me you were an excellent liar and not to believe a word out of your mouth, but there's some things a woman can't hide. Love is one of them."

She was unaccustomed to being so transparent, but she did not bother to deny what Molly said. It was the truth, and she was so sick of lies. Her shoulders slumped, and she lowered her gaze to the table. "Aye," she confessed, "I love him. A precious lot of good it does me."

"People never fall in love because it's good for them. They just fall in love."

"What Ethan loves is his cause."

"Aye." Molly smiled at Katie with affection. "Didn't I tell you he wasn't the man to set your cap for?"

"You did, but it's too late to remedy that now." Katie rose from the table, and memories of the exploits and the laughter she and Ethan had shared flashed through her mind. "Strangely enough, Molly, I wouldn't go back and follow your advice even if I could."

She started to turn away, but Molly's words made her pause. "Katie, you might try the White Swan. It's possible Dorothy or Joshua have heard some news of him."

She nodded and left the Mermaid. She stopped at her house to tell Stephens where she would be. Even though it was probably silly to think Ethan would return from his mission in the next few hours, and it was probably futile to believe he would come to her when he did return, she wanted him to be able to find her. Just in case.

The White Swan was as crowded with soldiers as it had been during Katie's first visit. But she did not see Weston among the redcoats in the taproom, and she felt reasonably safe entering the tavern.

Joshua was tapping ale for a group of thirsty officers, and Dorothy was nowhere in sight.

Aware of the possibility that Weston could make
an appearance, Katie chose a seat at a table close to
the door leading into the kitchen and tried to be patient as she waited for an opportunity to speak with
Joshua alone.

Dorothy passed her from the kitchen with a tray
of meat pies without noticing her, and Katie did not
call to her. She knew from their first meeting that
Dorothy did not like her or trust her, and she
would much prefer to speak with Joshua.

But Dorothy deposited the tray of food before a
table of soldiers, and when she turned around to return to the kitchen, she caught sight of Katie sitting
there. She gave her no welcoming smile, but she did
approach the table, and there was an anxious look
in her eyes by the time she reached Katie's side.

"Why are you here?" she asked. "Have you
heard from Ethan? Is he well?"

"I don't know," Katie replied. "That's why I've
come to you. I was hoping you had heard something of him."

"No, I have heard nothing." The barmaid's
shoulders slumped a bit. "But then, you would
know any knews of him before I would," she said,
sounding suddenly bitter. "You are his mistress, are
you not?"

Katie opened her mouth to reply, but a face in
the crowd by the door caught her eye, and she forgot whatever answer she had intended to give the

barmaid. Captain Worth stood just inside the tavern door, scanning the crowd as if looking for someone in particular. Katie could not help the curse that sprang from her lips. "God's blood," she muttered, "when will this nightmare end?"

"If you find it such a nightmare," Dorothy said, "perhaps it would be wise of you to leave."

Katie paid no attention to the barmaid's acerbic words. She started to her feet, thinking to run out the back, but Worth caught sight of her, and it was too late to run. He started toward her table, and she sank back down in her chair, wondering what he was thinking to approach her so openly.

Dorothy noticed that Katie was paying no attention to her, and she glanced over her shoulder to see whom Katie was staring at so intensely. Katie improvised an explanation. "There's that dreadful Captain Worth, the redcoat who accused me of stealing his watch," she whispered.

"You stole Captain Worth's watch?"

"Ethan didn't tell you about it?"

Dorothy shook her head. "Ethan does not confide in me," she said, and again Katie caught the bitterness in her voice.

She wanted to assure the other woman that, mistress or no, Ethan didn't confide in her, either, but Worth was approaching, and since she did not know his purpose, she wanted Dorothy gone. "You'd best go about your business. If Worth arrests me for theft, I wouldn't want him to think you know me."

Dorothy seemed to agree, for she started to depart, but Worth reached them before she could leave, and he greeted the barmaid with obvious pleasure. "Mistress Macalvey," he said, removing his hat and giving her a long, lingering glance of masculine appreciation as he bowed. "It is a delight to see you."

To Katie's astonishment, Dorothy smiled back at him. But perhaps it was not so astonishing, since the barmaid was also one of Ethan's spies. "A pleasure to see you as well, Captain. You would like ale, of course?"

"It astonishes me that you remember what I drink, ma'am. You have so many to serve."

Dorothy slanted him a look that was openly flirtatious. "It is good that the king's soldiers are here to provide us with protection," she said. "My brother and I profit by it in more ways than one."

"Indeed, and I can assure you that we do our best to see that the streets are safe and the taverns prosperous."

Katie moved restlessly in her chair as the other two exchanged bantering small talk. What did Worth want of her that he made a point to come to her table? He must have a purpose, but she could not imagine what it might be.

Finally, Dorothy departed to fetch the captain a tankard of ale, and Worth sat down opposite Katie. "Good evening, Mrs. Armstrong."

"Are you mad?" she whispered "To come to me so openly?"

"What of it? This is a Tory tavern. Do you expect Whig spies to be lurking about watching you?"

That was exactly what she expected, but Worth, of course, did not know that the Macalveys were truly Whigs. "It is always possible," she said in a cool voice that belied her anxiety. "I assume you have a reason for coming to my table?"

"I do." She watched as the captain pulled a letter from his pocket. "I came to your house to give you this, and I was told by your butler that you were here. It is from Lowden, and he is quite put out that you have not been to the marketplace these past two Saturdays."

He slid the letter to Katie across the table. She snatched it up and thrust it into the deep pocket of her cloak just before Dorothy returned with two tankards of ale. The barmaid placed them on the table. "There you be, Captain," she said, and left them once again.

To Katie's surprise, Worth's glance lingered on the barmaid as she walked away. "What a lovely woman," he murmured under his breath. As if suddenly realizing he had expressed his admiration aloud, Worth frowned and returned his attention to her. "I'm sure Lowden wants a meeting with you, and that is one appointment you'd best keep, little thief. Or you'll find yourself in a cell at Castle William."

His warning was unnecessary, and the note he had given her felt heavy as a stone in her pocket. If

Lowden wanted a meeting with her, surely he could have chosen a safer method of demanding it than a letter that could fall into the hands of anyone.

Katie rose to her feet and gathered her cloak around her. "I have no doubt the idea of me in gaol pleases you enormously, Captain," she said coldly. "But I have no intention of doing so to please you."

She left the White Swan, and she did not pull the letter out of her pocket until she was safely home. She read it in the parlor, where there was a fire burning in the hearth and she could burn the note afterward.

It contained no surprises. In fact, it was exactly what Worth had told her. The viscount demanded a meeting with her. He reminded her that she had only seven more days to gain proof against Holbrook, and she was expected to be at the Stag and Steed one week from tonight at midnight to hand it over. Katie muttered an oath, crumpled the parchment into a ball, and tossed it onto the fire. As if she needed reminders from him.

She watched the letter burn to ashes, wishing the man who had written it a similar fate. But she had the sickening feeling the viscount was not going to die and burn in hellfire before next week. She couldn't possibly be that lucky.

Dorothy studied Captain Worth in the White Swan without seeming to do so, and she wondered what on earth he had been doing talking to Katie. He had walked right over to her table, sat down with her, had a drink with her. And what was he doing passing her letters across the table?

Oh, yes, she had seen it with her own eyes. Worth had given Katie a note, and though Katie had snatched it up from the table quickly enough, Dorothy had seen it clearly, a folded sheet of parchment slipped into Katie's cloak. Nor had Dorothy missed the other woman's guilty glance around the room. What was it? A love letter? A Tory secret? Either way, it only confirmed Dorothy's suspicions that Katie was not what she seemed. The girl might be having a love affair with the British officer. Or, worse, she might be a Loyalist informant. If that were so, Ethan was in grave danger.

Ethan. Heavens, it hurt to think of him at this moment, not knowing where he was, if he were safe. For seven days, she had been waiting with all the concern Katie only pretended to have for word that he had returned. And it was pretend. Dorothy didn't believe for a moment Katie's concern was genuine. How could it be, when she met with a British officer in a tavern taproom?

But Dorothy also knew Ethan desired Katie. She had known that the moment she met the other woman. It was obvious in the way Ethan had looked at her that he wanted her. It was also plain to see that she was playing him for a fool, spending his money, buying clothes, going to parties.

When it came to Katie, Ethan was blind, Dorothy thought angrily. Blinded by a pretty face and a talent for deceit. She had never trusted that girl. Never. She had warned Ethan about her that night, but he had not listened. He had made that girl a trusted comrade. He even pretended the girl was his mistress as a ruse so that she could help him spy on the Tories.

But was it pretense? Surely, Ethan would not have a mistress, especially not one so thin, so brash, so deceitful. If Ethan had needed a woman to play the part of his mistress, why hadn't he chosen her? Why had he given that assignment to a virtual stranger, when she, Dorothy, was perfectly capable of handling such an assignment?

She had always been there for Ethan, ready and willing to do whatever he asked, be whatever he wanted. She would have played the part and would have done it willingly, had Ethan wanted her to do so, but he had not. Despite her loyalty, despite her sacrifices for him and everything she had done for him, Ethan did not love her. He did not want her. He wanted instead a pickpocket, a common street thief who accepted mysterious letters from redcoat officers.

She had to tell Ethan about that letter as soon as he returned, and then his feelings would change about his little pickpocket. Oh, yes, they would.

Sudden doubt flickered through her mind. Would he believe her about the letter? Ethan might realize her feelings for him and conclude she was lying about the letter out of spite. He might take Katie's side. Then what would she do?

That girl could betray him at any moment, lead him into a trap, get him arrested and hanged. Dorothy knew she had to convince him of Katie's duplicity. Somehow, some way. But she didn't know enough. She needed more information.

Ribald laughter interrupted her thoughts, drawing her attention to the group of redcoats seated around a large table on the other side of the taproom. Captain Worth had moved to their table and was sitting with them. An idea flashed though her mind.

"Ethan, you're blind," she whispered. "Katie is not what she seems. I know it, and I'm going to make you see the truth about her. By the time you return from Concord, I'm going to have evidence of her treachery."

She ran her hands through her hair and pulled the top of her chemise down a bit lower to reveal as much cleavage as she dared. She donned a clean apron, then filled a tankard with the tavern's finest ale. Tankard in hand, she crossed the room to where the group of officers sat laughing and talking.

The group of officers looked up as she approached, and the exaggerated sway of her hips caused more than a few of them to stare at her in open appreciation. But Dorothy kept her gaze fixed on only one man. Giving him her prettiest smile, she set the tankard before him on the table. She slid sensuously onto his lap and put her arms around his neck. "So, Captain Worth," she murmured, her lips brushing his ear, "tell me again what a pleasure it is to see me."

Katie spent the evening sitting in the parlor, waiting as she had every night for more than a week. She sat in the dark after the servants had gone to bed, listening for the sound of Ethan's carriage or the sound of his footsteps coming up the walk. But, as on every other of the past seven nights, the only sound she heard was the rhythmic tick of the clock that finally dulled her senses enough for her to fall asleep.

But this night proved to be different from the previous ones. When the latch on the front door clicked, Katie was instantly awake. She sat up on the settee, turning toward the doorway of the parlor. In the light of the candle that burned on the table beside her, she saw a tall, dark shadow standing by the door, a shadow she instantly recognized.

"Ethan!" She jumped to her feet, and she could hear herself gasping with relief as she ran to him.

His cloak was torn and dusty, his hat was gone, beard stubble covered his face, and he looked as if he'd had a long, hard ride. She reached out, touching him, running her hands over him to be sure he was real. "You're alive," she murmured over and over again. "Thank God, you're alive."

"I am very much alive," he answered in a weary voice, "though there was a moment when some had cause to wonder."

Katie stilled, her hands on his chest, and looked up at him. "What do you mean? Where have you been all this time? What—" She broke off, suddenly noticing the deep, angry gash across his temple. "Ethan, you've been hurt," she breathed, touching her fingertips gently to his temple. "What happened to you?"

He didn't answer. Instead, he gazed down at her for a long moment without speaking. In the candlelight, Katie saw something come into his eyes, something she could not define, something hard and fierce and hungry.

His silence alarmed her. Slowly, she lowered her hand from his forehead. "Ethan, say something. What happened? Are you all right?"

He did not answer. His manner was so odd, fierce and yet restrained, as if he were making a great effort to hold back some powerful emotion. Silence hummed between them for a long time before he finally spoke. When he did, it was not what she expected. " 'Tis incredible," he murmured, "how a man's thoughts change when he has escaped a close brush with death. Everything falls into place. Everything is given its true importance."

"Death? What do you mean?"

He reached out and laid his palm against her cheek. "I mean, I was shot. By our dear friend Weston."

"You've been shot?" Panic flooded through her, and her voice rose frantically. "By Weston? Ethan, for God's sake, are you all right?"

"There I was," he told her, "in a tavern outside Concord, having a pint of ale and an enjoyable evening, when who should walk in but our dear friend, the lieutenant." One corner of his mouth turned upward in that wry, one-sided smile she loved. "Can you believe it? Of all the officers for Gage to send on a mission, it had to be Weston."

"And he shot you?"

"I tried to slip out the back, but Weston recognized me and followed me out. Before anyone could stop him, he pulled his pistol out of his coat and took a potshot at me. Since he saw my Liberty medal that night at the White Swan, and I was now running away from him, he obviously shot me thinking he was doing his duty to king and country. The idiot. He got tarred and feathered by a few of the locals for his trouble, I'm told."

"But what happened to you?"

"The bullet skimmed the side of my head, that's all. It knocked me senseless. One of the farmers took me to his home, and his wife dressed the wound. When I woke up, I found myself lying in a farmhouse bed, with a nightmare of a headache and a concussion. It's taken me two days to recover enough to get on a horse and get back."

He lifted his hand and touched her face. "When I awoke in that farmhouse, do you know what the first thing was I thought about? Not Gage's mission in Concord," he confessed, his fingertips caressing her cheek. "Not where to hide all the powder in Lexington or the fact that we are about to go to war with our countrymen. No, I was not thinking about any of that."

Though she did not know anything of Gage's mission or powder in Lexington, she did know how hard Ethan's heart was pounding beneath her hand. "What were you thinking about, then?" she whispered.

His fingertips slid from her cheek into her hair, and he tilted her head back. "You," he said simply, his gaze scanning her face with a hungry ferocity that almost frightened her. "I thought I might never see you again. I love you."

19

$\mathcal{H}$e heard her breath catch, felt her lithe body tense, sensed her withdrawal. Grasping her shoulders, he said, "I mean it, Katie. You are mine. I won't let you go, ever."

She shook her head. "Ethan—"

"We're getting married." He cut her off before she could deny him. "You'll not be my mistress, you'll be my wife. You'll share the future with me, no matter what it is."

"It's impossible," she said, that jaded note in her voice. "It'll never work. I'm a street thief, and you're a gentleman. These things don't happen."

"Oh, yes, they do, my little thief." He pulled her against him roughly, kissed her hard, and pulled back. "Oh, yes, they do. Because when I saw you in North Square that morning two months ago, you stole not only two meat pies, a merchant's watch, and a redcoat's purse, you stole my soul. You stole my heart. And you can't give them back."

He caught a fleeting glimpse of something—
pain, perhaps—in her expression. She buried her
face against his chest, but her body was rigid in his
arms.

"Are you crying again?"

She shook her head. "No," she mumbled against
his dusty shirtfront. "But you don't understand. It
can't happen. I can't marry you. Ethan, you don't
know the things I've done—"

"I don't care." He pulled her chin up. "I love
you."

"You don't even know me." She jerked her chin
sideways, but he would not let her look away. He
held her chin fast in his fingers.

"I love you," he repeated, and kissed her again,
gently this time. "You don't believe me?" he asked
against her mouth.

"You might think you love me now," she said,
"tonight, but you don't. Ethan, I—"

"Do you love me?" The question was abrupt, demanding, but he'd have no subtle word dances
here. "Do you?"

She didn't answer. She simply raised her eyes
and looked at him. He could read nothing there.

Ethan didn't wait for her to evade the question.
"I can see I'll have to get my answer another way."
He grabbed her hand and started for the stairs,
pulling her with him.

She did not resist but came willingly, and he
knew it was not her body she held back from him
but her heart. As much as he wanted her body, he

wanted her heart even more. And, by God, he would have it before this night was over.

Inside her room, he shut the door behind him, took her into his arms, and kissed her again. "Do you love me?"

She kissed him back, but she did not answer his question. He turned her around and unfasted the buttons down the back of her dress. With each one, he could hear her agitated breathing, he could feel her holding back a part of herself. He knew why she had put it between them, but he was not going to let her keep up that wall. Whatever she had seen or done in her life, he didn't care. She was his, and that was all that mattered. "Do you love me?"

He pulled the dress from her shoulders and down her arms. It caught at the flare of her hips, and he left it there for the moment. He pulled the laces from her corset, one eyelet at a time, and he could feel her body tremble. He tossed her corset aside. "I'll have your answer. Do you love me?"

She shook her head from side to side, but she did not speak. He pulled off her chemise and trailed wet kisses down her spine that made her shiver as he fell to his knees behind her. He untied the ribbon at the top of her petticoat, then grasped the soft folds of both her dress and petticoat in his hands and yanked them down to fall in a swirl of dark wool and white linen around her ankles. He removed her drawers, pulling the linen past her hips and down her legs, revealing her soft, creamy skin.

Fully aroused, Ethan's body was already taut as a bowstring with the effort of holding his need for her in check, and the sight of her bare, shapely buttocks and long legs was almost his undoing. Her body was ready for him, all his instincts told him that, and it took every ounce of discipline he had not simply to stand up and take possession of her then and there. But first he would hear her say she loved him.

He sat back on his heels, closed his eyes, and drew a deep breath. He let it out slowly, striving for control, struggling for patience. *Wait,* he told himself desperately. *Wait a little longer.*

"Ethan?"

He opened his eyes and looked up to find that she had turned slightly and was studying him over her shoulder, a puzzled frown on her face at his sudden hesitation. Grasping her naked hips in his hands, he leaned forward to press a kiss to the luscious dent at the base of her spine. "Do you love me? I'll have those words from you, by God, if I have to steal them."

"Bloody hell, Ethan," she cried, vexed by his persistence. "You sound like a thief." She tried to pull away, clearly not liking this game, but he grasped her hips and held her there, kissing the small of her back.

"I'll have you say it, Katie."

He slid one hand to the front of her body, spreading his fingers across her stomach to caress her there, as he slid the palm of his other hand down the outside of her thigh to her knee. He pressed kisses up and down her spine as he unfastened the garter that held up her right stocking and pulled the wisp of knitted silk down to her ankle. She lifted her foot, and he removed her stocking, garter, and slipper in one swift motion. He cast them aside, then repeated the move with her other stocking. He rose to his feet, put his hands on her shoulders, and turned her around to face him.

She grasped handfuls of his shirt in her fists and tugged upward, pulling the white linen over his head. Standing on tiptoe, she kissed him fully, leaning into him, and he could feel the tips of her breasts brush his chest. When she pulled back, she met his gaze, and her fingers began to unbutton his breeches.

He could feel her knuckles brush against him as she unfastened his breeches, and he sucked in his breath sharply, let it out slowly. "Oh, God."

Katie started to kneel so that she might pull the black fabric down his hips, but he grasped her wrists to stop her. "Do you love me? Do you?"

She didn't answer. His hand slid into her hair, held her still, and he began trailing soft kisses along her jaw, her throat, her ear. "You love me, I know it. Say it."

A soft moan escaped her, but she still did not give him what he wanted. His hands cupped her breasts, caressed her body, pushed her gently back onto the bed. He stripped himself of boots, breeches, and linen and covered her body with his own. He slid his hands beneath her buttocks and entered her.

She gasped his name as her body yielded to his, but it was not his name he wanted to hear. He began to move within her, a slow slide and thrust that turned her gasps to quick pants. Her hips rocked against his, urgent now, wanting completion, but nothing would be complete until he had the one thing she kept from him. "Do you love me, Katie?"

"Ethan, oh, oh, please." Whimpered, frantic words but not the right ones.

He clenched his teeth, keeping back his climax with all the will he had. He repeated his question with each hard thrust he made into her, relentless. "You love me. Say it, admit it. You love me."

He couldn't do it. Once more, and he wouldn't be able to hold back. He surged into her again.

She arched up to meet him, and the words came tumbling out between soft cries of feminine release. "Yes, Ethan, yes. I love you, I love you. Please. I love you."

He climaxed inside her, a shuddering, explosive release. Now, now, he had her heart. He had wanted it, taken it, claimed it as his own, He laughed, remembering how she'd called him a thief. He wrapped his arms around her and held her tight. She might have called him a thief, but damn it all, he felt like a pirate.

Ethan was unaware that he had fallen asleep until he awakened, but even without opening his eyes, he knew that Katie was still lying beside him. He could feel her there, the slender shape of her body pressed against his side, her head pillowed on his outstretched arm. He could smell the warm, enticing female fragrance of her skin and hear the soft, even cadence of her breathing. She loved him.

He opened his eyes. The candle was out, but the soft gray light of early morning filtered in around the shuttered windows. Turning his head, he saw that Katie was still asleep, eyes closed, lips slightly parted, and the sight of her sent lust coursing through his body. Her profile in the dim light was exquisitely beautiful, and yet it was not her beauty that reignited his desire, it was memories of the night that came flooding back at the sight of her beside him.

Those memories overwhelmed his senses: the taste of her mouth, the touch of her hands, the feel of her skin, the sounds of her passion. Most of all, the sweet, erotic admission she had made. She loved him. Lust rocked through him, and he moved toward her, intending to kiss her awake.

The sound of a raised male voice and frantic footsteps on the stairs gave him pause, and the tap on the door told him that his intentions for Katie would have to wait. He lifted his head and saw the maid, Janie, peering timidly into the room. Their eyes met, and she blushed crimson at the sight of him in her mistress's bed. She lowered her gaze with a bobbing curtsy. "If you please, sir," she whispered. "A gentleman by the name of David Munro is below and says he has to see you at once."

Ethan did not ask why. If David had come to Katie's house in search of him, it had to be important. He rolled out of bed, causing Katie to make a soft sound of protest in her sleep, but she did not awaken, and Ethan decided it would be best to let her sleep. He dressed quickly, but he did pause long enough to lean over the bed and press a kiss to her lips before he left her.

The owner of the Mermaid was waiting for him at the bottom of the stairs. "Do you want to talk here?" David asked, glancing through the open doorway into the parlor, where Stephens was busily polishing silver.

"Not if it's important enough to bring you here at dawn to find me." Ethan pulled his dusty cloak from the coat tree and started toward the back door of the house.

"Glad to see you're back from the country," David commented as they left Katie's house and began walking toward the alley and the Mermaid Tavern beyond.

"How did you know I'd returned?"

"Nothing's ever a secret for long in Boston. Joseph came to see me this morning. He also saw Joshua. He told us both that the two of you rode back together late last night. With all that's been happening this morning, I sent Daniel to your house, but your servants told him you had not returned. I guessed you might be with a certain pickpocket we both know, but I didn't know for certain until her little maid came scurrying down the stairs red as a beet to confirm it."

They crossed the alley and entered the tavern. "What has you in such a stir, David?" he asked, giving Molly a nod of greeting as they passed through the kitchen. "What has been happening this morning to cause so much urgency?"

"A great deal," David answered as they crossed the taproom, empty at this hour of the day. "Adam Lawrence is here. He returned from Virginia yesterday. Joseph is also here, as I said. I'll let them tell you."

When they entered the tavern's private meeting room, Adam cast only one glance at him and immediately grinned. "You look like hell," he said, taking in Ethan's dusty, rumpled clothes and unshaven face. "What happened to your head?"

He touched the side of his face with a grimace. "It's a long story." He glanced at Joseph. "Did you tell them the troops did not march on Sunday as we'd thought?"

Joseph smiled. "How would you know?" he joked. "You slept through the whole day."

"What do you mean, he slept all day?" Adam glanced from one man to the other.

"It's a long story. Suffice to say I've been in Concord for a week helping move ammunition. Joseph has been doing the same in Lexington. From all the activity we were seeing among the regiments and in the harbor last week, we assumed the Regulars were coming out to confiscate the powder, and the rumor was they would march to Concord on Sunday. They did not."

"But they will," David said. "That's why we fetched you. They are going to march. We just got the date wrong."

Ethan sat down at the table, and the others followed suit. "How do you know this?" he asked.

"People have been coming in and out of the Mermaid for the past hour with reports about the behavior of Gage's troops. They are doing just what they did last week, only more of it. They aren't being very subtle about it."

"They don't have to be. They think they have all the power, and by showing it, they hope to intimidate us. But do we know it's real this time?" Ethan asked. "We could be jumping the gun again when it's nothing but a sham."

Joseph shook his head. "Most of the dockside whores are Yankee girls, God bless them. They are getting word from seamen coming ashore on errands for Admiral Graves and others that something big is coming within a week. It has to be the Concord march."

Ethan nodded. "I agree. And they'll march by the Lexington Road. It's far and away the best route for a regiment on the move. The question, then, is when they plan to do it. I'll see what I can find out. If—"

A knock came at the door, and Dorothy Macalvey entered the room and closed the door behind her. "I apologize for interrupting, gentlemen, but it's important."

She nodded to Adam and David, whom she

knew, then turned to Ethan. She smiled uncertainly. "It's good to know you're back safe. I'm sorry to come here, but I'm sure I wasn't followed, and I heard from Joshua that you were back in Boston."

"Like I said," David murmured, "nothing stays a secret for long."

Dorothy stood there, twisting her hands together in agitation. "Ethan, I need to speak with you right away. It's important."

"Is it about what's going on with the regiments?" he asked. "Have you heard something?"

She shook her head. "No. I mean, I have been hearing rumors for days that the Regulars are coming out, but that isn't what I need to talk with you about." She glanced at the other men in the room and hesitated. "It's something else."

"Can it wait until tonight? I've got so much to do here."

She bit her lip, clearly not liking the delay. But after a moment, she agreed. "Very well."

"Good. I'll come to the White Swan."

Dorothy nodded and left them, closing the door behind her.

"Is it wise of you to go to the White Swan?" Adam asked. "After all, the last time you were there, Lieutenant Weston—"

Joseph started to laugh. "I don't believe Lieutenant Weston will be able to do much of anything for at least a few more days. He should be making his way through the muck of the Sudbury Marshes right about now."

Ethan grinned. "He's probably lost."

Adam and David looked at the other two in complete bewilderment. It was Ethan who told them the story.

"I was in Lincoln hiding cannon with the farmers, and Weston walked in, along with another fellow. They were both dressed in the clothes of country farmers, but, of course, I knew they were officers, probably sent by Gage on another of these reconnaissance missions. After our little encounter at the White Swan, I didn't know if he would recognize me, but I decided not to give him the opportunity. I slipped out the back door of Brook's Tavern, but he had already spied me and came after me, brandishing his pistol. He took a potshot at me before anyone could stop him, and the bullet grazed the side of my head. I was knocked unconscious, but I was not seriously hurt. Some of the locals overpowered him, tarred and feathered him, and dropped him off in the Sudbury Marshes late last night. He probably won't be back in Boston for at least three more days."

All of them laughed, enjoying the story, but after a few minutes, Ethan brought their attention back to the subject at hand. "If the Regulars are still going to march on Concord, we have to learn when that will be, if we can. Perhaps Dorothy will know something by tonight. David, do you know if Andrew talked with Paul Revere about a system of couriers?"

"Yes, and I believe they have worked out a plan."

"I am meeting with Paul this morning," Joseph said. "I will find out what system has been planned, and I will let you know as soon as possible."

"Excellent."

The meeting was adjourned. David returned to the taproom to begin getting ready for the day ahead. Joseph departed for his meeting with Paul Revere. Adam started to leave the room as well, but Ethan detained him. "Did you make the arrangements with Willoughby in Virginia?"

"Aye. The papers are signed, and I put them on your desk at home. He didn't want to sell her indenture, but I raised the price until he agreed. It was a great deal of money."

Ethan didn't care about that. "Good work, Adam. Thank you."

Adam looked at him curiously. "For a man who is alive when by all rights he should be dead, who had to be dragged out of the arms of a beautiful woman this morning, and who is seeing ten years of hard work coming to fruition, you don't look very happy."

"I'm not happy. If our information is accurate and the troops do march, it will mean war."

"Of course. It's happening, Ethan. Everything we've waited ten years for is coming at last." He began to laugh, but he caught Ethan's expression, and his laughter faded immediately. "Why do you look so grim?"

Ethan looked back at Adam with sadness. "War is grim, my friend," he said. "Very grim indeed."

20

By the time Ethan reached the White Swan, he had heard confirming reports from at least two dozen people—troops all over Boston were preparing for something serious. Though he had been unable to find an excuse to call on Lord Percy or William Holbrook, Ethan had heard from two other informants at Province House that afternoon that preparations on land and in the harbor meant Gage's troops were going to march on Concord.

But when? Ethan wondered as he entered the taproom of the White Swan. He had to find out.

Though he was fully occupied with thoughts of war throughout the day, vivid memories of the night before flashed across his mind at unexpected moments. Every time Katie stole into his thoughts, he pushed those thoughts away, for they were distracting him from what he needed to be thinking about.

Dorothy saw him come into the tavern, but she

was busy serving ale to the soldiers crowded into the place. Forced to wait, Ethan took a seat at a table in the corner and allowed his mind the luxury he had denied himself throughout the day, memories of Katie warm and passionate in his arms, of her whispered confession. She loved him. He still couldn't quite believe it.

He regretted that he had been forced to leave her this morning without even a good-bye. But she was probably waiting for him right now, and that realization made him impatient to finish whatever business Dorothy had for him and be gone from there. The thought of returning to Katie not only aroused his desire but also filled him with a warmth and pleasure he had never felt before in his life. He wanted her, he wanted to hold her, please her, make love to her, and keep her safe. He meant what he had told her last night. Gage's Regulars and King George and talk of war be damned. He was going to marry that woman as soon as he possibly could.

"Ethan?"

The soft calling of his name interrupted his thoughts, and he looked up to find Dorothy standing beside his table. She took the chair opposite him at the table and opened her mouth to speak, but she closed it again and looked at him helplessly.

"What is it? You look the picture of misery this evening."

"Ethan, I need to tell you something, and I don't know quite how to do it. It's about Katie." She took a deep breath, and her eyes met his in a hard, level stare across the table. "Ethan, she's a spy for Lowden."

"What?" He stared at her and started to laugh. "You're joking."

Slowly, Dorothy shook her head. "No, I am not speaking in jest. Katie is a spy for the Tories. She works for Lowden."

Ethan felt a wave of pity for the girl opposite him. She was in love with him. She had been for a long time. "Dorothy," he began, "you—"

"I'm not doing this out of jealousy," she said, correctly interpreting his thoughts. "I have knowledge of her treachery."

"Knowledge?" Ethan felt a hint of impatience with this. "Do you have proof?"

"No," she admitted. "But once you listen to what I have to say, I think you will at least wish to investigate further."

He leaned back in his chair. "I'm listening."

"They hired her." Dorothy answered simply. "Lowden hired her to find out all she could about John Smith. He promised to buy her indenture and free her. He also promised her a great deal of money."

When he did not reply, she leaned forward in her chair and said, "Ethan, I told you before, you cannot trust anyone. I am not asking you to take my word for this. Investigate, and see for yourself. I know the truth, but you must prove it to yourself before you believe me."

"How do you know she is a spy?"

"I know because Captain Worth told me."

"Worth?"

"Yes, you know who he is. The man who supposedly had his watch stolen by Katie. It wasn't stolen. They staged the whole thing between them so that she could gain some sympathy in the Mermaid and infiltrate your network of spies."

He shook his head. "I don't believe it."

"It's true, my dear." Dorothy looked at him, and her soft brown eyes were not without compassion. "I learned it all from Worth."

"How? Did Worth simply volunteer all of this information to you?"

She did not reply, but her eyes grew a little rounder, and Ethan felt a heavy knot forming in his chest. "Dorothy," he murmured. "My God. What have you done?"

"We all do what we have to do, Ethan." She raised her plump chin with a hint of pride. "I had to find out the truth about her. It was the only way I could think of. Worth is a very talkative lover."

He looked at this woman who loved him, who had lain with a man to find out information that could possibly save his life.

Only if it were true.

Ethan studied the grave expression on Dorothy's face, and doubt suddenly rippled through him like a shiver. He also leaned forward in his chair. "Start at the beginning," he ordered in a harsh whisper. "Tell me everything you know."

* * *

The clock chimed the midnight hour, and Ethan did not come. One o'clock, and he did not come. Katie curled up on the settee in the parlor, her worry finally giving way to exhaustion. She knew he had much to do, she knew from Janie that David Munro had come for him early this morning, she knew there would probably be many more nights like this in future, but he would come home to her. *He'll come home,* she thought again as she drifted off to sleep.

The clock chimed two, and she woke with a start. The candle on the table beside her had sputtered out, the coals of the hearth were banked in ash, and though a hint of moonlight filtered in around the drawn curtains of the parlor, the room was dark. Something had woken her, but she could not discern what it was. Not the clock but something else. She fumbled for the flint on the table to light the candle.

A spark flickered, illuminating the dark for an instant.

"Don't."

The voice out of the darkness startled her. She jumped and dropped the flint.

She realized it was Ethan who had spoken, his voice floating to her through the open doorway from the foyer into the parlor. She stood up. "Ethan, thank heavens you're home. Did you just arrive?"

He did not reply, and Katie frowned. Her eyes were becoming accustomed to the darkness, and with the tiny bit of moonlight coming into the parlor, she could now see his tall, powerful form in the doorway. For no reason, a sudden sense of foreboding spread through her. "What's happened?" she asked, and started toward him, then stopped when he did not answer. She should run to him, fling her arms around him, kiss him, but she did not do any of those things. She could not say why she remained where she was, a few feet away from him, out of his reach. "Why are you so quiet? Why are you standing there in the dark?"

He did not reply for a long moment. "The dark?" he repeated in the cool, ironical voice she remembered from their first meeting at the Mermaid. "It seems I have been in the dark for a long time now."

"What do you mean?" Even as she asked the question, she knew the answer, and the foreboding inside her escalated into fear. Hairs rose on the back of her neck, and all the survival instincts she had gained on the streets of London warned her of danger.

He knew. Somehow, some way, he knew the truth. *Oh, God.* Katie sucked in a sharp breath, trying not to panic.

"Did you really believe you could continue this deception of yours indefinitely? That I would never find out you are one of Lowden's informants?"

Think, she told herself. *Think of another lie.* But she was sick of lies, sick of deceptions, sick of waiting in dread for this moment, which she had always known would come.

"No, I knew you would eventually find out the

truth," she answered, and it took all the will she had to keep her voice steady.

She heard him let out his breath, as if he had been waiting for just that answer. "At least you do not insult my intelligence by trying to deny it."

He had not moved, and though she could see the shadowy outline of his form in the doorway, she could not see his face. She desperately wanted to light a lamp, thinking she might perhaps read something in his expression that would give her hope. But she did not dare move. "No, I do not deny it."

He said nothing, and she decided her only hope was to tell him everything. He would probably never forgive her, but at least he might understand that spying for Lowden had never really been a choice. "Do you remember that day in North Square, when you first saw me?"

"I do," he answered, and started toward her. "I remember how beautiful you looked. Like an angel, I thought."

For a moment, she wondered wildly if she should try to duck past him and run, but she remained where she was. *He won't hurt me,* she thought. *Ethan would never hurt me.*

"An angel," he repeated, halting in front of her. A slash of moonlight coming in between the curtain and the window frame lit a white line across his face, but it did not help her, for she could read nothing in his expression.

She opened her mouth to continue her story, but

374 *Laura Lee Guhrke*

suddenly, he wrapped an arm around her shoulders and pulled her hard against him. "Tell me, angel," he said. "Tell me the truth. If you can."

She took a deep breath, then began to talk, getting the words out as rapidly as she could, hoping that her explanations would satisfy him enough to keep his anger at bay. "Ethan, listen to me. When you saw me that day in the marketplace, Lowden saw me, too. He had an arrest warrant drawn against me, and he knew about Willoughby. He offered me the same bargain you did, only he offered his first. I had no choice but to spy for him. But I've told him nothing. I spied on the rebels, yes, but—"

"Spied on the rebels?" he asked, his voice so icy that she began to shiver. "Or did Lowden hire you to spy on me alone?"

"You alone."

"Gage's orders to arrest the rebels will be arriving within a day or two at most. When that happens, how many redcoats shall I expect at my door to place me under arrest?"

"You will not be arrested, Ethan," she whispered. "I have not told him who you really are."

"You are such a liar. A beautiful and talented liar."

She sighed. "The problem with being a liar," she said wearily, "is that when you do tell the truth, no one believes you."

With one arm securely around her, he lifted his other hand to her face. The tips of his fingers glided down her cheek, then he curled his hand around the side of her neck. His thumb forced her chin up so that he could look at her face in the dim moonlight.

"You've never told the truth in your life," he muttered. "And you won't tell it now, it seems. So, perhaps I should stop wasting precious time and kill you without trying to get any more information from you first."

The cold, speculative way he contemplated her death frightened her more than the hand at her throat.

"Ethan," she whispered hoarsely, rigid with fright, knowing she could not escape from the prison of his arms. "You won't kill me. You can't."

"Indeed, I can," he assured her, his breath hot and harsh against her cheek. "I could break your neck with my bare hands. The thought tempts me enormously."

"You won't kill me," she repeated obstinately. Even with his cause in jeopardy, she refused to believe it. Besides, she knew she had one weapon with which she could defend herself.

She forced her body to relax in his embrace, and slowly, ever so slowly, she melted against him. She spread her hands across his chest, and she could feel his heart thudding beneath her touch. She waited a moment, holding her breath, but he did not move, and that gave her hope. She slid her hands up his chest and cupped his face. "Ethan," she said in an aching voice, "I did not betray you. I swear it on my life. I told Lowden nothing but lies, and the reason is because I love you."

A cry of rage and pain tore from his throat, putting an end to her explanations and her hope. His fingers curled around her wrists, and he wrenched her hands away from his face as if her touch burned him like acid. He shoved her backward.

"Get out of my sight!" he shouted, his voice filled with such loathing that it tore her heart in half. He pulled something out of his pocket and slapped it into her hand. It was a sheet of parchment. "There is your indenture release. Go, run while you can, and never let me see you again."

She knew his heart was lost to her forever, and the survival instincts that had carried her through most of her life took over. She ducked past him before he could change his mind.

Hugging the sheet of parchment to her chest, she raced through the darkened house to the back door, and after losing a precious moment to fumble with the latch, she jerked it open and ran out into the alley. But she did not stop there. She kept on running mindlessly, though she knew in her heart that Ethan was not following her.

She ran until her side ached. She ran until her lungs burned. She ran and ran, until finally exhaustion overcame her, and she stumbled, pitching forward and falling hard, scraping her elbows against the cobblestones as she landed, her certificate of freedom beneath her.

Shaken, she lay there for a moment, then slowly rolled over, grimacing at the pain that shot through her limbs. She sat up, but she did not get to her feet.

Gasping for breath, shaking with fear and heartbreak, she sat there on the cobblestones of an empty alley and simply could not find the strength to stand up.

Ethan's words came back to her with all the harshness of a whip.

Get out of my sight, and never let me see you again.

She slammed her hands over her ears, but she could not blot out his words, and she had the sick feeling that the contempt in his voice would haunt her for as long as she lived.

Katie did not know how long she sat there on the cold cobblestones of the alley. She did not know if she had injured herself during her fall. She only knew that her heart hurt far more than her body. In the gray light of dawn, she watched a regiment of Regulars march along the street past the alley where she sat. Though she knew she could not sit there forever, it was a long time before she found the will to move.

Finally, she got to her feet, grimacing at the pain that shot through her limbs. The sleeves of her dress were torn, and the skin on the inside of her wrists and forearms was scraped raw from her fall, but otherwise she found to her relief that she was uninjured. The last thing she needed just now was broken bones. A broken heart was enough.

Katie took stock of her situation. She could not return to the house. That much was clear. On the other hand, with soldiers marching through the streets, she did not like the idea of remaining outdoors.

She didn't even have any money with her. Katie dug into the pocket of her skirt and pulled out two British pence. She stared down at the pair of coins and felt an absurd desire to laugh. She had no home, no clothes but the ones on her back, nowhere to go, and tuppence in her pocket. Her situation, she decided, was pretty grim.

She looked down at the pavement and saw the sheet of parchment Ethan had shoved into her hand. Her freedom. It didn't seem to matter much right now.

She knew the wise thing to do now was exactly what Ethan had suggested. She was free of Willoughby, at least, and if she could get out of the city, she could be well away from Boston before Lowden discovered she was missing and exercised that arrest warrant. She bent down and picked up her certificate of freedom from indenture, folded it, and put it in her pocket.

The regiment of soldiers had passed by and was far down the street when Katie stepped out of the alley. She slipped her two precious pence back into her pocket and began walking in the opposite direction of the soldiers, listening to the precise tap of their boot heels echo behind her. She had no clear idea of where she was going or what she was going to do, but she knew she did not want to follow a regiment of marching redcoats.

Katie had taken only a few steps when she

stopped walking and frowned, thinking hard. Ethan had told her the other night that the troops had been expected to march on Concord Sunday but had not done so. He had also told her they probably still planned to conduct that mission, but he did not know when.

If she could find out exactly when Gage's troops planned to march, she could let Ethan know.

Immediately on the heels of that thought came another one, a discouraging one. He would not listen to her, and even if he did, he would not believe her. Why should he?

She turned a corner and halted again, her speculations ended by the sight before her. On the next corner, a soldier was harassing a newspaper seller, a boy of perhaps ten years old. As she watched the redcoat shoving him and laughing, she realized that though the boy was not Daniel Munro, he easily could have been. Daniel had worked for the *Boston Gazette*.

The soldier grabbed a handful of newspapers from the pile by his feet and tossed them contemptuously into the air. Sheets of newsprint scattered to the wind. He then grabbed the boy and twisted his arm behind his body. The child let out a howl of pain. "Bloody lobster!" the boy shouted, and kicked the soldier in the shin.

The redcoat let out a curse, then whirled the boy around to face him and backhanded the child across the face.

Without thinking, Katie ran toward them,

knowing she had to do something. "For God's sake!" she cried, grabbing the soldier by the arm to keep him from hitting the boy again. "He's only a child. You can't do this!"

The redcoat paused and looked at her, stunned. Then he began to laugh as he easily pulled his arm from her grasp. "Who's going to stop me?" he asked contemptuously, looking her up and down. "I am one of the king's troops, and selling this atrocity that passes for a newspaper is a criminal act against the king."

"Who says so?" she demanded. "Gage hasn't declared them against the law."

"It's speaking against the king," he roared back at her, clearly showing that his rage, like that of most soldiers in Boston these days, was at the boiling point. "It's treason to say anything against our king, and you colonials aren't going to get by with it any longer! Get out of the way, girl. You can't stop me."

Katie stared at him, frustration and fury welling up inside her. Images of Willoughby and the girl he had brutalized flashed through her mind, and she felt as helpless now as she had then.

Ethan's words that day he'd gone off to Concord came back to her.

There is a better way to live than at the whim of another, be he a king or a master, and we are willing to risk our lives to find it.

At the time, she had scoffed at those words, thinking them unrealistic nonsense. But now, as she felt herself shoved aside by a soldier who was about to beat up a boy who had simply been selling a newspaper, those words suddenly made sense.

Katie set her jaw. She was not going to stand by and let this happen. "Captain, please," she implored, and shoved the boy aside to step between them. With the boy behind her, she put a hand on the redcoat's arm and smiled up at him before he could even think of setting her aside again. "Perhaps," she said in a softer voice, "we can come to some sort of terms about this that are agreeable to us both."

It was so easy that she wanted to laugh. Comprehension of her meaning dawned on his face, and he grinned. "Well, now, that's the friendliest thing a Boston girl has said to me since I got here."

"Really?" She slanted a look at him from beneath her lashes, a look as old as time. She moved as if to clasp her hands behind her. In reality, she counted off on her fingers for the boy behind her— one, two, three.

He was a smart lad. The moment her fingers indicated three, he whirled around and began to run. "Go, go!" she shouted to him as she darted past the redcoat and took off in the opposite direction. With an oath, the soldier started after her, but he had taken only a few steps before he evidently decided his duty to destroy seditious newspapers was more important than a pesky rebel woman or a boy. As she ran, Katie glanced over her shoulder just in time to see him set the newspapers on fire.

She ran for another fifty yards or so, then ducked into an alley. She sank back against a wall, and at the same time she was gasping for breath, she burst out laughing. She knew she would probably never meet that boy again, but she felt a great sense of satisfaction knowing that she had helped him get away from that bully of a soldier, and she couldn't help the triumphant amusement she felt. It was amazing how easily the attention of some men could be distracted by a smile and a bit of eyelash batting.

I make myself the exception.

Ethan's words that night in the White Swan came back to her, and Katie's amusement quickly faded. He always had been the exception. Her feminine wiles had not worked on him. Perhaps, she thought wryly, that was why she had fallen in love with him.

Pain shot through her again at the memory of how he had cast her aside, but she knew it was all her own doing, and she could not hold him accountable for the choices she had made. She could not blame him for no longer trusting her. She also knew there was nothing she could do to change the past. The important issue that had to be faced was what she was going to do now.

After all, she had to do something.

Katie stood in the alley for a long moment, thinking hard. If she could learn somehow exactly when Gage's troops planned to march on Concord, then she could carry that information back to the Mermaid. By now, Ethan had already warned them about her. There was a good chance no one would believe her, but she knew she had to try.

In every problem she had ever faced before, she had always run away. She had run away from Miss Prudence, she had run away from more constables than she could count, she had run away from Willoughby.

This time, she was not going to run away, even if it meant her life was the price she paid. She squared her shoulders, brushed the dirt off her dress as best she could, and started making a plan to acquire the information Ethan needed. He was lost to her forever, but she would not leave him. He might not welcome her help, but she was going to give it anyway.

The oddest thing about it all was that she wasn't going to do this just because of the man she loved. She would do it for him, and for Molly and David and Daniel, and that boy who sold newspapers, and everyone else who wanted a better way to live.

"I don't believe it!" Molly burst out, rising from her chair in the back room of the Mermaid to face the tall, dark-haired man at the head of the table.

Ethan knew Molly could not be objective when it came to Katie, but he was frustrated nonetheless by her blindness where that girl was concerned, perhaps because it reflected his own. He had trusted Katie, and all the while she had been working for Lowden. That thought of her brought back all the pain and rage he felt, and talking about how she had deceived him was nearly unbearable.

His gaze swept the table, resting briefly on each person present. Molly, David, Dorothy, Joshua, Andrew, and Adam. All of them were people who had been worthy of trust, who had proven themselves time and again. Why had he been so ready to trust a girl he knew was a liar and a thief?

Because he had fallen in love with her. Why not admit it? Like a callow youth, he had been blinded by love.

He closed his eyes, fighting against his anger at Katie and at himself until he had banished it to a far corner of his mind. If he was angry, he could not think objectively, and dealing with the situation would become even harder.

While Ethan was occupied with these thoughts, the discussion of Katie went on around him.

Molly was still defending her. "Katie a spy? It's nonsense. Whatever Dorothy says, there must be another explanation." She glared at the dark-haired woman who sat across from her. "There are some who'll say anything out of spite."

"That is not fair!" Dorothy also stood up, and her brother, who sat beside her, put a restraining hand on her arm. "I did not—"

"Ladies, please," Ethan interrupted in a weary voice, gesturing for both women to sit back down. "May we return to the point? Katie cannot be trusted. She is a Lowden spy."

"I must admit," David interjected his voice into the discussion, "like my wife, I have a difficult time accepting such an idea. I was genuinely fond of the girl."

"As was I," Joshua added. When his sister glared

at him, he added hastily, "But, of course, she did betray us."

"Are you certain of this?" Andrew asked, glancing from Ethan to Dorothy and back again. "Are you both truly certain?"

Dorothy gave an emphatic nod of her head. "Captain Worth told me that Katie had been hired by Lowden for the specific purpose of finding John Smith. He'd had quite a bit of ale earlier in the evening, but he knew what he was saying."

"I'm certain as well," Ethan said, careful to keep his face expressionless as he looked at his friend across the table. "I confronted her, and she admitted the truth to me. She has been an informant for Lowden ever since she began working here. Molly, you remember that first night when she was on the run from the Regulars, and Captain Worth followed her in here with two of his men? Worth told Dorothy that the entire scene was staged to gain our acceptance and trust."

Adam spoke for the first time. "But Katie has known for weeks that you are John Smith. If she has been working for Lowden all this time, you should have been arrested long before now. Why has Lowden not put Ethan Harding under arrest?"

"My guess is that until now, Gage has refused to allow it. You know he has been reluctant to arrest any Sons of Liberty. We know specific orders to do so are on the way to him from London at this moment. My sources at Fort Hill tell me those orders were aboard the *Dartmouth,* which docked this morning. They will be in Gage's hands by the end of the day. My guess is that Lowden plans to have me arrested the moment those orders can be carried out."

"I cannot believe Katie told Lowden about you," Molly said stubbornly. "Even if Gage would not let you be arrested, your Tory sources, especially the ones in Gage's circle, would never have continued to give you information had they known your true position. Every Tory friend of yours would have been told not to tell you anything. Yet that is not the case. Even now, you are still getting information from Gage's underlings. Katie did not tell them about you. I'm certain of it."

Ethan thought about it for a moment, then nodded slowly, granting her that possibility. "If so, what would be her reason for remaining silent?"

Molly raised her eyebrows and gave him a pointed stare, her meaning plain as day. That look carried with it a glimmer of hope, and Ethan felt all his anger returning in full force. The woman was a traitor, he reminded himself, even as he remembered how it had felt to hold her in his arms.

He rose from the table so abruptly his chair nearly tipped over. "Cast aside these silly, romantic ideas of yours once and for all!" he told Molly savagely. "The girl did not keep silent out of any loyalty or devotion to me, I assure you. She must have had another reason."

"What reason?" Molly countered. "She could have demolished your entire web of informants by now, yet she has not."

He sat back down, striving for the objectivity he needed. "Lowden may know everything she knows and may be choosing not to act on it for reasons of his own that we know nothing about."

Molly made a sound of impatience. "Ethan, really! Why are you always so ready to believe the worst?"

"You forget, she admitted the truth to me. She admitted that Lowden hired her."

"I have not forgotten that, and I'm not saying she's innocent. What I am saying is that there might be reasons why she agreed to spy for Lowden in the first place. Good reasons. Like being hungry and being on the run from a brutal master."

"And once she was in our circle, she changed her mind and became a Whig like us?" He shook his head. "Oh, no. That lass values her own skin far too highly to risk it for an idealistic cause. No, my guess is that she decided to play a waiting game, pretending to be loyal to both sides, dangling me and Lowden like a pair of marionettes, waiting to see which of us came out on top. Whichever way it turned out, she would gain her freedom. And she has—from me. Lowden also promised her a great deal of money. If she had not told him about me before, she will certainly do so now."

"I don't think so," Molly said, then pressed her lips tightly together and was silent.

"We'll know soon enough which of us is right," Ethan told her. A ghost of a smile touched his lips. "If Katie has betrayed me, I will be in chains on a prison ship in the harbor within a day or two at most."

"Don't say such things!" Dorothy cried. "You'll need to get out of the city, that's all. The rest of us are leaving tonight by boat to Charlestown. Come with us."

"I cannot leave," Ethan told her. "There is too much to be done here. I must find out when Gage is sending the Regulars to Concord."

"The longer you wait, the harder it will be to get out of the city, my friend," Andrew pointed out. "With all of us gone, you will be on your own. Unless you have a great deal of influence with Gage and can get a pass, you could find yourself stranded inside the city. And if Katie has told Lowden the truth about you, I don't see how Gage can let you go."

"There was a time when Ethan Harding had enough influence to get such a pass, but I am certain Lowden already knows I'm a Son of Liberty, thanks to Katie. I can hardly expect to be able just to walk out of town. Andrew, are there any forgers hereabouts who can get me false papers?"

"It's doubtful. Most of the printers have already left town. Everything is in such turmoil, it's a blessing that John Hancock and Samuel Adams left the city."

"What about other Sons of Liberty?" Ethan asked.

"My sources in the mechanics union tell me only Dr. Warren, Paul Revere, and yourself have remained behind."

"What about the rest of us?" Dorothy asked. "If Katie has betrayed you, might she not have told Lowden about all of your informants?"

"Even if she has, the rest of you are in no danger of arrest," Ethan assured her. "Gage has no orders to arrest ordinary citizens, and I cannot imagine him doing so. But it is still wise of you to leave Boston while you can."

"Ethan is the one in real danger," Joshua said. "He is the only Son of Liberty among us." He turned to Ethan. "Dorothy is right. You must come with us tonight."

"I cannot. Not yet. There is still much to be done here. I will remain here with Paul Revere and Joseph Warren as long as I am able, and I will do whatever I can to avoid arrest once Gage receives his orders."

"What if Katie has said nothing about you to Lowden? What if you are not arrested?" Molly asked.

Ethan sighed and looked at her with pity. "Molly, I stopped believing in miracles a long time ago."

21

There was nothing for it, Katie decided. She had a plan for how to find out when Gage's troops were going to march on Concord, but to put her plan into effect, she needed the right clothes for the occasion. Clothes that Elizabeth Waring would never have conceived of making for her, even when she had been Ethan's mistress. For the clothes, she needed money. Quite a lot of money.

Hoping to heaven and hell she didn't get caught, Katie spent the morning dipping in the marketplace. Her luck held. Within two hours, she had enough coin to buy what she needed, and whether it was the devils or the angels who answered her prayers, she didn't get caught.

She set off for Mt. Whoredom. There she bought the props to stage the most colossal bluff of her life. She wandered the edge of the prostitution district until she found an inn that was a cut or two below respectable but was clean and not too seedy.

She got a room there, making certain it had a bed with a wood frame canopy. She then ordered a bath and sent a runner with a perfumed letter to Sir William Holbrook.

Most men, Katie knew, were very predictable, provided a woman could accurately assess their character. Sir William was no exception. Like a puppet on a string, he came to her at the inn that night, just as she had expected. When she opened the door of her room to let him in, his reaction told her that she had also lived up to his expectations. Even more, his fantasies.

She wore a red silk peignoir, loosely tied at her waist. Beneath it, Holbrook could catch only glimpses of the blackest, laciest, tightest corset Mt. Whoredom had to offer. Those two garments and a pair of black satin mules with heels were all she wore.

He was staring at her so hard his eyes bulged out like a pair of chicken eggs. The man was already starting to sweat, and she didn't even have his cravat untied yet.

She closed the door, trying to do what she knew prostitutes always did. She worked to distance herself from this man and this situation, until she felt almost as if another woman were doing this and she were merely watching it. It wasn't all that difficult. After all, unlike prostitutes, she had no intention of fulfilling the age-old bargain. Not even close. This was a game. She took a deep breath and turned to face him. The game was about to begin.

"Would you like wine?" she asked, and gestured to an opened bottle on the table beneath the window. Without waiting for an answer, she crossed the room and poured a bit of the red liquid into the two glasses on the table. Smiling, she offered him one and took a sip from the other.

She smiled. "You are very quiet, William. Have you lost your tongue?"

He lowered his gaze, watching as she made a casual move to reveal one of her legs. He swallowed hard. "Harding does himself well, I must say. Where did he find you?"

She laughed, a husky, sensuous laugh. "Let's say instead that I found him. He is quite generous with his money, and not a bad lover." She gave Holbrook a long, soft glance over her wineglass. "But tame, I'm afraid. Very tame."

"That's too bad."

She stepped closer and touched his lips with her fingertip. "I knew from the moment we met that you were anything but tame."

He reached for her, but she stepped back again, laughing. "William, you move too fast. We have plenty of time." She took a sip of wine and licked a drop from her upper lip. "Anticipation heightens the excitement, believe me. And before long, you are going to be very excited."

She set her glass of wine back on the table. She strolled past him to the bed and the pile of silk cravats she had laid there earlier. Idly, she picked one up in her hands and turned to him. "Cravats, you know, are a wonderful thing."

She fingered the cravat, staring down at it thoughtfully, letting it slide back and forth in her hands almost as if she were caressing it. When she glanced up, she saw that Holbrook wasn't looking at her. He was staring at the long strip of silk in her hands. "Silk is the most erotic fabric," she told him, wrapping the ends of the cravat slowly around her fists. "Strong and soft. Perfect for us. Wouldn't you agree?"

He didn't even bother to nod. She knew his imagination was running wild. He licked his lips. A drop of sweat ran down his cheek.

"Look at me, William."

He lifted his gaze to her face, and she smiled. "Take off your shirt and your waistcoat," she ordered.

Without a qualm, he obeyed, still staring into her eyes. Once he had obeyed that command, she gave him another. "Come here."

As he came toward her, she slowly shifted their positions. It was like a dance, and she was leading him. Without his even being aware of it, she maneuvered him until the backs of his knees hit the footboard of the bed. "Hold out your hands."

He held out his hands. *Like a lamb to the slaughter,* she thought, and wrapped the silk around his wrists. Slowly, she lifted his wrists and tied his hands to the wooden canopy overhead.

"Pull on it, William. Is it tight?"

He tugged and nodded.

"You're sure? It has to be tight." She laughed softly. "After all, I wouldn't want you to get away."

He tugged hard on the cravat and nodded again. Satisfied, she slid her hands down his sunken chest and round, soft belly as she sank to her knees and began to undo the buttons of his breeches. She carefully avoided his aroused penis. After all, she wasn't going to touch the damn thing, not even for secrets of state. Leaving on his linen underdrawers, she slowly slid the breeches off his hips, and he was whimpering before they got to his ankles.

She glanced up at his face and felt suddenly alarmed. He was so red, she hoped he didn't have apoplexy before she could find out what she needed to know. But it wouldn't be long now.

She flattened her hands against the sides of his legs and stood up. His whimpers increased as she passed his penis without touching it. He started begging, and she pressed her lips against his, not for the purpose of arousing him further but to silence him. Men who begged were so distasteful. It was time, she decided, to end this.

"Patience, Sir William," she whispered, her breath hot against his mouth. "Have patience. We have to wait for your wife."

"What?" The word came out in a strangled gasp, a combination of sexual arousal and sudden shock. "My wife?"

She pulled back, smiling at him, and gently patted his cheek with her fingertips as her bare knee slid sensuously between his thighs. "She should be here very soon."

He shook his head wildly, as if unable to take in what she was saying. "What do you mean?"

She opened her eyes wide. "I invited her to join us. With your, shall we say, unusual proclivities, I thought you might enjoy what the French call a *ménage à trois*. It's quite pleasurable. Have you ever done it before?"

"You're joking. You and I, with my wife?" The last word came out in a squeak.

Katie pressed a kiss to his lips. Against his mouth, she said, "Don't you think it would be exciting?"

"Not with my wife!"

"Oh, very well, then, if you want to spoil the party." She stepped back and calmly turned away, ignoring the indignant splutterings of the man tied to the bed.

"What is this about?" he demanded. "What game are you playing with me?"

She pulled at the tie around her waist and removed the peignoir, then tossed the swath of red silk over her shoulder to land at his feet. "This is no game," she answered, kicking off her shoes. Choosing to leave the corset on, she began to dress in her old clothes, and as she did, she explained. "When I sent a letter to you, I also sent one to your wife, a letter signed by your secretary, telling her that you need her desperately, that it was a matter of supreme importance, with instructions to come here at exactly ten o'clock." She paused in the act of buttoning her dress and bent down to look at his watch, which was still fastened by its thin chain to his waistcoat. "That's about fifteen minutes from now."

"What do you want, madam? Money?"

She laughed. "Sir William, I didn't do all of this for money. Harding gives me plenty of that, I assure you."

"What, then? What do you want?"

She did not answer but finished dressing as if he had not even spoken.

He waited only a few moments. "What is it you want from me?" he cried, the agony of uncertainty obvious in his voice.

"I want only one small thing from you." Finished dressing, Katie walked over to him. Keeping far enough away so that he could not kick her, she said, "I want to know when Gage plans to march on Concord."

"What?"

Clearly, this was not what he had expected, for he began shaking his head in apparent disbelief. "Gage is marching on Concord? Where on earth did you hear that?"

She smiled at him sweetly. "I am losing my patience. When do they march?"

He tried to bluster it out. "Mrs. Armstrong, I don't know what you're talking about."

"I have played enough games with you to last a lifetime, Sir William. That information is all I want from you. Speak it, and I will let you go. Tell me that one, small fact, and your wife will never know about our little assignation. If you don't tell me what I want to know, I will simply leave you here for her to find you."

"But I don't know when they march! I'm not privy to that sort of information."

She sighed with mock regret. "This won't do, my dear fellow."

He licked his lips. "I'm telling you, I don't know when it will be. I don't know."

She gave Holbrook a pitying glance, from the hands tied over his head to the breeches down around his ankles. She clicked her tongue. "What will your wife say when she finds you in this condition?"

"I'll tell her I was forced. That thugs—"

"What? Kidnapped you, pulled your breeches down, then left with your pocket money?" She laughed. "Of course. All thugs do that."

"I'll think of something credible to tell her."

"Hmm, you do that. But whatever you tell her, I advise you to think of it quickly. I judge you have about ten minutes left, if your wife is a punctual woman."

"Be damned to you."

Katie shrugged. "I wonder how long it will take for the scandal to leak out. Gossip is such an insidious thing."

"You can't prove any of this ever happened."

"Since when have gossiping ladies ever needed any proof? You know as well as I that accusation is enough to ruin a man. Besides——" She gestured to the peignoir. "As for the thug story, what sort of thugs do you suppose wear those?"

He stared down at the pool of red silk, and a look of such misery came over his face that Katie actually felt sorry for him. "The night of April eighteenth," he mumbled. "Four days from now."

She let out her breath in a rush of relief. She reached into her pocket and pulled out a vial of holy water. This stuff had always served her well, especially in her dealings with Holbrook. For her to return him to a suitable state of dress, he had to be unconscious. She couldn't risk having him over-power her. After pulling out the cork, she pressed the small vial to his lips. "Drink this."

He pulled his head back from the bottle in her hand as far as he could. "Are you going to poison me now?"

"Don't be stupid," she chided gently. "It's not poison. You're only going to go to sleep, and I swear to you that when your wife arrives, she'll simply find that you've had a bit too much to drink."

"I don't believe you."

"You don't have a choice. But don't worry, Sir William. I will keep my word. No one will ever know about this." She reached behind his head and grabbed a handful of his hair. Pulling his head back, she pushed the opening of the bottle between his teeth and tipped it so the liquid ran into his mouth. As she had expected, he tried to spit it out. But he involuntarily swallowed enough of the drug to have the effect she needed. Within just a few short minutes, he passed out. His head lolled sideways, and his whole body sagged. The silk scarves were all that kept him from falling to the floor.

Katie studied him with mingled disgust and pity. It would be no more than he deserved if she did nothing, if she left him to his fate, but she could not. She was a woman of her word. She untied the scarves and let him fall back onto the bed. She stuffed all the props she had brought into the small valise she had carried them in, including one of the two glasses. The other she left on the table, along with the bottle of wine. She then buttoned his breeches and left him snoring in the room, looking for all the world like a man who had gotten drunk all alone and passed out.

When the maid came in with his breakfast in the morning, she would find no trace of Katie there, and there would be no gossip or scandal to haunt Sir William Holbrook, as she had promised him. Katie's efforts to leave no trace of their rendezvous were not for his wife, of course. She wasn't coming.

Ethan was so weary he could hardly stand. He had spent all day and most of the evening contacting every source he had, but the results had been meager, to say the least. His contacts at Province House seemed to know nothing of the Concord mission, other than the fact that it would take place soon. If they did know the date, the subtle tactics of Ethan Harding, a man who had absolutely no interest in politics, had not been successful in learning it. Any of the prostitutes, mechanics, and seamen left in Boston who were the paid informants of John Smith also knew of the mission, but, like those high officials at Province House, they could not give the specific date. Though he had not slept for two days, Ethan's weariness did not stem from a lack of rest. Its cause lay somewhere deep in his heart.

He left the house of Dr. Joseph Warren, the only Whig leader other than himself and Paul Revere who still remained in Boston, his spirits lower than they had ever been. Joseph was as much in the dark as he about Gage's plans. Joseph's only news was that the governor had officially received his orders to begin arresting Whig leaders, and each man had advised the other to leave town. They both appreciated the advice. Neither took it.

All his friends were gone by now. Molly and David had closed the Mermaid a few hours before and had left Boston with their son, the Macalveys, and Adam Lawrence, slipping out in the night to the wharves, where a boat had ferried them across the river to Charlestown. Andrew had left for his family in Worcester, and Colin had departed for his wife's relatives in New Hampshire.

Ethan knew it would be wise if he left as well. Now that Gage had his orders, it would be only a matter of time before he was in a cell at Castle William if he stayed. He was sure Katie had given Lowden his name long ago, and the viscount had only been biding his time, waiting for the orders to arrive before arresting him. Katie had denied giving his name to Lowden, but Katie was a liar. He had always known that.

He closed his eyes and willed her away. He could not think about her, he would not. And he certainly couldn't stand in front of Joseph's house all night waiting to be arrested. He had to go home, gather what money he had tucked away, and leave for Charlestown. He began walking through the dark, empty streets.

His steps did not take him to his house. Instead, almost without realizing what he was doing, Ethan found himself standing in front of the house he had leased for Katie.

Slowly, he walked to the door. It was unlatched, and he opened it. Compelled beyond understanding, he walked inside. The servants had fled Boston hours before, and no one had bothered to close the curtains. In the moonlight, he could see the lamp that stood beside him on the small table. He lit the lamp and looked around him.

The moment he did, memories of Katie filled his mind and overwhelmed his senses, memories of playing chess, of laughing at the butler's wooden countenance, of the day they had walked through this house together and the pleasure she had taken in even the most trivial things. The linens, he remembered, had delighted her, and the bathtub. And that big bed with the soft, thick mattress.

Ethan, look, a real bed, with a feather mattress!

Her voice, filled with all the wonder of a child at

Christmas, echoed from upstairs down to where he stood in the foyer. He closed his eyes, and in his mind he saw her falling back onto the bed, laughing with joy. He could feel every curve of her body beneath him on that bed.

Something brushed his leg. Startled, he looked down to find Meg twirling her round orange body between his ankles. She meowed loudly, as if quite indignant. He bent down and scooped up the animal with one hand. "What's the matter, sweeting?" he murmured. "Did everyone go away and leave you behind?"

Meg meowed again and snuggled into the crook of his arm. She happily began to knead his palm with her claws, oblivious to any pain she might be causing. He stood there and let her.

I know we're playing out this charade that I'm your mistress, but giving me presents is carrying it a bit far, don't you think?

Her tears that day had astonished him. He would swear those tears had been genuine, one genuine thing in a love filled with lies.

No, he corrected himself. There was another. His love for her was genuine.

God, how he loved her. Even now, when he was about to be arrested because of her treachery, he could not destroy it. He had the feeling he never would.

The door latch clicked, bringing him out of his reverie. He whirled around and found her there, looking at him. "Ethan," she whispered.

The grandfather clock ticked away the seconds as they stared at each other. The only sound in the silent house.

It was Katie who spoke first. "I came for Meg." A soft smile touched her lips. "I never expected to find you here."

"Take her." He thrust the kitten toward her so abruptly Meg gave an angry howl. "Take her and go."

Katie stepped through the doorway and closed the door behind her. She came to him and took the indignant Meg from his hands. But she made no move to leave. Instead, she just stood there, looking at him with the kitten cradled in her arms. "Ethan, I'm so sorry. I never meant for any of this to happen."

Something snapped inside him. "Go, for God's sake!" He stepped back, away from her, afraid of what he might do if he were close enough to touch her, close enough to kiss her. He was afraid he would forget what she had done, that he would weaken, relent, forgive the unforgivable. "Get out of here."

"I will. But before I go, I have something I must tell you. It was the purest luck to find you here. Believe it or not, I've been looking for you everywhere. I never thought you would come back here."

He had never thought it, either. When she stepped toward him, he took another step back, shaking his head. "Stay away from me, Katie. Stay away."

"Ethan, listen to me. I know Gage's plan. I learned it from Holbrook. The Regulars are coming out tomorrow night. I wanted you to know."

He did not believe her, not for one tiny instant. "Holbrook doesn't know when the mission will take place."

"Yes, he does."

Ethan made a sound of derision. "And he just volunteered this information to you?"

She cleared her throat. "Not exactly. But how I got him to tell me isn't important. What's important is that you know about this. I hope it helps you win your fight."

Did she never stop trying to deceive? "What is this?" he demanded. "Doesn't Lowden have enough proof against me yet? Is this a trap?" He glanced down her body and back again to her face, a pointed glance. When he spoke, he wanted his words to hurt. "If it is, Lowden is a very intelligent man to send such attractive bait, but it doesn't tempt me, my dear."

He succeeded. She pressed her lips together, and he knew his hurtful words had caused her pain. He felt no triumph.

"This is not a trap. I am telling you the truth." She gave a tiny, humorless laugh. "I know there is no earthly reason why you should believe me, and if you choose not to, then that's your choice. But I had to tell you."

"Why? What reason could you possibly have for telling me this?"

Her face softened, reminding him of how she had looked right after lovemaking, and Ethan felt everything inside him start to crumble into dust.

"I am doing this now," she whispered, "in the hope that you'll be able to forgive me," she said. "Someday, when you have this new nation of yours, when you have a wife who loves you and half a dozen children who adore you, maybe you can look back on this time with me and forgive."

He did what he vowed he would not do. He stepped toward her. He touched her face. "Katie—"

The door burst open, interrupting whatever he had been about to say, and a group of redcoats crowded into the doorway. Ethan did not even take time to think. He shoved her behind him as the soldiers began to enter the house. "Run, Katie!" he shouted. "Run, now!"

She did not obey him. She did not run. She did not even move. Bayonets were lowered and muskets pointed, and Ethan knew he was going to be arrested. Still, he kept himself between Katie and the soldiers.

Through the open doorway, a sharp command was given from outside. With their muskets pointed at him, the soldiers parted into two halves, and another man entered the house, walking between them to stand before Ethan. It was Viscount Lowden.

"Harding, it is a pleasure to see you again, sir." He bowed, and Ethan was astonished by the courtesy. Even when arresting a man, it seemed peers of the realm still retained their good manners.

"I wish I could say the same, my lord," he answered warily. "What is the meaning of this?"

"I have bad news for you, I'm afraid. Mr. Harding, your mistress is under arrest."

"What?" He did not need to pretend his astonishment. Turning, he looked at the woman who stood behind him, but he could read nothing in her face except an intense and haunting sadness.

She stepped forward and shoved the cat into his arms. "Take Meg, Ethan, and leave Boston while you still can."

Two of the soldiers came around him and seized her. They started to drag her away. Ethan reached out to stop them, but Lowden laid a hand on his arm. "I wouldn't advise it, sir. Don't intervene, or we will arrest you as well."

"But what is this about?" he demanded. "Why are you arresting her?" *And why the devil aren't you arresting me?* "What has she done?"

"She is a thief. She is also a Whig spy, and she will be tried for her crimes and hanged." He smiled and patted Ethan's arm. "You had no idea, did you? You poor fool. I think you'll need to find yourself a new mistress, my dear fellow."

With that, he turned and followed the soldiers who were dragging Katie out the door. Ethan watched them go, but he knew that with six armed soldiers surrounding her, there was nothing he

could do to prevent them from taking her away
without risking her life, and he did not try.

I told Lowden nothing but lies, and the reason is be-
cause I love you.

Her words of the night before came back to him
with startling clarity. He remembered his brutal
handling of her and the panic in her voice as she
had tried to explain, as she had tried to justify, as
she had tried to tell him the truth.

Ethan felt cold, but it was not the night air coming in through the open door that chilled him. It
was the icy wind of truth that made him cold, truth
that whispered to him and made him realize he had
made a terrible mistake.

The beady little eyes of a rat blinked at her in the
dim dawn light that filtered through a slash high in
the wall of her cell, and Katie kicked at it with a
curse that would have sent Miss Prudence racing
for soap. The rat scurried only a few feet away, then
set its gaze on her again, studying her. Mocking her
as well, she imagined. Or perhaps it was really
thinking she looked just like a large hunk of roast
mutton.

Katie huddled back against the damp stone wall
behind her and rested her forehead against her bent
knees. How odd that she was probably going to die
in a hangman's noose, but she was not as afraid of
that as she was of a disgusting creature the size of
her shoe. Why did all gaols have to have rats? Evidently, prisons everywhere were pretty much the

same. Castle William might be in Boston Harbor, but it was just like Newgate. She had come full circle, it seemed.

The clang of bars echoed down the damp hallway outside her cell. Katie lifted her head and heard the tap of boot heels getting louder, coming closer.

"Good-oh," she mumbled to the rat. "Must be time for breakfast. If it's to be my last meal, I hope it's roast chicken."

Her mouth watered at her own mention of food, but food was not forthcoming. Instead, a gaoler appeared, keys jangling in his hand as if to unlock her cell. Katie's heart gave a leap of hope, but that hope died the moment the guard stepped aside and another man came to look at her through the bars.

"My dear Katie, I hope you had a good night's rest," Viscount Lowden said, speaking with such heartiness she wanted to spit on him. Too bad she'd never learned to spit that far.

"Lovely," she answered. "This inn is superb." She gestured to the jug of brackish water, the trencher where not even a crumb of stale bread remained, and the rat, who still sat with his nose twitching. "Fine dining, entertaining company. I even have a view of the harbor. Too bad I'm not tall enough to look out."

"Be of good cheer. You won't be staying here long."

"I don't imagine so." She pushed the hair out of her eyes with a weary hand. "Did you just come to gloat, or do you have a purpose for this visit?"

"To gloat, of course."

"Of course." She waved her hand toward him as if it didn't matter to her in the least. "Gloat away. I won't stop you."

"Actually, I do have another purpose. I wanted to tell you personally that your trial is scheduled for this afternoon. You'll be convicted, of course, and hanged tomorrow."

"Damn. And I was planning a holiday in the country. What am I charged with? Refusing to co-operate with a blackmailing viscount? Silly me. I didn't know that was against the law."

She could tell her light, careless tone bothered him. His mouth tightened to a thin line, and he did not reply. What on earth had he expected? Weeping? If so, he'd be disappointed. "Really, James, don't pout. I'm sorry if you didn't get to arrest John Smith, but it isn't as if you've gotten nothing for your pains. You got me, and I'm much prettier than Holbrook."

"Cease this prattle! You'd best keep a civil tongue in your head, or—"

He broke off, and Katie took advantage of the moment. "Or what?" she asked as she stood up and sauntered over to him. "That's the rub, isn't it? I'm going to die, and I don't care." She gripped the bars and looked him in the eye. "So there is nothing you can do to me now. I'm not afraid of you anymore."

"No? Perhaps that is because I am not a young and handsome officer." He turned and made a beckoning gesture with his hand. A redcoat stepped sharply forward out of the shadows, an officer whose vacuous face she recognized at once.

"Weston," she breathed. "Bloody hell."

"Yes," Lowden said with obvious pleasure. "Lieutenant Weston."

The lieutenant turned toward her. "Witch," he ground out between clenched teeth. "I hope you hang."

"That will be enough, Lieutenant."

"Yes, my lord." Weston stepped back, but he still glared at her with all the hostility of a man who had been made to feel an utter fool by a mere woman.

"Lieutenant Weston has been in the country for the past fortnight," Lowden told her, "but he returned to duty this morning. Now, I had you arrested last night because you did not keep your appointment with me and bring me proof against Holbrook before Gage's orders arrived. Since you did not fulfill your part of our bargain, I felt fully justified in having you arrested. I located Weston here this morning so that he could testify at your trial this afternoon, and he told me some very interesting things. In fact, he is fully prepared to tell the governor all about John Smith. And about you, my dear."

She gripped the bars more tightly in her fingers. "What does this man know of John Smith?" she asked, attempting to bluff. "Has he proof of Holbrook's sedition?"

"Alas, no, not against Holbrook. But that doesn't

matter. After all, we both know John Smith is not Holbrook but Ethan Harding."

Ethan. No, no, not Ethan.

"Ethan?" she repeated, shaking her head. "I told you before, my lord, Harding is not the man. I heard Holbrook's name distinctly that night at the Mermaid. Besides, poor, muddled Harding couldn't plot cheating at cards, much less a revolution."

"Yes, that is what you told me. But I have a different opinion. I don't believe Harding is as big a fool as he appears. In fact, I am guessing that Harding is John Smith and you have known it for quite some time."

She made a sound of contempt. "Guessing? Is that the best you can do, my lord? Have you any proof of your guess? Gage will expect some. Inconvenient for you, I know, but there it is."

"We will know soon enough if my guess is a correct one. When Lieutenant Weston sees Harding, I'm sure he will be able to identify him as the man who was in Concord a few days ago calling himself John Smith and hiding powder stores from the king's troops." Lowden paused, and Katie felt despair settling over her and seeping into her bones like the chilling gray fog of a winter night. Once Weston saw Ethan, it would all be over.

Lowden smiled as if he sensed the effect his words were having on her and took great pleasure in it. "Weston will also be able to tell the governor of how during a gallant attempt to rescue you, Harding's Liberty medal was revealed."

Katie was clenching the bars so tightly that her hands began to ache. "If Harding were the man, I would have told you."

"Not if you had developed an affection for him." The viscount shook his head in mock disapproval. "Really, Katie, I had expected better of you than that. Don't you know that falling in love with your protector is in very poor taste?"

She scowled at him and did not reply.

"So you see, my dear," he went on, "we have all we need to hang Harding for sedition. He will be tried before the governor."

"If we can find him," muttered Weston under his breath.

It took Katie a moment before Weston's mumbled words sank in. When they did, Katie's hope soared again, and she began to laugh. "You can't find him?" she cried. "Oh, that's rich indeed. What are you going to do? Have his trial without him?"

"Enough!" Lowden roared. "We will find him, and when we do, he will be tried, convicted, and executed. As for you, you will not live long enough to see it happen. You will be tried this afternoon for your theft of the good lieutenant's purse, both Weston and I will testify against you, and you will be hanged. Unless, of course, you would care to add your testimony to the case against Harding? Tell us where he is hiding? And give us the names of all his informants?"

Katie looked at Lowden. His dark eyes bored into hers, and she suddenly realized why the first time she had seen him, his face had reminded her of a death's head. There was no life in his eyes. They were flat, black, and cold. Like death.

Katie smiled into that dead face. "Be damned to you."

"I have no doubt I will be damned soon enough," he answered. "But you will pass through the gates of hell long before I do, my girl. I am certain of that."

She was certain of it, too, but that didn't matter. Nothing mattered except that Ethan had not been arrested.

The viscount leaned closer to her. "We will talk again as you are led to the gallows. Perhaps then you will be more willing to tell me what you know."

Lowden and Weston walked away, and the moment they were gone, she bent her head and prayed with all her heart to a God she had never believed in that Ethan was safely out of the city.

22

~

$\mathcal{T}$rials of mere street thieves were simple, straightforward, and far more concerned with expediency than justice. Katie expected to stand before the magistrate only a few short minutes, long enough to hear Weston's condemning testimony, before sentence would be handed down. Since this was her second offense, she knew she would be immediately dispatched to the hangman.

She stood in the dock as Weston was sworn to tell the truth, and she could have told the bailiff not to bother. After all, she had stolen the money, and Weston didn't have to lie in order to see her hanged. She did not turn around, but she knew Lowden was seated somewhere behind her, waiting to tell how he had seen her take the officer's money. She imagined he would have some plausible tale for how he acquired Weston's purse from her, and then he would present that evidence to the magistrate. She would be asked if she had any last words, she would swear up and down she was innocent, the magistrate would not believe her, and that would be the end of it.

Though Katie was resigned to her fate, that did not mean she intended to go to the gallows on her belly. She kept her shoulders back and her head high as Weston launched into his tale, but he had barely said half a dozen words when a stir began at the back of the room.

The magistrate held up one hand to halt Weston's testimony and frowned at the two young bailiffs who stood guard by the doors.

Katie turned her head and saw that one of the bailiffs had opened the door leading out of the courtroom. He was speaking in a low voice to someone outside the room.

"What is this commotion?" the magistrate demanded impatiently.

The young man turned from the open doorway to the bench. "Sir, there is a gentleman here who says he knows the accused and has information important to this trial. He requests permission to speak to this court."

Katie stiffened at those words, suddenly afraid. The bailiff must be referring to Ethan. But if he knew of her trial and had come to speak on her behalf, he must also know Weston was here and would recognize him. Would he walk right into the lion's den? Surely not.

But he did. When the magistrate gave permission, the bailiffs stepped aside, and Ethan sauntered into the room, dressed in his finest walking suit and linen, looking for all the world like a man being presented to the king.

Katie looked at him in despair as he came forward to face the magistrate. She slowly shook her head as he passed by, silently pleading with him to leave before it was too late, but he barely spared her a glance.

She saw Lowden rise to his feet, she saw the satisfaction in his face and the smile on his lips. When she turned around, she found that Weston was subjecting Ethan to a hard stare, and she knew it would be only a moment before he confirmed this was the man he had seen in that dark alley with her outside the White Swan and at the dim tavern near Concord. Her despair deepened into agony.

Mother of God, what was Ethan thinking to come here in an attempt to save her? He would only succeed in dying with her.

"Mr. Harding," the magistrate greeted him in a pleased tone of voice, and she realized the two men knew each other. "It is a pleasure to see you, sir."

"And you as well." Ethan bowed. "I hope you are in good health, Jonathan?"

"I am, Ethan. And you?"

Honestly, was there anyone in Boston Ethan did not know? Katie pressed the knuckles of her clenched fist to her mouth as the two men exchanged pleasantries. They could be the dearest of friends, and it wouldn't matter. Ethan could not possibly think his acquaintanceship with the magistrate would save her, and by making the attempt, he was forfeiting his own life.

"You have information bearing on the matter before my court?" the magistrate asked him.

"I do," Ethan answered, and gestured to her. "This girl is indentured to me."

"Indeed? I was unaware of this. What do you know of her crime?"

"I know she did not commit it."

A stir rippled through the few spectators present.

Lieutenant Weston leaned forward in his chair beside the magistrate. "She stole my money. As for you, sir, I know who you are."

Katie held her breath, waiting, but Ethan ignored the interruption as if good breeding forbade any reply. "I witnessed the entire incident in North Square," he told the magistrate, "and I saw nothing to indicate this young woman stole from this officer. They—"

"I said, I know who you are." Weston stood up, fists clenched at his sides. "You are a Whig traitor."

Ethan stiffened. "Be careful what you say, sir," he warned in a bored voice. "You are becoming offensive."

"Indeed," the magistrate said, frowning at the officer. "If you have an accusation of sedition to make, Lieutenant Weston, I hope you are prepared to present evidence of it to another court. For now, you will be silent."

"Wait." Lowden spoke for the first time as he

strode forward. "If the lieutenant can prove his claim, then I have the authority to take Harding into custody. Do you have evidence, Lieutenant?"

"I do, my lord."

As if Lowden didn't already know about that evidence, Katie thought in disgust. She felt as if she were watching a play on the stage, with every man before her acting out his particular part. Ethan acting the innocent gentleman accused of an appalling crime, Weston acting the outraged officer only trying to do his duty, and Lowden acting the peer of the realm who had the right to take over the entire show.

Lowden faced the magistrate. "I believe this officer has the evidence to prove his claim, and I would like to hear it."

"Would you, indeed?" The magistrate frowned. "My lord, you may be a viscount, you may indeed have the authority to take this man into custody, but that is not the purview of my court. I am here to preside over the trial of this girl for theft. Any other matter should be taken to Governor Gage. Now, step back and be silent."

"How dare you speak to me in such a way?" Lowden said, his voice shaking with fury. "I am a representative of the king's chief minister and a peer of the realm, and I will not be told to be silent by some colonial magistrate! Harding is a traitor. As for the girl, she is not only a thief, she is also a spy for him, and I will see them both hanged before the day is out."

"Heavens," Ethan drawled carelessly. "First the girl's a thief, then she's a spy. I am a traitor. What is this man's next accusation? Are the bailiffs now secret informants for the French?"

Several chuckles from the observers behind her caused Katie to feel a faint hint of hope. Ethan was attempting to make the whole thing seem rather ridiculous, and he was beginning to succeed.

Lowden sensed it as well. "Laugh if you like, Harding," he said between clenched teeth. "I will take this matter before the governor, Weston shall prove his claim, and I will be the one laughing when you dance on the end of a rope. And your mistress will hang with you."

Ethan shrugged. "If the magistrate is amenable to the idea, I would be pleased to accompany you to the governor's office." He turned to the man at the bench. "Jonathan, with all these silly accusations of sedition and spying and such flying about, perhaps this entire matter should be put before the governor. What is your opinion?"

"I believe you have the right of it," the magistrate agreed with a sigh. "If this girl is somehow involved in Whig chicanery, it is beyond my jurisdiction. I shall send a message to Province House at once, notifying Governor Gage that you require an audience with him forthwith. The bailiffs will escort you."

Katie saw Ethan's shoulders relax slightly, and she realized an audience before the governor had been his intention all along. What she could not understand was why.

Governor Gage was not in the mood for long, drawn-out stories. Ethan could tell that the moment the four of them were ushered into his office. Given tonight's mission, that was not surprising.

As Lowden launched into his tale of how Ethan Harding was the rebel spy John Smith, of how Harding's mistress, Katie Armstrong, had assisted Harding in seditious activities, of how he knew this because he had originally hired the girl to spy for him, and half a dozen assurances that Lieutenant Weston was prepared to confirm all this, Ethan saw the governor's frown etch deeper and deeper into his forehead. Ethan also knew Gage did not like Lowden. He did not like him at all.

"Do you mean to tell me, my lord," he said, cutting off the viscount's diatribe in midsentence, "that you are accusing Mr. Harding and Mrs. Armstrong of sedition?"

"I am."

Gage turned to Lieutenant Weston. "I see you have finally returned to duty, Lieutenant. What is your part in all this?"

Weston explained the events leading to this moment, from the theft of his purse by Katie to the pistol shot he had fired at Harding outside Concord.

"That will be all. Step back, Lieutenant." He turned to Ethan. "This is a serious accusation, sir. What have you to say?"

Ethan lifted his hands in a gesture of bewilderment. "I am at a loss. I was a witness to the incident in North Square between Weston and Mrs. Armstrong, but I saw nothing to indicate she stole anything from him. He seemed to be making ungentlemanly advances toward her, and she clearly rebuffed him. As for the incident at the White Swan, he contends I wear one of those ridiculous medals, and I can assure you, I do not. However, the fight between us did take place. What the lieutenant has failed to tell you is that he was once again making unwelcome advances toward Mrs. Armstrong, and I came to her aid. He was, to put it bluntly, attempting to assault her person. He tore her dress."

The governor's frown got even deeper. He turned to Katie. "Is this true?" he demanded. "Were you subjected to assault at the hands of my officer?"

Katie played her part with all the skill of a true actress. She nodded, then immediately ducked her head in shame. "It is true," she confessed in an agonized whisper. "Lieutenant Weston attempted to take advantage of me, and Mr. Harding came to my aid."

"This is preposterous!" Lowden cried. "What does this matter? They are traitors, and I want them hanged for their crimes."

"What you want, my lord, does not concern me overmuch," Gage responded dryly. "Be silent." He returned his attention to Ethan. "And what of the viscount's contention that you are the rebel spy John Smith? What say you to that, Mr. Harding? My officer swears he saw you in Lincoln and contends that you were there to move munitions and powder out of my reach."

"I?" Ethan looked utterly appalled. "Gad about the countryside in the cold spring air moving gunpowder?" He straightened the lace of his cuffs and sniffed with disdain. "What an idea!"

"You wear no Liberty medal?"

Ethan spread his arms wide. "I will submit to a search, sir," he said with dignity, "if you feel it necessary."

"Of course he's willing to be searched," Lowden said with mounting irritation. "He probably isn't wearing it now. He'd be a fool to do so. That proves nothing."

"Since Harding is the accused, I believe the burden of proof is on you, my lord," Gage reminded him. "And I will not tell you again to be silent."

He returned his attention to Katie. "Mrs. Armstrong, I am not quite clear how you came to be hired by the viscount. Please explain."

"I didn't want to be a spy, sir," Katie said with a sniff. "I mean, I'm only a woman, and all this talk of Whigs and Tories bewilders me, I must confess. But the viscount——" She broke off and bit her lip. "The viscount forced me to become a spy. He told me he had seen me stealing in North Square, and he threatened to have me arrested. But I swear, I am innocent of that crime."

"Innocent?" Lowden stepped forward. "This girl wasn't innocent the day she was born. If you don't believe me, pull off her glove. She bears the brand of a thief and was sent here on indenture."

"Indeed?" The governor looked at her with a new light in his eyes, as if reconsidering his opinion of her given this information. Ethan caught his breath, wondering how Katie would respond.

She drew herself up with such injured dignity Ethan wanted to laugh. No matter what the lie, trust Katie to be convincing. "I admit, Governor Gage, that I have done wrong in my life," she said softly. "I did steal once in London a year ago, bread from a baker's stall." She spread her hands in an appealing gesture reminiscent of an innocent child. "I was destitute, I had no home, no family, no friends to aid me. And I was hungry."

"Oh, heavens," Lowden groaned, "let us all pity the poor, destitute child."

Gage turned on him, his face turning brick red with anger. "Viscount Lowden, I will not tell you again to be silent. Now, step back, and keep your mouth closed."

Fuming, the viscount obeyed, but his tightly pressed lips caused Ethan to wonder how long his silence would last. Ethan knew if Lowden continued to interrupt, Gage would have him removed, and that could only help Ethan and Katie.

"To continue," Katie said, "I felt I had no choice but to do what the viscount demanded of me. I agreed to spy for him, even though I knew if the rebels found me out, they were likely to kill me. But I found no evidence against Mr. Harding at all."

Gage subjected her to a long, hard stare. "But you are his mistress, are you not? You might be compelled to lie for him."

"So I might," she agreed. "For his kindness to me has known no bounds. He bought my indenture and freed me. However, I am not lying, and I believe the viscount's failure to provide anything but accusations proves I am telling the truth in this affair."

"I have had enough of this!" Lowden burst out. Stepping forward, he shoved Katie out of his way and faced the governor across his desk. "I will not listen to this traitorous witch a moment longer. I am a representative of Lord North, the king's chief minister, and I will not be told again to be silent." He pointed a finger at Gage, and Ethan noted his hand shaking with rage. "You have avoided taking action against these Whig rebels long enough. I demand that you arrest both of these traitors and sentence them to hang for their crimes."

"By God, sir, you will make no demands on me!" Gage slammed his fist against the desk. "I am a general of His Majesty's Army, I am a gentleman, and I am governor of this colony. It is I who wield the power here, not you."

He gave Lowden no chance to respond. Instead, he swept on. "Don't think I don't know your purpose here. Spying on me for North, sending dispatches to him filled with lies. I know your ambition is to usurp me and take my place. I have known that from the moment you arrived. I have also formed an opinion of your character, and it is not a flattering one. You may be a peer of the realm, but you are no gentleman, sir."

"How dare you speak to me in such a fashion?"

"I do dare, sir. Viscount or no, your conduct in this affair has been appalling. Making accusations against British citizens without any proof and using fabricated accusations to force young women into becoming informants only confirm my opinion of you. It also gives me the excuse I have needed ever since your arrival to have you removed and sent back to England. There is a ship sailing for Liverpool in the morning, and you will be on it." He turned to the two soldiers who stood at the doors into his office. "Sergeant Field and Sergeant Ellison, escort the viscount out of Province House, and see that tomorrow morning when the *Westminster* sails for England, he is on board."

"I will have you court-martialed for this," Lowden told him in a fury as one sergeant appeared on either side of him and began pulling him toward the doors. "When I have made my report to Lord North," he shouted over his shoulder as he was hauled away, "you will be fortunate if you do not face a firing squad."

"I have no doubt you'll try, my lord," Gage muttered. He turned to Lieutenant Weston, who was still standing by the window as he had been commanded. "As for you, Lieutenant, I have as poor an opinion of your conduct as I do of the viscount's. Officers under my command do not assault young women, regardless of their circumstances and station. They do not fire pistols at citizens not proven to have committed a crime. I have given express orders to all my officers not to use force or intimidation on the local populace, and you have disobeyed those orders in both these instances. You are dangerously close to court-martial."

Weston set his jaw and did not answer, clearly feeling that silence was preferable to court-martial. "You will spend one month in the barracks with both your pay and your duties suspended. You may go."

Weston bowed and turned away, stiff and silent as he walked out of Gage's office.

Gage then turned his attention to Ethan. "As for you, sir, I have always been of the opinion that you are not as foolish as you pretend to be, Mr. Harding. Given that, I have no doubt—no doubt at all—that you have done at least some of the things of which the viscount accuses you."

Ethan had no idea if he would be freed or sent to Castle William. All he could hope for was that Katie would be free to go.

"However," the governor continued, "my orders from London are very specific—I am to arrest only Whig leaders, and I have been provided with a list of those leaders. Your name is not on that list. In addition, there is no evidence to indicate you are in any position of power within the Whig cause. The only evidence against you is the word of Viscount Lowden and Lieutenant Weston, both of whom, it would seem, have a personal ax to grind here."

Gage took a deep breath and let it out in a heavy sigh. "This matter comes down to the word of Lowden and Weston against that of Mrs. Armstrong and yourself. Your two versions of the events leading to this moment differ considerably, and there is no way for me to determine who is telling the truth and who is not. If I were a wagering man, I would bet that both yourself and the viscount have told me nothing but lies. Still, the fact remains that nothing can be proven against you, and I will not arrest men without hard evidence of wrongdoing. You may go, but if you are indeed a Whig spy, I would urge you not to try to leave the city. My soldiers are everywhere, and you would not get far without a pass."

"No, sir," Ethan agreed, knowing that was nothing less than the truth. "What about Mrs. Armstrong?"

Gage looked at Katie, and, to Ethan's astonishment, he smiled at her, a sad, compassionate smile. "Mrs. Armstrong, I am truly sorry for the indignities you suffered at the hands of my officer and the viscount. You have my abject apologies. If Mr. Harding were truly the kind and honorable man you paint him, he would not keep you as a mistress." He frowned at Ethan. "And sir, if this unfortunate girl was indentured to you and you took her for a mistress, you have abused your position as her master. The fact that you have since freed her does not change that."

Ethan tried to look contrite. "Yes, sir."

Gage returned his attention to Katie. "My dear child, what do you want out of all this?"

Ethan caught his breath, wondering what she would say.

"Governor Gage, all I want is to leave Boston, find a nice quiet place to live and a hardworking, steady fellow to marry, and stay out of all these complicated political affairs. I have had enough of Whigs and Tories to last a lifetime."

Ethan frowned. She couldn't possibly mean that. What was she really up to?

"And so you shall, my dear." Gage pulled out a sheet of parchment and picked up his quill. "Here is a pass to leave the city," he said as he began to write. "I would advise you to do so first thing to-morrow. Try not to travel alone if you can."

He blotted the sheet and handed it to her. She accepted it meekly. "Thank you, sir."

Ethan could not believe it. Not only was she free, she had managed to connive a pass out of the governor to leave Boston, which was far more than he could have hoped for. He took her arm and began pulling her toward the door, wanting her out of there before Gage changed his mind.

Once they were safely out of Province House, once they were in his carriage and on their way to his house, he allowed his jubilation to show. He laughed a long, hard laugh of disbelief. "My God, it worked," he told Katie as he fell back against the seat of the carriage. "The most colossal, unbelievable bluff of my life, and it worked."

It took him a moment to realize Katie was not laughing. He turned his head to look at her, and what he saw in her eyes caused his laughter to fade away. Something in the way she looked at him twisted his heart with a joy far greater than outwitting Gage.

"You came for me," she whispered in disbelief, and reached up to touch his cheek. "You came back for me."

Ethan turned his head to press a kiss into her palm. "How could I not? I love you."

"How could you?" She shook her head. "After I spied on you, after I lied to you."

"But you didn't betray me. I knew it the moment Lowden and his men burst into your house. They arrested you but not me, and I knew that I had made a mistake, the worst mistake of my life."

"I should have trusted you, I should have told you the truth, but I was so afraid. I didn't know what you would do, and I didn't think even you could save me from the viscount's threats. I didn't think you would want to, once you knew the truth."

"You aren't the only one who hasn't been honest, Katie," he reminded her. "But when the moment came to save yourself, you did not. You saved me instead by refusing to speak against me. How could you think I would not do the same for you?"

"I heard Lowden had constables out looking for you, but you were nowhere to be found. I was certain you had left the city. I had hoped you had escaped. But then, there you were, striding into court, and I was so afraid they would hang you." Her voice broke on a sob, and she threw her arms around his neck, burying her face against his shirt-front.

He stroked her hair and smiled. "Are you crying again?"

She shook her head. "No," she choked with a sniff. "I never cry."

"Oh, then you must have something in your eye."

She laughed with him and sat up, brushing away the tears she said she wasn't crying. "But how could you take such a risk? You must have known about Weston by then. You must have known he would recognize you."

"I found out this morning he had returned to duty, and when I learned of your trial for the theft of Weston's purse, I knew he would be called as a witness."

"That's my point. You knew, and you came anyway."

"I also knew there was no other way. I couldn't break you out of Castle William, so my only option was to get all four of us in front of Gage and see if I could bluff our way out."

She stared at him as if he'd lost his mind. "You had it all planned?"

"Of course. I knew if we could just get Gage to

give the final word, we would have a chance. I know the man, I know how he thinks, and unless Lowden had evidence of which I was unaware, I felt there was a strong chance Gage would let us go. But, of course, it meant telling some outrageous lies." He smiled at her, that wry, one-sided smile she loved. "You see, I took a page out of your book. I crossed my fingers and lied like hell."

She laughed. "What a marvelous idea."

"Yes, wasn't it?" He paused, and his smile faded. "I am hoping you have another one."

"Another idea?"

"For how I can get out of the city. I have to get word to the countryside of what you told me last night, that Regulars are marching tonight. I found Paul Revere this morning and told him, but both of us have the same problem—how to get out of Boston."

She held up the document Gage had given her. "That's no problem. I have a pass."

"Yes, and I couldn't believe how you finagled one out of him. I thought I'd ask Gage to give us both passes, but when he indicated he had suspicions regarding my loyalty, I decided not to push my luck. So you can leave, but I can't."

"Of course you can." Katie leaned back against the carriage seat. "A spot of forgery is clearly indicated."

"Agreed, but we'd still need someone skilled enough at forgery to do the work. Most of my contacts have left the city by now, and I don't know anyone still in town with the talent to—" He broke off and stared at her, understanding dawning in his eyes as she started to laugh. "Can you do it?"

She turned her head and smiled at him. "Did I ever tell you about the time Meg and I did our forgery swindle?"

He grasped her hand and pressed it to his lips. "Did I ever tell you how much I love you?"

"Yes," she whispered, "but tell me again. And again. And again. For the rest of my life."

Trull's Inn and Tavern, located by the wharf in Charlestown, had been doing a brisk business all evening. If Tory informants had been watching the place, they would have found it highly suspicious to see so many people running in and out. Their suspicions would have been justified. Every few minutes, another person arrived with news of the movements of Gage's Regulars.

Daniel Munro was supposed to be asleep, tucked safely in a bed upstairs, but he had no intention of being left out of things. He tiptoed downstairs to find out what was going on.

He found his father and mother in the taproom with the Macalveys, and he kept out of sight by the door, listening.

"He'll be here."

Daniel recognized his father's voice, and he wondered who was expected to arrive. Paul Revere, maybe. But his mother spoke, and Daniel knew it wasn't Paul Revere.

"Ethan will come," David said. "He knows to meet us here. If what Joseph told us is reliable, and Ethan doesn't arrive, I'll be the only one to ride north tonight, and I can't cover all that distance by myself. Many people won't be warned."

"I'll do it," Joshua said.

"You can't make such a hard ride with your leg, and if Ethan doesn't come soon—"

"Ethan will come only if he hasn't been arrested," Dorothy Macalvey said, and the shaking in her voice made Daniel roll his eyes. She sounded as if she was going to cry or something.

"Ethan won't be arrested," Molly said fiercely. "Last we heard, John Smith wasn't on Gage's list."

Daniel frowned. What did John Smith have to do with this Ethan person? He didn't understand. Dorothy started talking again, and he leaned closer to the door, but he needn't have bothered. She sounded really scared, and she wasn't bothering to be quiet about it.

"It may not matter. If Katie told Lowden about John Smith, that he is really Ethan Harding and has been spying on the Tories for years, Gage could arrest him anyway."

Daniel frowned again, thinking it out. John's real name was Ethan? But why hadn't John told him that? Adults, he thought with disgust. Didn't they know he could keep a secret just as well as anybody?

"Keep your voice down, Dorothy," Joshua admonished. "For God's sake."

She paid no mind to that. "Katie betrayed him, and he could hang for it."

That was it. Daniel had heard enough. He ran into the room with a shout of fury. "Katie didn't say anything to the Tories!" he cried, stopping just inside the door with his fists clenched. "I don't believe it. She wouldn't tell."

"Daniel Munro, you're supposed to be in bed!" Molly came over to him and grabbed his ear. He hated that.

She gave his ear a hard tug, and he let out a wail of protest. "Katie isn't a traitor! She isn't! She isn't."

"Young man, you are going back upstairs." Molly started pulling him in that direction by his ear, and Daniel gave another wail, but he was saved from a return to bed by the opening of the front door.

Two figures came in, their dark cloaks billowing as the cold spring wind gusted in after them. Daniel saw Katie's short crop of golden brown hair, and he gave a shout of joy. "Katie!" he cried, running to her.

She opened her arms, laughing, as the boy hurled himself at her. "Watch out," she warned, and reached into her pocket. "You'll hurt Meg."

She pulled out the half-grown cat, who let out a loud wail of protest, and thrust her toward the boy. "Take her while I get my cloak off."

Daniel accepted the animal from her and glanced at the tall figure who had entered with her and was now pulling off his heavy cloak. "John! You're finally here. We've been waiting forever."

"We have." David stepped forward, shaking his head, looking confused. "What goes on here, Ethan?"

"It's a long story," he replied, and Daniel frowned, remembering what he had overheard.

"You lied to me," he accused. "All my life, I've thought you were John Smith, and now I find out you're somebody named Ethan."

"For heaven's sake, Daniel," his mother said, "who cares about that now?" She glanced from Ethan to Katie and back again. "This is a surprise. It's so late, we thought sure you'd been arrested."

"I have not been arrested," he assured her, and gestured to Katie. "Although Katie almost got hanged because she wouldn't tell Lowden who I was."

He noted their bewildered faces. "It's a long story. What news have you of Gage's Regulars?"

"Joseph Bramley was here a while ago, and he said they are definitely on the march. He was on his way to Lexington. Paul Revere has already gone that way."

"There are many soldiers on the roads," Katie put in. "We had the devil of a time avoiding them to get here."

David shook his head, clearly befuddled. "How did you get here?" he asked. "Last time we saw Ethan, you were a spy for Lowden, and he was on the verge of arrest."

"As I said, I haven't been arrested." Ethan could see that he was going to have to explain before he could get any more news about the Regulars. He led them all into the taproom, everyone sat down, and as succinctly as possible, Ethan told them everything that had happened during the last twenty-four hours. Though the situation had been grave at the time, when he got to the meeting in Gage's office, he couldn't help laughing.

"Of all of us, Katie fared best. Gage was so charmed by her, by how she had been taken advantage of by Lowden and myself, she came out smelling like a rose. I swear, when she connived a pass out of the city from him, I could hardly believe it."

"So she didn't give your name to Lowden?" Dorothy spoke for the first time, clearly disbelieving. She turned to Katie, bristling with disapproval. "But Worth said you were Lowden's spy. He gave you a letter from Lowden. I saw him do it, and he told me Lowden had written it to you. And now you expect us to believe—"

"Dorothy, that's enough, I think." Ethan cut her off. "She didn't betray me, or any of us, and that is what counts."

"I knew it!" Daniel cried, hugging Meg to his chest and giving Ethan a grin of pure satisfaction. "I told them, but they just wouldn't believe me."

Ethan glanced at David and Joshua. "Is anyone going to tell me what has happened so far this night, or am I going to have to ride to Lexington and ask Joseph?"

"Joseph stopped here on his way to Lexington and told us that there were riders spreading the word, but no one has gone north to Tewksbury," David answered. "I was just about to go to Chelmsford and warn them, but there is no one to go to Tewksbury."

Ethan looked at Katie, and he saw the fear in her eyes, the same fear he'd seen there before he went to Concord. He shook his head. "No, David. I can't go. Not this time."

"Someone has to."

"It won't be me."

The gazes of the two men locked, and no one spoke.

After a long silence, Molly cleared her throat and stood up. "I'll fetch some hot soup for Katie and Ethan. Look done in, both of them."

Molly left the taproom, and the others rose to their feet and followed her out, although Daniel paused in the doorway, the cat in his arms and an agonized expression on his freckled face.

"I knew it wasn't true," he said passionately. "I knew you hadn't told the Tories anything, Katie. You couldn't do anything like that. I tried to tell them, but nobody would believe me."

Katie smiled at her young champion. "Thank you, Daniel."

He scowled at Ethan. "Maybe next time, all you adults will listen to me. Maybe next time, you won't lie to me about your real names. Maybe everybody will start to figure out that just because I'm a boy, it doesn't mean I don't know anything. I've got more sense than any man."

With those words, Daniel departed, slamming the door behind him to show just how disgusted he was by the behavior of adults.

Katie laughed, but Ethan did not. "He's right about that. Daniel definitely has more sense than I do. I was convinced you had betrayed me. You tried to tell me the truth that night, but I—" he broke off and tilted his head back to stare at the ceiling. "God help me, I did not believe you."

She heard the loathing in his voice, just as she had only two nights before, but this time that loathing was directed at himself, not her.

"What changed your mind?" she asked. "That Lowden did not arrest you last night?"

"Yes, but it didn't matter. That night when I saw you there, when I saw Lowden taking you away, I didn't care if you had done anything or not. I didn't care about anything except that they were taking you to prison, and all I could think of was how scared you were of rats and how I had to get you out of there."

That was love, she realized, looking at him. Thinking only of your beloved, regardless of the past, regardless of the hurt you had suffered. Katie knew she was a fortunate woman indeed. She also knew what she had to do.

She rose from her chair and knelt beside his. "Ethan, you need to go. You need to ride north to Tewksbury and raise the alarm."

He turned to her, touched her cheek. "How can I leave you now?"

"For the same reason you have always had. Because you want a world where people are truly free."

"It means a war, Katie, probably a long and dangerous war, and an uncertain future."

"I know." She put her arms around his neck and kissed him. "But I've never thought much about the future. I've spent my whole life living only for the here and now. Why should I change?"

He started to speak, but she silenced him with another kiss, a long, full, lush kiss filled with all the promise of a future together, and she had no doubts it would happen.

Finally, she pulled back with a sigh of contentment. "Besides," she said, "I think our future is very bright. We love each other, and we are helping to create a brave new world."

He laughed softly. "I thought you said women never do anything for an ideal."

"We don't." She smiled. "Ideals be damned. I'm thinking of all the children we're going to have, and how someday their father will be able to sit with them by the fireside and tell them how one night, in April of '75, he helped create a nation. Now, go. When you return, I'll be waiting. Through all the battles to come, and all the hardships, and all the joy, I'll be waiting. I love you."

Ethan stood up, pulled her to her feet, and took her hands in his. "About all these children we're going to have."

"Yes?"

"Under no circumstances are you going to teach them how to steal pocket watches."

She gave him her very best innocent stare. "But, Ethan, you said yourself the future is uncertain. Our children should have some extra skills to fall back on."

He frowned at her, and she could tell he was doing his best to look stern. "Pickpocketing is not a skill I want my children to learn. I'd prefer them to take up a worthy trade."

"Oh, very well," she conceded. "I won't teach them pickpocketing. After all," she added with her usual optimism, "I can always teach them forgery instead. Or lock picking. Or everything their father taught me about how to be a spy."

Ethan groaned, and this time it was his turn to silence her with a kiss.

Return to
a time of romance…

SONNET
BOOKS

Where today's

hottest romance authors

bring you vibrant

and vivid love stories

with a dash of history.

PUBLISHED BY POCKET BOOKS

Step into a web of small-town scandal...
the Southern way.

Breathless

Another romance
to savor from

LAURA LEE GUHRKE

and
Sonnet Books

SONNET
BOOKS

POCKET BOOKS

2402